The
Wintering

Also by Joan Williams

THE MORNING AND THE EVENING
OLD POWDER MAN

The
Wintering

Joan Williams

HARCOURT BRACE JOVANOVICH, INC.

NEW YORK

First edition
ISBN 0-15-125225-4
Library of Congress Catalog Card Number: 78-134571
Printed in the United States of America

A B C D E

For my sons,
EZRA DRINKER BOWEN
MATTHEW WILLIAMS BOWEN

The pursuit of truth
is a wholly individual matter,
logically independent of the tradition of past thought,
more likely to be arrived at by a departure from it.

—DESCARTES

The
Wintering

Often, in the long-
ago summer, he had lain wanting only to daydream. But when he
sought sleep without dreams, Poppa intruded again. Hot and perspiring, Poppa came around the house; his question, having fes-
tered in him unbelievably long, burst out at last. "But what do
you want to do?" Poppa said. The boy's answer was the only one
Poppa probably had not considered: "Nothing." Wordless then,
floundering at air like a toy monkey on a string, Poppa rounded
the house again. Respecting his father, the boy did not laugh
aloud.

Over and over, his mother said, "I declare, he's spurted so, I
think growing's taken all his energy." She irritated him. Why,
when he had been shaving a year, couldn't they leave him alone?

The sun burned wrathfully and only shadows from the muscadine, twining up the porch's cedar supports, meeting in the
eaves, gave spattered relief. It was a summer of drought. The side
lot wavered distantly in heat as if seen through tears, and Poppa
seemed to saddle Molly in dust. They came up out of the side lot
and passed him as silently as ghosts. His final glimpse was of the
beautiful, flame-colored horse with Poppa rocking in perfect co-
ordination until, colliding into sunlight, they were gone. His

mother's pale face appeared behind the screen door. "Why didn't you help your daddy catch that horse?" she said. "Go pitch him down some hay, at least. You know his blood pressure," and fear fluted her words again. Jessie's young face, in sorrow, watched while he went out the back door and slammed it. His mother, watching too, seemed in scattered pieces behind the back porch's latticework.

Inside the barn, he leaned against a horse's sticky side, thinking that here he could be content with the horse eating and sleeping and emptying and filling its bladder with the monotony of people, only never bothering him. But he could not hide. At suppertime, someone would come looking for him. He took the fork and pitched hay, knowing as long as he remembered the afternoon he decided to leave home, he would know again the smell of barn on a hot afternoon.

From a bed, his since childhood, he could see the moon in slivers through night-dark pines and could hear not only night's myriad and familiar sounds, but also the crunch of Jessie's feet on gravel as she came from town. Her cabin in lamplight, long ago, had been safety when he looked out from his room. Often, he went there when he was small. Even in sleep, he could know the smells inside that cabin again, of coal oil and simmering firewood and their own smells, sitting close to the fire to play cards. Beyond the lamplight and without the fire had been cold corners of darkness.

On the morning he ran away, he got up before daylight to pack underwear and a toothbrush, having no need for or attachment to clothes hanging in a half-opened closet. The kitchen windows were pale as death with dawn. He cut a slice of Jessie's weekly cake and left the cake box carefully askew and crumbs scattered as evidence. Then, eating the cake, he went down the hall where dawn was a grey pall at the front windows. Roosters crowed like echoes of one another around the world, it vast and

4

he alone. Daylight meant heat and the stench of ragweed along the roadside, as if something were rotting in fields. Dawn's mist lifted to reveal town, and he passed between two rows of white stores with hens roosting on their porches. Everything was still except for a wolfish grey dog slinking across the road and water dripping from the town pump, as ceaseless as time. The dog's eyes were as haunting as a skeleton's, but thrown cake, it whined for more. An incline took town from view, and he stopped to look back and saw the dog, still hungry, watching him out of eyes that were hollow and accusing.

He accepted a ride from a farm couple and, jostling in the pickup's bed, watched the farmer's shirt rub red his pocked neck and watched his wife's black elastic hatband slip up and down as they went over bumps. Eroded gullies flew by and at intervals cabins with dry dirt yards full of flowers, standing out from the dust like stars separate from the dark. He seemed floating in dust when he jumped from the truck. He crossed a highway to wait beside a Negro. "Hot," he said. "Sho is," said the Negro.

Suddenly, the bus was there, as things appear in dreams, without warning. He felt disconsolate and wanted to talk to the Negro, in back, his last link with home. But mirror-smooth and white, the gravel roads disappeared, and he was among city streets, a stranger. He saw a waitress in a restaurant, who was cooking, and a clock on a building read five. Outpouring crowds from office buildings carried him along the street to a park; there he drank from a fountain with chewing-gum wads looming up through the water, seeming larger than life-sized. Old men sat on benches in dejected attitudes of rest. An orator in a flowing brown robe stood on a crate. Lying in grass to listen, he woke to a stab of pain. A policeman with a bloated face cried, looking down: "Move on!" He went back between the old men, who now were grinning, while the orator called, "Repent!"

When he passed the restaurant again, the waitress emerged

and said, "Hey, what's your hurry?" Her mouth in darkness seemed a bloody gash against an evening soft as new-plowed ground. Having answered, "Looking for a place to stay," he followed as she beckoned down a block with a river hidden at its end. Entering her boardinghouse was like entering a hole, her face too white and close in the gloom. Had he, at last, accepted the proverbial ice-cream cone from the stranger as he had been warned always not to do?

"Sugar," she answered. "What's yours?" When he replied, she recoiled and repeated, "By-run?"

Two wieners appeared to be dancing in boiling water until the landlady turned off the gas jet beneath them. She came toward him with eyes big behind thick glasses, making him think of things never told, and he averted his glance. "Fifty cents, Sugar," she said. "The same room as last time. Last name?" When he had answered, "Shelley," he followed Sugar's wide hips, swinging up the stairs before him. Laughing, he read the paper again, Re'cd from Byron Shelley 50¢. Swinging open, a door revealed a frail room, beyond which the sun sank magnificently into a river, blood-red, while he stood grieving for all things dying.

Watching smoke rise from the bed, he said, "I'm hungry," and Sugar crushed out the cigarette. They went over napless carpet through the silent house and stood on the front steps, where he cried, "I am the best of Byron and Shelley and Keats!" He was embraced afterward by surging crowds, then the image disappeared, as if a movie screen had darkened, and the audience gone. CAMILLE read a marquee under which women emerged, weeping, and turning their backs seemed to shun him on the street. In the restaurant, Sugar's handbag, a disintegrating straw, lay on the table. She took from it a scarred gold compact decorated with a sequined lady, half-gone. She put beside that a pint of whiskey and said, "You lost your girl or something?"

"I don't even have one. Why?" he said.

6

"Because," she said, "you're quieter than the dead."

There were too many questions, he thought: like home. Then he had thought the one word he had been telling himself ever since dark not to think. He saw again the grey pall at the front windows. Running home through dark when he was small, he had seen his mother's silhouette move in lamplight from the window to the door. She had called, "Where were you? Where were you?" And Jessie, carrying stove wood, had come from the kitchen crying, "Is it him?" He had been safe, then.

"Where's that ice!" Sugar said. The waiter set down a bowl full of cold blue cubes. "What'd you do, spit and wait till it froze?" she said. The waiter's voice formed two soundless words, like hollow cries of pain. "The same to you," she said.

His stomach wanted to reject whiskey never tasted before. Instead, he and Sugar went lightly down sidewalks rising and falling like furrows in the starless night. Along the street, a car careened crazily and a rummaging dog overturned a garbage can, leaving spoilage in his way. A woman sang. From a window someone yelled, "Shut up, you old whore," then he knew it was Sugar whose singing filled the lonesome night. Craters were streaked tears on the moon's face. "That or-bed maiden," he cried, "with white fire la-den Whom mortals call the Moon, Glides glimmering o'er—" and he ran off after scraps of things, like ashes rising in the wind. "Good Christ, you're on a jag," Sugar called, following. Light broke the darkness of their room like the impact of glass shattering stillness. Sugar moved from the switch and said, "Lay down," and they passed between them, on the bed, a soggy container of coffee she had bought.

He was grateful, for it was unexpected that Sugar could say nothing. He lay thinking that tomorrow, at the window where now he saw blackness, he would see the river, solitary and drifting, too. Freedom was drinking coffee with a whore when at home, people would be getting up for chores.

"That all you got," Sugar said, turning her head. "A tooth-brush and a clean pair of B.V.D.'s?"

"Top clean, bottom clean," he said, trying to make a joke. But it would not work, and when his voice wavered, he shut up.

"You some kooky rich kid or what?"

"Do I look rich?"

"No. But something's different about you," she said. He sank back into the darkness of the room again, having escaped nothing after all. Being himself, he was somehow different. Sugar's voice, in semidarkness, seemed unattached when she said, "You sleep, honey?" Coming a long way back from sleep's brink, he said, "Getting there." She moved closer and her huge breasts offered every possibility of suffocation. How could he save both his pride and his virginity? He wanted to lose the latter, though not here.

"Look, Sugar," he said. "I'm just a country boy."

"Shoot," she said. "I'm just a country girl."

Hoping sickness would answer, he loped down a hall with a single bulb burning at its end, but a finger down his throat only caused gagging. He came back into the room and said, "I don't feel so hot." She said, "Me neither. Cheap whiskey."

Removing his socks, he saw the Mississippi with the sun rising as it had fallen, blood red against the sky. He had thought that if it were daylight, they could not make love. But Sugar dragged him toward her over the scant sheets, while he dug his heels into the mattress. Scared to death, he had to laugh. His arms folded stubbornly across his chest when she held him. It was like being tickled with a feather as she touched him, there. It was good, but being held against her was like suffocation, so that he fought his way up, in despair over death, and was weakened. She released him and lay like a beached whale, taking deep slow breaths.

"Sugar," he said, "I guess it just wasn't my time, and I'm sorry." In the silence and the separating dark, listening to her sigh, he felt all the other disappointments of her life and her slow acceptance of this one. Sitting up to tell again that it had been all his fault, he wailed instead, "Sugar, I'm not but fifteen years old. And I've run away from home!"

"Why, boy," she said, sitting up and covering her breasts. "You go right back on home, you hear." He saw her face a final time, tender and anxious, before he heard himself sobbing.

Dreaming, he remembered and woke wondering whether there were any difference between the two: dream and memory. He had laughed in sleep, as he had all those years ago, at Poppa, floundering like a toy monkey on the end of a string before rounding the house. Then, as now, the sun had been on his face in splatters like hot grease, coming through the muscadine only grown more gnarled, older. The nature of his dream had made the journey back from his drugged sleep a longer one than usual. And, without opening his eyes, he knew by the feel of the sun that it was almost noon and that the rain had stopped. He wondered how long he had been lying in the hammock on the porch. As he had known in dream when Poppa rode away on Molly that someone was watching him from behind the screen door, he knew that now and opened his eyes.

Jessie's grey hair stuck in wisps from a skullcap, the top half of a woman's stocking, twisted at the top of her head like a balloon's end. "You all right?" she said, meaning that moment when, with the same effort with which he had propelled himself awake, he propelled himself into a sitting position and swung his feet from the hammock to the porch, deck-grey and wetted by blown rain.

"So-so," he answered. Sitting up, he was sickened by the back swaying of the hammock and the smell that clung faint and near and as invisible as memory. Paraldehyde, he thought. This siege must have been bad and long if they had called a doctor. He wondered if time lost had been really lost or whether he would eventually remember everything.

When he let the hammock go, it swung softly toward him and moved him several stumbling steps forward. They must have been the first in some time, for he was stiff. He wondered again how long he had been lying there. His steps seemed without aim or stability, as if he were a child learning to walk.

"Can you eat?" Jessie said.

Everything was indeterminate and without purpose and unwanted, he thought. "Soup, I guess," he said. Though feeling sick at the thought of food, he needed something.

Jessie went ahead of him down the hall, the whites of her heels visible one after the other in a pair of his old slide-in bedroom shoes. He stood adjusting to the hall's dimness after the porch speckled by sun and shadow. His hand trembled reaching behind him to close the door, gently.

Dizzy, he sought something steady to look at, feeling the need to lose everything. He called after the flapping heels, "Just broth, bouillon, something light," swallowing rapidly. The hall was warm and smelled of age. Moving down it slowly, he was pervaded by the dream- and memory-smell of horseflesh and barn and hot afternoon. The wallpaper had an English hunting scene, in black and white except for red jackets, and had been long faded. Floor to ceiling, he confronted a confusion of men and horses and beagles with ecstatic tails, jumping and running and scrambling beneath brush. It was too deadly serious, he thought, studying the paper at eye-level. For years, he had believed there had to be some joking fox's face hidden in all that confusion, the clue to what the hurrah was about.

In the kitchen, he sat down and watched Jessie stir soup. "I'm going to get after those vines in the pine copse today," he said.

Noticing he was already wearing old work pants and a T-shirt, he wondered when he had put them on and why. Even sitting still, he perspired in the hot sticky aftermath of the summer rain. The last thing he remembered was going into town properly dressed to have his Seconal prescription filled. By happenstance, as he came out of Chester's drugstore, he had seen Cole, the Negro bootlegger.

"You got something I can wash down some pills with?" he had said.

"Suh," Cole had answered.

He remembered racing along the softly crushed, red gravel road, his pickup behind the Negro's, and going around back of a rural store he knew the Sheriff owned. Why not keep the whiskey closer to town, at the jail? he had wondered, going back through the pine-sweet, shining countryside with an old tarpaulin thrown over a case of beer and several bottles of bad Scotch, wishing for a bootlegger who knew more about whiskey. "Hardly no calls for Scotch," Cole had said. "We gets the cheapest."

Now, watching Jessie set down consommé, Almoner wondered whether anything was left to drink and where it was. The soup's steaming smell thrust upward. It was like the smell of a wet chicken or a wet hound, and suddenly he tasted again the first can of warm beer chasing the first capsule. He remembered little beyond that except a progression of daylights and darks. But what day or week it was now, he had no idea. He had managed, finally, to know nothing but darkness. Spooning soup wearily and without curiosity about those missing days, he recalled a sensation of glitter and gorgeousness, which meant he had spent time on a chaise in the dining room. Imprinted on his memory was the gleam of crystal, in bright sunlight let in through the muscadine, and that would have been the chandelier. He had a connecting memory of some green outdoors scent, lilies-of-the-valley, but not growing in spring's moist ground along the edges of the porch. He thought the scent had been Amelia's ritualistic perfume. He remembered opening his eyes and glimpsing her standing in some light-colored, sprigged dress, holding a white patent-leather pocketbook off which sun bounced as dazzling as snow.

If she had spoken, he might have responded, but she had instead only looked, and closing his eyes, he had kept them resolutely closed, without being able to help his mouth's corners turning up, like a cat's mouth. Exasperated, she had turned and gone sharply away, leaving to trail across the air the smell that made him want to possess something as unbelievably sweet. He had seen her as if through one-way glass. That would be his choice now in life, he thought, to see but not to be seen and to know things but not to have to contend with anything else. He had felt stretched beyond himself by forty and had had, then, a surfeit of the feeling for ten years.

At forty, he had thought life had to be faced as being made up of many shortcomings. And thinking this moment of Inga, he wished there were some way of supposing her somewhere besides in the house. The pain of recalling was too sharp, but something always brought him back to it. He spooned soup rather sullenly, and Jessie, noticing, stood at the sink with a hand kneading her back.

"You got the misery?" he said, stopping the spoon, solicitously.

She only mumbled and pretended inability to answer because her lip was too full of snuff, though it was not. He was able to interpret this as awareness of his feelings; their thoughts scattered in varied directions, but in the way she stood and he ate, they meant compassion for each other. He was wondering what point there was to reaching on and on outward into life if, now, he was to be so overcome with some indefinable need that not even Seconal and beer could deaden it. Spoon resting in empty bowl, he thought, staring down at the table and mentally composing a picture which he titled Emptiness.

"Is that axe still on the back porch?" he said.

"Was," Jessie said.

Jammed into an old cotton basket beside a saw, which was also rusty, the axe came out, dull-edged and with a scraping sound that set his nerves vibrating as wrongly as musical strings plucked by some untutored hand. And his nerves kept vibrating as they did at the sound of Amelia's voice. She had followed him into every room of the house, once. He could not escape. She had stood even outside the bathroom door crying, "Everything's falling apart, the yard's a mess. If you're not going to fix it up, you got to at least get some Negro to." Flushing had barely drowned her out. He had been angered into action when the toilet would not flush immediately a second time, as she droned on. Going for his tools, he had fixed the toilet to flush when needed, and she had watched disbelievingly. In the dining room now, the sideboard's door clicked shut. He made it almost from the kitchen before Inga came in, wearing a soft fawn-colored robe, the softness, the fawn, like her eyes, he thought. Sniffing for sherry, he smelled, so far, only the sweet scents of her bath. Her hair was damp at the base of her neck and pulled up onto the top of her head, then stuck with heavy gold pins. Artificially colored now, he supposed. But her hair had the naturally progressed look from virgin gold to her present age, and he anguished over what age could do.

"I have a headache," Inga said. "What should I take for it?"

"Aspirin, fresh air, try those," he said. Jessie, having gone to the back door to spit, had come back. "What us going to have for supper?" she said.

"Ask the mistress of the house," he said. Going by Inga, and wondering why she had on silver dancing shoes, he then smelled menthol from her medicated eye pads and the bittersweet smell of her cough syrup, which was heavy with codeine. A moment, that smell seemed to take him back into his own drugged sleep, and he struggled to keep his eyes open. Inga's voice was thick, her eyes were heavy, and the medicine was a whiff on the hand she raised in a gesture not hopeful of detaining him. In the hall, the telephone rang as he passed it. He answered only to sever himself from his previous conversation. Inga's hand had continued upward to her forehead, and she had said, "Oh, Jessie. Is the pain never to end?"

"Hello," he said.

A male voice young enough to quiver and quivering on a rising note rushed at him, without pause. "Mr. Almoner, sir, this is Borden Lake Decker, you went to school with my mother, Winifred Lake, Winnie they called her (Would the boy never breathe? he was wondering, smiling), and I go to Princeton (here he did breathe, waiting hopefully, Almoner thought, for at least a fraternal grunt, but he was silent), and my roommate is here, Quill Jordan, *Quill* Jordan, from Delton, you know (but he was not to be impressed, either), and we're both English majors at *Princeton* (yes, I got that), and we admire your work so much (whispering in the background), and, oh yes, Quill's writing a senior thesis on your work, and could we possibly come over and just meet you a moment? And, oh (more whispering), there's a girl here who wants to be a writer, too."

Whew, Almoner thought, though the young voice seemed not at all breathless. He said gravely that he was sorry, but he was leaving that moment on a fishing trip, not to return for several days.

"Oh," the boy said. His voice sank deep enough to hold a more masculine hint, as if he had touched the bottom of disappointment. Still, Almoner thought, he was not going to relent. The boy said, "Thank you for this much time, I know how you guard it."

Then why had he called? Almoner wanted to ask.

The boy cried as if he were within hailing distance. "But I want to tell you, Mr. Almoner. You're not forgotten at Princeton!" Then the phone was clamped down, abruptly, on his own confusion.

Almoner was chuckling and almost laughing continuing down the hall, but he was touched by the sincerity. And, I'm not forgotten at Princeton, he reminded himself, thinking of the vast gap between them that the boy would think that would matter. Yet it meant something to be told he was not forgotten. He had attended the university only a year. It had receded in his mind into all the university campuses he had ever visited. He went back into the sun, realizing he was appreciative, too late, of the boy's wanting to comfort him.

Crossing the porch, going into and out of the speckling shade of the muscadine, he was aware again, with a seasick feeling, of the light and dark of sun and shadow on the grey porch. He descended two steps down from it and crossed the sunlit yard toward the pine copse where it was hot and airless. Lifting the axe with effort, he was grateful for the shade and hacked at heavy tenacious kudzu vine grown in from the road and choking young trees. Old rain loosened, and drops glanced away like flint sparks from the gum-scented trees, while the afternoon grew muggier.

The work should have been done earlier, before the sun was out or after it had gone down. But it was a kind of punishment to lose through perspiration both liquor and medicine. He felt himself like a candle melting, perspiration flying from his elbows as he swung the axe above his head. He smelled on himself the stale smell of his obliterated days and nights. Beyond the copse, he faced gigantic and now flowerless forsythia bushes guarding the house. They swam before his eyes. Wiping perspiration, he drew an arm across his face and thought, Damn, did he have the d.t.'s? when a maroon Chevrolet appeared. However, it ground real gears beyond his cattle gap after slowing for it, then travelled toward the house with its wheels bearing, Ferris-wheel-fashion, wet leaves. He watched it curiously as if it had nothing to do with him; people in his house seldom had visitors. His brain was still dulled and received slowly a second image: that it was Roy Scarbrook who had just passed.

Starting toward the house, Almoner set the axe against a tree. He thought of Roy and his ever-wide, proprietary grin as he had seen him last, among his counters with their overhead labelling signs slightly wavering, Men's, Women's, Children's Wear, tittilated into motion by an old, revolving-bladed fan fixed to the ceiling. It must have been last summer, Almoner thought, when he had done his most recent shopping for himself and had purchased the khaki pants he wore now. Shaking hands with Roy Scarbrook, presently, would seem a continuation of that day, the year having evolved with his having almost no memory of it.

Roy, in a shiny plaid suit and with a pink cornflower in his buttonhole, was almost to the front door before Almoner realized the grin seemed recent because of a newspaper picture when Roy was elected Rotary president. It's going to be some other damn thing about promoting the town as a spa and needing me to help, he thought. He considered going back to the pine copse, but Roy, at the door, stuck his head forward and back, like an apprehensive but curious bird, apparently having been asked to enter and obviously reluctant to do it. Almoner would laugh, later, thinking what was strong enough to propel Roy forward eventually was ingrained, old-fashioned middle-class manners.

He gained the steps as Roy relinquished the door, having held it to the last possible moment, his hand remaining now behind him and in touch with the screen. Through it, having reached the porch, Almoner saw a face come forward as pale as death and looking disembodied. Thinking back to his dream, he almost instinctively called "Ma!" before seeing it was Inga encased in an invisible-looking dress. It was less than smoke-colored and drifting and its fragility was due mainly to age; the bodice once had been covered with iridescent sequins; now failing, they clung like fish-scale remnants on some half-cleaned fish. She came totteringly on the weak heels of the aged silver dancing shoes.

God, Almoner thought, she had done it all in exact sequence, the sweetly seductive bath, then her hair and her make-up and a nap in her robe; her dress had been donned a moment before the beau's arrival. Now, she held out a hand. For the corsage? Almoner anguished over life itself as much as over what it had done to Inga.

"Roy," she said. "I thought if we had a little talk, we could—" but Roy was backing out of the screen door he had never made a step beyond. He stepped aside to avoid colliding with Almoner.

Roy said, "We pressed your wife a little about her bill, but forget it! She can have all the time in the world to pay." His words floated back on the departing car's exhaust, while Jessie was still coming to answer the doorbell's summons.

Wide-eyed, she said, "Miss Inga, honey, you come lie down. I'll fix you some nice eye pads and your head won't hurt."

Amelia was a sliver of face at her own door. "I've never been so embarrassed," she said, shutting it again.

Jessie waited and then followed the sad drooping hem over its owner's doorsill and shut that door. Almoner made no sound laughing; again, dappled by leaf and shadow and sun as he crossed the porch, he felt confused. Though he was full of sorrow, he could not stop laughing. Moving from the muscadine's shelter and retracing his way across the yard, he retrieved the axe and re-entered the pine copse, where the shade had deepened. Mosquitoes thrust themselves against his ears. Pine needles, except on the bottommost layer of their mat, were dried and warm. What had she been going to do? he wondered, laughing. His mood changed when he thought that she could not have carried anything off and that was sad. And now added to the weight of his afternoon's work and to the weight of his life was knowledge of this new bill. How many times had he come up and gone down those porch steps, he wondered. Leaning on the axe handle, he went back again in memory to the morning when he had come home at the urging of the woman, Sugar, and found his parents dead. Gone: he hesitated over that word even now.

It had been a summer of drought. The pine copse had been scorched and browned. Having been told as little as possible, he had gone to see for himself the thin tire tracks crisscrossing, as if made by an erratic plow, the crumbly dry furrows of cotton land. An old Negro sharecropper living on the edge of the field had told him about the little car coming along travelling too fast. He had said that inside there had been a white man and a white lady, settin' forward like she could make the car go faster, and time they passed a cotton wagon, the car swang out of control and went off acrost a field. Sont ahead two tires, the old man had said, turnt over and burned. He had shaken his head sadly saying, "Another nigger got the tires."

He had gone back across the field at a walk, not running as he had come, like a boy. The sounds in his brain now as he worked his axe were the old echoes, Ma! Poppa! Jessie had explained how they had covered the countryside, once they discovered he was missing, and had found the farmer who had left him at the highway. They had been on their way to Delton when the accident happened, at that moment of dawn when he had been staring out over the river, solitary and lonesome.

To care for him and for Amelia there had been Jessie, who moved into the house, and old relatives. One by one, the latter had been buried from the house. The grey pall had seemed never to be lifted from the front windows. In despair, he had one summer gone to Europe on a walking trip and stayed long beyond his intended time. Then when he had come back there had been in the house only the three of them, he and Jessie and Amelia, but not the same two he had left. For Amelia had seemed a child then, as frail and crushable as a kitten. But she emerged from puberty an old maid. Male callers, after rising to greet her, were asked to fluff out the pillows again. Continually his comings and goings had been questioned, until he had thought of marriage as an escape, though wide-eyed Southern girls had seemed as empty as Kewpie dolls.

Switzerland had touched him deeply, and there he had spent his longest time at a small pension where cows had been bedded behind the thin walls of his room, their sounds and smells reminiscent of home. (Companionably at sunset, he and Poppa had always driven in their own cows for milking; he had heard again the sounds of Poppa urging them on and of the dull clanking of their bells.) He had seen in the Swiss mountains far-reaching sunsets similar to his own countryside's, and tiny wild flowers, like fallen stars in stubby pasture grass. Soft evenings there had been full of the same enormous country stillness; his past at home had fused with his present there. His time had been spent with the household's youngest daughter, who had chosen his souvenirs, and on whom he had lavished chocolates and lavender sachets. He had written her from home. Yes, she had written back, she remembered him good. He had felt endeared to her not only because she remembered him but because of her misspelled and scrabbled English. Returning to visit, he had brought her back his bride. Now, she was calling at the front window: "Jessie! The shade won't come down!"

Hidden from the road, he watched the descent of the tasselled shade as Jessie darkened the front room. The loneliness of the countryside was all around him and near only grazing cattle. A mourning dove called but another did not answer. He resumed hacking at the vines, his mind wandering, still drowsy and not himself. But would he ever be again? he wondered. This present sensation of order would be temporary: the axe, his upraised hand, the tangled vine at his feet. Soon he was thinking of the drugged man in the hammock and of the young bridegroom with aspirations. "Not," he had cried repeatedly, "to be a *Bürgermeister!*" But Inga always had had deaf ears. Almoner thought of himself, at the axe's next descent, as a monk locked up to copy laboriously for years, who at last had finished the work, but himself had been broken and done in. But even to his own satisfaction, the work was done; that was worth a lifetime, wasn't it? Envisioning manuscript stacked up behind him, he heard imaginary applause, and from the house he heard Amelia and Inga shouting to one another, irritably.

By God! This time the car was yellow. He stopped, his hatchet midair, as much surprised as before, knowing this one could not be wiped away along with perspiration, either. He stood motionless, like a wild animal trying to hide. The cattle gap had caught the driver unaware, and he had stopped the car, straddling it. Almoner knew they had to be strangers, for any car as long as a city block, in this town, would be familiar. It was being driven backward between the forsythias. He swore at the eyesight of the young. The boy, driving, had glimpsed him and was getting out, his head seeming on fire, his bright orange hair singed by evening sunlight. He kept still, though the situation was hopeless, while the boy came on, smiling fearfully. Even before hearing his rather high voice, Almoner knew it was the one who had telephoned. What had he said: that he knew his mother? If so, the name was lost. But he had fobbed him off, obviously enough, with a lie, and that he had come anyway was too blatant, like his hair. With a quick mental image of himself trapped there, Almoner thought, there was no way out. But, thrusting aside pines, the boy offered him one.

Her room was cast in summer darkness, which could only mean rain. And, not opening her eyes, she felt an imagined sense of the ocean's bottom; though, unintentionally, she was thinking of the ultra-green underwater of chlorine-filled swimming pools with which she was familiar. The wallpaper in her bedroom was blue and green and in an adjoining bathroom the paper had a pattern of shells. Truant ivy across her windows cut light, its shadows flickering in independent spots on the ceiling. She imagined with her eyes still closed that flickering to be exotic and wildly patterned fish. The roof of tiles was slanting and there a pale pigeon had managed to secure itself and was cooing. Any coolness in summer was a relief. She drew up a sheet which had a feel of dampness like fog and rubbed her feet against towels now rough and dried. The night before her mother had laid them across the bed wet for the attic fan to blow over them. Remembering that coolness now, and suddenly that it was the morning she was going, Amy opened her eyes. Her mother came that moment on silent bare feet across the hall to stand in the doorway, looking older. Her voice dryly held sleep as if not to relinquish night, with nothing ahead in her day. "What time are you going?" Edith said.

"At nine," Amy said. She shut her mind abruptly against criticism from her mother, and wished she had lied. For Edith immediately was breathless. "Why didn't you get up earlier then? You won't be ready! You'll go out again looking like a tack," she said. Sighing and assuming the burden unasked, Edith went to the kitchen and began slamming about pots and pans, the noise meaning if Amy did not have sense enough to hurry, she did.

Listening as water rushed into the sink to grow hot, for the coffee to make sooner, Amy removed her pajamas and left them in a dispirited heap on the floor, where they had slipped from a hook. She stared into the disordered closet where there was almost nothing to choose from and nothing appropriate to wear. Her father's frequent and disgruntled appraisal came to mind: "With all the money she can spend on her clothes!" At breakfast, her mother would say the same. Amy picked out a dress at random, feeling all of them were wrong. As consciously as putting stoppers in her ears, she told herself not to mind what her mother said; and she would not mind really being told what was wrong, if only someone would tell her what was right! Her white slip looked grey. Feeling inert and withdrawn, she came into the kitchen where her mother stood cooking. And, turning her head, Edith's look said plainly, Why couldn't Amy ever look as nice as the other girls?

Made to feel self-conscious, she swung her legs, childlike, beneath the table but then saw her sandals had muddy heels. Why hadn't she noticed when she put them on, as other girls would have? She had seen only, dressing, that her skirt had a spot, and she had tried to press a pleat carefully over it. Before, her mother had said that the sandals might be right for walking about a muddy campus, but they were wrong for Delton where people dressed when they went out. As Edith poured coffee now, her eyes roamed. "Are you going out with something all over the front of your dress?" she said.

"It's not all over, it's only a spot," Amy said. However, since she had come downstairs, it seemed to have grown larger. She longed to put down her head and cry about its being there at all.

"Why can't you look better with the money you can spend on your clothes?" Edith asked in exasperation. She wondered whether Amy was ever going to grow up. She wondered the next moment whether she ever wanted her to; bringing Energine, she scrubbed at the spot.

To Amy, her mother's head seemed so vulnerable bent solicitously at her knee, and her scalp was so babyishly clean, that she wanted to care about the things her mother did. Smelling her mother's perfume from the day before, Amy remembered her dressed beautifully to go out, bending over the crib to say goodnight and tickling with her hair. People ought to have some

visible connection to kin, to make explainable why you felt bound to them: because you were all bald, for instance. Her stockings were not the same shade, and Amy was grateful her mother had not noticed. Having congratulated herself on putting on stockings at all, to discover they were not mates only reconfirmed that almost everything she did went wrong. But she had had on one stocking, and so she had put on another.

Edith had opened the back door and stood staring out with some private thought. But turning, she said only, "It might clear," and birds fluttered away on wet wings at her voice.

Amy said, "Quill will have his top down whether it rains or not." She hoped to share with her mother amusement, at least. But Edith was not to be won over and remained across the room slightly frowning. "It'll serve you right for going," she said. "It's ridiculous to miss that luncheon." With aimless anger focused at last, Edith twisted her mouth. Amy looked away thinking that when she left, her mother would say, "Have a good time."

When she bent over her breakfast, mud inside the sandals slid uncomfortably toward her toes. Leaning against the wall and admitting that she did look tacky, Amy wondered what to do with the rest of her life. Her head felt toppled, as if it needed to be braced. Supporting her chin with her hand, she hoped her life would pass quickly.

Edith, wondering whether Amy would ever learn to sit up straight, said, "Where'd you get that dress?"

"Near school. Why, don't you like it?" Amy said, knowing of course her mother did not, or she would not have asked in that tone. Edith's shrug implied Amy might know what girls wore at that school but it was not what they wore in Delton. But that was her dilemma, Amy thought, that she belonged neither here nor there. She wiped perspiration that sprang out along her hairline. The rain had dwindled and birds drank in the house's gutter.

Edith had been looking out; staring back at Amy, she spoke as if she were dying. "All my life," she said, "I've wanted to get out of the South in the summertime."

Amy thought how annoying for people to spend their lives doing what they did not want to; she would not. When Edith bent over her coffee cup her face sagged—either in age or in disappointment. Amy felt sorry for her mother; she met her mother's eyes over her cup's rim.

"Did you hear a car?" Edith said.

But Amy had already taken from her pocketbook a small mirror and was putting on lipstick. She hurried to the living room where the French doors were closed against blown rain. There, through small wet panes, she saw Quill stopping to put on his seersucker jacket. Behind him, windshield wipers had been left running on his car, giving her the feeling he had little time to spare here, and feeling protective toward home, Amy wondered if she would ever be able to leave her mother. The cathedral ceiling in its far reaches held gloom settled like tufts of fog. She tried to remain hidden as Quill came up the steps in his duck-footed way. But seeing her, and doubling up his fist, he made a great show of pretending to knock on the glass wildly. He tried so earnestly to make people laugh, it seemed rude not to. Amy opened the door and smiled broadly. Politely, he kept his eyes from flickering over her clothes. He was dressed meticulously and his clothes became him, as her father's seemed always to belong to him. He even had his shirts custom-made with tiny monograms. As she tugged open the French doors, her father came out on the porte-cochere overhead and leaned over the railing and smiled down in his flushed way. "Hey, boy, how's the squash?" he called.

"Fine. How's yours?" Quill's face grew redder as he glanced up. Her father's ringed hand pressed against his middle to imply

flatness and trim and that he was fit as a fiddle. Those, Amy thought, would be his words if he said any. However, he only held together the flaps of his silk robe and went back inside to shave after calling, "Good to see you, boy."

She had been aware of Edith's running upstairs; now, she appeared having put on bedroom shoes, softly padding. Amy went quickly toward the car and whispered, "Come on. Let's go. Hurry."

Quill had to stop. "Fine," he answered. "How're you, Mrs. Howard?" Weariness overcame Amy as she knew her mother would tell him. Edith touched the neck of her pink robe, and her cheeks flushed the same pale color. She was happy to have conversation with someone, though her eyes stared about wearily at morning, and her hand held without interest the doorknob to her house. "I'm fine," Edith said weakly, which meant that she was not. But it was not young people's worry, her smile said, bravely. In the car, Amy clenched her fists; her feet pressed against the floorboard hard.

"Does your momma think you're crazy, too?" Edith asked. If only Quill would not answer, Amy thought, saying, "Mother, we have to go."

"Amy hops around like a flea," Edith said. "Does your mother think you'll see this man?"

"She said we'd have a pretty drive," Quill said. Edith's eyes shone and her smile grew. She saw that was a nicer and more subtle way of putting it than she had. Perhaps she was often too blunt; had that made Amy so shy? She said softly, "You won't see him."

Amy, with an intense look, had urged Quill into the car. He started the motor, and as they backed out of the drive Amy saw Edith watching as if to make the moment of their having been there last. Amy smiled and waved and Edith waved back thinking, My baby. While they were still within hearing distance, she cupped her hands as if to yodel and called, "Don't forget Dea! And have a good time!"

Quill's foot went to the brake. "What did she say?"

"Nothing," Amy said. "Go on. I heard. I have to stop a minute and speak to my aunt." She leaned against the seat thinking how irritating it was to be told, like a dog, to Speak! In public places, Edith was always nudging her and saying, "There's so-and-so, don't forget to speak." If she were playing bridge at home, she would say, "The girls will be here, don't forget to come in and speak." Otherwise, Edith said, ladies talked about rudeness and the upbringing of someone's child and whether or not they were going to turn out right.

Halting the car at a red light, Quill removed his coat and laid it in careful folds on the back seat. At a filling station, opposite, where her family traded, the proprietor knelt changing a tire but did not recognize Amy in the unfamiliar car. When she waved, he made no sign in return; then she was taken on, melancholy at not being known. Signs above them read QUILL BLVD. It was lined with car lots whose shimmery signs and triangular paper announcements rattled in the wind. The galore turned even the fine mist tawdry, Amy thought. Customerless salesmen stood at windows staring out with thoughtless faces, and people leapt gutters full of water to catch busses. Damming up gutters as a child, and sifting through debris, she often had found money and pretty stones, which she called by the names of exotic jewels; luck had been comfort in the loneliness to which she had seemed born. Having aspired then to being grown, she had never suspected that could also mean insecurity and more loneliness. Amy was grateful that Quill did not mind silence; she kept watching life along the street. Women came from cavernous supermarkets, followed by white-aproned clerks obscured by grocery sacks. Once, she had asked her mother why she did not shop for weeks

26

ahead. And Edith had said, "You don't know anything about running a house, and you never will. You'll never have your nose out of a book long enough!" Eventually, Amy had understood. This morning, Edith had announced happily that they were out of coffee. With purpose, she would go out shopping later. Amy felt guilty, staring out at the rain-struck people, having never seen she was not responsible for the emptiness of her mother's days.

Quill's expensive shirt had a smell of being freshly laundered, hand-ironed, making Amy think wistfully of feeling cared for. When the light changed, his face took on a greenish, electrified look. Seeing his profile in repose, she thought for the first time that Quill was handsome. He felt watched. He turned and his eyes expressed, silently and excitedly, "We're going!" She nodded, but kept her true excitement inside. They left the final sign reading QUILL BLVD. It was easier to have a freer sense in tangled countryside, too poor even for pastureland. The smell of rained-on ground rushed to the car window when she lowered it; the rain had almost gone.

In its polished loafer, Quill's foot pressed the accelerator harder. Though his hands were pudgy, they were inordinately clean and their nails looked buffed. They held fastidiously the rosewood steering wheel, which had a mellow shine like good furniture, cared for. He gave Amy more of a feeling of being disordered. She moved her own feet farther from that polished shoe on the accelerator. It seemed unfair that all Quill had to worry about was losing weight and admission to a certain club at Princeton. He was telling her now about a new diet, consisting only of grapefruit. She sometimes turned her head, as if listening. As they went through a small town, she was attentive to the clay soil washing redly toward the sidewalks. Wasn't her life passing repetitiously? Years had accumulated in which she had known Quill, and always he had been either gaining or losing weight. But at twelve, when she had been in dancing school, he had been the only boy ever to ask her to dance. She looked at him now, thankfully, remembering her terror. She had never really gotten over it. She thought how even her father had said, in those days, she was cute. But she had never been able to make animated conversation with little boys, as instructed by Edith. Trying to rattle on gaily in conversation, she had failed. After mingling at the punch bowl, she would then not be chosen as a partner; always, she had to dance with another superfluous girl. Feeling guilty about that, she had never told Edith, who had wanted her to be popular and to attend. Keeping unhappiness to herself, Amy had believed strengthened her character; she had been very early concerned about strengthening it. But, at dancing school, something besides shyness had kept boys away, some difference in herself she could not explain. And wishing that it had a name, she turned to Quill with pretended interest and said, "But don't you get tired of nothing but grapefruit?"

"Of course," he said. "And I cheat." The diet was his father's idea, who was frantic about Quill's appearance. Quill had to succeed him as president of the bank founded by Grandfather Quill, for whom the boulevard had been named. Once, Quill had confided eagerly that he really wanted to be a painter. "Then aren't you going to?" Amy had said. He had replied in a flat voice, "I have to be a banker instead." Robust and hearty and wearing slimming dark suits, he would sit in the gilt-laden old foyer greeting depositors, and his soul would be a painter's. Flecks of gold had appeared in his green eyes when he spoke that day of painting. In the light of this rosewood dashboard, he had one night read her *The Prophet,* with the car doors open to night and the aged smell of the Mississippi, a cavern of darkness down the bank from them. Innocently, she had said, "But would your father really care if you didn't become a banker?"

"Care!" Quill had half-screamed, in astonishment. And the

28

word Care! had flown out into the darkness, like a rallying cry. How, she had wondered, did people reconcile themselves to things against their nature, or quell rebellious hearts and manage to laugh, as Quill had. But she had wondered also, shortly, whether people should.

Quill's father had said that fatness might imply sloppiness for depositors, and instability might be implied if Quill bet publicly on games. He could not even play bridge, which he loved, for money. Luckily, his father had been happy with the narrow life to which he had been born, but was it fair to deprive his son? Since she seldom could answer her questions, Amy kept staring silently out at the countryside. Repetitiously, the tires seemed to be crying, You're going! She had thought it good that Quill's father cared about something and that he cared so much, wondering about her own parents' interests. She leaned on the windowsill now, wishing her brain would rest. Always, she had to be wondering about something: God or justice or things like that, without answer. She would like to know, for instance, the reason for suffering: why some people had to and others did not. She wondered that now, watching the landscape go by silently. She had never had anyone to answer her questions, but then she had never had anyone to ask, either. She had been worn out with inconclusiveness when she began to read Almoner's books, and had gotten from them the feeling that everything she had ever asked herself, he had. He would answer all her questions when she saw him, she felt.

Talking about his diet, Quill had said, "I'm starving. You got anything with you to eat?"

She shook her head. "What did your father think about our going today?"

Drawing down his chin into triplicate, Quill intoned several times the words, "Waste of time," his voice mockingly deep. It was strange, his father thought, that a man would write books which didn't make any money and go on writing them. He had been grave about such queerness, with all the implications that word had. Quill shook his head, imitatively.

"No one would think a thing if we were going to see a movie star," Amy said. "Everybody went crazy thinking Ava Gardner was coming to Delton." They were satisfied with themselves, and exchanged smiles. Then Amy turned toward the window to watch a boy straddling a horse, riding across the horizon. She waved at a small Negro boy running alongside the road, with empty pop bottles, toward a general-merchandise store.

Fused behind rain clouds, the sun suddenly appeared as if a curtain had been drawn aside. One might applaud, it shone so well. Feeling warmed, Amy considered confiding to Quill her fear, her loneliness, and that she had a deep need for a lasting friendship. But, holding to reserve, she only gazed out longingly at the passing countryside, conceding all these years later, since dancing school, that silence was still natural to her. Suppose she revealed her innermost thoughts to someone and they did not care! No one else had needs as desperate as her own, she thought. She wondered if people whom they passed on the roadside glimpsed, at the car window, a small face, forlorn and wondering.

The road ahead went straight, without curves; that seemed to be Quill's future, while hers was fraught with danger and unpredictability. Hers was as jumbled as the static Quill got on the radio. Pushing buttons to clear it, he winked, meaning, look at the buttons. They read BCIKU, rather than BUICK. Baby, Can I Kiss U? Despite his wink, Quill had never had that feeling for her, and Amy wondered why. The buttons changed gave her a sense of belonging, if only to a fad of her generation, for everyone she knew changed the buttons in their families' Buicks. Feeling so often the need to run away in all directions at once, Amy found stability in anything predictable or repetitious. She might at this moment, even, be the daughter her mother wanted: any girl in her crowd out riding and receiving winks. Yet the evasive difference existed. Not having wanted to go to the luncheon, she had not gone, but felt guilty at breaking convention.

Quill interrupted her reverie saying, "I can't wait to ask Almoner about that long passage at the end of *Reconstruction*. Nobody knows what it means, exactly."

"Something about being glad and hating, too, that the South lost the war, isn't it?" She wondered if that were her own interpretation, or one come back from some forgotten seminar. Her interest in seeing Almoner was not to discuss his books, and she felt disappointed that was Quill's reason, though suddenly, she realized it was the obvious one, that it was why most people would want to see him. Still, she was disappointed it was Quill's reason. Almoner, simply, was to open for her all her locked-in feelings. He would understand her past, as she felt she understood his. Everyone was imprisoned by his past, she had read. One stared out from behind it as from the bars of a cell. It had been a Russian who had said it, she remembered, obviously someone dark and brooding.

"At Princeton," Quill said, "everyone thought the passage meant more than just that the land was wasted. It has to be symbolic of something bigger."

"It does?" she said. "Well, I never understand symbols unless they're so obvious, they're awful." And she did not understand the significance of living, she thought, watching in envy gigantic crows lift themselves from fields of dead corn to fly over treetops into the distance, freely. Compassion in Almoner's books was what mattered to her, and she changed the subject. "Are you sure Borden knows we're coming?"

"Certain," Quill said. "His momma phoned this morning and wants us for lunch."

"Lunch," Amy said. She had not thought they would take time to eat. If it were arranged with Mrs. Decker, then nothing could be done. Even the thought of Borden's mother made her feel ill-at-ease. What had she thought of their going?

"I can't imagine a girl wanting to go out there and see that man!" Quill cried, in imitation of Mrs. Decker's pretentious tones. "Don't let it matter what she said." He patted Amy's knee, knowing she would worry, anyway.

Amy's voice grew smaller; she pleaded. "Don't let her know the whole thing was my idea!" He was reassuring, but Amy looked terrified staring ahead at the road. He looked down at her legs, which she had stretched out with a weary motion. They were good. He wondered why he had no desire to take her hand resting on the seat near him. She looked pretty and that violet shade was her best color, though her dress was terrible. But why had she worn those shoes? Her intentness made him remember how she had said that, even if it were wrong for his father to want him to be a banker, at least his father cared: implying her own did not, he supposed. But what did she think his father cared about, Quill wondered. Certainly not me, he thought. Not myself.

A long time, a water tower had been ahead as if suspended in the sky. They passed beneath it now, circling through the square of a small town. "Halfway there," Amy said, letting out a relieved breath. Even Quill might be bored by her long silences, but the landscape was conducive to dreaming, and she kept staring out silently. Here was a tangled world of greenery. Even telephone poles to their topmost were covered thickly with tangled kudzu vine, which covered road banks and filled ditches. Brightly colored birds darting in and out of it fostered, too, a feeling of jungle. Having seen Quill glance in distaste at her shoes, Amy saw in horror that she had left, as a country child might, long yellowish streaks of dried mud on the carpeted floorboard. She had to think of the practical, as usual, and tried surreptitiously to brush them away.

"Leave them," Quill said. "The car needs vacuuming anyway."

Blushing, Amy wished momentarily to be someplace else. But someplace else could be worse. Her debutante friends soon would be selecting from orderly closets dresses appropriate for the luncheon. She said, her voice faint, "Did Mrs. Decker say anything else?"

"That Almoner drinks."

"Well, so does she." Amy turned angrily. "She's always crocked at the club."

"That when he's drunk, he runs around his yard, naked, reciting poetry." Quill bent over to beat the wheel rapturously, laughing. Sinking against the seat in laughter, too, Amy said, "I'm afraid though, it's not true."

Under no circumstance, her aunt Dea had told her mother, should she let Amy go out there to meet Almoner. And then, after hanging up, and knowing she could not stop her, Edith had made great shaking fists crying, "Oh, why can't you be like the other girls?" At noon, those girls would be eating chicken à la king out of crispless patty shells. Though she had made her decision, as so often happened, Amy had a conflicting second thought: Should she be at the party, about to sip sherry? She gave directions down her aunt's familiar washed-out driveway, and promised not only Quill, but herself, that they would not stay long.

Uncle Joe appeared on the porch, which was laden with ferns. From his receptive face, Amy could tell he had been watching for the car. Was he shorter than she remembered or was the effect caused by his wide-legged baggy pants? He seemed the same width as height. Then no longer did she consider his appearance, not even that he had come out in run-over tan bedroom shoes, for the moment he saw her, he cried, "Sugar!" and patted

33

her repeatedly. Did he remember the time when she was little, and he had swatted her playfully on the rear and burst a boil? They went into the house laughing, where abruptly Amy halted to think, This is my uncle and this is his house. She found a similarity to her learning to ice skate at school; then she had gone wobbling across a slick pond, which had seemed ever widening, and finally had reached the opposite bank where she had grabbed onto a tree for safety. The secure feeling of the tree came to Amy now, as she stood thinking, This is my uncle and this is his house. He called her always Sugar when her father never had. "Son," Uncle Joe had said, meeting Quill.

Uncle Joe padded across the room to pick up his pipe, filling the room, once again, with the aroma of honeyed smoke Amy remembered. She stared from one to another. She hoped they realized she could not assume the responsibility of a conversation, though it might be hers since they were strangers. At Joe's suggestion, she and Quill sat on a brown horsehair sofa with spots worn amber, a place to nap when she was small. Waking, she would have cheeks as bristling and red as when her father, teasingly, rubbed whiskers against her before shaving. Summer with its distinct smells came now through the open windows, past the ferns in their old green pots. From them rose the smell of enriched earth and dampened peat moss. She thought of woods that had been behind the house and of gardens and earthworms turned up after rain and of her cousins chasing her, dangling them. "How are Josie and Bubba?" she said.

"Fine and hope to see you," Joe said. "But we couldn't tell them to come over because we didn't know what time you'd be getting here."

Always suspecting adverse criticism, Amy began to defend herself. "I didn't know what time, either," she said. "Quill was a little uncertain. Then there was traffic and the rain. I was afraid they'd be sitting around waiting if I wrote them." Uncle Joe's calm face said he had not meant anything, she did not have to defend herself against him. And realizing that, Amy had sense enough to hush.

Joe said, "Sometime, you got to come just to see us. You didn't today, did you?" and he gave Quill a wink.

"We did come mainly to see Almoner," Amy said.

"Hep my time. That's what your aunt said. I told the woman I finally was going to have her locked up. How come you want to see that rascal?"

Quill dared glance at Amy, but barely. Things were so much as she had predicted them, they could not help laughing. Why they laughed escaped Joe, and he could be easily led to another topic. Amy said, "We just want to see Almoner. But where's Aunt Dea?"

"Ran uptown, sure did," Joe said. "Said you'd come as soon as she left, and you did." But were they going to leave? The boy was edging off the sofa. "She's coming right back."

While Quill suggestively rattled the car keys in his pocket, something she could not define held Amy. That she had not spoken to her aunt, as her mother wanted? Feeling some bond, she said, "Well, if she'll be right back, we can wait longer."

Amy gazed out at the ragged drive, refusing to look at Quill, which meant, she had not wanted to have lunch at Mrs. Decker's, either. Standing, Quill edged about the room impatiently, and Amy thought she saw it as he did. Silence bore down heavily on the small house from all the surrounding fields. Inside was heard only the ticking of a grandfather clock, enormous in the tiny entranceway. Its slow rhythmic pendulum seemed to say not much went on around here. On either side of the mantel were shelves, without books, used as whatnot cases. They held inexpensive ornaments, like china swans with backs hollowed to hold candies and nuts, which held, instead, an accumulation of rubber bands from Sunday morning papers. Reasons for existence seemed to be the over rained fields outside, where cotton stood worrisomely low. Long after the house itself and the people in it were gone, clocks would tick and the land would exist, the silence said. But people, and particularly strangers, cannot stand too much silence. When conversation died, and since he was the host, Joe looked toward the window. "It's fairing up," he said.

Making up for the impoliteness of wanting to leave, Quill agreed. "Yes sir, I believe it is."

"Aunt Dea's coming." Amy went quickly to the door, with Quill following. He was introduced and took Dea's groceries. "We'll put them in the kitchen," she said.

Coming back inside, Amy glanced up at Blue Boy, who seemed enigmatically to stare down from a wooden frame. A table beneath him held a tarnished bud vase and a single yellow paper rose, making Amy remember that in meager moonlight this house had had a kind of goldness, that after she had said good-night, Aunt Dea's face had declined into shadow. By the time Uncle Joe said, "Nite, Sugar," Josie beside her would be asleep. Bubba in the next room would signal by kicking against the wall, until Uncle Joe said only, "Sonny," then he would quit. And always the bedcovers had had a smell of oldness, as if taken from newspaper-lined trunks.

Dea stood now in the kitchen doorway, tying on an apron, saying she was sorry they could not stay for noon dinner. Then, for the first time, Amy looked at her and thought, this was not her aunt but her father's sister. Fleeting resemblance was in Dea's dark eyes, with a heavy fringe of lashes, and in some stance of her feet, despite their being in wedge-heeled red shoes. What point, Amy wondered, was there to common memories from childhood if afterward people were to be so separate and different? Matching her breath to Josie's in sleep, she had tried to draw herself closer. Amy had thought she would not be lonely if only she had a sister. One summer visit, she had slept with her hand beneath the pillow, but her tooth had been gone in the morning. A nickel had replaced it, and she had known there was no fairy. At home, she was left quarters, but Uncle Joe had given what he could. Afterward, she overheard her mother laughing. "She wants us to give her only nickels from now on, like Joe," Edith had said. Amy's father had been taking up ice. "If we'd left her there long enough, she'd have been glad to come home," he had said.

"I'm sorry you can't stay," Dea said. "I'd hoped you would have forgotten all about seeing that man."

"Forgotten?" Amy said. She could not laugh in front of Dea. Quill took sudden interest in some farming magazines on the maple coffee table. Dea sighed decisively, then blurted out, "He hasn't been seen in town for a week. That means one thing, he's on a spree. Amy, you have no business going out there even if this boy goes, you hear?"

Quill flung himself back exaggeratedly on the sofa, as if reeling from a blow. "You see him? You actually see Almoner?"

"Of course," Dea said. "He lives here. Why wouldn't we?" And Joe looked curiously at the boy, waiting to hear. "Only a million trillion people would like to see him," Quill said, managing to sit up straight. Joe began to study his pipe, which was not drawing right. He said offhandedly, "Shoot, don't anybody around here think anything about seeing him. Most probably hope they don't. Right, Mother?" He and Dea nodded, backing each other up. Smiling a little to himself, Joe said, "When he's not on a spree, he's fishing. I'd like to know when he writes all those books he's supposed to write. They say he's got some influence up yonder in New York, though. And a group of us here, farmers and merchants, want to build up tourist trade and turn our hot springs into as important a place as the one over yonder in Arkansas. There was a great big ho-tel here once that burned. We need some backing to build another. We thought Almoner might interest some folks up North. But a group went out there and he wouldn't even see them."

"Honey, wouldn't even see them!" Dea said, explosively.

"I tried to get him on the phone, and this nigger woman, been with them a long time, said he wasn't home. But I know good and well he was. How come I know is the vet was out there seeing about one of his cows sick and phoned and told me I could catch him. Then she says he wasn't to home."

"Any of them will say anything they want to, I believe," Dea said. "Except that little wife of his. I feel right sorry for her sometimes. She seems lonely. I think it's been hard on her having two other women in the house who were there first."

"Well, she's a foreigner," Joe said. "Maybe she didn't know anything about running a house."

"Lord help us. I imagine running a house in a foreign country is the same as running one here. Same old sixes and sevens," Dea said, wondering at the look of surprise Amy turned on her. She had been sitting like a correct little girl, her knees pressed together so hard they showed white places, though chewing on a fingernail. Then she jerked up her head in such surprise her hair flew away from her shoulders. Did Amy think because she was a housewife, she never got tired of it? Dea wondered. Edith had said Amy had some crazy, idealistic picture of life, that you shouldn't have to do things you didn't want to. Amy would grow up, Dea supposed. She hoped she would get over being so quiet and thoughtful. Why had this boy come along on this wild-goose chase today? Smitten with Amy was the only reason Dea could guess.

What would Aunt Dea do if she didn't do housework? Amy had wondered. Having bitten the cuticle, she now had a sore-looking red place. Damn it. Why couldn't she have pretty long nails like her mother's. Tucking fingertips toward her palms, she decided she had misunderstood Dea's tone; probably, she had been just tired. The cross look on her face had gone already. Sighing, Amy thought that nobody had problems like her own.

"He never has done a lick of work I could see," Joe was saying.

Politely, Amy said, "Who?"

"Almoner," Joe said. "Ain't that who we been talking about?" He gave her a kidding look, thinking she must have had her mind on this boy. Immediately, they had looked at one another, though not exactly as if they had been bitten by the love bug. A moment later, they were leaving.

Amy trailed her hands through ferns on the porch, pulling them until leaves came loose, then pulverizing them between her fingers into a remembered fuzzy mixture. She hoped they had not left rudely, unsure what she had said. With some appropriate saying, she had maneuvered them outside. Pressed hard against Dea a moment, she felt a child again, remembered hiding behind the fern tubs in hide-'n'-seek. It was difficult to realize once she had been so small, the ferns had been taller than her head. Pressed now equally hard against Joe, she wanted to sink against him and confide and sob. "Come back, Sugar," he said, and his voice seemed to tremble as if there were things he understood. But suddenly fearing he was going to see right inside her, Amy drew back with her heart full of love, her eyes unrevealing. "Don't worry," she said. "I'll be back."

"Don't you get mixed up with any Yankee boys now, hear." When he cautioned her, he winked at Quill. The remark seemed the result of narrow-mindedness and stupidity to Amy. Perhaps she was right to keep, tightly, everything to herself. As they stood together, Dea and Joe seemed safe against the world, she thought, lonesomely. Everyone waved. As they drove off, she remembered from childhood that Joe's favorite expression had always been, "Depression years, a nickel was hard to come by." And thinking of the one he had spared beneath her pillow, she looked back and again wanted to cry.

When the car was out of sight, Dea turned to confront other plants on the porch, feeling angry that they looked puny after all her care. She could pitch them all over the back fence with easy grace. She unpacked groceries, while Joe settled before television, though there was nothing on now but reruns. Inattentive to it, he called, "Amy seems younger for her age than most girls." But he wondered why she looked so unhappy when she had everything in the world. Some look in her face kept returning, and he said, "On the other hand, she seems older in some ways." He had not meant to start a long conversation, but Dea appeared in the doorway saying, "Seen too much at home, I imagine." Why had he started talking if he wanted to watch television? A sports program was coming on, and he looked glued to it. She returned to the kitchen thinking of her brother, Mallory. Fancy doodle, she called him, seeing him crying "Teatime!" at four in the afternoon when he was mixing up martinis. Amy probably even knew about that place called The Cotton Stalk out on the highway, where all those River Street businessmen went to drink beer and meet women and God knew what else. Only she did know, Dea thought, because there was a motel right next door.

Truthfully, she did not like being a farmer's wife and never had. She felt resentful, too, that Mallory had made money and Joe had not. Her hand strayed uncertainly over shelves, as she thought of Amy hellbent on finding the life she wanted.

"Hon, what's for dinner?" Joe called.

Dea felt that moment like crying and could not answer.

"HON, what are we eating?"

Thinking of what was in the icebox, Dea said, "Ham."

And Joe murmured, "Again," but meant to be heard. He strolled to the kitchen because there was a commercial on television. He saw by Dea's face that she did not want ham, either. He thought of things he ought to tell her, that he knew he had not come up to her expectations, for one thing. Almoner, now, might be able to put those things into words, and for that, he could envy the man. Inadequately, he tried to tell her everything by saying, "I love you. I sure do."

"I know it," Dea said, patting his hand. And she was grateful he meant she would never grow too old for him. Yet she was glad to be able to draw his attention to the window, having seen that Old Bess's calf had escaped into the road again. She watched Joe cross the yard to head the calf back to the side lot, admitting she felt envious of Amy and her young friend. Suddenly, she had a premonition of Joe's early death. She would live then in long loneliness, regretting even the passing of these days, Dea thought.

The town, Amy had thought, would have some look comparable to Almoner's greatness. She stared about it in disappointment. All the little stores, with flat roofs, seemed squashed together and faced a railroad station in the center of town. The tracks, from a distance, seemed to end at a crumbly red brick Court House with white pillars. In reality, they curved on beyond it and stretched across the flat Delta, following briefly a willow-banked, somnambulant and yellowish river. In all directions, parked cars fanned out from the station. Negroes, who congregated about it on benches, liked the might and windiness of passing trains. Few stopped. For the most part, they were expresses rushing on toward New Orleans. The silence which descended after a train had gone lay vastly heavy over the countryside. People pausing to watch the train had loose clothing blown about in its breeze and seemed to stand in frozen wonderment at the thought of other places. Now, at standstills and as if mesmerized, people who had watched the train pass remained. Even Quill's car, halted in its presence, seemed to quiver. The train sent back thin whistling cries as lonesome as the bearable loneliness of the countryside itself. And in its aftermath, pursuits resumed by those who had watched seemed negligible. An old man in a stationmaster's black suit came out, totteringly, to inspect flowers in a garden along the tracks, which was surrounded by a little white wire fence, like intertwined croquet wickets, of that height. His flowers grew voluptuously, though some straggled in a dark red line along the ground as if something wounded had gone by. Others were yellow blossoms on thin stalks as if the sun had graciously scattered pieces. It was high now and bright.

Unevenly along the end of one block were Negro stores with bluish-looking screen doors. Quill drove across the tracks. Amy could smell popcorn from a movie where already children had formed a Saturday-afternoon line. Some store windows held bent faded placards and tricolored bunting, heralding politicians, left over from the Fourth of July. A man, cutting diagonally across the street, seemed an artistic person, wearing a slouch hat and smoking a pipe. "That might be Almoner!" Amy cried. Neither of them knew what he really looked like for he had refused pictures for many years, even for book jackets. Immediately, Quill had clapped his foot to the brake, causing a number of car horns to blow behind them. "Oh no," Amy said. "Go on. It's not."

"How do you know?" Quill said.

"That man spit on the street, and Almoner wouldn't," she said. Pretending not to observe Quill's exasperation, she told herself as he drove off erratically that he was anxious. She knew inwardly that Almoner would be tall and would seem protective and even if he were old and grey, he would seem dark and mysterious.

She grew more anxious, staring with dread at two lines of sentinel cedars guarding Mrs. Decker's old house. Her bitten fingernails were hard to keep clean. Amy dug at them as if they were soon to be inspected; her hands nervously touched her hair. Most often, she walked with her eyes looking down, so now saw paint peeling at the base of the house's columns, though at eye-level they were more freshly painted. It seemed typical of the false front put up by Borden and his mother, who had lived for years in genteel arrears. Their thinking was that who they had been born made all the difference. Propped to the house against rain, old wicker furniture was mindful of hidden faces. This gave the place an uninviting air, despite crapemyrtle flowering gorgeously pink at the front windows. Quill twisted a brass doorbell, like winding a clock, which caused an alarmed ringing in the back of the house. Calling out as shrilly, Mrs. Decker came along the hall on tall thin spike heels, crying in time to their staccato beat, "Yoo hoo yoo hoo yoo hoo." She threw her arms around Quill's neck and her upturned face read, Wasn't it delightful that she was so small? Did he realize the top of her head barely touched his chin?

Her shoes were tiny as an elf's and were dyed aqua to match her dress. Amy was more aware of her own sandals, broad and flat like a clown's shoes. She abandoned the idea of ever being groomed and hugged her pocketbook against her chest. Mrs. Decker acknowledged her briefly. "You're not," she said, "making your debut and not even going to the luncheon? Surely, you didn't give that up for this expedition!" However, she did not listen to Amy answering that she had. Instead, Mrs. Decker led Quill toward a velvet love seat in the living room.

Left to follow, Amy glanced behind her and prayed the woman would not notice the yellowish dusty streaks she was leaving across her polished dark floors. She sank into a wing chair opposite the love seat and tucked her feet beneath it. But that moment Mrs. Decker saw them and wondered, Why those shoes? The thought quite clearly reflected itself in the puzzlement on her face. The eyes she lifted to Amy's face admitted that Amy was pretty, but did she never change expression? Amy stared back at her with such fear in her eyes, Mrs. Decker felt she had to say something. "Your hair," Mrs. Decker said, which caused Amy immediately to begin apologizing for its being stringy. One thing Mrs. Decker hated was for young people to interrupt, and in the way she bit her lip she made that quite clear. When Amy was silent, she was able to begin again. "Your hair," Mrs. Decker said, "looks lovely there in the sunlight." Then she looked at Amy a little queerly: what had made her so defensive? Again, she glanced briefly at the shoes, wondering why they were muddy. Quill's, however, were polished and clean. She had not thought him the sort of boy to have gone off in the woods with some girl.

"Thank you," Amy had said shyly, drawing back into her chair. "My mother never thinks my hair looks nice."

"Well, now it looks like an angel's," Mrs. Decker said. "Howard?" she repeated. Did she know Amy's family in Delton?

Her parents had not been born in Delton, Amy answered, but had moved there from Arkansas when she was born.

That accounted for things, Mrs. Decker thought, and Amy probably had not even been invited to the luncheon. Somehow, she made that thought obvious before turning her attention back to Quill.

Not only had Mrs. Decker seen her shoes but the swooping ring left by Edith's attempt to clean her skirt, and Amy drew her pocketbook over it. Trying to appear interested in Mrs. Decker's conversation, she looked instead as forlorn as a child waiting apprehensively outside a principal's office. Appearances kept up in this room were as fragile as the old china mustache cups collected on a side table. Mrs. Decker's world, she thought, could be as easily shattered by a few hard facts as it could be improved by a little hard cash. How had Mrs. Decker acquired an air of total confidence? Amy wondered, staring at her liquor-mottled complexion. She tried to find some remainder of the unconventional girl Mrs. Decker must once have been, for early she had run away with an itinerant portrait painter and caused a scandal. Only Borden had come of the marriage and she had had to creep back home in shame; then her father died, having lost all the family money. Mrs. Decker, since, had painted cake plates and crocheted baby clothes and let herself be prevailed upon by her friends to sell them. She lived by pretense, Amy thought, staring around the threadbare room, and that was something she hated. The free spirit, the passionate heart Mrs. Decker must once have possessed were entirely missing in this purplish-faced woman. Staring at her, Amy felt fearful about her own rebelliousness.

Borden came up the driveway in an old car, sitting with envious bravado on its high, outmoded seat. It might be the thing he wanted most in this world to be doing. The car door slamming in the small town's stillness had an important sound. Borden dressed flamboyantly, seeking status, and wore now a pink shirt and a bright red tie, somehow blending with his carrot-colored hair. Waving a bottle in a wrinkled brown sack, he apologized for lateness. "I had to wait outside the pool hall for Cole to finish his game!" He and his mother caught hands ecstatically a moment, provided with another unsurpassable anecdote. Since the others were having a drink, Amy reluctantly agreed, as she would not hurry lunch by declining. But she cast a grateful look toward the dining room where Borden mixed drinks when he said they ought to go soon. Pouting daintily, Mrs. Decker agreed to tell Mary to hurry lunch.

But later, nibbling a cherry from its stem, Mrs. Decker said whoever heard of only having one drink! Borden, indulgently, said that she might have a second, but she would have to take it to the table. Coming along after Mrs. Decker, Amy felt that Borden's tolerance was something she lacked, which she must practice. She tried not to mind Mrs. Decker's fingers drumming incessantly, like a pecking hen's head, while she talked (and talked). Amy could not help but feel angry that people like Mrs. Decker and her own family, leading such uninteresting lives, were disparaging about Almoner, who had done so much for the

45

world. Did they never think of the comparison? Maybe the bourbon was making her so hot and so sleepy. She would sleep at the table if they did not leave soon. Maybe it was only boredom making her eyelids want to close. The luncheon seemed it might stretch out the entire length of the hot summer afternoon. Amy opened her eyes wide and looked toward the window, hoping brightness there would keep her awake. She watched maids with their small white charges stroll past and return later eating ice cream. Borden and his mother kept on giving the endless details of things not important in the beginning, as her family did; looking back, turning her head from one to another, Amy wished Edith were in her place, she would so much enjoy the conversation.

When Mary appeared with an asparagus soufflé, Mrs. Decker commanded they praise it. Mary indulgently stood and stared beyond them, while they ooed and aahed. And though they were like fools, Amy thought, there was no way not to join in. She made little murmurs, then watched Mary swing back through the kitchen door, gladly. At least, eating stopped the continousness of the conversation, though with their mouths full, they had to stop and, again at Mrs. Decker's command, exclaim over the rolls Mary brought in. Who else still made their own? they were asked.

"Take two while they're hot!" Mrs. Decker cried, as Mary circled the table.

Tears welled up in Amy's eyes. She did not want to live a life without meaning or purpose. Wavery yellow lines converged in darkness behind her closed eyelids, into nothing. At last, opening her eyes, she saw a possibility of the luncheon's ending.

Mary had come through the swinging door with strawberry shortcake. But this, Amy saw immediately, presented her with more difficulty. With hands able to crochet so deftly, Mrs. Decker, with one movement, lifted onto a small server a cake with a pyramid of strawberries and then a topping of whipped cream. All at once, the serving arrived safely on her plate. Amy knew she would not be able to manage and waited apprehensively for Mary to approach. And, of course, her cake did waver in midair. Mary obligingly lowered the tray. Amy looked up at her gratefully, but not changing Mary's bland expression.

Mrs. Decker had noticed that lowered tray. She glanced away politely. Amy stared at the others, already eating, before realizing she had nothing left to choose but a dessert fork.

Mrs. Decker's fork securely bore on its end a soft berry, waiting to meet her mouth. She said, "I don't have time to read, but if I did, I wouldn't want to read Jeff Almoner's books! Depressing, I hear. Why read about what I've been around all my life? Maybe they're good." In a silent moment afterward, she asked them to consider another possibility, before poking the berry into her mouth and chewing mouselike at its seeds.

Amy was furious listening to her chew and regretted all the insincere compliments she had felt it necessary to pay Mrs. Decker: on the centerpiece of sweet peas and on all her old family things. And, infuriating Amy, Mrs. Decker had accepted all the compliments as if they were her due. Now, her fork plunged again at air. She let a word impressively hang. "I," she had said. She waited until she had their attention. "I," she repeated, "blame publishers, that's who. If they wouldn't publish depressing books, people wouldn't write them."

"You read then only for entertainment?" Quill said.

Amy, having wanted to ask the question, was annoyed that she had not had the nerve. Like an admonishing finger, Mrs. Decker's fork wagged again. Amy wished to God she would put it on her plate and keep it there. "Yes, I do," Mrs. Decker said. "Life is hard enough." She stared around at them with almost wet eyes, meaning they would understand when they were older.

Amy toyed with her fork, knowing that escaping things was

one of her own tendencies. But she did not want to escape life reading books; she wanted to find out about it. What Almoner wrote was a mirror for her soul, Amy felt, and he had touched even corners of darkness which before she had feared.

"Let's don't be depressing!" Mrs. Decker was crying. "Quill, whose debut did you think the prettiest?"

"Lydia Fontaine's," he said.

"Oh. So did Borden," she cried, leading Quill from the table.

Coming afterward with Borden, Amy inadvertently brought along her napkin. While waiting for her to return it to the table, Borden seemed to stare at her speculatively and as if also wondering about her clothes. Amy felt her sandals had grown looser and flatter, and they made slapping sounds across the floor. She stood in the living room before the blackened empty fireplace; imaginatively, she warmed her hands, listening to the conversation about Lydia's party, feeling she had no invitation to join in. But neither had Borden been invited. Simply, she did not know how to fit herself into situations, how to belong.

In this room, with its musty odor of wallpaper, while the others talked of the debut, Amy smelled the party's aroma. It had been a satisfactory mingling of carnations and champagne and girlish odors of perfume and the more masculine scents of liquor and cigarettes. Enviously co-ordinated, the decorations all had been pink. Most memorably, Lydia had worn a wreath of rosebuds in her hair.

Amy stepped obediently from the fireplace when Mrs. Decker issued an invitation to "the little girl's room." They went along a hallway overhung with paintings by Mrs. Decker, all of single magnolia blossoms broadly opened and flat to the canvas and with centers like staring yellow eyes. At night, it would seem cats stared from the walls, Amy thought. Insecurity and a longing to be liked compelled her to say how good the pictures were. In this instance, Mrs. Decker was not pretentious. Looking as if Amy were crazy, Mrs. Decker said, "My dear, they're not good. They're terrible. It's only finger exercise for my arthritis."

Amy sidled into the bathroom, leaving Mrs. Decker at her dressing table. The day's tenseness led Amy to sit unusually long on the coldish enamel toilet seat. To hide her noise, she thought of turning on the faucet, but was fearful of being chastised by Mrs. Decker for running up the water bill. She knew Mrs. Decker would be careful of hers, as Aunt Dea always had been. Amy emerged blushing. However, Mrs. Decker's face, newly painted, revealed nothing. Passing Amy, she closed the bathroom door. Amy regarded in the dressing-table mirror her own smooth face, which needed no make-up. She stared at a wall holding pictures of Mrs. Decker when she was young. The same sorrowful feeling bore down on her, which she felt at Aunt Dea's house: that time merely passed. Where had it gone? Mrs. Decker might have been asking herself, staring in the dresser mirror. Amy, seeing through a window that all the outdoors was dry, realized she had not imagined the length of the luncheon. For Mrs. Decker, it had been the high point of a day. Amy thought she did not want to live merely to die, and wished upon herself one fantastic adventure after another. She pulled stealthily open a dresser drawer, wishing her tendency were not to peek; even, she looked into other people's medicine cabinets! The drawer contained only a lot of little jars, like Edith's. Many had greasy tops, revealing Mrs. Decker was not thoroughly meticulous. Amy was glad for information about other people's lives. It helped her understand her own.

She was waiting politely near the hallway when Mrs. Decker came from the bathroom. Of necessity, their mouths formed smiles, and they had to say something. Mrs. Decker went out. "So much hot weather."

"Hasn't it been hot," Amy said, trailing along.

"And September will be hot, too. It's worse every year."

That exchange brought them into the living room where, as soon as Amy entered, Borden said, "Sorry, old girl, but you've been shot down in flames. I phoned Almoner. He says he's not going to be home."

"He really doesn't want to see anyone, I think," Quill said.

"Did you tell him who you were?" Mrs. Decker cried, astonished.

While the boys nodded, Amy wondered what identification Mrs. Decker considered herself to have. Her own, vague as it was, had fled. She felt like crying.

"Did you tell him you went to Princeton?" Mrs. Decker said.

"Told him everything," Borden said. "Mentioned Quill's family. That we were Princeton tigers. Everybody's one for always, except him, apparently."

"He only went to Princeton a year," Amy said.

Nevertheless, Borden's shrug meant. "And I told him about Quill's thesis."

"We told him a girl was here who wanted to be a writer," Quill said.

Amy turned toward him, angry he had said that in front of Mrs. Decker. It was too personal to have revealed to her. Quill gave her an apologetic look. He had told Amy not to be intimidated by the woman. It was not his fault she had been, his arched eyebrows meant. Amy shuddered when Borden suggested they play bridge instead. "I don't play," she said quickly, not caring about Mrs. Decker's aggravated look.

"If Amy just wants to meet a writer, there's Agnes Jones here in town," she said.

"Momma! She writes about tuberous begonias," Borden said. Even his patience had a limit. "We could just drive by and look at Almoner's house."

That would be like getting out to stare at an automobile accident, Amy thought. Quill had agreed, and she would do anything to leave. She took Mrs. Decker's flaccid hand.

"Do come again, dear," Mrs. Decker said.

"I'd love to. I had such a nice time," Amy said, turning up the corners of her mouth.

The porch furniture seemed still in shame, turned toward the house. The day had grown jubilant in the sun; the tall cedars admitted its sparkle. Borden's hair was a fiery gloss atop his head, as he stood asking if he might drive. When he raced the motor boyishly, Amy forgave him everything, seeing that he endured pretense for his mother's sake. That was an admirable quality, and one she might lack, Amy thought. Knowing that she was too quick to judge people, she exclaimed most cordially over the houses Borden pointed out and listened to the repetitious histories of the people who lived in them. Small-town people wanting to drive around and look at houses as an entertainment bored Edith. Often, she had not wanted to come to Dea's for that reason. Amy felt expansive, pretending interest for Borden's sake. Eventually, however, she ran out of platitudes. As if receiving some silent signal, Quill took them up. Amy glanced at him, gratefully.

She was free then to draw inward, which was preferable, and visualized her school, near mountains turned purple at dusk, a cloudlike filminess descending from them. Nearby was a green and placid river, with a tamed quality different from the Mississippi. The first river made her want to dream along its banks. Here she felt torn in many directions like the stronger river on a rampage. Her environment had a hold on her from which she could not divorce herself, any more than the river could separate itself from its levees.

Climbing from the car, being confronted unexpectedly by a breeze, Amy stared round as if this were some foreign land. One after another, the three went down the stony path toward the springs. There, water trickled from a grotto over speckled brown rocks, slickening them. They laughed at paying dimes for dented cups to drink the water, watching old people with angel-white hair seriously lifting theirs. Inside, the cups smelled of mildew. While Quill and Borden walked about exploring, Amy remained in one spot and felt how singularly alone, how small she was in comparison to the gigantic and unhindered sky, going on and on everywhere. Eventually all the old people went away. The Negro attendant sat sleepy and bored. Distantly, Borden and Quill were laughing. Amy kept staring at the thin trickle of water, as if it might grow, knowing she was always waiting for something to happen. While the Negro fell asleep, she stood beneath the expansive sky, thinking restlessly that what she wanted was the future.

"Come on, Amy."

The others were already at the car and thought she was following, then Quill called. Amy went back reluctantly the way she had come, seeing Borden sitting at the wheel and turning it grandly. "The dreamer," Quill said, getting out and letting her slide into the front seat.

"I didn't realize you were ready to go," she said.

"Obviously," he said. "We wondered how long you were going to stand there."

Amy settled in dreamily between them, mentally adjusting a long trailing gown: honored for something she did not bother to name; but even Mrs. Decker paid court. She remembered Quill's once saying that she would be all right if only she knew what she wanted. Amy tried to think what he had meant by that remark, feeling she knew exactly what it was she wanted. She wanted to go wherever she had to go to find out whatever it was she had to find out. That made sense to her, though to explain it to Quill, or someone else, she knew it would sound evasive.

Along the roadside were tangled wild-primrose bushes, devoid of blooms since spring. Tumbled among them now were black-eyed Susans, their strong yellow color more appropriate to the blaze of summer. Suddenly, the countryside ended abruptly at high shielding forsythia bushes. Borden, having driven through an opening in them, set up a clatter of metal that rang in the still country air. A dog barked off somewhere. The car seemed to have sunk down into the cattle gap. Silence came after the dog hushed, until Borden said, "This is his driveway."

Quill breathed one word that was not a question: "Almoner's."

The three sat woodenly and staring ahead, like children trans-fixed by fairy stories. That might have been the gingerbread house ahead, with a pinched-looking roof and tall front windows and a narrow porch with an empty hammock. A shout seemed to ring out in the car, startling them.

"There he is!" Borden had whispered.

"Almoner," Quill said, again hardly breathing.

But feeling they were prying where they did not belong, Amy said, "We ought to go." Borden had driven hastily off the cattle gap, grinding gears. The three seemed to cling together without touching. They must hear her heart beat, Amy was thinking. "I'm going to ask if he'll just speak to us," Borden said, climbing out; and too late, Amy reached across the seat for his coattail.

She watched him go down the slope toward the grove of trees where they had glimpsed Almoner, who, by disappearing, seemed to be hiding. Watching Borden's red head recede, she kept thinking how this silence and this waiting and this intrusion all were wrong, and nothing could be done about any of them now. Like a kite or a leaf blown, at the whim of the wind, she went at random anywhere, anywhere at all she was taken, with-out plans of her own. Then when things went wrong, there was nothing she could say, nothing at all. There was no one she could truthfully blame but herself, she admitted.

Over the car's hood, yellow moths hovered with their wings

folded tricornered into sails. Then, like a flotilla of small boats, they floated away, at once, into the day. Amy, watching them, thought that she bore these moments of dread because she had borne silently so many other stresses in her life: not being the way her mother wanted, her father's martinis, being an only child. Inadvertently and through some fault of her own, she had many times been embarrassed. Often she had been lonely or bored or felt forgotten. She had been tearful and had felt a stranger to happiness always. Only at unexpected moments did happiness ever overtake her.

This time Quill's whisper seemed loud inside the car. "He's coming!" But the sound was as full of foreboding, to Amy, as storm wind. Thinking back to all her stresses, she knew she would somehow endure this one.

Almoner came along the incline, brushing pine needles off his shoulders. He was neither as tall as she had imagined nor as elderly. Once he said something to Borden, who bent down to listen attentively. When they arrived at the car, it seemed part of the awryness of the whole afternoon that she could see nothing of Almoner's face but his chin. Leaning down to the window, Borden said that he had apologized for their rudeness, and Mr. Almoner had agreed to speak to them for a moment. As if pulled by a string, bending promptly to the window after Borden's speech, acknowledging their names, Almoner extended his hand past Amy to meet the one Quill stuck toward him.

"This is a great honor, Mr. Almoner," Quill said.

"Thank you," Almoner said.

When he stood straight again, Amy could see nothing but his chin. She had neither spoken nor given him her hand. The intrusion made it seem not right to ask even that. With bent shoulders, Almoner was already going back down the incline and toward the sheltering trees.

Amy never moved, though when Borden backed the car his

54

elbow jabbed her uncomfortably. The flowerless tall forsythias gradually shut away the house. The afternoon had begun to darken. Their car wheels, on the gravel, sent startled birds into flight from weeds and left them swaying. Small brown rabbits ran in fear, helter-skelter, out of the way.

Quill's whoop seemed to shatter more than the quiet of the countryside, to ring out over the world. "He touched this!" he cried, raising his hand into the air. "Almoner touched this! I'm never going to wash it!"

Amy, wishing she could close herself into silence, wondered why she had never noticed before how many freckles Borden had. When he leaned past her to speak to Quill, even his lips had an orangish tinge. She heard him in disbelief. "Almoner said he was tired of folks coming here to see if he was a freak," Borden said. "And what was worse, he was for free. Nobody had offered to pay to look yet!"

Amy kept on staring at Borden's spotted face hanging in air before her, until Quill leaned around to look back at him. Then his face was like a ripe red tomato about to burst and kept growing redder as he laughed. They were laughing helplessly, their hanging mouths exposing fillings. Amy closed her eyes and sank on the seat between them, horrified.

It was lonely; it was evening. The station inside had a dimness like lamplight long ago. The stationmaster stood in his doorway, his flowers now all faint and pale as first stars, seeming as evasive as the early moon. Bug-spattered street lights let out along the darkening streets lariat-thin lines of yellow. In fields and ditch banks, katydids and locusts screamed as if fearful of the night, which crept along and left visible the merest shadows of cotton. Clouds formed were mauve and black. Against them, Negroes seemed lean brush strokes, going home between cotton rows, children running ahead. Dim light was far-spaced cabins. Except for a single light in back, Dea's house was dark. Passers-by, mindful of supper being eaten in the kitchen, might long themselves for home. Any light seemed something safe, Amy thought. With fields enveloped and the road darkened, she and Quill seemed to be travelling far reaches of black space.

At her own house, shadowy evergreens seemed bent solicitously toward the windows. Apologetically, Quill said that he must hurry as he had a date with Lydia. "Coal Black," he called her. He went out to his car, in his duck-footed way, then waited until Amy went inside. His headlights bent into shafts of yellow as he left and poked about the living room as a stranger might, searching. The house seemed ravaged when the headlights departed, at last, from the French doors, leaving them blank. Quill had admitted that Lydia never had anything important to say. Then he had cried, "But her hair is so coal black, it gets to me!" Amy felt not only deserted but mystified watching him go.

When the car lights had gone, she tiptoed about appreciative of finding nothing, and no one, not belonging to the house. Touching a piano key, she sent into the silence a single sound. When silence again followed, it seemed that a voice had cried out and been stilled. The music lessons she had taken many years had abandoned her and Amy's fingers came away from the keys. Rusty's dog basket in the kitchen was empty; she mourned that he had not been let out merely to come back in. Though the icebox seemed empty, she ate finally something left over in little capped boxes and wandered further to perform before the hall mirror a half-remembered ballet step left from other pointless and vanished lessons. In half-pirouette, she wondered whether she might wear rosebuds in her hair as an ordinary event. Climbing stairs laboriously, inexplicably exhausted, she accidentally found a note, which said that her family had left her but only to go out to dinner.

In her own mirror, she found her face changed since that moment when she had been at Mrs. Decker's dressing table. No longer did she have any look of belief, since Almoner was not to save her. But what was worse, she had brought him more suffering. Amy pictured him as always alone; even now he might be brooding, after supper, that again today someone had come to stare.

With stealth equal to Quill's headlights, she searched for Edith's good blue stationery, hidden in her mother's room from cleaning ladies who could not resist it. Amy wrote at her dressing table, her hands shaking so that she pretended hardship, that she was poor and in an unheated house in winter, drawing closer to the light bulb for warmth.

Dear Mr. Almoner:

I know you have a secretary and probably you will never see this but I have to write it anyway, as I am the girl who came there today when you told us not to, and I wanted you to know it was not for the reason you thought, to stare at you, but because I like your work so much. I am unhappy and I know you are unhappy too. I wanted to tell you you shouldn't be so unhappy and lonely when you have done so much for the world. There were so many things I had wanted to ask you because I know you have thought and felt and suffered everything I ever have and I wanted to ask you the reason for suffering. Why some people have to and others don't? In the end do you gain something from it? I knew after reading your books I could ask you everything and you would answer and I could tell you everything about myself, that my dog just got run over, and you would understand. Could I come again by myself? You don't have to worry as I know all about your drinking and that doesn't make any difference to me. My father drinks too. So don't worry or be embarrassed. I hope I have not bothered you again by writing. But I

57

couldn't go on thinking that you thought I came there to stare
when I so much did not come for that reason, at all.

> Sincerely,
>
> Amy Howard

Light crept beneath the door as silently as an intruder, startling her as much. And standing there, Edith apologized and said she could not imagine Amy's not having heard them come home. Who on earth was she writing that intently? Faint pink glitter in Edith's dress matched the color of her shoes. Her breath came in puffs after the stairs. Around her middle, flesh folded over her belt.

"I borrowed some of your good stationery," Amy said. "Is that all right?"

"Of course." Edith looked expectant.

"I'm writing to Leigh, that boy at school," Amy said.

"The one you like. Is he really going to come visit us sometime?"

"He says he is." Edith kept staring, and Amy moved her arm nonchalantly over the letter.

Frowning to sort this day from another, Edith said finally, "You didn't go to dinner with Quill?" Indifferently, Amy said that he had a date with Lydia. Did she care more for Quill than she pretended? Edith wondered. Why else sit there looking so friendless or lonesome, like an orphan crouched over its supper, and wearing those shoes? Good heavens! She did not like, really, having her good stationery taken and must remember stationery as a present for Amy at Christmas. Then Edith had another idea. "Are you taking your thyroid?" she said.

"Yes," Amy said, wondering how long her mother was going to stand there. Tipping the lampshade, Amy sent light in the opposite direction. Was it the letter her mother was staring at so strangely? She couldn't read from that far away, could she?

Did the light hurt her eyes? Edith wondered when Amy tipped the shade. Her eyes looked more haunted staring out from the shadows. Edith looked around at the chrysanthemums printed on chintz, thinking how she had created this perfect young girl's room and that her daughter sat in it with a hangdog look, which was not inherited from her side of the family. Amy seemed never to have belonged to the decor, at all. She had tried so hard to impress on Amy that pretty girls were not necessarily popular, that personality counted. She would bet Quill had not asked Amy to dinner because she had not said two words all day. However, since Amy got invited places frequently, she must be different when she was out from when she was at home, Edith decided, sighing. Amy had looked down in the dumps even mentioning she was taking her thyroid. But Edith thought in a rush of emotion, My baby. When she went forward to kiss her, Amy bent a little backward over her letter, stiffening. Edith thought that she must smell too much like garlic and retreated to the door. "We ate at the new French restaurant," she said. "I had snails. Delicious but garlicky. Whew!"

Amy sat, without expression, listening while Edith told who else had been there and what they had had for dinner and about the decor, while Edith wondered what had made her eat so much when, leaving home, she had promised herself to eat hardly anything. She tried to perk up Amy by suggesting that she go to the restaurant; Edith told about the elegant dessert cart, thinking how when it had come by she had seen cheesecake, her favorite, and said, "Would just a smidge hurt?" and Mallory had said, "Help yourself, healthy to have an appetite," then he had kept on staring at the girl in the jersey dress across the room until even the girl had become annoyed. "Homemade petits fours, hmm," Edith said.

"They sound delicious," Amy said.

And Edith thought how she had eaten what Mallory left of his petits fours when she had finished her cheesecake, how he had inclined his wine glass toward the girl, and how she had said then, "She is pretty," and Mallory had said, all innocence, "Who?" Her thought then had been that the worst thing of all was being married to a fool. That was still her thought while she and Amy listened to him downstairs locking up and singing "Have You Ever Seen a Dream Walking." She and Amy listened, their eyes not quite meeting.

Tired, Edith said, "Don't let the bedbugs bite," and went out feeling lonesome and left open the door she had found closed.

"I won't," Amy said, trying to smile.

She wondered what her mother expected to find out by leaving the door open. Edith's bedroom light switched on silently. The silver-blue glance of her room shadowed the hall; it made Amy sad, for when she thought of her mother, she thought of things that were lovely: her clothes and her perfume, none of which seemed in the end to matter. She wondered if her mother was happy. Taking her arm from the letter, which was slightly smeared, Amy hoped Mr. Almoner would not think she had cried writing it. Undoubtedly, he might think she was some kind of nut, anyway. What was it like, she wondered, to be her mother and to think about nothing but eating in the newest restaurant in town, considered the best only because it was the most overdecorated. Listening to her mother's ritualistic night sounds, she thought it would certainly be easier to be her mother, or to be Lydia. Yet with all the difficulties of her life, she would not choose theirs. She would not fill up her life with inane things. Edith's curtains were being closed, with their usual smoothly running little click, across their antiqued rod. Amy stared at herself in the mirror, seeing fear reflected in her eyes and something mischievous—some promise of womanhood at last, she thought. Edith's heels crossed a bare section of floor and, afterward, came the ritualistic sounds of the manipulations of her little jars.

Cleaning her face, straining her neck, her mother stared at herself in the mirror nightly, without thinking anything, Amy supposed. And knowing if she reread the letter she would never send it, Amy sealed it shut.

Number three is the trees. Color some of them green. Color some of them brown. Put in touches of red. It is a fall scene.

Edith's brush hovered over the picture like a bee over a flower, as she was fearful of dipping the tip into the cup of red paint. Why had they made the picture so hard? If only the trees could be as easy as the grass and the sky. She reread: One is the sky. Color it blue. Two is the grass. Color it green.

But the solidly blue top half of her picture, running and too wet, did not look like sky. The blue was beginning to streak toward the solidly green bottom half of the picture, which was grass. With her heart palpitating, Edith touched the brush tip to the red, then to the canvas. But a red dot on a brown branch did not look like an autumn leaf, at all. The mothball smell of clothes, however, being packed into Amy's trunk meant winter and that she was going. She had not wanted Amy to see her unhappy. Leaving the room, she had said, "Do your own packing. You're old enough." Maybe she had spoken more sharply than she had meant to, for Amy had looked hurt. When she had come back from the grocery, everything she and Amy had laid out between them in the room had been packed but remoteness.

Was it hopeless? Edith stared at the dots, her nose almost touching the picture. She thought how at Christmastime, Poppa had brought home barrels of apples and the house had been full of people and she had complained about always having to give up her room. Now, she watched squirrels run about the gutters and the sun slant over her silver toilet articles already polished to perfection and thought how gladly she would give up what once she had coveted, privacy and silence, having had enough of both. If only this house would swell with people and smell of December apples. Instead, it would grow more empty with Amy gone. She had said, "I hate to see you go. The phone never rings," not able to say what she really meant. She wondered if Amy had understood.

Amy sat on the front steps drying her hair in the early autumn sun and lifted her head as the postman came down the block whistling, as usual. "We always know when you're coming," Amy said, accepting mail.

Amy had to get married soon, Edith decided, looking down at her. There would be grandchildren then and she would have something to do. She hated blaming Amy for anything, but why couldn't she just be happy and married like the other girls? She looked so sweet and pretty, bent over a letter with her hair drying bright as brass in the glare. Only a few days, and she would have her whole house silent and empty, Edith moaned.

The postman was gay and whistling still, despite stopping to tie a handkerchief around his neck to catch perspiration. Staring down, Edith thought Amy's hair fine as a baby's, with each separate strand gossamer in the sun. As Amy got up and came inside, Edith remembered the first pair of little kid shoes Amy had worn; scuffed, they were in a bedroom drawer now. She was determined Amy was going to have that beige cashmere coat in the Town Shop window, for then she would be all the same color, tawny. Maybe her eyes would not stare so from her face; maybe she would not do things like racing boyishly up the stairs yelling. Edith wanted to be sweet but, that moment, her blue sky reached her green grass and mingled. She said bitterly, "I can't understand screeching. Who wrote you? Who?"

Her mother's crossness doused her like a dampener a fire. Amy had been coming into the room, happily, holding the letter. "Almoner," she said reluctantly. Edith's face remained blank. "That writer Quill and I went to see."

"My goodness. I thought somebody had sent you a million dollars," Edith said. For a moment, Amy's hangdog look had actually been gone. Edith had felt hopeful. Now, she saw the look return. Smiling and bubbly and cute, Amy had been for a moment like the other girls. Edith said, "You're so much prettier smiling, Amy. You must remember that." Maybe it was Amy's age that made her turn sullen. "Why did he write you?" Edith asked.

A look of solitariness about her mother had made Amy consider for a moment that she might understand; now, pressing the letter against her and· wondering how to escape the room, she said, "I had just written him first to say I enjoyed meeting him." She went toward the door.

"What did he say in the letter?" Edith said, detainingly. She could not help staring at Amy's hands, holding the letter against her. She sighed, supposing there was no sense making her have a manicure because she would not take care of her nails once she got back to that school.

"He just said he enjoyed meeting us," Amy said. "But now I have his autograph." If her mother mentioned her nails again, she was going to scream. She tried to divert Edith's attention. "Isn't that nice?"

"I guess so," Edith said vaguely, trying to remember the man's name. Still, Amy was going toward her room. "Remember what I said about smiling."

"Mother, I don't want to keep hearing about all that," Amy said, feeling desperate for so much weightier advice. "Do you think I ought to write him again?"

"I wouldn't bother the poor man to death. He's probably busy."

"I'm sure he's busy," Amy said. Though her mother was too fat, she seemed frail sitting in the washing sunlight by the window painting that terrible, numbered picture. And sensing how the orderliness and the silence in the house would intensify when she was gone, feeling devastated by the situation, that this was her mother and this was her mother's life, Amy longed for another way to remedy the situation, not having produced grandchildren. "Mother, your picture is so pretty," she said.

"Pretty! All streaky and with those red dots!"

"Well, they don't matter," Amy said hopefully.

"Of course they matter," Edith said. She was already tired of watching squirrels run around the roof, her winter's occupation. "You have your head in the clouds, or your nose in a book. You don't know what matters. Why don't you put white iodine on your fingernails?"

Amy was usually afraid to speak up for herself, but had not meant unkindness and feeling hurt again by her mother's tone, she said in retaliation, "I know one thing that doesn't matter is that coat in the Town Shop window." She fled quickly to her own room, having sided with her father, who had said the coat was too expensive, though she found no joy in having done it. To wear that coat would be embarrassing. But as soon as the saleswoman had said, craftily, that soon the coat would be gone, for college girls came in constantly to look at it, her mother had decided she must have it, Amy thought, holding the letter close before opening it.

Dear Miss Howard:

I remember of course your coming. If nothing else I would remember your hair as the sun struck it just so, but I remember that your eyes were the color of violets, like something you wore, and that you said nothing: that perhaps struck me most. Silence is a commodity hard to come by; you did not gush, like most. I had thought you were going to be some book club woman; anyway someone altogether different. But I saw at once you did not want the usual from me. I looked at your face and thought of spring with violets, tiny wild ones, deep in the woods, not culti-

vated, but growing naturally, belonging. Some long winter was over and suddenly it was spring, shy Miss Howard.

But I don't think it best for you to come here again. What can I tell you? You know a great deal more than I believe you think you know. But if you have some questions, write them to me and I will try to answer them. It is I who must apologize for being rude that day. And if I do not answer right away, don't worry. You have time to wait for things.

Almoner

Beginning now, the first of October, I'm going to keep a diary. Not really because I want to but because my English professor says it's a good way to practice writing. But nothing ever happens to me to write about. Except of course hearing from Almoner. Nothing ever happens to me to write about except, of course, that I heard from Almoner. The point of this is, I guess, to practice sentences. I have to remember and not just jot things down. But do you know what happened? It makes me so *mad*. The last Sunday before I came back to school I had a date with Quill and showed him A's letter and then right before a crowd of people at the club he said, "Amy got a letter from Almoner. Boy oh boy oh, I don't see old Almoner writing to me!" Then everybody laughed. Stupid insinuation. I can't stand it! I kept saying, "But I wrote him first—and no one would listen. They kept on laughing and making jokes. Oh g— damn them all. I think Quill is as superficial as the rest, after all.

Here, I'm going out with Leigh and that's all. I like him I guess but I don't know why. Because he's not like them in Delton I think. *That's* not a sentence. Be careful! old Amy. He doesn't know or care anything about sports; he never wants to sit around on Saturday afternoons and listen to football games. However he wants to listen to opera which I don't like either. Maybe this is my trouble. What *do* I like? But I am trying to learn something about music and art from him since I don't know anything. But yesterday I was humming a popular song and he said, "I think you must have been a typical American teen-ager in high school," and I said, "Of course I was—why wouldn't I have been?" And why wouldn't I have been? Anyway, I'm glad I was. I wouldn't want to have been like him. They lived in Europe then and he doesn't know anything about what we were all interested in. Even if I want to be something better now and not like the rest of those girls I'm glad I went through that. I'd rather have been an American teen-ager than to be more cultured. Then I wasn't trying to be anything more than what I just was, and it was so much easier. It's hard to be something more; though even then I did feel different. It was as if always I was watching myself being.

Tonight Leigh and I walked down a road from school and through the grounds of an old people's home and sat under a tree and leaves that were left were all dry and rustling, like dry whispers of the dying, and saying they were dying. But next October there will be leaves again and I thought they were asking me where I would be. Sometimes I think things do communicate with us. When I was much younger I thought Rusty could talk. I remember begging him to talk and promising that I would never tell anyone if he did. I remember always being so lonely; there seemed never to be anyone in the afternoons to play with but him. Tonight I thought of all those sleeping old people and of how young I am. It's hard to be young but there is the ever-wonder of tomorrow and things to come.

Mother wrote me and said not to write Almoner any more. I think she suddenly remembered after I left I had said he did and she probably mentioned it to Aunt D. But my English professor says I ought to write him again, that it's fabulous he wrote me—which I think, too. So I do not know (as usual) what to do?????

I woke up today and it had been raining. Sprinkles have continued throughout the day. And suddenly I noticed all the bright red, orange, yellow leaves are gone. There are only a few dull gold ones left and all the others are dried brown. It's windy. The leaves loosen from the trees and rise from the ground blowing in whirlpools and the landscape is desolate but nice, brown with purple coming down from the mountains. The river is skimmed with ice. Soon it will snow and then

66

everything will seem so secretive. Yesterday I walked with Leigh to an old barn and on its front there was an old clock with hands stopped at a quarter to eight: daylight or dark? I wondered to whom it had meant something.

Last week I wrote nothing down; it was just a week, a series of cold windy leafless days. I only remember the sky was repetitively blue. I cannot remember today at all. Only that it was day and now it is night, solid at the windows. If I had tried could I have made this day into something? Probably I shouldn't have just let it pass. Yet Almoner says I have time to wait for things, though I don't feel like I do; I want something to happen quickly. It was, after all, a day in my life. What is the purpose of my life? Can each person living have some significance when there are so many millions of people? Someone came to my door and knocked and when I did not answer went away. I'd rather ponder the mystery of who it was and what life she has lived and will live that I will know nothing about, though we will be under the same sky, than to know who it was. Only now that she has gone I'm becoming obsessed with wondering who it was and what she wanted? Oh damn; why do I have to wonder? Everybody else is down the hall having a birthday party; probably they wanted me to come; they are making so much noise. I wonder simply, gratefully, though I don't want to go, Who thought of me? It's too late; they're going into their rooms; bedroom slippers scuffling all about. A train whistling is going by in the black valley between the dark mountains and I can hear it faintly and always that lonesome sound makes me think of going home, though I don't want to be there. Or, always I want to go but then when I'm there I don't want to be there. Why is that? That train is going the wrong way for home and it's so different here with people at stations having red noses and wearing galoshes, which no one in Delton would do, even if the weather were bad. I bought a terrible-looking scarf but it's warm. Edith sleeps all winter in those satin sleeveless gowns. She'll be pulling her curtains now and creaming her face; immediately her cold cream's smell has come. All my childhood is lost. I'm not sure I want to live. I want to go home until I'm there. I feel so lost.

It's as if some second presence is always with me making me want to run away from wherever I am and do something different from what I'm doing. It's the same as I wrote a few days ago about going home. Always I feel I am waiting for something. But what? And then I feel I'm not living life waiting. Suppose tomorrow I died? Does Edith ever see any lack in her life?

Since I wrote last, we've gotten a new dietitian; the other had to leave, and this one is an older man and I feel so sorry for him because he seems so lonely belonging neither to the faculty nor the students. He is always wandering around. Yesterday I passed him and I could tell he wanted to talk but I sort of looked down at my books and hurried on and I know I was flaunting not needing him and being young. And yet the whole time I was doing it I didn't want to be cruel. So why did I do it????? I wonder if I'm like other people or not. As soon as I passed him, he began whistling. Oh my God, the sound was too lonely to be stood and I ran to the coffee shop. I'll never forget that. Please God, don't let me be cruel. I'll promise anything if I'm not. Off the hall, doors keep opening into laughing and talking but I've shut my door again. I don't want to think or hear the train whistle but there it goes again. Time goes so slowly. There are sights, sounds, dark insights muddled together like a kaleidoscope inside, all colors, but then Monday follows Sunday in never-varying stretches.

Guess what? I got another letter from Almoner! I had written him in November but I was afraid to tell even you for fear he would not write again.

Dear Miss Howard:

While telling me you did not know the exact questions to ask, you asked them. But they are questions not to be answered in a letter. All of them are things I most likely can never answer. Do you remember I told you that from the beginning? But they might be attempted when a man and a woman are at peace together. Don't worry that you ask them at twenty, which is the age I assume you are, without quite knowing why; it is far better

68

to ask them than to be a vegetable, like too many young people.
And meanwhile, read Housman.

Almoner

I'm not sure what he means about a man and a woman being at peace together. Is it what I think? If so, that seems embarrassing for him to say.

I can hardly believe it's almost the middle of December. We've had a lot of snow. My English professor said keep on writing Almoner. Copy below.

Dear Mr. Almoner:

Thank you so much for your letter. I really did not think you would write again and I'm so glad you did. And yes you were right in guessing twenty. But I've become twenty since seeing you. Twenty will not come again and take from seventy springs a score, it leaves me only fifty more.

See, I listened and I always will listen to you. What else should I read? Well, I do worry about having so many questions and it's nice of you to say not to worry about having them. Somehow when you tell me you don't know answers, you give them to me, as you said about my questions. And if ever I should know anything I would certainly want to tell you and to see if you don't think so too. Do you think the happiness of knowing things you know and what you think is enough to make up for the unhappiness of knowing them?

Sincerely,
Amy

It keeps on snowing and I'm getting worried I might not be able to fly home for Christmas. I'm neither a woman or a girl. I'm nothing, nobody. Edith has said I'm an embarrassment. Suppose I do turn out to be some odd queer old maid like families keep in upstairs rooms? One time I walked around the block when it was raining. Then neighbors asked Mother why I was out walking around in the storm.

Nobody could understand if you said you wanted to feel rain on your face. She said it had something to do with a science experiment at school, because people already thought I was queer! I didn't make my debut when I could! My head needed to be examined, Mother said. She told my father and he drank four martinis before he said the neighbors ought to mind their business. Then at dinner I kept finding him staring at me and wondering why I had done it.

I spent the weekend reading *Don Quixote*. Almoner sent it! Isn't that fantastic that Jeffrey Almoner writes to me and sent me a book. It was wrapped up badly in gift paper but I kept thinking, imagine that he had wrapped it up himself and for me! He enclosed a note saying he had written me a letter but had decided not to send it. I wonder why?

Dear Mr. Almoner:

We had so much snow at school they let me leave earlier for fear I would not get home for Christmas, and I did not have a chance to write you and thank you so much for the book. You were so kind to send it to me and I feel I should send you a Christmas present too but I just did not know what to send. Or whether it would be all right to anyway. Though I am trying not to worry about what other people think. I wondered if maybe you did not send the letter because it was a criticism of mine? If so, I would not care and would like to know what was wrong with it. I go back to school soon after the first and would love to see you again.

Sincerely,
Amy

P.S. I would not bring any other people.

P.P.S. Do you have a certain conception of what you think a short story ought to be?

I'm ashamed to say I've done nothing but go to parties and so haven't had time to write in you at all. But I had to tell you about his coming in tonight with his face more pocked-looking and flushed and saying, "I've been made a deacon in the church!" And I said, "Why, Daddy, that's great!" That moment I thought, Mother sees. She stood in the doorway looking at him half-mad and half as if she pitied him and we looked at each other and looked away. I wonder if we'll die without telling one another what we are thinking. Sunday morning he was there in his lintless grey suit, smiling at everyone, a white carnation in his buttonhole. Sunlight bearing colors of the stained-glass windows fell on us all in crazy confusion. "Hallelujah!" we sang. On the altar a red poinsettia suddenly shed a leaf; it bled for us all; it lay like a giant drop of blood on the expensively carpeted steps. He showed us to our seats. My daughter; my wife; my good soul! In her handbag Edith had his aspirin which he ate all during the service. He had meticulously gargled. But I could smell on him the left-over smells of the party, the same as the living room smelled this morning. And last night he put his arm around a neighbor and thought his hand was hidden beneath her arm and his fingers were feeling the edge of her breast. Oh God, why did Rusty have to die? He is my father and I couldn't even say to Mother what's the truth: he was made a deacon because they want his money. But does he think there's another reason? That's the point. That's what all my life I'll wonder and never be able to ask him. I promised to try not to be cruel. And since I can't ask I'll know my own father less well forever. Whatever he does on Saturday night is atoned for, he thinks, by struggling up for church on Sunday morning. Like Catholics and confession. One time a maid we had said to me, "White folks go to church on Sunday and Klan meeting on Monday; how come?" I guess she was not really expecting an answer because I was too young to know what she was talking about. So I just told him it was great he had been made a deacon as if I thought it was an honor he had acquired after hard work and he grinned and kept on brushing his suit. But I saw Mother in her room staring in the mirror as if she were putting on make-up, though it was already on. Does she feel something missing in her life after all? Once she told me a man ought never marry a terribly rich wife or inherit himself enough money to live on.

I want to see you too. I knew it suddenly this fall after I had been fishing. The road plunged; leaves overhung. And I saw your face, the way I remember it, though now it might not be right at all. It would not work for you to come here, which means subterfuge. Have I the right to start you on this? No. And so refuse if you want.

I certainly don't refuse. I want very much to see you and not to ask about short stories. I want to know about inanity and why everything is. Tell me where to come?

The train station Monday at ten. Call if this is not possible and if I sound strange, don't worry. I'll understand your message.

"But why, if you are meeting the girls for lunch, don't you want to wear your new coat?" Edith said.

Amy caught herself in time from saying that the coat was too dressy. It was not too dressy for the Forrester, where she had said she was going. "The coat's just so pretty. I hate to get it dirty," she said.

"No sense saving it," Edith said. "I've done that too much in my life. Put good things in the closet, waiting to wear them. The time never seems to come." At Amy's window, framed by chintz ruffles, Edith looked out, the seams of her pink robe grown tighter and giving.

Was that the summing-up philosophy of her mother's fifty years, Amy wondered: that the time never seems to come. She determined not to end up with it being hers and brushed her hair with strokes fearful and angry.

The fine strands flung themselves about freely, and Edith suddenly wondered about Amy's hurry. "Why are you going to town so early to go to lunch?" she said.

Amy answered blithely, "To spend my Christmas money!" knowing that her mother would understand shopping, looking at

72

her in a womanly and conspiratorial way. She must remember to bring home packages, Amy thought. "How long can I keep the car?"

"I only have to run to the grocery later," Edith said. "But you can't go to the Forrester like that, in a skirt and sweater." And no, she shook her head, not even if Amy put on high heels. Amy had held up a pair. Seeing her mother was going to be adamant about the way she dressed going to the Forrester, Amy, conceding, dragged from the closet a forgotten dress with a stand-up collar and a row of militarily marching buttons.

"Why haven't you been wearing it all along? Becoming," Edith cried, knowing she was never going to understand her daughter. She held out the coat, determined Amy should wear it, and when the fur collar was fastened beneath Amy's chin, Edith cried, "Oh, you look sweet as a little kitten!" She forgave Amy's disappointed look when she had found it under the tree. At Christmas, Mallory was not tight with money and had not minded her buying the coat; he was jovial at the Christmas season about everything. Edith followed Amy to the door to remind her, "If you see anybody I know at the Forrester, don't forget to speak."

Nodding from the car, Amy wondered if her mother had taken seriously that she was shopping and going to lunch with girls, or whether she had taken the easiest way out and pretended. Her mother might even find out the lunch had not taken place and never say so. Often, Amy thought, she longed to be confronted with things, as if someone cared. Why had Mr. Almoner been so secretive about their meeting? She supposed because he was married. But she wanted to know him as a writer, which had nothing at all to do with his being married.

He appeared self-contained, though somehow aware of his own aloneness, sitting on a bench in the station. Unmindful of the crowd, Almoner stared at something on the ceiling. Probably he was astounded at all this ornateness for a train station, too, Amy thought, as she always had been. There were gilded frescoes and stone gargoyles, which she stared at as if for the first time. She hoped she and Mr. Almoner would think the same about a lot of things. Through arched remote windows came a celestial pale light giving the station interior a churchy feeling; despite the crowd, everything seemed hushed. Almoner was touched particularly by one shaft. Approaching him, Amy had the feeling she ought to kneel. Standing directly in front of him, she bent, half-whispering, "Mr. Almoner."

He quickly removed a package from his knees and stood, doffing a checked cap. "Miss Howard? I'm glad to see you."

In the station, servicemen were making goodbyes, while Negroes with bursting heavy-corded packages headed out a gate marked Chicago and old people watching them cried. One hand met Almoner's; Amy brought her other hand to the fur collar as if to cover it.

"I'm glad to see you, too," she said, knowing the coat was overdone.

While Almoner appeared well-dressed, on close inspection, his clothes were somewhat worn. That meant simply, Amy thought, that his mind was on more important things. His raincoat evidently did not even shed rain, for the sleeves were darkened alarmingly. She was sorry to have nothing to offer but to go back out into the day, which was awful. The station was worse: stuffy and full of smells and of people slunk down on benches sleeping with open mouths, homeless-looking and exhausted. Passing back through the room, Amy worried about looking privileged, feeling eyes turned toward her which were not. She only hoped, damn it, that Mr. Almoner did not think she was dressed up to prove something, noting his shirt had a frayed collar. Outside, on the station's top step, they stared at the city as if it were a puzzle dumped all around them.

74

"Where shall we go?" Amy said.

Holding up his package, Almoner asked if it would be too much trouble to take it to his typist. That was his excuse for coming. He looked at her a moment as if wondering if she understood. Amy only said it would not be trouble and wondered what that Almoner asked could be. He was unbelievably modest. If only he had not had to think up an excuse for coming.

The package was on the car seat between them like an unintroduced person and they drove several blocks before Amy dared ask, "Is it a new book?" Her breath, blown outward, hung about the car like odorless smoke and dissolved against the windshield, on whose exterior rain had begun to freeze. Holiday traffic moving at a snail's pace was tangled because of the weather. Why does rain always make traffic worse? Amy had asked and fallen silent, thinking what an inane thing to have said to Almoner.

But he said he had never been able to figure that out himself. It was certainly a fact. He returned a smile, though Amy's had been relieved and small. To her, her remark seemed not so totally worthless.

But staring out at the worsening streets, she was afraid of being responsible for Almoner's safety. Perhaps he was not as bored as she had worried he would be. But suppose she had a wreck and Almoner was killed! Or, almost worse, suppose she had an accident which only caused their names to get in the paper and their meeting to be known. Juxtaposition with the famous Amy found exciting and wondered if she would really mind publicity lifting her above the crowd. Almoner was certainly old-fashioned and courtly, asking her permission to light a small cigar; she tried to imagine telling him he could not smoke.

Until the moment Amy had asked him about the package, her voice timid and fearful, Almoner had thought them having a silence unusually companionable for strangers. "I hope it's a book," he had answered.

75

Amy had wondered what that answer meant. Was it a book or not? She feared appearing stupid, asking him to explain, and put the answer down to a writer's idiosyncrasy. She felt on tenterhooks because of the silence between them. Now that he was here, she could think of nothing to say, absolutely nothing at all, and felt resentful that being so much older and more intelligent, he did not keep up a conversation. She had circled, in silence, the typist's building several times, without finding a place to park.

He would have to run in while she was driving, Almoner said. Sorry to be a bother. . . .

But he was not! Amy said, unable to imagine Almoner being a bother. She watched him disappear and the revolving door flash brass. She was tired, however, of driving these cold slushy streets. Would the typist have sense enough to be humble? And imagine that an Almoner manuscript had been on the seat beside her! That moment, Amy recognized a friend of her father's waiting to cross the street. To avoid that corner, she adroitly turned into a parking lot and went out its second entrance, surprising herself at how quickly she had adapted to secrecy and intrigue and deviousness. Hiding things, she thought sorrowfully, came too naturally to people. It was strange to be hiding in her own city, and she noticed alleyways and the dark entrances to little shops never noticed before. She could not help being irritated, coming repeatedly to the building's entrance without ever finding Almoner at the curb. Then, driving on, she concentrated on two inward pictures: the girl out shopping that her parents saw and the girl she wanted to become, with a life far different from theirs.

The rotund proprietor of a cheese store, whose window was full of his hanging wares, had begun to nod from his doorway, Amy came past so often. She thought that like this day with Almoner, this block of stores would be forever imprinted on her mind. A Negro in white spats swept the foyer of the typist's

76

building; a woman with bluish hair dressed mannequins in lacy black underwear that was not exactly nice. Forever preserved in her mind, these people would never grow older, though Amy felt pressured by the passage of time, despite being young.

Almoner, dashing a hand against his cold nose, stepped hurriedly and apologetically into the car. Amy's awe made her want to sacrifice anything for him; she did not want apology. "I haven't minded driving around," she said, "but where shall we go now?"

"What is your wish?" he said, in his formal and old-fashioned way, which always struck her. She had no wish; she only wanted to do what he wanted. "I'm afraid," he said, "I know so little about the city. But I think we should go someplace neither of us will be recognized."

Amy instinctively had already begun taking them from the center of the city. And now as they passed through a rather seedy section, she realized they were directionless. "Do you like the river?" she asked, at last.

"Of course. And if I had thought of it, I would have known you did." He looked away from her erect profile to gaze again through the rain-spattered windshield before softly confiding. "Once," he said, "I wanted to go down the river willy-nilly in a boat, the way the wind took me."

"And you never did?" Amy said, surprised.

"No." His eyes were speculative, turned toward her again.

"I'm going to do everything like that I want to," she said confidently.

"You're young. Maybe you'll choose the right life to enable you to do all the things you want."

She was puzzled by his voice, some tone of regret in it similar to one often in her mother's. Surely Almoner, having his work, had a fulfilled life, she thought. They came, at last, from one of the city's saddest parts to a bluff overlooking the river, which in the frost-ridden and sunless day appeared not only sluggish but totally without sparkle; lifeless and still, it lay as if it were a gorge only.

"I'm afraid we'll be cold sitting here," Amy said, staring down.

"Not too cold." He spoke in a positive voice. Having stared in silence down at the water, too, he said, "Dawns and sunsets on the river are beautiful."

"I've never seen either," Amy said. To see both over the river, she considered now a goal, watching frost melting on the windshield slide inward to form a heart's shape. "We're looking through a valentine." Then, furiously, she blushed and thought what a stupid remark.

"Yes, it has formed a heart," he said. "The edges are like that lacy paper they put around valentines. I wonder if there is any significance?"

Significance? Amy thought, trying to be totally mystified. "Look!" She drew his attention to the window. "See that barge. I've never been farther down the river than that. But I'd like to go down it to New Orleans. I'd like to go everywhere, I guess."

"I do wonder what the future holds for you," he said, in a way which surprised her; though what surprised her more was that he reached out and put a hand on her arm. Amy sat stone-still and embarrassed, wondering what the gesture meant. At her stillness, because of the resoluteness with which she kept her eyes ahead, he not only took back his hand but moved closer to the car door.

Partially to gloss over the incident, partially to break the silence, Amy ran over in her mind, frantically, topics of conversation and found them all lacking. Finally, she said, "Most people I know wouldn't care about coming here to sit. But I've done it a lot." Only Quill would share such times; however, after considering, she decided not to mention his name. Then Almoner sat with a grave face, while Amy told him about walking around the block in the rain, once, and how everyone had reacted.

78

"You'll have to be tough, have a tough hide if you want to be a writer," he said. "Believe in yourself, or no one will. You can't worry too much about what other people think."

But did not worrying about what other people thought mean not to worry about hurting them? Amy wondered. Fearing that she ought to know, she was afraid to ask. She kept on roaming about in her mind for something else to say. Almoner, poking about in his pockets for matches to light the cigar he had stuck in his mouth, looked pensive. Amy considered that he was thinking merely about where he had put a light. However, he looked as thoughtful once he had pulled a packet of matches from his breast pocket, lit the cigar, and sent a spiralling roll of smoke to break open on the windshield. He sounded abrupt saying, "Miss Howard, your letter came at a time in my life when I needed it most. That day, I tried to think of something to compare it to. And I thought of wind through apple trees. I needed an image with great freshness, fineness, sweetness. Before your letter came, I had been going along feeling like a used-up—"

Urgently, Amy looked at him and said, "You're not used up!"

"—bloke," he finished, looking grateful and smiling at her. "You brought back something of my own youth."

"I was so scared about writing you," she said, "I don't know what I said."

"You told me," he said, not daring to laugh, "a great deal. Even about a dog you had that got run over."

"Oh no! I couldn't have." She began to laugh. "I'm embarrassed."

He laughed quietly. "Yes, yes," he said, like a low quick murmur, "you did. But I hope you'll never be embarrassed with me." He pinched the end of his cigar, looking down at it. "Assuming, that is, that you aren't finding this meeting too unsatisfactory and that you'll risk another."

Who, Amy wondered, would pass up a chance to meet Almoner? She had been wondering whether she could risk telling her friends at school about seeing him. They would not consider, first, that he was married. Since she was no one and he was famous, she could not see why that mattered; still, not wanting to face that fact, she knew that it mattered. "Yes, of course, I want to meet again," she said, not looking at him; she stretched restlessly beneath the steering wheel. "I am getting very tired of just sitting here, and I'm cold. Would you like to have lunch, or do something?"

"Lunch! I wasn't thinking. It's way past your lunchtime." He had held close to his face, in a way which reminded Amy of her father looking at the phone book, an old-fashioned round watch. "At my age, I don't eat much in the middle of the day. But where can I take you that you can get what you want?"

"I don't know where we can go that you won't be recognized, or that I won't see somebody I know. Except there's a place near my old high school that has great cheeseburgers, and no one else will be there now since it's vacation. Unless you want something better than that?"

"Coffee will do me, Miss Howard," he said. "Let's go where you want."

As Amy started off, driving again back over the same slick wet streets, she wondered if his calling her "Miss" were a custom left over from his day of dating. He sounded entirely too quaint. She said, "Please call me Amy."

"All right. But then you have to call me something else. Either Jeff or Jeffrey. Which do you prefer?"

She preferred to go on calling him Mr. Almoner, which seemed proper. She said, however, "Jeff."

The air coming from the car's heater had grown too hot. Amy lowered the heat and the car became gradually too cold. She then kept alternating the temperature, which would never adjust correctly, and that gave her an unsettled feeling. The day was more dismal with sleet falling now, and slush in dreary little globs was flung about by the windshield wipers.

"Your fine letter deserves something better than this," Almoner said quietly.

And "this," Amy thought, must refer to the day and their wandering around in it so aimlessly and to being cold; shivering for some time, she had tried to hide it.

"It must have taken courage for you to write it," Almoner said. He moved slightly toward the middle of the seat and again placed a hand on her arm. "It was fine, damn it."

She sat stiff as a board, wondering that her letter could have been so meaningful. And glancing once at her stolid profile, he took his hand away. She said, with a slight rush, "Remember Quill, that boy who came down there with me to see you? He got an A on his thesis about you."

"I'm very glad to hear that," he said unconvincingly.

Amy pressed a little harder on the accelerator and turned them with a bump into the drive-in. She glanced at the rickety fence surrounding it, with the same signs she remembered. A carhop started toward them but Almoner signalled that they would be going inside. Though he got immediately from the car and started around it, Amy met him by the hood. He supposed young ladies in this day and time did not wait to have doors opened for them. He did take her elbow, going up the steps to the entrance. "And is he—if this is a term you use today—your boyfriend?" he said.

Without meaning to be rude, she drew her elbow away, having never liked anyone holding it when she was walking. "Quill?" she said. "No, he's just a friend. I don't have a boyfriend." Sensing that Almoner wanted to know, whether he would have asked or not, she thought she might as well tell him.

They stood, a moment, adjusting to the dim interior before crossing the room toward a booth. The waiter who had started out, Amy was thinking, had been Sill, whom she remembered from high school. She was surprised that he looked no older. So much time seemed to have passed since she had come here as a high-school girl and yet it had been, really, only a few years. Had she not changed at all, either? Certainly, this place looked the same. Outside, in one corner of the fence had been the same Budweiser ad she had stared at while letting, for the first time, a boy unbutton her blouse; discreetly those nights back in high school when she had been brought here to neck, the waiters had come and gone, setting up or taking down trays. And now inside, the green booths had their same sticky look of being freshly painted, though they had not been. Many of the scratched initials, evident on the tables and the walls, she remembered, all of them still imbedded with dirt and food. Colors from the nickelodeon swirled about the room in the same pattern of lavenders and greens, coloring her face and Almoner's until they sat down. From the washrooms they had passed came the same odors of a pine-scented cleanser.

Once they had given their order, Amy stared thoughtfully at her folded hands, unable to think of anything to say. Having criticized Quill for wanting to ask Almoner questions about his books, she did not feel free to do so; only by the river had she asked a few tentative ones. Almoner stared up at a clock on the wall. While digging at food in one of the scratched initials on their table, Amy thought how she hated being shy. She conceived of her insides as crying out to end her loneliness, knowing she might sit here endlessly, silent.

As if it took effort on his part, Almoner said, "This fall, I almost came up to your school to see you."

Then her mouth dropped open a little, and Amy looked up in astonishment. "You did!"

"Yes, and if I had, I was coming to call on a young woman.

That's why I didn't come, because I didn't know whether you would want me to."

"Everybody would have been thrilled," she said, looking down at the initial again.

"I wasn't coming to play literary," he said firmly. "I was coming to call on a young woman. You may even want me to stop writing you letters, not to complicate your life."

"How is your writing me letters going to complicate my life?" She looked up.

"I might fall in love with you."

"Oh. That would be complicated," she said softly, looking in relief at the waiter approaching, his tray high above his head, recognizing their order by her pink soda. She bent immediately to the straw when her glass was set down.

"I may have to come to New York in the spring," Almoner said, watching her drink. "Could you come down from your school to meet me? We could have good food and good talk in New York, and freedom we'll never have here."

Amy, letting the straw go, looked at her lipstick mark on it, the same strawberry color as the soda. "I have a vacation at Easter. Would it be then?" she asked.

"Yes, I think it would be then." He smiled. "Did I tell you I like very much what you have on?"

"I'm glad," she said immediately. "For once, even my mother liked what I have on, and she never does."

He said, "Your nails, too, I like those. Not all painted like so many women's, but natural. Your hands look older than you are. I don't mean that unflatteringly, but they have a strong honest look about them."

"Good heavens," she said. "My mother thinks they're the very worst thing about me, my nails all bitten."

"And today your eyes are not violet at all. Look up a minute.

No, they're greenish like your dress. Do they change with the color you have on?"

"I don't know."

"No one's ever told you?" he said. "There seems to be so much you've never been told."

"I feel I don't know anything, despite college," she said.

"You don't need college to be a writer," he said. "Why don't you give it up?"

She had bent toward her straw and stared at him instead, her lips open. Then she sat back and said, "I've almost gotten my degree. My parents would die if I quit. My mother went to a finishing school. She's horrified enough that I go someplace we can wear blue jeans to class. And my father's horrified because he thinks everybody there is a Communist and that I'm going to be one. Everybody's a Communist to him who's not as conservative as he is. I'm sure you'd be one."

"Certainly. A writer is always suspect. Well, I suppose if you've put three and a half years into it, you might as well get the degree. But do you have time to write, with all your studies?"

She tied her straw into an intricate knot. "I suppose I do," she said slowly. "But I never do write anything, except a diary. Or rather I write little things sometimes and throw them away because they always seem silly."

"They might not seem silly to me," he said gently. "Why don't you show me something you write. The same thing might come out of it that comes out of your letters. Something you're not aware of yet."

"I'm really not," she said. "It doesn't seem to me anything could come out of them."

"When you're older, you'll know. I suppose I wish you'd never reach the point in your life of needing something, a new start, as I did. But since you are sensitive and intelligent, I'm afraid you will."

That moment, a patron put money into the nickelodeon, and Almoner sighed apprehensively. Then, to his relief, the music was soft. They were quiet again, listening to a Negro man sing, rather sensually, "You Always Hurt the One You Love." Looking at Amy intently, Almoner said, "That's for you."

She had, unexpectedly, felt an emotion rise in her which she compared to jungle cats roaming restlessly around cages; the restaurant was near a zoo and frequently, on afternoon dates, she had wandered about there before being brought in here for something to eat. She was as distressed by Almoner's words as when he had touched her in the car. He was no longer looking at her but staring into his empty coffee cup. And, unable to think of anything but ending the moment, she said, "What time is your train?"

"At four," he said quickly. "If that's too late, you can take me now."

As quickly, she said, "Oh no. I wouldn't dream of letting you wait in the station alone that long. But I don't know anything else to do, do you?"

"No," he said. "I'm afraid I'm not much help to you."

"I guess we'll just have to drive again," she said, beginning to slide out of the booth. Their hands met reaching for the check.

"Oh," Almoner said, laughing. "Were you going to take me to lunch?"

She said, "I did suggest eating, and you only had coffee."

"But don't you realize," he said, standing beside her now, "that I'm a famous author. Therefore, I must be rich."

"Well, good heavens then," she said, laughing, "by all means, you pay." But going along with him toward the cashier, she felt still worried, though the check was small, knowing that he made very little money from his books. That was one of the outrageous things she had somehow by her presence wanted to make up to him.

Deserted now, the parking lot was an expanse of asphalt slick with rain, shiny as tar. The descendent grey afternoon had brought on lights in houses early. It seemed much later than it was. Though her bottom felt paralyzed with sitting, Amy climbed into the car, unable to think anything but that she would be glad to get home.

They went along in silence for a while. Then Almoner said, "I almost wrote you first, you know. I felt I owed you an apology. I was going to get your address on some pretext from that Decker woman. And then when that blue envelope came, I knew it was from you. Now, I almost know what your letters are going to say before I open them. I think if you had come alone that first day, we would have talked right away and intimately, not as strangers."

"Oh yes, I've thought that, too. I was so sorry afterward I hadn't come alone, I can't tell you. I had thought about it, but I was afraid to."

"Amy, you'll never get anywhere being afraid," he said. "If I haven't already told you that, it should have been the first thing I ever told you. And if I have no chance to impress anything else on you, let it be that."

"All right," she said, thinking it was easy to be told, and to agree to not being afraid; but then how did you actually go about it? "Aren't we, though, going to meet in the spring?" She glanced at him, wondering if he had forgotten suggesting it, or whether she had been so boring that he had changed his mind.

"Let us meet," he said.

"But we had decided." He sat a little queerly, his head dropped slightly. She looked at him cautiously. "We will meet!" she said brightly, glad that he sat up.

She drove the most circuitous route she could to the station, passing time; they spoke mostly of the bad weather and of the increasing difficulties of ever finding a parking place in the city.

86

At last, she found a place a short walking distance from the station and they started toward it down a block where, above them, now glitterless reindeer arched on their hind legs and met over the street, having been forgotten since Christmas. Walking along, she and Almoner glanced inside a dilapidated apartment building and both saw a Negro woman standing and pressing her hair; remarking on her expression, each found they had seen the same minute details in the room.

Almoner slowed a moment and, looking around, said, "Is there a park near here, with a fountain?"

"There's one in the middle of the city," Amy said, slowing. "A developer wanted to tear it down and build a shopping mall. A lot of old people got up a petition to save it, so he built all these modern buildings around it, and it looks stupid. Could that be the one?"

"I suppose so," he said. "And I'm sure it does look stupid. I hadn't realized how much the city has changed. I'm not sure I should let you go back to the car alone at this time of day."

"It's fine. I like it here," she said, liking being somewhere no one else she knew would be, as she felt about going to the river. Then, several Negro children ran past them, laughing; flashing white teeth, their grins seemed to separate from their faces in the gloom.

"Have you ever noticed," Almoner said, "how their voices are not raucous like white people's?"

"No," Amy said, carefully considering and wanting to know and to see everything as Almoner did. She was not, she thought, afraid of tangible things like dark streets, but all day, without courage, she had wanted to ask him a question and now forced herself. "Do you mind our long silences?"

"I hadn't noticed them," he said. "There's not enough silence."

They had been about to cross a street and suddenly Amy extended her elbow. He took it as the light changed. In the mo-

87

ment they hesitated, about to step off the curb, a man rushed from a building behind them and vomited into the street, spattering one of Almoner's shoes.

"Excuse me," said the man afterward, throwing a handkerchief to his mouth and running back from where he came.

"Now that man has really been raised politely," Almoner said, grinning. "Imagine being sick and begging pardon."

"He certainly was sick a lot," Amy said. As they started across the street, she looked protectively both ways.

"Yes," Almoner said. "Good metal at the bottom of his stomach. But I'm afraid I've brought you to a bad spot."

"No, I like it here," she said, pressing his arm reassuringly. His humbleness, she thought, was part of his greatness; she could imagine how mad her father would be if anyone vomited on his shoe!

Almoner, slowing, said considerately though, "Won't you go back now? No need for you to see me onto the train."

To abandon him to wispy twilight, Amy felt, would be to abandon him to further loneliness, and she could not do it. "It doesn't matter about its being dark," she said. He came rather laggingly up the station steps, rubbing his lips as if guessing they had a bluish cast, while she waited. If they met ever again in Delton, there had to be something to do besides drive endlessly around, she thought. "Do you remember a letter you wrote me once but said you never mailed?" she said. "Why not?"

At the top step, he had paused to catch breath. "If you have to ask," he said softly, "you're not old enough to know."

Inside, at the newsstand, he bought a paper. Amy stood before the array thinking that his smile had implied there was a great deal she did not know. She did want to know everything he did and wondered how she might learn it all; it was so much more difficult if one was a girl to have a free life, with any degree of wildness in it. Her hand had lingered over a news magazine, but as if of its own accord strayed to a fashion magazine. Almoner, glancing at the headlines of his paper, had started off toward the proper gate, without realizing Amy was not behind him. At the moment she closed the magazine, the aproned vendor leaned down with an extended hand.

"Miss," he said, "your father forgot his change." His newsprint-blackened hand dropped the money into her mittened one.

Almoner was turning, perplexed, as she reached him. "Did you think I had left without saying anything," she said teasingly. "No, I'm not going to leave you. I feel responsible for Almoner. You've got to get safely on that train."

"Yes, that's what I've needed," he said, looking happy. "Someone to take care of me. Perhaps our roles are to be reversed. You're to be the teacher."

"Oh no," she said. "You're the teacher, but I can see to your safety for the world." She dismissed the idea of repeating the vendor's mistake and thought instead of the faces of young men, outside, which had bothered her; observing Almoner take Amy's elbow, to draw her closer as they went across the street, the young men had made some joke among themselves, and one had looked back. She had been surprised, realizing she had no outward appearance different from girls who went out with older men to get from them what they could. Probably those young men had surmised that this coat, which she did not even want, was a reward.

Buckets of sand along the station platform held cigarette butts and ugly tobacco-juice stains; against one post a drunk loitered, while a legless drooling pencil salesman half-lay nearby. Yet in their midst and among the sooty grey stones, Amy felt her life expand. Her heart soared knowing Almoner. She watched him drop the change into the pencil man's tin cup, noting that piecemeal light, filtering through the station's platform roof, turned his hair silver. He removed his somewhat funny checked hat, his eyes grown serious.

"No goodbyes," he said.

"All right. I won't say goodbye." She hugged herself against the cold. "Spring then. That's not so long."

"It seems very long to me," he said.

Parting from someone, Amy always turned to look back. She waited but Almoner went on, unnoticed among workmen and women who had come to the city for after-Christmas sales and now dragged along, by upward-extended arms, small children who resentfully scuffed their shoes. What was the point of achieving? Amy wondered, watching him go. Why struggle, when people who never did anything had lives that turned out happier? His back seemed unnaturally erect; he was an alone figure in the crowd, disappearing. She wondered also why being deceitful worked. On the way home, she stopped at one of the city's most exclusive shops and had a saleswoman pick out for her an expensive suit. At home, Edith was ecstatic and said it was the most becoming thing Amy had ever owned.

"Except for my coat," Amy said winningly.

More pleased, Edith said, "I hadn't been sure you liked it."

Lifting his first predinner martini, having inspected the suit, her father meant it as a toast. "Well," he said approvingly. "Well." He was careful to avoid putting fingerprints on his frosted glass. At dinner, he stared at her with his eyes shining. Edith smiled continually from her place at one end of the table, beaming, and her look said plainly, Amy was learning to be like the other girls, at last.

Mister Jeff laid on the sofa, say he got wore out in Delton and wasn't going for the mail, so I had to be the one go. Sho would have to be Jessie bring home trouble. That letter on the hall table

90

since noon. Miss Amelia been wanting to open it all day, curious as a cat. Finally, Miss Inga come down at suppertime and read it. Didn't say nothing till they were eating. I could hear the forks against they plates and then this sound like that old bullfrog down in the pond at night, "Old goat old goat old goat." Miss Inga kept on going. The do' is swole open. I could see Miss Amelia looking from one to the other. "What's going on?" she say. Miss Inga taken the letter out of her lap and act po-lite saying, "A friend have been kind enough to tell me my husband is running around juke joints in Delton with a young woman, very young."

"Juke joint!" Mister Jeff say. Seem like he always can find something to laugh about. "For heaven's sake when?" Miss Amelia say. "The day he took his precious manuscript to the typist," Miss Inga say. "All ten pages?" Miss Amelia say. Then he turn white. Seem like they oughtn't do Mister Jeff that way no matter what.

Jessie's sister nodded.

Then he starting off from the table, and Miss Inga held up the letter. "Don't you want to read it?" she say. He look back and say, "There's enough without having to read it at my own dinner table." And Miss Amelia say, "Enough what?" And Miss Inga say with her head bowed, "Lying misery defeat." Then Miss Amelia say, "Oh, shut up." She the onliest one take dessert. So then he laid down some more with a book on his stomach but the whole time I cleared up, I didn't see him turn no page. Miss Inga's shadow was going all over the room and she walking up and down telling him she wasn't going to put up with it and he not saying nothing. Usually he say something make her just shut up. Some reason he ain't saying nothing. Then I thought, Mister Jeff care. He ain't taking no chances on saying nothing because this time, Mister Jeff care. Seem like I be glad he be happy tell you the truth, though I see Miss Inga's side. She got tired of talking to herself, finally. I had did mopped and they come in tracking up the flo'. Then Miss Amelia read the letter and say, "You know why Reba's done this, don't you? Because you didn't invite her to that party you gave for Jeff's publisher ten years ago. I told you she'd get even no matter how long it took."

Miss Inga shake her head saying, "Ten years," not thinking 'bout Miss Reba. Miss Amelia say Miss Reba get her hair done on Fridays and so it would be all over town by now. "Tall and blonde and wearing an expensive coat and alligator shoes," Miss Amelia read. "Are we supposed to think he gave her those? We've outlasted others. We can outlast this one."

"But where will it all end?" Miss Inga say.

"At the grave, I guess," Miss Amelia say. "Jessie, what's the matter with you?"

"Rabbit done run over mine," I sayed.

Then they fixing to go on to the picture show. Get they mind off it, Miss Amelia sayed. But they ain't going to get they mind off it. Like I can't keep my mind off Vern. I keep telling him church ain't meeting no mo', it's taking up collection. And everybody full of hate when the Bible say love. Too little love. Black and white folks going to be fighting out yonder in the road. Mark my words. It's all laid out in the Bible. History just goes round. "Love," Vern sayed to me. "What white man love me?" I sayed, "He give you a job." "That white man where I plow at need me bad as I need him," he sayed. Then he gone off to another meeting. Preacher got a new car, Vern ain't. Sets up to the lunch counter, they close it down.

"It takes the process of time," Jessie's sister said. "Like you may want you some field peas in the wintertime, it takes till the summertime to get them."

"I see," Jessie said. "And I guess that what us going to do: see."

But, that evening, Miss Amelia tell Miss Inga to stop crying and run put her face back on. She had some wrinkle-erase cream on her dresser and sayed it would hide the red around Miss Inga's eyes, go use it. Miss Inga say, "It won't hide the wrinkles though, will it?" And Miss Amelia act like she don't hear. So Miss Inga sayed to me, "Will it, Jessie?" And I sayed, "No'm."

"It's like you sayed, Sister, everything going to go according to the process of time," Jessie said.

That evening, waiting on the porch to go to the movies, Inga had seemed like a little bird huddled on its perch, Amelia had thought. They had stared back in at Jeff with the book still on his stomach, and he never turned a page, she had noted. The winter-dry muscadine had scraped the porch's eaves with a groaning sound that reminded her of arthritic old people complaining about their swollen joints. The car's headlights, bending obliquely, tore through the forsythias, and the car rattling over the cattle gap had made a sound as if something had been dropped hollowly into frozen ground from a distance. How old she felt, Inga had thought. How much better Amelia seemed to be bearing up under life. She wondered what her secret was, and for the first time, having often wondered why Amelia had never married, she had thought that it was because she had had sense enough not to. It aged you, Inga thought, having realized when she looked into the mirror that the hair rinse she had put on was not enough; tomorrow she would go to Billie Jean's.

"If we had had children do you think things would have turned out any differently?" she said.

Meaning to absolve Inga of that guilt, Amelia said, "Probably he would have cared more about his work, anyway."

Anyway, but how cruel, Inga thought, wanting desperately to reach out and touch someone. "His work," she said vehemently.

Vurk, Amelia repeated inwardly, jarred. If only Inga had been able to get rid of her accent better. She remembered how odd she had looked when Jeff brought her home wearing black lisle stockings; right away, she had given her some silk ones. Inga had wanted to milk. As kindly as she could she had said, "We have Negroes to do that."

She said, now, "Inga, don't you ever miss your home?"

"Why, this is my home!" Inga said.

"Well, I mean where you came from, then," Amelia said.

Inga answered, a little lost, "Home to me is where I live."

"That's certainly not the way I am, at all," Amelia said. "I sometimes wonder what in the world would have happened to me if I had married a man I started to once. He got transferred afterward to St. Louis!"

Was Amelia telling her something finally, or had she at last only understood, Inga wondered. She had left her country and Amelia wouldn't move out of her county if she had to. She had married for love, Inga thought. Was that a mistake? At the ticket window, she drew up her coat collar feeling pierced by eyes on the young woman selling tickets. And inside the movie, she thought she was going to scream if Amelia did not stop sucking popcorn hulls off her teeth and scraping the popcorn against the insides of the cardboard box. She thought of her early years here when on pretty mornings the smooth magnolia blossoms had given off their lemon scent. When she went to open market all the men around the station had stared and she had swung her basket teasingly. How much she had liked bending over the great bushels of peas to run her hands down to the cool wettish depths at the bottom, but one day she had realized the old countrymen gathered around to stare down the top of her dress, which had changed those lovely moments. Nothing ever did stay the same. If only Jeff had worked at the lumber mill like everybody else. And why should she have invited Reba when she hardly knew her? If only she had not chosen that time to try to defy Amelia and go against her advice. Did defiance ever work? The time she

94

had put Jeff's manuscript in the garbage, she had not let Jessie burn it. She had told him afterward it ought to teach him to keep carbons. The pages, found at last, had been smelly and smeared. Before he went back to the house, she had asked what he would have done if she had let them be burned. And he had answered, "Kill you or leave you," she could not remember which, as they would have been the same.

On the street again, Amelia said, "Did you enjoy the movie?" wondering why Inga kept her coat collar up to her nose.

"Yes," Inga answered, though Amelia knew she had no more idea than a puppy dog what the whole movie had been about. Negroes came down the rattly wooden steps from the gallery.

"Hidy, Vern," Amelia said, recognizing Jessie's nephew from his painted-on leather jacket. He lowered his eyes as if not to see her, then at the last minute spoke. She wondered if he mumbled because he didn't have good sense and someday was going to ask Jessie.

"Let's look in the jewelry store," she said. While there, a couple were reflected stopping behind them to speak. The station's lights dimmed as she and Inga turned around. It was nine o'clock and not even an express would pass through the remainder of the night.

Holding a large knitting bag, the woman said, "Dea Ellman, Amelia," since it was obvious Amelia could not place her.

"Joe," said the man, lifting his hat.

"Of course," Amelia said. "And you know my sister-in-law, Inga."

"We were about to have a quick Coke or something at Chester's," Joe said. "Won't you join us?"

It was the most astonishing invitation Amelia had ever had, but then it was not an invitation, at all. It was a command, she thought, ruffled. The man had taken her arm and was guiding her toward the drugstore before she could answer, and Inga had been taken in tow by the woman. Silently, they sat while Chester smeared the marble table top, wiping it before he took their order. Each mentioned something to eat, though no one cared.

"We stay in the country so much, we hardly ever see anyone we know," Dea said, trying to look amiable.

Know? Amelia thought, wondering when she had last seen these people. What was the point of all this? When Dea said she could not remember when they had last seen a movie, and Joe started to answer, Amelia cut in quickly. "None of them are worth talking about," she said. "Inga, your coat's trailing on the floor." She wished Inga could at least say Boo once in a while; it was like dragging a child about with her. Inga blushed, and Joe helped her straighten the coat.

Chester brought the order and it took time to remember who had asked for what. Dea gave Joe a definite nod and taking a great swallow of his Coke, he knew he had to begin. "Some folks like to tell a tale like there's more to it than there is. And I believe Reba Royal is one of them," he said. "Though don't misunderstand, I'm just as crazy about old Reba as I can be."

"Amy only came here to see Mr. Almoner because of her friend who's writing a paper about him," Dea interceded.

"Amy?" Amelia said. They did not know as much as Dea thought they would. "Came here?" Inga said. Amelia gave her a kick under the table, and she was silent. "Of course," Amelia said.

"My niece," Dea said. "She used to want to be a stewardess and then a nurse and now she thinks she wants to be a writer."

"Till she gets married, of course," Joe said, winking. "You know how these things go."

No, how did they go; that's what they were wondering, Amelia thought. She looked at them questioningly.

"After she came here with her friend who's writing the paper she wrote Mr. Almoner to thank him for seeing them, then evidently he wrote her and proposed lunch in Delton," Dea said.

Or she did, Amelia thought.

"We think it's nice for young people to be interested in Jeff's work," Inga said.

"She's gone back to college in Vermont now," Dea said. "She's too serious about studying for a girl. And I hope she will marry soon. She's a pretty girl."

"I'm sure of that," Amelia said.

"What Reba's telling don't sound as simple as it was," Joe said. They were running around together all over Delton was the way Reba told it. "And naturally Amy's mother is upset and we thought just to come out in the open and talk to you was the best way to handle it."

"If we all just sit tight and keep calm, it'll seem like Reba's just talking off the top of her head," Dea said.

"Yes, I think that's the best way to handle Reba," Amelia said slowly. Later, having argued gently over the bill, and Joe having finally paid it, they stood outside on the sidewalk and shook hands all around. There was nothing else they could do for now, they agreed.

Dea and Joe waited until the women had driven off safely and then headed toward the country. Driving through the darkened town, they turned moon-struck faces toward houses with lights on later than usual, wondering why they were: such small things were their main concerns. Something must be good on the late show, Joe decided. They paused to admire a new stop sign at the corner of Main. When they at last turned into their own driveway, Dea made a mental note to take the greenery off the mailbox tomorrow. Concern made her poke inquiring fingers into the fern pots inside the house now, and she found they were dry. She had to water them and Joe was almost asleep by the time she stood by the bed putting on her gown. But if she talked, he would go immediately back to sleep.

"Did you notice how Mrs. Almoner says 'work' so funny? 'Vurk,' " Dea repeated.

"Switzerland or Sweden. Where was it she came from?"

"I don't know," Dea said. "Someplace. I am certainly glad we got that talk off our minds."

Joe yawned. "Somebody has to write books, I reckon," he said, turning on his back. "But I certainly can't imagine a man sitting down wanting to do it."

Dea got into bed and smiled a little complacently. "It certainly isn't like a man getting up and going to an office in the morning, or to the fields."

The furnace popped and the clock in the tiny entranceway struck the half-hour. She could smell cloves stuck into an orange, hanging in her closet, which a granddaughter had given her for Christmas. The odor reminded her she needed to make a dentist's appointment, as his mouthwash had the same smell. Turning over, Dea knew she would sleep well with that talk over. She was glad to be rid of their duty.

While his black dog ran ahead, Almoner, holding his gun close, stood uncalmly at the edge of an autumn-scarred field. A plane crossed overhead, a silver sliver against the totally blue sky. Was it hers?

"So you had lunch with Almoner," Quill said. He had been tugging so mightily at his seat belt Amy had been wondering whether it were going to go around him. And as immediately as they had gotten on the plane, he had yelped for a Bloody Mary, trying to be so suave. Now, she gaped at him. "Don't look so astounded," he said, grinning. She had turned to glance at

Borden behind them with his head bent over a magazine. "Don't worry," Quill said. "He knows. How did you think you could get away with something like taking him to the Frog Pond?"

Laughing, his jowls hung, and he looked like a bloodhound, Amy thought. "Will you hush," she said. Surrounded by his laughter, and feeling still astonished, she put her head back remembering once when she had been floating down a rapid river that she had been sucked into a whirlpool, had had the sensation of drowning, and all her thought had been to open her mouth desperately and gasp. "How did you find out?" she said.

"Mrs. Decker called my mother. Some woman from down there had brought her daughter up to enroll her in school here and saw you."

Cars minute as fleas went by below with her mother in one, driving home from having brought her to the plane. She couldn't know, or she would have said something, Amy thought, which meant that Aunt Dea did not know either. She knew them well enough to know if they had known, they would have said something. Why had she taken Almoner to the Frog Pond? she wondered, opening a magazine: to try to disprove his feeling there was a need for secrecy, which she had not wanted to believe. She had wanted it all to be innocent and he had ruined that when he touched her arm.

"I don't see anything wrong with having lunch with him," she said. "That's why I went to the Frog Pond."

"Boy oh boy oh, I don't see old Almoner asking me out to lunch," Quill said.

She was silently furious the remainder of the trip. When they landed, Borden hung back as if she and Quill might have something to say to one another that was private, but as noncommittally as strangers who had happened to share a seat, they turned their backs on one another and parted.

I've wanted to write you letters ever since you went back to school, but I don't know how to sign them. I'm afraid you don't want me to sign them the way I want to. Write and tell me and then I will write you.

Jeff

If you won't write, then send me some of your work. I can always help you with that. Maybe that's the only reason you came into my life, after all.

It has snowed all day on top of the foot we already had and it makes me feel so far from Delton, where it's almost spring. I've been trying to think of some good titles. A. says they are important. If I think of a good one, maybe I can think of a story to go with it. I wanted to know him and not feel so much as if there were no one else like me in the world. But I don't know what to do about the insinuations in his letters.

Thank you for sending the piece, though, in addition, I would have liked anything, even a scrap of paper with your name. The little girl going out to burn sparklers in her yard alone while her parents were having a New Year's Eve party made me want to cry. It is difficult to adjust to the fact that we are all alone. Maybe that's why I wrote books, to cope with this frustration. I have to tell you because, so far, there has been between us only honesty, which is why in so short a time I know our relationship is different, that your writing is not yet right. But if you work it will come right; what I thought would be is there, what comes out of your letters: remember I told you what it was at the river that day?

Jeff

I didn't write, I guess, because I didn't know how to tell you to sign your name. Any way you want to, I guess. But thank you very much for reading the piece. Do you know somebody saw us at lunch that day and told Mrs. Decker who told Quill's mother. I'm sure a lot of people know. My mother doesn't seem to or she would have said something. But do you think your family does? I hope nothing happens. Here, it is still cold and bleak. Many people have gone away for the weekend and it is lonely; but I like this kind of loneliness: when you choose it. But I have been just thinking about myself and I know I think about myself too much. I just don't have anything to write about; that's why nothing I write is right. I feel I have got to live, then sort of stop, and then write about what I've lived. I've tried to grow up since knowing you; but I don't think I have, completely; because I don't think I want you to sign the letters the way I think you want to. I hope you will understand the kind I mean when I say,

Love,
Amy

He should have known, Almoner thought. He said, "I should have known; if you'd burn my manuscript, you'd open my mail. Why didn't I suspect? Just tell me this. With your interest in the dollar what made you pick this one? Why not the one from New York, the publisher's. They've sold more books. Or this one from Hollywood. It's bound to have a money-making scheme. Why this plain white envelope from Vermont?"

"There's one way to put a stop to it. I'm going to see her father. Mallory Howard, in Delton. Are you surprised I know so much?" Inga's legs visibly trembled as she entered the hall. One hand groped for her room's door handle, missed, touched, while her voice came thick and smelling of codeine. In the moment of smelling it, reliving all he had ever known of separation and death, Almoner shuddered. "I'm surprised at nothing," he said.

"I didn't burn it," Inga said, lingering at her door a moment. But he was gone.

Amy:

She has opened your last letter. I should have been more vigilant, watchful. I've torn up all your others. To rip them up was like tearing myself inside. She was expecting the letter. I don't know how. She knows your name and has threatened to see your father, though I don't believe she will. I hate to frighten you, Amy. But I must. I have to warn you. Now, maybe you'll understand really the risks ahead, if you continue to see me. Only you can decide whether it's worth continuing. Whatever you decide, this may force you to grow up at last, despite yourself. If there are to be any more letters, we can't risk them here. I will rent a box under the name March Walsh. Do you remember him, a minor character in Reconstruction? *A favorite of mine. Write me, if you will, so that it arrives here on Saturday. If the box is empty then, I'll understand.*

Jeff

Dear March:

I'm writing on Wednesday assuming it will reach there on Saturday. Are you still coming East this spring?

Amy

"And so," Leigh said, "Almoner's coming East to see you." He was meticulous and had made his way carefully through early spring's mud ruts. On the Vermont hillsides, gouges that were ski trails revealed lonesome-looking rocks. Forgetful, Amy had set her overnight case down on wet ground, where in places snow was accumulated and swirled through with dirt. Leigh, swinging her case to the overhead rack on the train, swung it carefully away from his overcoat with its beaver collar. Amy ducked beneath his arm to settle by the window. "Not to see me," she said, looking up. "To see his publisher."

Leigh fit with difficulty long legs behind the seat in front of them and said, "How convenient. Just when you have a vacation."

"You sound like some old biddy from home!" Amy said, hissing.

"Oh, Amy," he said. "Are you really so naïve?" He flipped open *Time* Magazine to the political section, sighing weightily, with no time now for anything lesser than the world situation.

"He has to see his publisher," Amy said, slowly and distinctly. How had she even in fantasy thought of marrying Leigh? In that coat and carrying an umbrella, he seemed slightly effeminate. She turned to a novel opened on her lap. But the landscape offered a deer delicately nibbling newly revealed grass and fields full of water warming in the spring sun; clumps of evergreens stood, drenched and dark-looking on the hillsides. Unhappily, she could not avoid her own face in the train window, or her staring eyes, looking out at a swollen stream tumbling over boulders. The stream, for some time, followed the tracks as the train, on and on, wound circuitously out of a valley. Watching, her reflected eyes in the window were never steady.

Leigh, with some curiosity, looked up and said, "Where are you meeting him?"

When she answered, "His hotel," Leigh twirled an imaginary mustache and cried, "Ah-hah!" Amy grabbed her suitcase from his hand as they left the train. "See you on the milk train Sunday night," he said, slipping off easily between commuters.

She found them, however, an onslaught and herself in the way, with men breaking irritably past her, flinging aside their briefcases and their faces angry. She longed to have gone downtown to the party with Leigh and longed it more when she lost her way, having ducked into a tunnel which did not lead her, as she had expected, upstairs into her hotel lobby, warm and dry. Instead, she emerged onto a slushy street, where a taxi darted immediately from the curb, its driver turning his head as if not to see her and its tires spattering her coat. The hotel was so close she felt she had to walk, but had an oppressed feeling now. She went down the friendless block, convinced her hotel reservation would not have been held. And to tell herself that crying would not help did not make the tears stop.

Ladies in the city, she noticed, wore tidy boots with openings for high heels, while she wore galoshes with buckles; they squished and flapped as she crossed the hotel's marble floor. The lobby was full of the rapturous squeals of young ladies in silky clothes, greeting one another, and full of the mewling of a string quartet in the palm-leaved cocktail lounge. Amy began quickly to swelter, as she wore beneath her coat a heavy tweed dress whose pockets were puffed with notes from her last class. Always, she cried at inopportune moments. Though the clerk reassuringly presented a reservation card for her signature, she could do nothing about tears falling down her cheeks. In her pocketbook was a shredded tissue, which bore little resemblance to a Kleenex, but saying that she had a cold, Amy managed to blow her nose on it. Protesting that she had only one little bag, she was about to pick it up. The porter's shunted face made it evident one did not carry one's own luggage. Amy afterward tipped him too much, making up for her blunder, her own ineffectuality, hoping he would like her, she admitted.

The desk clerk phoned her room to say that a message had been left previously by a Mr. Almoner, who was expecting her at six. Her suède gloves, with their sheepskin lining, lay on the dresser, and she could not go out wearing them; washing the mud spatters on her coat had left the nap rubbed-looking. Her mother would say, at its present length, her hair needed cutting. It did need to be set. Maybe she was wan from not taking her thyroid, though never before had she thought it mattered. Amy observed herself, unhappily, in the dresser mirror.

Deeply fearing salespeople, and particularly in New York, she nevertheless went back downstairs to an arcade of shops in the station's basement. She was no longer sweltering, since she had changed into the dress with the military buttons and stand-up collar. However, her galoshes still clomped, making her cling to the thought that intellectually she was superior to salespeople; being intimidated by them, she always bought things she did not want. Were silvery-grey galoshes, with little tassels, really what other college girls were wearing, as the salesman said? She doubted it. But having tried on a pair, and thinking she heard a lining rip, Amy was afraid not to buy them.

In a glove store, a haughty saleswoman said, "Young lady, I don't think you know what you want," the remark irritating since it was true. The woman's aqua-tinted eyelids rolled up in her head, meaning that except for someone's indecision, the store would be closing. So that, feeling she must buy something, Amy held up several pairs of limp gloves for the saleswoman to choose. "Which?" Amy said. Too late, she found out the gloves were all French kid and twenty dollars a pair. She knew that it was ridiculous to have been afraid, as ridiculous as wearing these gloves, with tiny difficult buttons reaching to her elbows. Turned loose on the world, standing on a moist curb, ineffectual and ill-at-ease, she again wanted to cry. The gloves, which had been smartly crushed at her wrists by the saleswoman, when Amy lifted her arm for a taxi looked only wrinkled.

Almoner, opening his door, sent light fleeing from behind him into the corridor, where Amy stood. "Here you are," he said. "In your coat I remember. May I take your things?" He reached for gloves she held wadded in one hand.

"Here I am." She stood hesitantly in the room. "It's nice to see you." She looked around in disappointment, realizing it was foolish to have expected anything but an ordinary hotel room; expectation usually led to disappointment, she was learning. He held out his hand for her coat. "Aren't we going out?" she said cautiously.

"We're going, shortly, to a party my publisher is giving," he said. "But it's a little early." He placed her coat on the bed.

"I'm not very dressed up to go to a party with (almost Amy said grownups) your friends," she said.

"You look very nice. In fact, Amy, I see now you're going to be beautiful. If you aren't exactly yet, you will be." He studied her attentively.

She shook her head. "I'll never be beautiful, but it's nice of you to say so." Though with a little more confident tilt to her head, Amy went to the window and stared down. Below, people seemed hunch-backed bent against the wind and while she was disappointed to have been privileged, which never seemed fair, now Amy was glad to be inside this room. Pensive, she had not realized Almoner had come up close behind her. When she turned, at his touch, he put his lips briefly on hers.

And, "There," he said, "did that hurt?" There had been, he thought, no more pressure than a flower but there was none in return.

"No," she said, not smiling.

"Well then," he said, "why do you look so troubled?"

"Because you want to kiss me," she said. "I'm afraid you don't want us just to be friends."

"I'll be whatever you want me to be, Amy," he said, moving away. "I won't kiss you, or talk of love if you don't want that." She continued to look out the window, her face turned slightly away. "Though I've wondered if you didn't accept the possibility when you wrote me that first time, or at least when we decided to meet?"

She shook her head somewhat petulantly, feeling accused.

Then, needing to place guilt elsewhere, she thought of her mother's saying that older men sometimes went out with young women to keep from feeling old. She said, testingly, "Maybe you just like me because I'm younger."

"It wasn't your face in the train station that day," he said. "I wouldn't have recognized you if you hadn't spoken first. I never really think that, in actuality, you are a schoolgirl. Now why do you look troubled?"

"I don't know," she said. "I just don't know what to say when you talk about love. And everything troubles me, I guess."

"You'll always know trouble." Amy was toying with a tassel on the window shade, turned half away. "You've been so frightened by your past that you'll always be hurt because you're gentle and sensitive," he said. She turned so that he could not see her face at all, and he suspected tears. "But I think you have a toughness, too, Amy. You can cope with just being hurt. But don't be frightened. I wish I knew everything that had ever happened to you. I could help you better. Anyway, I'm here, if that helps."

"Yes, thank you." Her voice was tiny, muffled against the window.

"Would you like a drink now?" Amy shook her head. Almoner mixed himself one, moving to a bureau across the room where there was a bottle and glasses. Turning from the window, she came further into the room. "I'm sorry you've had so much trouble in your life," he said, watching her prowl about inspectingly. "But I'm satisfied in a way, too." She stopped then to look at him questioningly. "You'll find, eventually, that trouble didn't hurt you," he said. "Suppose your heart breaks; it'll heal. It will be stronger. I know you want to be able to believe in people and life, to trust both."

"Shouldn't I?" she said quickly.

"I think so. Other people you'll know in your life will tell you not to."

"That seems a sad way to live." She perched, almost tiredly, on the arm of a chair.

"Just don't be afraid of being hurt. It's inevitable if you're going to reach out for experience. And that's what you're after, isn't it?"

"Oh yes," she said, brightening. "I don't want a life like my parents or most of my friends. Simply social, you know?"

Crossing to the bureau, Almoner put more ice in his drink, that instant having wanted so desperately to touch the face he thought so tender. He leaned against the bureau. "Of course, I know. I turned my back on my past, too, didn't I? Isn't that partially at least what brought you to me, that you sensed it?"

"I guess so. I don't know exactly what brought me. Feeling in your books was the only name I had for it."

He started impulsively toward her and saw the frightened look on her face. "I'm sorry. I forgot again. I don't want to put any more pressure on you." He remained, however, close. "But you are my love, you are. I can't help that. And I can't believe my luck in finding you, or rather in having you find me."

She accepted being teased about that and laughed with him. Moving again to the window, she could see a crowded intersection, the surrounding streets black and emptying. Amy felt Almoner full of probing questions, sitting down behind her; and she would feel less fearful down there, with those strangers. What exposure about herself did she fear so much? When she looked back, her attention went quickly to a round table in the center of the room, holding an enormous basket of fruit and nuts. Going to it, she read an attached card. "The management sent you this! I've never known anyone that important before," she said. Grateful for his kindness, she knew no other way of telling him. It seemed a shame that the fruit would go to waste, as he could not eat this much in a month. Feeling an obligation to the management which had been so nice, Amy began to crowd small things one after another into her mouth, raisins, kumquats, and nuts.

Putting down his drink, Almoner said, "I think we'd better go to the party before you spoil your appetite."

He worried about her feet getting wet, but Amy, sensing the new boots were dreadful, insisted on leaving them behind. Often, at the movies, she wore gloves to keep from biting her nails but did not like wearing them, or to have her hand held when she had them on. Nevertheless, she left one gloved hand in his hand as they were driven up Fifth Avenue; he had taken it as immediately as they got into the cab. And once, pressing her hand hard, he said, "Amy, know this, that anything I have is yours."

She thanked him, wondering what he meant, supposing only money, though surely he knew she had enough of that. Knowing she could not attribute his remark to stupidity, she felt a vague sense of her own ignorance. That feeling carried over when she stood on the sidewalk and gazed at the lavish, monumental apartment building where the publisher, Alex Boatwright, lived. When Almoner had paid the driver, and they went inside, she sensed more how the party was going to be beyond her. A red-coated doorman opened polished glass doors into the subdued rich glitter of a mirrored lobby. They stepped from a quiet small elevator immediately into Alex's apartment, which was a new experience for Amy and confusing. She had expected to step into a corridor of closed doors. Looking about foolishly, she thought that she stood a moment too long before understanding. All around her were blurred older faces. Rooted to the spot before the elevator, she heard the inaudible whisper going about the room: "Almoner's come!" All eyes had turned their way.

Alex Boatwright came, with extended hand, to the foyer to rescue them. He stared at Amy from what seemed a great height, giving her a queer feeling that he knew as much about her as she knew about herself. But would Jeff have mentioned her to Mr. Boatwright? Introduced, he nodded a great shaggy head and looked at her kindly. She went across the room between him and Almoner feeling safely maneuvered, occasionally nudged, like a little boat between larger ones.

"What may I get you to drink?" Alex asked and bent to hear her when they reached the bar.

"A martini would be fine," she said.

"A martini would be fine for this young lady," he repeated, though the bartender had heard and already reached for a pitcher. She wondered why, with a little smile, Mr. Boatwright had repeated her order. Holding her glass, she stood between them like a child with something to pacify it, while they talked across and above her head. She was eventually separated from Almoner by other people crowding around to talk to him. When Alex's attention was taken, too, Amy wandered toward windows, full-length at one end of the room. There, Almoner presently joined her, having noticed her alone; but he said nothing, as if he felt, too, the enormity of everything, as she did: not only of night and the city below them—simply of everything; that was the only word Amy could think of. They were forced, eventually, back into the room by others. As they went from group to group, he sometimes touched her elbow, guidingly. Irritated that she was so inadequate, she felt annoyed by his possessive touch. She wondered several times about Leigh and the party she might have chosen.

Might he get her a refill? Almoner asked. Amy shook her head, guarding against losing whatever wits she had. Never before had she been to a party where women wore long dresses, unless it was a dance. She was so much the most underdressed female at the party that she forgot to worry about her appearance. She sat on a footstool near Almoner's knee, considering herself hardly distinguishable from its pattern. She grew used to the fact that anyone who spoke to her was going to ask the same questions: How she had met Almoner and what she did? Oh, they then said, what school? without really caring. They wanted to know so obviously, she thought, not only more than she told them but more than they dared ask. At home, her father and his friends drank quickly, seeing how much they could "put aboard" before dinner. Without drinks, Almoner and Alex Boatwright sat now discussing a vague sonnet. Amy wished she could tell her mother about the ice sculpture and about the crêpe suzettes for dinner, fantastically thin. She longed, in a burst of enthusiasm, to write her mother about everything!

Almoner, tuned to her moods, said in a low voice, "I told you in New York we would have good food and good talk."

An exchanged glance between them acknowledged several things, that freezing day by the river when they had first risked meeting, that undeniably there would be more meetings, that truthfully no matter how nice it was here, they preferred their own part of the country. Almoner then went for coffee, thinking that the glance between them had been as intimate as one between lovers, wondering if he and Amy ever would be.

As soon as he left the table, the woman sitting next to Amy said, "How nice that you know Mr. Almoner. How did you meet him?" Her rising eyebrows were dyed heavily, black as ravens' wings. Amy watched their flight.

"He's a friend of my aunt's really," she said. She smiled innocently, believing the woman could not think there was anything between the shy, ill-at-ease girl she saw and the famous man. Surely the woman must see she had been brought along by Almoner as unthinkingly as he had brought his coat. The woman's eyebrows lowered and her nose quivered. She was affronted by being lied to. She turned, as Amy did, to watch caterers who, as if they were magicians, folded away tables and transformed the foyer into a place for dancing. Beyond, Almoner had been stopped by admirers and stood uncomfortably, holding de-mitasses. Not even saying "Excuse me" the woman left the table. Conspicuously alone then, Amy was grateful when a youngish man came up, bowed, and asked her to dance. She rose, thinking that men just beginning to grey at the temples were handsome, always. He was not so old, either, probably about thirty, she judged. He turned out to be rigid and untalkative, however, and she began to wonder why he had asked her to dance. Unheed-ingly, he kept hitting her in the eye with a white carnation in his buttonhole. Assuming their silence was her fault, falling back on her mother's advice, Amy talked wildly about whatever came into her head: how thin the crêpes had been, the ice sculpture, whether he had read any good books lately. He kept woodenly pushing her about until the music stopped. He then, unexpect-edly, asked if she would like to go to a jazz concert in the Village the next afternoon.

"I'd adore it!" Amy cried.

"Do you think Mr. Almoner would go?" he said.

"I doubt that," she said.

But shouldn't they ask him? the young man said insistingly, starting her across the room. Forced to introduce them, Amy re-peated the invitation, which Almoner declined.

"I'm sure you would like to go, though," he said generously.

"It's all a bit indefinite," the young man said.

"It sounds great," Amy said.

"Mr. Almoner," said the young man. "I run a literary lecture agency. You wouldn't be interested in one lecture, or a tour?" He then ruefully threw out his hands, meaning he had anticipated Almoner's negative reply. With another stiff bow, he retreated across the room.

Was she still invited to go? Amy wondered, watching him. Almoner later was helping her into her coat, and she glanced across the room at the young man, who stood by the bar. He managed to miss that glance, turning quickly to have his glass refilled. More than she had wanted to go to the concert, Amy knew she had wanted to go out with that sophisticated young man. That made her too guilty to tell Almoner what she had learned, that night, about the ways of the world. How gullible she had been and how duped. When they went down in the elevator, she told him, instead, how often she had been questioned about knowing him. That the implications attached to the questions had bothered her hung explicitly in the air, though Amy did not say so.

"Of course," Almoner said understandingly. "Here, I'm lionized. People were curious. Why had I chosen you?"

"Certainly not for my fascinating conversation," she said wryly.

"You had the guts to be yourself," he said.

"What's myself, though?" she said.

"Someone who is seeking something beyond what most people her age are," he said. "You behaved like exactly what you are, a properly brought up young lady at her first big New York party (and frightened to death, he thought)."

"Oh, was I awful?" she said, mortified.

"Awful?" They had by now been bowed through the glass doors by the obsequious doorman and stood on the sidewalk. Her face, reflecting the city's night lights, seemed to him a small white flower in danger of being trampled on. He said, "Amy, you were charming. And you are modest. Not many women are that any more."

Feeling unconvinced, and that she had been only stupid and shy, Amy felt exhausted by the evening. She pulled her coat tight about her and said, "I'm cold and tired. You're so close to your hotel, you go on there. I can take a taxi alone to mine.

"I'm sorry we're not staying closer together," he said.

"I stay in rooms just for college girls," she said quickly. "It's cheaper."

"That's a sound idea," he said. "But I can't let you go around in the city alone, at this hour." At his whistle, a taxi leapt away from a curb as immediately as a horse reacting to a crop.

Amy said agitatedly, "But I've often gone around by myself this late at night."

"I'd hate to face your momma, though, if anything happened when I was in charge of you." He gave her a little tug toward the door he had opened.

Amy determined, sitting back in her corner of the cab, that he was not going to get out at her hotel; glum and silent, she wondered how to keep him from it. She stared at the driver, humped over his wheel, feeling that the taxi was like a stealthy rat roaming these dark side streets, while everyone in the city slept. Then, the taxi's tires slithered along the curb, as it drew to a stop. She reached immediately for the door handle. Almoner, in his corner, did not move and said, "Will you be sleeping late tomorrow?"

She regretted having felt so meanly toward him. "No," she said, "I don't want to waste our time together sleeping."

They arranged a meeting for the next morning. The doorman had been patiently holding open the door, and she stepped out quickly. She watched the taxi go off, but Almoner did not look back through the rear window. The doorman had hurriedly crossed the sidewalk and seemed huddled against the building. Inside, a dance had just ended. There came down red-carpeted steps, toward the street, an outpouring of formally clad young people; not their faces, but wilted corsages of the girls, showed the lateness of the hour. One young man burst through the door as Amy started inside. Thinking she was one of them, he called out that she was going the wrong way. He made a grab at her but

Amy escaped, then looked at him from the lobby. He stood on the sidewalk, looking back at her in surprise, laughing.

Blinking against the bright cold morning, Amy said, "I don't think there are any bars open on Sundays until one. You want a drink this early?"

"At my age, it's sometimes necessary after a night out," Almoner said, surprising her since he had not had much to drink. "Walking may clear my head, if you don't mind. I slept very little."

"I'm sorry," she said, seeing that he was pale. Taking his arm, she drew him toward her as if to take him from someone's earshot. "I stayed awake awhile wondering about something you said. Why did you choose me?"

"Why, I told you," he said, looking better. "Someday, you may be beautiful."

"Seriously," she said.

"Though this morning, I think you may already be beautiful, Amy." They were walking rapidly because of the cold, their eyes blinking against gusts of wind. She felt he had evaded her question. Sensing it, he was serious. "I think you were chosen for me," he said, his arm tightening against hers. "Didn't you know that? Call it fate or destiny or God or whatever you will." Her face glistening with cold was bent toward him intently. Since neither cared in what direction they were going, he suggested they turn a corner and not face the wind. They walked more comfortably. "I don't think persistence is your nature, Amy. But you persisted and wrote me that letter after I had rebuffed you. It seems a miracle, or something akin to one, that brought you back into my life again."

"It seemed that night that a voice did tell me to write it," she said. "No. On my own, I wouldn't have done it."

"I think I'm to act as a catharsis for you," he said. "To free you from your past, to do whatever it is you want to do. Be a writer, if that's it. Though, Amy, I have to tell you, sometimes I'm not sure you know what you do want."

"That seems to be a general opinion," she said, lowering her head against more than the cold. "I guess that's what causes so much confusion inside me."

"I see in your eyes so much that's troubling you," he said. "Lift your head and look at me. They're bluish today. You must be wearing something that color. Yes, I see." She had drawn aside her coat collar to reveal a bit of of her dress. "I went searching for violets today before I met you," he said. "But I couldn't find a florist open. I'll find them eventually."

"Thank you for looking, anyway," she said. "I do hate feeling always troubled. But Jeff, it's not always about myself. I worry about the unfairness of your being unhappy and lonely. And"— she pointed to a man lying in a doorway, a discharge long as a watch chain hanging from one nostril—"I worry about people like that. Things I can't do anything about."

"It's all right," he said. "Worry. You have to."

She let out a little breath of relief, which bounded ahead of them, whitely, in the air. "I'm so glad to know you," she said, touching his cheek. "If only we were closer in age. Should I have been born sooner, or you later?"

He caught the hand that had touched his cheek and held it against his overcoat for warmth; she wore no gloves. "At your age, I was too busy working, Amy. I wouldn't have paid any attention to you if we had met then. It had to happen now, as it has."

"Most people say don't worry about things you can't do any-thing about. I thought that was dumb, but I wasn't sure. Most people want only to be happy, to think about things that are happy. And I do think that's being stupid." She stopped. "Here's a bar open now if you still need a drink."

He then drew his watch from his pocket and squinted at it. "I haven't been thinking again. Probably, you're hungry. Let me get a cab and take you someplace very nice. The Plaza?"

"Heavens no!" she said, wrinkling her nose. "I like places like this much better. Besides, there are tables for ladies."

Inside at one, a woman sat with her head bent down to flattened palms. A sick-looking man leaned from the next table speaking to her in sad monologue. He glanced up as Amy and Almoner came past, then extended his conversation to them. "It's nice to be remembered but what good does it do ya?" he demanded more loudly, since neither of the new customers spoke. "What good does it do ya?"

"None," Amy guessed.

"Right!" he said happily and drank his beer.

"I should not have ordered a whiskey sour in a place like this," Almoner said, though he had drained his glass. "I suppose beer is the only thing." She looked at the man who was sleeping next to his empty beer bottle, then twirled an orange slice in her Old Fashioned. "What will you be doing tonight after I leave?"

"I'm to have dinner with Alex and several of his friends."

"Oh, I'm so glad you won't be alone. I was worried." She chewed on the orange slice and tucked the peel into her glass.

Almoner ordered a second drink which slid about the table in its own morose wet circles. He bent suddenly across the table. "Amy, I have no reputation to lose. But you are a young girl and not to be harmed. I'm afraid my family and yours can picture me as no older than my heart is telling me I am. Only you do. I'm afraid the risks you take in meeting me may be too great, after all. I don't think you understand them."

Not understanding them fully, she said, "Of course I do. I want to see you."

He leaned back, his eyes urgently on her. "It's almost impossible for a middle-class Southerner to be anything else. But you wanted to escape your background and since I had done it, I thought I could help you. I wanted to save you some of the knocks I knew. But I'm going to fall in love with you. Probably, I already have. I keep trying to warn you what it could mean if you keep seeing me."

"I'm not afraid," she said.

"I almost didn't answer your first letter for that reason," he said. "I knew when I read it, this could happen. I dream of you in a way you don't want me to, Amy. And I hope those dreams will come true. I see you don't even want me to talk about it, and I won't if I can help it." He closed his eyes, then opened them tiredly. "I dread tomorrow."

"So do I! I have the most terrible French exam. I should have stayed at school and studied." When he closed his eyes again, she stared at his face worriedly and admitted, "I don't know what to say, Jeff, when you talk about being in love."

He said, "Don't say or do anything then. You can't help it if you don't love me, as much, in return."

"I do love you in some ways."

"Do the best you can. Do you want another drink?"

"I really think I'd better be going."

"You have time. Let's talk about your future. That may have nothing to do with me. Alex says if you want a job when you've finished school to come and see him."

"That's very nice of Mr. Boatwright."

"A job here might give you the same freedom as marriage, without saddling you with some champion of the middle class," he said.

That remark annoyed her; it was he who had not made the right marriage. She would make no mistake. And the sort of people she liked were not middle-class champions—Quill or Leigh. She did not go out with people who were dull and stupid. She said, "I do think I'd better go. I might have trouble getting a cab. You're so close to Alex's, there's no sense your coming all the way down to the station with me."

"No sense to it, at all," he said. "Except to be with you longer."

"Yes, but it wouldn't be very long. And there's really no sense to it."

"All right. If you're meeting a young man, I can accept that."

"It's only a boy who's taking the same train back to school," she said.

While he searched for change to leave on the table, she went ahead to wait on the freezing windy street, drawing in breaths. When he came out, they sheltered themselves against a building and hunched into their coats as if they were inadequate, kin to bums they had seen huddled in doorways.

"I'm to keep the postbox, then?" he said.

"Yes, of course. And I'll write on Wednesdays, so that it always gets there on Saturdays."

He said, "There." He had touched her lips briefly and drawn back. "We've used the kiss a second time. Did it hurt this time?"

She made herself smile. "No," she said. But she turned quickly toward the street and hailed her own cab. It drove off swiftly through a light about to change. Having been directed toward the station, the driver looked into the rearview mirror, his eyes filling it. Amy's glance met his there.

He said, "You must be going off for a long time. Your father's still standing on the curb, watching you go."

Almoner said, "I've put her into a taxi." He came slowly off the elevator and stood in the foyer.

"It's late to be starting such a long trip," Alex said.

"Yes, it is." Then not meaning to, Almoner said, "Alex, she's modest and tender. Not many are any more, but she is. I'm afraid I'm too old for the responsibility of this incredible luck."

"You are lucky," Alex said. "But don't worry about it, just deserve it. I thought at first she was pretty. But later, looking at her, I discovered she's beautiful."

"Yes, I've discovered it, too," Almoner said. "Also, that she's brave, and it breaks my heart."

"It should break your heart."

"I'm sorry to be a little unsteady. I was up half the night. I'm writing again, Alex."

"I thought so," Alex said, smiling.

"Let's don't talk about it any more."

"No, let's don't. Have another drink, instead."

French exam yesterday. Worst thing I've ever seen! I went to New York over the weekend and saw A. Had a nice time, but I should have stayed here and studied. God, just please don't let me fail. I don't think I did, but I didn't do well. When I was coming out of the exam, I had a phone call and guess what? It was Almoner! I assumed the call was from the city when the operator said who was calling, so I picked up the phone and said, "How are you?" Then he said, "I'm here, in the village. At the inn." He sounded apologetic, as if afraid I would not want him to be here, and in a lot of ways I did not want him to be, but I couldn't let him think so. So I just said, "My goodness," or something like that, and then he said all tumbling out, "I couldn't bear it, I couldn't bear it." And I said, "What?" Then he said he had drunk a lot at this party with Alex and couldn't bear his hangover and so just got on a train and came up to school. Wasn't that wild? He wanted to know if I would see him and I wondered how I could not have seen him; can you imagine my saying, "No," when he had come all that way? While we were talking it had begun to snow, and I said could he believe it when at home forsythia would be budding. And he said the snow reminded him of me: unharmed as yet, gentle, soft, a little cold to the touch. And I said, "Oh dear, I'm sorry." And he said, "You shouldn't be sorry, you can't help it, yet." My past had made me the way I was, he said, and I had to get rid of all the Sunday-school morality I had been brought up on in order to be free to write or do anything. Was he saying that to get me to do what he wants??? Or because it's right? I am trying not to be so afraid of everything if that's what he means. But I had to tell him truthfully I'd love to see him the rest of the afternoon but I had to study at night for a history exam. Yes, of course, I would have to study, he said; that he was always forgetting that in actual fact I was a schoolgirl, that never from the first moment had I seemed it to him, and that was why he kept forgetting how much older he was. He sounded worried about his age so I said it didn't matter to me. And he said, It didn't? He kept worrying that it did. And would I lie? So, of course, I said, "No. I wouldn't lie." And he said, "Thank you for that."

I told him how to walk out from town and meet me at that old barn, where the clock is stopped. In June, daisies cover that field as high as my knees and now the snow was almost as high, with only a few slightly worn paths through, and with new snow lightly sprinkled over it, showing colors, as it snowed only an hour and then the sun came out. He had boots, I was glad to see, and he was there waiting in front of the red blank barn and with nothing else around but the field of snow and as I was coming along toward him, we could only watch each other, and for a long time it was as if we were never going to speak; he never did say anything until I said, "I'm glad to see you," and then he said the same thing. There was nothing to do but walk. I said the fresh air would probably make him feel better. He said, to breathe the same air I did made him feel better and probably that was why he had come. The trees groaned so. That is an eerie sound, even in daylight, but I said that I liked it, did he? And he said, "No. Trees are our enemies; they wait for us in enmity and don't care whether we live or die." He thinks they hope we'll lose our way in the woods among them. I'm so glad to know a grownup who thinks this way and talks this way; most older people don't, or many people my age either; and I've always felt things had thoughts. But then suddenly he stopped and put his hand on my chin and said, "May I kiss you?" I felt embarrassed and walked on and he said despite what I had said on the phone, I must think he was too old. "That's it," he said, "isn't it?" Then I felt sad and I was sorry he was older, but I'd never tell him that. I worry mostly about his being married. But I want so much for nothing ever to hurt Almoner; it would seem unfair; and I said, "It's not it. I love you." And, in many ways, I do.

"I love you, too," he said. We linked arms walking on. Then he said, "But I have to tell you things I dream about I hope will happen." And I let his arm go, wishing he had not said that, and there was this tiny bug crawling along in the snow and I said, "Look at that! Where can it possibly be going?" We bent down to look and he said, "It must know, and I wish I did, so I could help it. It's the bravest thing I've ever seen. It should have expired long ago with winter." He was going to pick it up. I said, "Let's leave it alone. Let it find its own way."

History was not so bad. I feel sorry about A. coming up here for just an afternoon, but I did have to study. And it was sort of a relief when he left; I felt glad to be back in my own life, as I feel responsible when I'm with him about seeing that he is not bored, though he never seems to be; he's so quiet it's hard sometimes to know what he's thinking. I understand now what people mean when they've said that about me. I feel if it's just friendship there's nothing wrong in our seeing each other, even if he is married. I kept thinking, suppose he got sick or something when he was at school and I had to notify his family. He said he had tried to warn me of the risks I was taking; did I want to change my mind? I said, "No." But I don't know why he wanted to come so far for so short a time; I do want him to be happy; I hugged him goodbye.

Dear Jeff:

I felt so depressed after you left, though I was not feeling sorry for myself. I just have been very unhappy, even though I passed all of my exams. Isn't that wonderful! It's some sort of unrest, wanting something and not knowing what, I guess. Being this age should be wonderful but it isn't. It's terrible not knowing what one is and what one is going to do, if anything at all. Though not knowing, I can still believe in myself, which is one thing about being young, instead of old. Then your violets came. It was as if you had known how I was feeling. It was snowing again. I pinned them on beneath my coat and walked in that calm snow and felt the cold but smelled the violets. In a great rush I thought of you but so much else, my whole life; the little girl I was; wondering what I am now. I thought about people leading different lives in one life, for the first time that my parents have a whole life separate from me, had one before I was born, and I don't really know them any way except as my parents. I wish you could help my mother find something in her life as you're helping me. But don't lie to me either. And promise me you will tell me if you do think I'm stupid, or worthless, and will never become anything. And as you asked, here is a letter with something green in it. One of the violets and its leaves.

Amy, Amy, he thought; and her grief was his own; it was like her to send the violet. He put it in his wallet. Late spring or early summer, the pavement burned, and the post office had been a cool, brief respite where he had tried to read in a corner, but some *grande dame* had wanted to talk, or perhaps to peer at the letter. Was, as Inga said, the town full of talk? Somehow, he doubted that. Mud-hived cars clogged the street in the cold, late, wet spring, and the crops were behind; he felt sorry for farmers. "Dogtail cotton again?" he had greeted a farmer whose face was haggard, and then gone on wondering where he could read the letter. He did not want to give any appearance of hiding.

Dearest Amy:
Don't grieve so, though I told you from the first that it is better than vegetating. And believe that something will come of it, though we don't know as yet what. But never think you are worthless. Out of all I might have, don't you know I would not have picked you, if you were. You are not, you know, the only young woman ever to write me. And at my age this may be the

last cast I can make: don't you know that? Believe in yourself for me, if for no other reason. Write and say you will in your little girl's splash all over your lined school paper. I love you, I love you. I meant it that day in the snow. I do.

You be a little brig and I'll be the ocean for you to sail on, your sails taut, running free. It's been a long time, Amy, but I'm writing again, and you did that for me: gave me back what I had to have, a belief in what I was doing. I've needed someone to give something to, which was not money. I was tired of that. I needed someone saying Yes, to me, and to whom I could say it in return.

Never, never stop believing in yourself. Never write me again as you did. Because, next time, no matter what, no matter where you are, I think I would have to drop everything to come

Coming in, Inga said, "Do you like it? Do you or don't you? Jessie does and so does Amelia. She just *stood* over Billie Jean until she got it right. The older you get, I read, the lighter you should wear your hair, though I would have thought darker, wouldn't you? But you don't think it's too blond, do you? Pleas-s!" She dropped the final e, which jarred him. "Can't you take yourself out of the paper and look, one minute, Jeff?"

He said, "I'm buried in the paper wondering why someone's cut a chunk out of the sports page before I've read it."

"Be-*cause,* here's why." Vy, she said. Always she reverted more to her first language in anger. She took the ripped piece from an end-table drawer. "I thought you liked *blondes.*" Her hand went up gracefully toward her hair without touching it.

"So." He held the clipping. "She is graduated from college and is attending a cotillion. You hadn't learned it from your talks with her parents but had to read it in the paper?"

Vexed, Inga said, "And you didn't know she was home?"

"You cut out the news before I saw the paper," he said.

"Why tomorrow are you going to Delton?"

"I told you, to buy fishing gear on sale at Sears."

"Amelia and I want to go. We need to shop."

"Come ahead. I'm glad for the company. It's a long drive."

Edith, raising a shade, said, "It's almost noon. Weren't you meeting someone downtown for lunch? How was the dance?"

Sighing at the difficulty of waking up excited, Amy knew she would have to. She sat up and touched her head a moment longer to her pillow, resting on her knees. Another moment of silence and her mother would want to know what had been wrong. And nothing had been wrong with the cotillion; it had been planned beautifully, as always. She had been expected to go since she was in kindergarten (it was held to honor those graduating from college), and Amy could not make herself refuse to attend. Now she cried, "It was wonderful!" Equally difficult was being secretive about a day over which she felt expansive. She could avoid more questions by pretending to be the daughter her mother had always wanted, chatty and gay. "Guess who's engaged," Amy said. "Quill. Isn't that wonderful?" Once she had replied, "To Lydia, of course," she tried to think of other details her mother would like to know. But soon Amy was silent, wondering how Quill had given up or sold out so soon, to be a replica of all he had mocked by wanting to be a painter. She felt sorry for him.

Edith's smile wavered, as she worried about Amy's being left behind. Her voice came weakly. "I know their parents are happy they're all set," she said. "Two of Delton's most prominent families."

Amy wondered if other people when they saw themselves in mirrors were as surprised as she? Confronting herself in pajamas, she thought, That's me. That's how I look? and then going from the mirror had no image of herself. Though she had not wanted to marry Quill, why didn't he want to marry her? What was wrong with her? she had asked, staring.

125

"You're going to find yourself left if you don't watch out," Edith said, leaving. She meant Amy was too choosy and it was better not to be.

It would be so much simpler just to get married, Amy thought. Looking from the window, she felt jailed and sentenced to this solitariness. Below, a Negro man knelt weeding zinnias, his loose brown clothes similar to those of an old woman she had seen in New York rummaging in a trash can. Staring into the bright back yard, holding compassionately the two images simultaneously, the one here, the other on the sun-slatted street, having this double image which no one else could have, she felt the impossibility of people ever knowing one another. What, with all the longing in her heart, was she to do? Amy thought wildly.

At the bottom of the stairs, Edith waited. Though the weather was scorching, Amy came down in stockings and carrying short white gloves. She held them up gaily, as if they were the recognizable badge of some sister organization, like a sorority. Having belonged to the most proper one in college, Edith went still to alumnae meetings proudly wearing her pin.

How attractive Amy looked pulled together, Edith thought, smiling back happily. Friends had said Amy would get over whatever phase she had been in. How needlessly she had worried. Though she had one more warning. "The best husband material gets snatched up first," Edith said.

Amy mentioned a logical time for coming home. Edith did not need the car, unless maybe she might run to the store later. The back yard seemed emptied, the zinnias all weeded, the Negro had gone. However, the mingled flowers produced a glorious multicolor like the crushed ante-bellum costumes the girls had worn to the cotillion. Lydia had gained weight and with her thicker middle already looked like a matron, Amy thought. Cutting in on her, Quill had said right away, "Guess what?"

And if he had decided to marry Lydia what was she going to say except, "How wonderful, Quill." Then she had added, "I know your father's happy." And Quill had blushed and turned her over with an air of good riddance to a friend, Billy Walter; she had wanted to cry after Quill's retreating back, "Lydia never reads!"

Answering her mother's final warning, Amy had said, "I don't want to get married yet." But didn't she? The next moment, Edith had taken a package at the front door and opened it to a pair of yellow linen pants and a bright red blazer. "Is he going to wear those together?" Amy had said. Edith had answered, "Why, baby, that's fun!" Her parents went dancing every weekend now. One Sunday morning, recently, her father could not get up. When someone from the church had called, his lips had turned blue. Walking away from the phone, he had told Edith to talk. "He's been sick all week," Edith had said. "We should have phoned. But we thought, until the last minute, he would be better on Sunday."

Amy bruised some of the zinnia heads, driving the car reck-lessly from the driveway. She viewed them in sorrow, as their heads seemed bent. If only she did not want to exceed that from which she had come, ordinarily would have been, how much simpler life would seem. Why should she have more strength than Quill, a man? He had backed down. Tar bubbled in the streets; the pavement shone in the heat. She thought of turning back home. Edith, wandering toward the sunroom, had been eat-ing a bowl of ice cream, and a fan had made an indolent breeze. Staring into the bright day, Amy wondered suddenly if her mother had guessed whom she was meeting, as uncharacteristi-cally she had not asked.

Her own face, Amy imagined, softened as Almoner's did whenever they met. And his face, by now, was dear and familiar.

She accepted that her presence gave him something because he said it did, though she was still vague about what. In a corner of one eye, he had a small brown scar. Left over from chicken pox when he was small, he had said. The scar darkened when he smiled. Though now it darkened, he looked pale and bothered and as if he had been slightly afraid she was not coming. Twirling his cap around and around in his hand, he stood waiting. Amy realized he had something instantly to tell her.

"Suddenly they have no summer clothes," he said. "They've come with me." The scar grew lighter when he was annoyed. "They waited for me to say they couldn't come, so I had to say they could. They're shopping here and there. I have to pick them up occasionally and take them somewhere else. That way, they're keeping an eye on me, I suppose."

They would always have obstacles, they said. They had to laugh and went out into the day. "But we don't have much imagination," Amy said, as they emerged from the station. Despite a frantic exchange of letters, they had been unable to think of any place else to meet. "Does anyone besides me know you have no imagination?" she teased. "Probably somebody else writes your books."

But her light mood changed almost as soon as they reached his car; again, they were confronted with aimless driving. This time, the only differences were that it was hot instead of cold, that he was behind the wheel instead of her. The sun bore down on surrounding cars and came back in blinding flashes. Soon Amy had a headache and observed that at its edges, Almoner's hair had been turned by perspiration from silver to pewter grey.

Through plodding, sales-minded crowds, she trailed after him, with nothing she wanted to buy, or even browse among, in the sporting-goods department. Her only accomplishment in life, it seemed, was accompaniment. Being with Almoner was all the importance she had, though in Sears Roebuck no one recognized him. He looked across a counter at her. She smiled back meaning not to worry, that she was not bored, that she did not mind waiting while he picked out a tackle box. He came out with the kind he had always wanted. She said she was glad that he had it at last. Possibly she would never pinpoint what she had learned. Trailing along with him, she only felt her time was not wasted.

Liking aloneness and often seeking it, Amy was glad, nevertheless, to be sitting in the drugstore with a purpose, though it was only waiting for Almoner. The store's interior was consumed with the smell of frying hamburger. Smoke roiled and roiled out from the grill, while a gaunt woman stood scraping, over and over, the remains of other patties, without turning the one almost burning. She looked up, then brought Amy more coffee as requested, the saucer sloshed full, and went back to scraping.

The woman did not even consider running amuck, Amy thought in astonishment, watching her. She could not believe such complacency. There was the outdoors, hot but beautiful and heady as a filled spinnaker, and not once had the woman turned her eyes toward the window. She only kept standing there between the stacks of individual cornflakes boxes with their red roosters crowing and the individual red and white labelled cans of soup, now eating her crusty hamburger. Never, Amy thought, would she reconcile herself to deadliness.

Irritated and angry, Almoner came in, his blue shirt bearing wet splotches, like dark ink stains. Yet, he had found something humorous. His eyes were full of light. His lips trembled and straightened and trembled again. He and Amy fell against one another laughing, even before he spoke. "They'll be waiting for me to pick them up again in less than an hour," he said.

The woman was nearly asleep, her head bent over a newpaper she had been reading spread out on the counter. Though her customers were apologetic, she was not bothered in the least; at their order, she threw on two thin hamburgers and began to dirty the grill she had just cleaned. Smoke roiled up toward the ceiling, catching there around lights already coated with amber grease. The stool next to Amy was broken. She moved along the counter and Almoner sat down next to her. Soon, the woman would be cleaning the grill again and soon they would exchange these seats. Biting into her untoasted roll, Amy stared toward the door where smoke had rushed seeking escape and had collected, caught instead.

They drove afterward past their place at the river, it was too hot to stop, and on around the edges of the sweltering city. "You feel it, too, don't you?" Almoner said. "The pressures here. I feel like we're two balloons, and you're drifting off one way and I another. And I can't do anything but watch you go."

"Maybe it is the city," Amy said wanly. "I get awfully tired of just driving around."

"I too," he said. "We need a place of our own. But that's too risky here. But someday we'll walk and find bugs in the snow again, won't we?"

"I don't know." She felt hopeless about everything. She stared out at luxurious cared-for lawns and at houses with settled looks, where nothing seemed ever to have gone wrong.

"I don't seem to be able to get through to you." He longed to take her hand. But they seemed rather defiantly clasped together and secured to her lap.

"I'm sorry. That's my fault," she said.

"It's no one's fault," he said. "Or rather, it's the fault of everything. Having to hide, being made to feel guilty. I tried to warn you what it would mean if you wanted to keep seeing me."

"I know," she said. "I'm not sorry about seeing you."

Drawn up to the station's elaborate and gritty steps, she sat miserably, her eyes avoiding his. "You might as well go," he said, reaching past her to open the door. "I know you're busy, but write anyway. Please."

"I will," she said. "And I'm never busy. Is that postbox really safe?"

"No."

"I'll keep always writing on Wednesdays. Though maybe not every Wednesday."

"No. Even I don't ask that." He held her as she pressed against him briefly; their cheeks touched. "I thought I felt your heart beat," he said, letting her go.

Jeff:

I'm sorry I haven't written sooner. I wasn't sure you would want me to. I don't seem to be able to say the things you want me to. And I was moody and not very nice that day in Delton. And now, for the first time, I've felt really afraid. I tried to tell myself it didn't matter if we met. I guess it does. Did you know I. called here that day when she was shopping? She told my mother she wanted to ask me to lunch, that since you were so interested in my work, she was. When I got home, my mother asked me if I had seen you. Thank god, I told the truth. Then she told me your wife had called. I'm not, to any of them, a child, am I? To myself, I am. I guess that's the difference. I never thought of myself as being a threat to anyone; I feel so often threatened myself. You know, as no one else ever has. My mother says letters are proof positive and not to write you any more. She's afraid of my being named in a divorce suit. She believed me when I told her, on my part, it was only friendship between us. But she does not want gossip. I've been trying, of course, not to care about what the people I know think. I guess I have not succeeded. I'm afraid and yet I think we have to go on. This is all too important to me. I've never had anyone before; to share our feelings is worth anything to me. I can't believe she really once almost burned one of

131

your manuscripts. My mother said not to see you any more but, of course, I have to. But where?

Amy

Perhaps you had better not see me. I'm afraid this is all going to get turned into a sorry mess and all that we wanted it to be will be lost beneath and I can't take that. You are feeling more fully the grasp of that middle-class Southern background. It won't let you go easily. No one can really break away completely; you can only keep trying. When I didn't hear from you for so long, I wrote furiously on my book. Then when I heard, I wrote more furiously. But nothing will drive all of this out of my mind. But I keep believing, Amy, that some good is going to come from it all. I hope you do. Somehow, we'll achieve what we want: your freedom and our being together sometimes. Try to have faith. Inga did not mention the call, naturally; nor could I, or she would have known we had been in touch. We circle one another cautiously, like caged animals. I hadn't wanted, in the time I have left, to damage a young woman's life. I had wanted only to help it. So perhaps the risks are too great after all, and perhaps you had better not see me again. Here, then, is the kiss a final time * and will you accept it at last? And please, please forgive me if I have done you only harm. That was the very farthest thing from my mind. You, brief tender and touching as spring, helped me from the first moment I laid eyes on that face.

Jeff

That he was to see Amy again filled and sustained Almoner, as he parked his car a short distance from a town square. He remembered her saying that the water tower here had hung in the air so long ahead of her, the first day she had come to see him, that she had taken it as a symbol. It was halfway between her town and his. If she ever passed it that day, she would really see Almoner. Her face had bloomed openly when she said it; always, it

132

was so damned difficult not to touch her when he wanted. What a relief, she had said, when finally she had passed the water tower. Now, he stared up at the old steel structure thinking it had a kind of majesty.

The summer had droned on, as usual, with the heat relentless, and would have been unendurable without her restorative quality. But how much more time was there to be? The incredible thing was not so much that she had found him but at exactly the time when he had thought he could not go on. He felt desperate, sometimes now, about the frail hold he had on her, on everything. Look to this day, for it is life, he quoted silently: the fragment of an old poem, the rest not remembered. Was it possible that the remarkably clear day he had come out of the pine copse and found her waiting was only a year ago? It stood out in memory so clearly, there seemed nothing in his life before to remember. Though sweltering, he dared do nothing now but sit and wait, despite the pain near his heart his slouched position was causing. For reassurance, he touched a little box of pills in his breast pocket. The hot dry heat in this stillness filled the creases of his face and neck with perspiration. Perhaps his ankles would swell again. For momentary relief, he pushed back an old hat he was wearing low, its band stuck colorfully with fishing flies. Maybe he ought to have worn a false beard and a mustache and glasses, or maybe there was nothing to worry about at all, though he did not believe that. Not here, he thought. He kept cautious eyes turned toward the area around him, only occasionally staring off toward the square where Amy's bus would stop. Though he would not be recognized here for his ability at the typewriter he might be for his proficiency with the fly rod.

Beneath the corrugated tin porte-cochere, jutting over storefronts around the square, were the usual old men lounging in clean khakis, though from Almoner's viewpoint, their weathered and lined and curious faces were not visible. In any of these small towns near his own, he often saw recognition spring to the eyes of retired farmers, like these, spending out their days in indolence on the main street; and he had had younger men, white or Negro, wave to him from atop lumbering farm machinery on their way to or from fields, their strong arms bulging and impressive. Today, easily, word might get around that Almoner, the fishing champion, had been seen on the square. He pulled the hat low again. Some of the old men were playing checkers in leafy arbored places around the Court House, the road in sight beyond them widening into the highway down which the bus would come. He kept his eyes turned there now, wondering if he were a fool, reminding himself of the saying, none like an old one. But he believed in Amy and he was content with his own loss of despair. To him, this anticipatory trembling was worth any risk in meeting.

He watched through perspiration-blurred eyes women out shopping. The day seemed to shimmer in wavery colors, like prisms reflecting sun. Townswomen were recognizable by rouge and colored small earrings. The country ones had tight hair and dry skins and kids who went ahead but whirled and rushed into their mothers, butting them with their heads. If he were noticed, the magnified story of his being here would reach home long before he did, at sundown. He barely peered from beneath the hat now at the women going by, swimmingly, in lavenders and greens.

The bus was late and he was fearful. Then in a moment of inattention, it came and went. On the square, Amy stood at the curb. After seeing the car, she turned to face a store window, freezing as if not to be seen, like a doe he had come upon in winter woods, everything crystallized and still. He dared now ease straight enough to stretch his legs. The other passengers had gone. Having studied them, the old men had resumed checkers. Those only lounging again stared with vacant, lived-up faces at the dusty street, as usual in midmorning, quiescent and nearly deserted. Perhaps Amy should not be subjected to this sort of thing, after all, Almoner thought.

She stood out. Seeming to have foreseen that, she wore dark glasses, but a cheap white plastic kind. He guessed them an afterthought, that she had purchased them in the bus station. Around her hair, almost totally covering it, was her own heavy beautifully colored silk scarf. She wore a plain blouse and skirt, he guessed intentionally inconspicuous, and the schoolgirlish brown sandals he remembered, flat and buckled. Stares followed her. Simply, she did not belong among the bare decrepit storefronts and broken-in sidewalks or to the country quietude. Her walk was noticeably more brisk than that of the other women who passed. Almoner chuckled, speculating on how gossip would bound about supper tables that night: "Fellow with fishing poles on his car wait there thirty minutes before this girl come, then didn't get out of the car. Opened the door and she got in. They drove off and come back again for the bus in the evening." You could make a lot out of not much when you had nothing else to think about, he thought, opening the door.

"Here I am," Amy said, getting in.

As quickly as possible, Almoner drove out to the highway. "Yes," he had said, leaning past her and closing the door. "Here you are again." Now, taking her hand, he drove slowly along the empty highway thinking, Love, sweet love, and how her face seemed today unbearably young.

"Isn't it stupid?" she said. "I had thought when summer came, we could see each other often. But it's harder than ever. My mother didn't need the car today but said I couldn't have it. I think she guessed where I was going, though she wouldn't ask." She turned to look ahead at the road a little sorrowfully. "Life makes you lie. I had to say I was going to a swimming party. At the station, I put my swimming things in a locker. But, I'm here.

Maybe we ought to be spies instead of writers. We're getting good at intrigue, aren't we? Anyway, you're a writer," she said, her face mournful.

He pressed her hand. "You will be, if you work at it hard enough."

"No," she said wistfully. "I don't think I ever will be. I just don't have anything to write about. And, Jeff, my mother started in again, saying don't I realize how my seeing you looks to other people. An old man. You're her age. She doesn't call herself old. And your being a writer makes it even worse. That's a suspect thing. For heaven's sake, couldn't you do something sensible, like selling insurance?"

"Yes, I'm very suspect," he said. "I hardly work at all, you know. I've lived with that here a long time, Amy. You'll have to get used to it, too, if you're going to be a writer. Also, apparently, if you're going to throw in your lot with mine."

"I have to be honest, Jeff. If you were an insurance salesman, I wouldn't be here. All this is partly, you know, because you are Almoner. A great man. I can't be afraid to know you because of them."

"Amy, you are brave. And you are coming out of that middle-class shell."

"But it's not making me a writer," she said. "I keep going from one thing to another."

"Yes, I read about you in the paper going to parties," he said. "I think about you out with all your young friends. Always, you are laughing."

"Oh no," she said quickly. "Jeff, it's not like that at all. I'm hardly ever laughing. And I go to parties only because there's nothing else to do. I was talking about starting one story and never finishing it and starting another."

"There's something to do if you want to be a writer," he said, firmer than usual. "Write. You'll have to make choices between parties and work."

But what was she to write about? Why couldn't he understand she had nothing to write about. She said defensively, "My mother told me to see you one more time, to tell you I couldn't see you any more."

He let go of her hand to put both of his on the steering wheel. One foot, in a greenish rubber boot, went toward the brake and slowed the car to a stop. The road seemed to fluctuate and shimmer in the heat. "It's what I've been trying to tell myself was going to happen," he said. "Your people and mine are never going to see this situation except from their point of view. And what you have to take in order to come here isn't fair. I've been selfish. I'm sorry. I had better take you straight back. There'll be another bus shortly. Or should I drive you to Delton?"

"You're going to let them win?" In astonishment, her eyes grew darker.

He took her hand again and gripped it harder. "You are the dearest and bravest thing I've ever known. I'm very glad to see you, Miss Howard."

"I'm glad to see you, too," she said, returning his hand's pressure.

On either side, as they drove on, the countryside had a vacant look, being flat and brown. Its emptiness gave them the feeling that nothing could grow here, thrive or live. Almoner was searching for a particular place and indicated the back seat, where there was a picnic basket. "Jessie fixed me a lunch. But I noticed there was enough for two. And in that covered bucket, there's beer on ice. Somewhere down one of these side roads, there's a pond in some woods, where I fished once. It'll be cool there, if I can find it again."

To unstick her sweating back from the seat, Amy occasionally sat forward, the heat making her also drowsy. But she felt placid about driving on and on, accustomed to inactivity; her days at home seemed to consist only of fruitless long hours. Inert and miserable, she was unable to attach herself to any project. She felt constantly confused, and her attention when she tried one thing immediately leapt to something else. Still, Almoner travelled the rocky roads; the car drove outward from itself devilish-red clouds of dust, which skimmed fields. Their clasped hands grew moist and slid apart. Amy could not help but think about the missed swimming party, since she was so hot; and she thought about Billy Walter, who was cute and would have been her date. Her thoughts fluctuated, like the heat waves shimmering over the day. To be with Almoner was more important than the swimming party, she decided.

"Damn it," he said after a silence, "I've been thinking about the lying you had to go through to get here, that you'll have to go through again when you get home. An artist ought to be free."

"You're the artist," Amy said. "And you're not free. If I were a writer, though, would it be easier for us to meet?"

"We might have more obvious reason to, but it wouldn't be any easier here," he said.

The red gravel road led on, with grassy ditch banks beginning to encroach on it. She stopped watching it to say, "Would you like me if I didn't want to be a writer?"

"Like you, yes," Almoner said. "Perhaps even love you. But I think your wanting to be a writer makes what's between us stronger. You understand me in a way not many have. No one else has ever called me before—" He stopped, shyly.

"What?" she said.

"A great man," he said, his voice even softer.

"All your awards must have convinced you of that!" she said.

"They're not like having someone you care about tell you," he said. "Someone who hopes to gain nothing from it. But we've had

138

enough of this driving. I'm obviously still lost. That countryman ought to be able to give us some directions."

The man came along in a tottering walk on the road's edge, a cabbage almost as large as his head crooked beneath one arm. "How's the road ahead?" Almoner said, stopping.

The man, beaming with pride at being asked, said, "Gravel but tolerable." Even his ears, stuck out on either side of his head by his hat, seemed to blush. Headed for town, he wore clothes as if for Sunday, despite the heat. A white shirt was held together tightly at his neck by a red tie with a zigzagged yellow streak like cartoon lightning. Grinning further, he held out his cabbage for sale, which Almoner declined politely and respectfully. The man loped off into dust still floating like a phantom all around them.

Amy, watching him go, remembered the countryman's calm weathered face and thought of her father's silly flushed look when he had been drinking or dancing. His friends recently had exclaimed over his knowing the latest and craziest dance steps. Then Edith had found a receipt and confided that, secretly, he had been going to Arthur Murray's. Having invested in a new company, and appointed to make contacts, he and Edith kept going out dining and dancing, while she grew fatter from rich dinners.

She was sorry, Amy said later, they had not bought the man's cabbage. Almoner assured her it would bring a good price in the general-merchandise store toward which the man had been headed. Blending into the landscape, he had simply disappeared, belonging here and to the sun-struck road, in a way, Amy thought lonesomely, that she belonged nowhere. Was she responsible for her nature? Struggling to do what was considered the right thing, she never succeeded. Was that totally her fault? She continued to stare at the rusty-colored roads. They had travelled them like a maze, a test of endurance. The sky bearing down on the car was zealously blue and hot. They continually passed houses where, in fragmentary but windy shade, people sat in their yards and stared at them in countrified dull surprise. Losing his way, bringing them repeatedly past the same houses, Almoner began to laugh. "Think," he said, "what they'll all say when they meet in church on Sunday. 'Dashed right past my house two or three times!' 'Did the same at mine!' 'Turned around in my driveway twice, with me right there!' "

Amy, adapting quickly to seeing through his eyes, also laughed. "And nobody will know it was us," she said, delighted.

"Nobody will know it was us," he repeated. Almost giggling, they drove on with a carefree feeling they seldom had. As they backed a second time from a driveway, where people sat stoically beneath a cedar watching, Amy said, "It seems so funny to think of people living back here, so far from cities, from everything. It's like being lost to the world. But it's nice."

"Yes. And no evidence in the world of what they do to make a living," Almoner said. "But someone important must live up this road. It's gravelled to the barn."

"Maybe the road commissioner himself!" she said.

"Of course." He laughed appreciatively. And, chuckling, they went on retravelling the same dusty roads.

"Would anybody else like doing this," she said. "We are alike."

"We're soul mates, I'm convinced. I'm as sure of it as that some form of fate sent you to me. It's still unbelievable, to me, that we found one another." Her heart-shaped and smallish face looked happier than usual; he hoped so adamantly that she might someday find a love that would be the reason for her existence; she was his, though he had found her so late. Something akin to complacency appeared on his face.

Amy was sorry not to be able to match his exact mood. The wild red dust had begun finally to blow into the car, and they could think or talk then of nothing but finding a place to stop.

Seeing a deserted house, they decided to explore it. A soft cindery path led toward its rambly front steps. On them, they stopped and listened to the soughing of wind through mighty old cedars. When they were in the house, they gazed feelingly at the bedraggled reminders of lives far sadder than theirs. A crinkled Sears catalogue lay, as if wishfully, open on the kitchen floor; the walls of the house were unplaned and unpainted and smelled of the spotty fires of hard winters; flaky dark streaks went down them, where rain had poured in steadily. Ghosts lingered obviously and Amy whispered when she spoke.

"I wonder where the people went?"

"Probably ran away to avoid debts and went someplace just like this, or worse. And they'll start all over and end up the same." As he spoke, Amy moved closer. From the porch's edge, they stared away distantly, as the couple who had lived here might have done to contemplate their lives. Through a crack in the porch, Almoner saw, in the chicken-messed dirt beneath, a cache of empty beer cans. "The man probably hid them under there from his wife, a good Baptist. I'd imagine a beer now and then was all the little pleasure he had in life, too." The man's dogged life, his despair and frustrations and poverty seemed that moment their own. Cupping a hand to Amy's face, Almoner said, "I can't stand even vicarious unhappiness there. Let me spare you feeling responsible for other people's suffering, Amy. I've had enough in my lifetime for both of us, it seems."

"But I don't want to be spared, Jeff," she said. "How would I learn then, as you did? I don't want to go around being unthinkingly happy."

"All right," he said. "But if I can't spare you unhappiness, don't let me cause you any."

"I'm not worried about that," she said. "Don't you." Reaching up, she brushed the back of her hand against his forehead, lined with perspiration. Then, through trees, he glimpsed what he thought was water, shining. Was it a pond? Squinting in the direction he pointed, Amy thought so. Bringing things from the car, following one another along an overgrown path, they came out on a bank strewn with willow trees. Almoner gave Amy a lesson with his fly rod. She was more successful than she ever had been before, but they caught no fish. It was the wrong time of day to fish and too hot. "But, at least," he said, putting away the rod, "I'll go home with my line wet. Around evening, somebody will have a string of fish I can buy."

They went deeper into the woods, where it was cooler. And though neither of them was hungry, they unpacked Jessie's lunch and ate lackadaisically. Soon, in the heat, sandwiches left exposed began to dry, their edges to curl. Amy sat balanced on a tree root, running a cold can of beer over her face before drinking. Almoner carried a can of beer with him, pacing. Not even a bird sang and nothing else moved. His feet went soundlessly over pine needles but occasionally cracked open an acorn. "I had a speech all arranged," he said, "in case you were mad about the changes I made in the story you sent me. And thank you for all your letters, Amy. They help keep me going. They are so beautiful but heart-wrenching, too. They make me want to leap onto a white horse and rush to your house to save you. And I feel so damn helpless being able to do nothing."

"You do something. I can always reach out to you," she said. "I'm sorry to write you always sad letters. You have enough sadness. But that seems to be always the way I feel. I know that story's not good. And how could I be mad at any corrections you make? I only get mad at myself, for not being able to do better. And for not making myself work more."

"Before, when I've made corrections in your things, you said you were afraid the work wasn't yours then. I keep telling you it is. We've all learned from someone else, you know. Maybe only by reading, but we learned somehow." They were both startled as a twig snapped beneath his heel.

After looking around, Amy said, "Tell me the speech anyway."

He emptied his beer can and said, "It's about giving and receiving and not being afraid of either. Though giving is the hardest, particularly when people don't want to accept what you have to give."

Amy began immediately to collect acorns into a little pile about her feet, looking down at them; her voice was low. "I'm sorry, but I can't. I just don't feel that way. And it's not," she said, looking up, "because you're too old. I just don't feel that way."

He bent the beer can and tossed it to the ground. "I'm not pressuring you, am I?" he said. "I've waited a year. I can wait as long as it takes you to grow up."

"Are you mad?"

"How can I be mad at a child?" he said.

She said, concentrating on looking at the acorns, "Every time after I see you, I ask myself why I wouldn't. And I'm sorry. I think, maybe next time. Then the next time comes, and I don't want to either."

"I only thought," he said, "that it would be easier for me to help you if there were no more barriers between us. You know I'm not going to force you, and I'm not going to beg either."

"I'm sorry. I'm sorry," she said hopelessly. "And what would I do if I didn't have you to talk to about the sort of things we do."

"Yes, most people don't understand dealings of the heart," he said, sitting down somewhat tiredly. "They understand only dealing across counters with money."

Amy began abruptly to cry, turning and leaning against his shoulder. His face went down immediately to the top of her head. "Please," he said. "Please don't do that."

"No one," she said, "understands me here, but you. I've got to go someplace else."

"Don't keep running," he said. "There's not any other place. Places don't matter, don't count. It's all inside you."

"But I'm so lonely," she said, sitting up. She accepted a handkerchief he handed her and pressed it to her face.

"I've told you, writers have to accept loneliness," he said. "That's a cliché by now. But I think to accept life at all, you have to accept loneliness."

"Only when I see you, I'm not lonely. And we can hardly ever see each other."

"This secrecy is intolerable," he said. "And there's so little time."

"Is it time for the bus?" she said, about to get up.

"Oh no, there's plenty of time before the bus," he said. Leaning forward and toward the ice bucket, he drew out two cans of beer, dripping water. He bent over, opening them, and Amy stared at his back, realizing what he had meant by time. Her life, she thought, seemed so full of time, she had no idea what to do with it all.

He leaned back against the same tree and handed her a beer. After sipping his own, he said, "You've come a long way, Amy. And you're going to grow up some more." Then he put an arm quickly about her. "Hush. Hush. I didn't mean to make you cry again. I never want to do that."

"But you are so kind to me," she said, muffled against his shoulder. "And maybe next time I will."

"Yes," he said. "Maybe next time you will."

Someone nearby suddenly began to chop wood, and they drew quickly apart. Amy got up and moved away to sit against a more distant tree; she consoled herself by thinking she had been right to refuse. How embarrassing to have been discovered making love in the woods; and the thought that the woodchopper would have perceived them, an old man and a young girl, would not leave her mind. She cringed at the thought of having been discovered, of jumping up and straightening her clothes; even as a child, on outings, she had hated going behind bushes to go to the bathroom, pulling down her pants in the open air. Always, it seemed, she had been dogged one way or another by fear of exposure and discovery. Opposite her, he sat drinking his beer and not looking at her, until she spoke. "I brought a pencil and paper today." She hoped to lighten their moods. "I was going to ask you a lot of questions. It seems I ought to know everything about your work, but I never ask you anything."

"You don't need to ask those things," he said. "What you learn from this is enough, Amy." A wave of his hand took in the woods and meant also solitude and silence. Almost at the same instant, an orange and black butterfly lit on one of Amy's shoes. She remained perfectly still and hardly dared breathe. "It would be nice," Almoner said, "to be a butterfly. Come out and fly about and die in a few days. They have no knowledge of death and can't fear it then. Since they wouldn't harm anything, they have no reason to suspect harm."

"It's so tiny," she said. "It seems to have elbows and knee joints." The butterfly ran a careful antenna over its body, then flew up. Amy drew in a disappointed breath. However, it only drifted onto Almoner's hand. He held it up with the butterfly resting atop it.

"It likes me," he said.

"Maybe it wants to be a writer, too," Amy said, smiling.

Opening and closing its preening wings, the butterfly remained on Almoner's hand, while he touched it first to Amy's hair and afterward to her lips; then, it fluttered away with sunlit wings, settling onto one of their discarded beer cans. Pouring beer into his hand from his own can, Almoner held it toward the butterfly, which then flew out of sight.

"Oh," Amy said. "I'm afraid we made it mad."

"Maybe it wasn't too disgusted with us," he said. "It knows we're only human beings."

"What would I have done if I had never met you?" she said.

"Kept looking," he said, "as I did. Though, God knows, I'd about given up ever finding you."

Twilight came on, and bright green moss beneath the trees leapt out sharply, more brilliant. It seemed a soft carpet to lift up and carry away with them into the growing dark, as they carried the things they had brought from the car. As they stood, the sun's shafts drew upward and away from them. And into the cooler air, birds began to sing. Their path was fainter. They stumbled, following it again. The sun sank languidly behind the car and across the sun's path, birds appeared only as black wings. The countryside around them seemed aflame, the fields mellowed. Gullies, in shadows, were like caverns. As they drove back to town, Amy stretched out, realizing she was tired. "It does seem so stupid," she said, "that we have to hide to sit and talk."

"It wouldn't be comprehensible to many people," Almoner said, "that two other human beings would want to spend an afternoon sitting and talking, or not talking, as the notion struck them."

When they reached town, he parked the car the same distance from the square. Despite lengthened street shadows falling along the sidewalk, the corner where the bus would stop was clearly visible, surrounded by stores with lights on. Negroes, who were waiting on the curb, now bent to pick up bundles.

"The bus must be coming," Amy said hurriedly.

"Next week?"

"Yes," she said. "All right." She leaned across the seat and touched her mouth lightly to his. Then she started to get out.

"Amy," he said. "Sometimes I wish you hadn't written me that letter. My God, didn't you see what it would mean?"

"No," she said worriedly, glancing toward the bus stop.

"I wanted to save you any unpleasantness or unhappiness you didn't have to have," he said. "But I can't go on fighting like this."

"Fighting?" she said.

"My glands," he said.

"Oh. The bus is going to be here."

"Run then, damn it," he said. "Run."

'Next week or not?"

"Yes. Yes," he said, watching her run.

Jeff:

What's happened? Does your wife know about the day in the woods? She phoned and asked me to lunch. I said I could and then she phoned right back and said she wasn't coming to Delton, after all. My mother had a fit and said not to write you; the stuff about letters being proof positive. Now, she's written asking me to lunch there. I don't want to come but should I? What's going on? And I did say, Why couldn't I? Why didn't I? I missed you afterward. I wish God would help me. Nobody is so dumb and foolish as I.

Amy

Dearest Amy:

I bought crappie from a Negro walking along the road with a string of them, and nothing seemed out of the ordinary when I got home. I don't know why the sudden telephoning. Intuition? Something could have happened; someone could have seen us on the square that day. What choice do they leave us but back alley subterfuge? They can see nothing else for looking at us cross-eyed. As I was coming from the drugstore the other day, I encountered your aunt, and she looked at me so exactly like Amelia, I was confused for a moment. There's a difference in the air I can't put my finger on. Momentous housecleaning began, I in the middle trying to work. But to them I am the only one in the

147

house not doing anything and I'm sent to town for floor wax. Amy, I don't have time to lose this way. I must finish this book and soon. Impossible of course, but if only we could go off together and when I had finished working, there you would be with your eyes looking at me as I dream they will, to read the work and say simply, Yes, it's good, go on. Something as simple as that. Go on, Jeff, I believe in you. And I there to say to you, Yes. We need each other for that. But they'll leave me alone for a while, because coming back with the wax, I pointed out that time lost that way means money lost. They've even had the front hall painted and Inga insisted on new wallpaper and really I have no extra money. Always there are bills. If only we could go away.

And Amelia's been going about with a secret air and so I thought, at first, the plan about your coming here was her idea. But now I think her preoccupied air is because she has a beau. She had recently resumed church work with zest, and the choir director, now a widower, has begun to ask her out to dinner. Only I see now, as I'm writing, that Amelia resumed church work shortly after his wife died. Then Inga told me herself, that while the house was clean she wanted to invite you here as her guest to stop gossip. I don't think the town's full of it, as she says; rather, I know the town's full of gossip, but not about us, I mean. But how can I take the chance it's not? Always, you must be protected. How are they sure we are still in touch? It all goes around in my head endlessly. My work is suffering, and the time lost can never be regained. This time, I'm afraid you'll have to decide what to do. You see, despite running, you may be forced by all this to grow up, yet.

Jeff

While her new employer stared at her legs, Amy tried not to laugh and stared down at his blue socks with gold clocks. Since he wore no garters, the socks' droopy tops showed when he

148

crossed his legs. He had no more idea than the man in the moon that her alligator shoes cost more than he made in a week, she thought. He kept looking at her insinuatingly as if she must be pleased and as if assuming they would be going out together after work. Did he even realize, she wondered, that there were different kinds of people, that what he might consider life's highest attainment would have little interest for her. God! if only he would stop looking at her legs.

A greenish gold tooth on one side of his mouth shone when he laughed. He wiped saliva, afterward, from his mouth's corners, then stuck thumbs behind his lapels and leaned back and kept staring. A blister on one heel, from walking and job-hunting, made Amy ease off a shoe, which gave him further reason to look. Told at the employment agency that smiling pleasantly would help get her a job, Amy had smiled. Proust, Existentialism, the Renaissance—college courses fled through her mind, pointlessly, now that she was in the real world, out to make a living. His green gold tooth appeared when he told her a joke; he sat wiping saliva on the back of his hand. Suppose she mentioned reading *Rememberance of Things Past* in French? He would find that as pointless as she had found his joke, Amy thought, having smiled at it. Hired as a receptionist, she need not do much and felt qualified for less.

At some interviews even smiling pleasantly had not helped. How had others taking the test known, if A talked to B for C minutes at so much a minute, then so many minutes overtime, how much it would cost? The telephone company's personnel manager had shaken her head in pity. "You got none of the problems right," she had said. Trying then to smile, Amy had said, "Well, I was a Literature major in college." But in the elevator she had cried, for the woman's pity had seemed to be for so much else besides her inability to get the job. Graduated from college, she was not qualified to be a long-distance telephone operator.

As a receptionist, she was to address envelopes, having clipped from each morning's paper announcements of births and marriages. Then to the people involved, she was to send a letter suggesting insurance. It hurt that she had not been invited to Quill's wedding; he would throw away this form letter from some unheard-of company and never know she had typed it. Beating upon the typewriter keys with two fingers, she thought of adding, It's from me, Amy; here I am, lost! Every day she had been working, her employer had worn the same pair of socks, or did he have similar pairs? Today, he had a run in the shiny material. Tomorrow she would know whether he ever changed them. There was something to look forward to in this job, after all. Picking at something near his gold tooth, he went out to the "Y" for his daily swim. Resentful that he had this freedom when she had none, Amy immediately abandoned his correspondence for her own.

Dear Jeff:

Thanks for calling, though unfortunately my mother heard and knew who it was. I'm glad my note was satisfactory and that your wife thought my having a job was a good enough excuse for my not coming there. But the job is so boring and I'm not learning anything, except that the business world is dull and stupid. I'm sorry about not meeting in the woods again but it did seem scary to do it after she had called. When will I see you?

Amy

Dear Amy:

If it weren't funny, I'd beat my head against the wall. So often, when we could have been together, we've been apart to spare our families so they would be what they think they are, happy; or so at least others would not think they had reason not to be. They've forced us to secrecy. They may force us to something like having to go away to be together. Keep at the job for now even if it is boring. People need something to chafe against *and particularly artists, as I've probably told you. Bear down on your pencil now. Tell yourself that's how you'll get out of it all. Start something and stick to it, Amy. I tell myself by working like a mad man, I'll drive you out of my thoughts for a little while. But you won't go. You won't. When will I see you?*

Jeff

She would see about what was going on in this house, Amelia thought. Jessie was continually going out, frequently letting the back door slam, more than in all her other years here put together, and always wearing white. That did not mean a boyfriend, but she couldn't be going to that many funerals. Amelia could not think of a single Negro who had died these past few days. And always, what's-his-name, her nephew was waiting at the end of the driveway. Amelia remembered him as the cutest little colored boy. What had made him turn out so surly? She called, "Inga, was that the phone?"

"No."

Inga's voice came muffled from the hall closet, where she had found a once-fashionable pink straw hat, its wide brim decorated with cherries. Backing out, Inga closed her eyes against the suddenness of day. In that inward yellow-starred darkness, she had a brief flash of self-assertion, thinking, I live here. Opening her eyes, she stared at the white hall paper Amelia had chosen, after saying the green grass cloth she had wanted was too expensive. But at least, Inga consoled herself, she had made the decision to have new paper, and she knew triumph. Now everything in the house had not been here before she had come. Something seemed hers, one decision anyway. The new wallpaper quickly had become her point of reference; she referred to things as having happened before or after she had decided to have the hall redone. Yet, she thought ruefully, how much had happened before, how little since. Time fled. Looking in the hall mirror, Inga pulled the sadly flopping brim of the hat over her face, then lower.

Inga had known she was expecting Latham to call, Amelia thought. That was the reason for that look on her face, putting on that old hat, just as jealous as she could be. She held open the door onto the grey porch, while Inga felt her way along the hall. She stumbled slightly over the doorsill. Amelia was exasperated more when they were driving. Then Inga said the car's motion made her sick.

"I'm driving just as careful as I can," Amelia said.

Forcing her voice to be even, she called attention to things she thought of interest: the stationmaster's geraniums were the prettiest in years, Chester's was getting a new awning, Brother Milroy's wife was under the dryer at Billie Jean's and usually her day was Friday. Why would she be getting her hair done on Thursday? Brother Milroy's arthritis must be better. He was able to wave, in return. Amelia had waved at him in his yard as they went by. "He's waiting for Latham to go over Sunday's music," she said, a little note of proprietorship in her voice.

Inga gazed with weak eyes back toward town, trying to see the importance of all these little things, as Amelia and all who had lived here always saw them. Through blurred vision, she saw only little stores huddled about a tattered station and thought how the people here came out to see a train pass. But Amelia had managed to take away that little flash of self-assertion she had felt in the hall. Inga searched for it again, vainly.

When Amelia turned down a rutted driveway, Inga saw a figure holding open the house's door and knew it must be Dea. As they came closer, she saw the navy dress, the red shoes, Dea wore so often. Was it in kindness, as it seemed, that Dea took her arm and helped her past the doorsill?

"I haven't been out much lately," Inga said. "I can't adjust to the daylight."

"Hard to get used to our summers, I imagine," Dea said.

"Inga's been here a very long time," Amelia said testily.

She had heard these remarks so continously, so many years, that Inga merely sat down in resignation. Dea thought how pale she was, but Amelia was blooming like a girl. Proud as a peacock about Latham Peabody taking her to dinner regularly, she imagined, when everybody knew he kept a nip in his pocket and took it first, when his family were, supposedly, the cream of the Baptists. He had only one kidney and was probably just looking for somebody to care for him in his sick old age. Had Amelia ever thought of that?

Feeling a little stiff with one another, they spoke at first about inconsequential things, like ferns. "Yours are so pretty," Amelia said to Dea.

"They don't get too much sun, and I water them the minute they get dry," Dea said. They had gone to the window to look out admiringly. They discussed, then, gardening. Inga, asked questions, never had her mind on the subject. Natural, the others thought, exchanging a glance which made that plain. The afternoon lagged like the conversation, until Dea brought out iced tea and cakes. Amelia, bending to the tray, said she must try one of each kind. Though she was "sort of" on a diet, and she laughed at herself.

"I hate myself being tempted," Dea said. "I need to lose, too. But I so seldom get a chance to entertain, I thought it would be fun to have you over, instead of trying to discuss everything on the phone." Nibbling cake, the others could only nod in agreement. Dea glanced around at how soft the color in the room had grown, the sun lower. Her house looked so much prettier. She was glad to have waited to get to the point of the visit. "He's phoned Amy," Dea said. "And her mother wanted me to find out if you couldn't get him to stop. Amy is about over her hero worship, she believes, and her notion about being a writer. She could never have published anything. Anyway, she has a lovely job now and a boyfriend from her college is coming to visit her."

"Is she to be engaged?" Inga sat forward.

"In a way, we hope not. He's not a Southerner. But her parents are giving her a big party and she's very much back in circulation. Her mother and I've been telling her if she doesn't marry soon, she'll end up with dregs." Or as an old maid, she had almost said, forgetting about Amelia. Though with her skin blooming was Amelia possibly thinking of marrying at this late date? And wondering about it, Dea knew she was envious of beginnings.

"Jeff has been working so hard, I don't think he's been thinking about that girl," Inga said.

Vurking, Dea could not help repeating to herself, staring at Inga curiously.

Amelia set down her glass. "I feel tied. If we mention it, he'll know we've been talking. He speaks of going away for a while. Maybe that's the answer."

"Couldn't you say her mother had asked me to speak to you about his phoning? Surely, he doesn't want to seem an older man bothering some young girl," Dea said.

"She's not complaining," Amelia said quickly. "It's her parents. She must encourage him."

"I can't think for what reason," Dea said.

"Her reason is what we'd like to know, too," Amelia said. "What does she want? It's gone on so long, someone's getting something out of it." She turned on Dea a frozen smile.

Dea carried the plate of cakes across the room. She would certainly save the rest for her own family. Coming back to sit down, she said, "I don't get the impression, at all, that they've seen one another lately. Do you?" The others were forced to shake their heads. "I don't see, then, how what you suggest holds water. Maybe you don't realize, Amy could have made her debut."

"I'm sure she's a very nice girl," Amelia said. "But what does she want?"

Always, she had relied on the strength of others, Inga realized. But these two were going to go around and around the subject, and she was decisive. "There's got to be a reason they want to keep in contact, hardly seeing one another. Why? What is so strong between them? I'm going to find out."

(Vy. Vhat, Dea repeated to herself.)

"I'd like to know how," Amelia said, standing to indicate they must go.

Inga, plopping the pink hat on lopsidedly, said, "Let's put on our thinking caps." There was, however, only one way: to face the girl, at last. Dea, reaching for Inga's elbow again, helped her across the doorsill. The Almoners, she thought, were the type to sue.

On the porch, Amelia touched a finger to a fern pot. "Your ferns are dry now," she said.

This, on top of her remark about Amy, was inexcusable, Dea thought. "Maybe you don't have luck because you water yours too much," she said. After slamming the car door, Amelia would have driven off without another word, except that the highway was blocked by a slow-moving line of cars. She stuck her head from the car window to stare. "They go by like that every Thursday afternoon and on Sunday," Dea said. "Don't they think they're dressed up, though."

A slow thought penetrated as Amelia realized that all the Negroes wore white. Coincidence? Surely, Jessie was too old and had too much sense to demonstrate. And she had said herself Negroes were too uppity for her these days. Jessie wouldn't just mouth what white people wanted to hear, would she? Suspiciousness, Amelia thought, had become quickly a habit. All these years she had been able to count on so little changing; now nothing seemed certain. She was not, however, going to put any stock in the Negroes' carrying on, or believe that Jessie was among them. But nothing on earth would make her pull out to the highway now, though once she would have gone, blaring her horn, expecting them to halt and let her through.

"Don't back out yet," Dea said.

"I wouldn't dream of it," Amelia said. Their fingertips had met on the windowsill. In the silence, summer throbbed, intense as a drumbeat all around them.

"You can't get a lick of work out of any of them on these days either," Dea said. "Everybody says it. They'll take your money and give you the sorriest job they can." When the line of cars had gone, their fingertips parted. Amelia started the motor. "Well," she said, "I'll have to go without supper because of the cake, but it was worth it."

As they drove back toward town, Inga was still sunk into silence. Amelia was considering the threat this girl presented to her way of life, as the Negroes carrying on threatened it. She had never felt before the need to marry. But if Jeff went off with that girl, she would end up with Inga, who did not seem to realize that in the long run you had yourself to depend on. She was surprised then. Inga said, "I'm going to see her on Saturday, if she'll see me. She probably doesn't work then."

"Well, she'd certainly better see you!" Amelia said with hollow bravado. Entering the house, she began to hum some faintly remembered tune about unanswerable things.

Inga momentarily hid in the closet's darkness, hanging up the old pink hat. With all she had on her mind, her life possibly coming to an end, Amelia had no thought, except to sing.

Amy stared into her dim closet realizing that, as usual, she had nothing right to wear. As Amy looked blank, Edith stood behind her. "You never have the right thing like the other girls," she

156

said. "Now that you're working, you ought to buy some clothes." This was not her mother's real reason for complaining, her face grimacing, her tone almost groaning, Amy thought. Shaken, Edith said, "Who else gets themselves into situations like this. Oh, why couldn't you have been like . . ."

"Because I don't want to be like the other girls." Amy spoke out at last, flatly and finally, before going out of earshot, her heart not beating too fearfully.

On Saturdays, most downtown shops and offices were closed. The nearly unpeopled streets had a funereal hush. They were like war-struck streets, deserted and dreading, after an air alarm had sounded. To dispell the quiet, Amy thought of blowing her horn, even without reason. When she started down the street, palsied heat waves danced ahead. Tanned from his honeymoon, but nervous and thinner, Quill was leaving his bank at its Saturday closing hour. Electric chimes saluted noon, whirring and ringing and playing the Londonderry Air, which sent a flurry of starlings over the drained streets, as if exulting to the music. Wanting to confide in Quill that she was meeting Mrs. Almoner, Amy thought that she could not. Though it did seem like fate to see him when they had begun everything together so innocently. Life seemed made up of circles and this the completion of one. Amy and Quill, acknowledging one another formally beneath the hotel's awning, inquired about one another's health and answered, in turn, that they were fine, thank you. Longing to say more, Amy's eyes sought Quill's, to find in them some signal that said go ahead. She met only a yellowish cast, as a pond holds scum, hiding what is beneath. Quill mustered a moment something of his old teasing manner. As Amy started indoors, he said, "Spending your Saturday afternoons in hotel rooms now, young lady?" Then he went on, having settled his hat at an even more correct angle.

What, Amy wondered, could be made out of two people sharing an experience and the life of only one being changed by it? In the lobby her attention turned to avoiding wet places on a marble floor, which a Negro was mopping. At the hour planned, arriving at the flower shop, she was surprised by the frail lady who rose, evidently recognizing her, and spoke.

"Mrs. Almoner?"

On the vulnerable-looking lady, neat coils of gold braid atop her head wavered as she nodded. The real depths of her eyes were obscured by dark glasses. She apologized for not removing them but daylight hurt her eyes. Amy, feeling overgrown, bent to hear the faint voice, having the wavery quality of a fine dangling silk thread. She was as glad not to have taken her mother's advice to wear high heels as she was glad not to be able to meet, clearly, Mrs. Almoner's eyes.

"May I take your arm?" Inga said. They reached the top of stairs leading down into the dining room, and she felt uncertain.

Amy, saying, "Of course," received through her crooked elbow weight like a feather's. "Be careful," she warned, "the steps are damp, too."

When they stood in the doorway, holding arms, Inga shivered in cold air from the air conditioning. The hostess approached and Amy asked for a table sheltered from the draft. She guided Inga across the room and around tables and chairs. Curtains drawn against the bright day left only white tablecloths and summer zinnias, as centerpieces, to relieve the room's dimness. They settled, their order was given, and Inga shivered slightly again. "Too hot outdoors, too cold in," she said.

Amy agreed. Their heads shook in mutual distaste over the stores already displaying fall clothes. "I'm still looking for white shoes," Amy confided.

Inga had seen some on sale in a shop down the street. On a scrap of paper from her purse, Amy wrote down the store's name.

A discussion of clothes continued until the waitress brought their order.

"It's nice," Inga said, "that you're so tall and can wear those low-heeled shoes. I've always felt I had to wear such high heels. And lately, they make me feel off balance and dizzy."

"That's too bad," Amy said. "Could you need to have your glasses changed?"

"Yes, that does need to be done, too," Inga said. "I'm always putting things off. For instance, I've wanted to meet you for a long time. Jeff thinks so highly of the possibilities of your work. I'm sure you have other things in common, too. Of course, what I want to know is, do you want to marry him?"

Amy sat back from the table in astonishment. Her lunch went untouched and the congealed salad began sadly to melt all over her plate. "No." Not only had the abruptness of the question surprised her but that anyone had thought of the possibility of her marrying Almoner.

Puzzled, Inga pushed her glasses toward the bridge of her nose. "Then why do you want to keep seeing him?"

"His books mean so much to me. And I want to be a writer, too." Amy looked embarrassed.

"It's my opinion that men have a change of life, too. At about fifty. I think that's happening to Jeff. But I don't understand why you want to see him if you don't want to marry him."

"I told you," Amy said. "Because I think he is a great writer. And I want to be one. If you wanted to be a painter, wouldn't you want to meet Picasso, or somebody like that?"

"No. I would see no purpose," Inga said.

"I don't know how to explain then," Amy said, surprised.

"I don't think a man and a woman can just be friends," Inga said.

"Not when you're young maybe. When you're older," Amy

said confidently, "I think things must be different. Feelings I know change." She was thinking how long her mother and father had slept in separate bedrooms.

"I do not consider myself at fifty too old to fall in love," Inga said.

"Oh no! That's not what I meant," Amy said, having meant that exactly. She had not meant to blurt it out meanly, having no desire at all to hurt frail Mrs. Almoner. It was sad, though that she had expectations of someone falling in love with her at fifty.

"Do you have a young man?" If Amy gave the correct answer, all her others would seem more trustworthy, Inga felt.

"Sort of," Amy said. "A boy I knew at college is coming to visit me soon."

Inga had not touched her own lunch but sat back, a hand grabbing her throat, as if relieved to have avoided choking. "Oh. I'm so glad to hear that," she said. For the moment, they were silent. Inga stared at flowerlets of cauliflower on her plate, which were turning brown. Amy nibbled at a soggy potato chip and looked about at other diners, who seemed to be enjoying their food. Her table for some reason had no bowl of flowers. The lack created an expanse of white tablecloth between her and Inga. A little girl, leaving with her mother, ran along between tables. Having plucked flowers from her own, the child waved them once gaily toward Amy's face, like a flaunt.

"There's to be," Inga said, her eyes wandering from the little girl, "a Fish-o-rama at the springs. Fly-tying contests, the kinds of things Jeff likes. Would you and your young friend come as our guests?"

"That sounds nice. He admires Mr. Almoner's work, too."

The waitress looked apologetically at the untouched food, removed their plates and presented the bill. Amy and Inga bent over it, arguing slightly before agreeing to go Dutch treat. When they stood, Inga immediately took Amy's arm. Guiding Inga carefully back across the room, around tables and chairs, Amy felt in care of something as light and defenseless as a bird. To Mrs. Almoner there was a sweet air she could not help but find appealing, in some ways missed in her mother. Certain of mistakes she would never make, Amy wondered why the Almoners had not been able to get along.

She was positive it was Amelia waiting at the flower shop, though there was no introduction. The commanding woman, with a tortoise-shell comb stuck in the back of her hair, accepted Inga's weight by extending her own arm. On her face was a look of dismissal, which caused Amy to flee. Barely did she nod at Mrs. Almoner in goodbye.

Surely the two women watched her. Amy, trying not to run, feared her slip was showing. Sticking a hand into the collar of her dress, she pulled at a strap. A barbed remark from Amelia would not have surprised her. In fantasy, Amy replied with an innuendo about the choir director. Wouldn't, she thought, Miss Almoner be mad to know she knew about him!

She felt trapped an instant by the revolving door, before being flung freely to the street. There, the bells were striking untriumphantly and meagerly the half-hour. With a feeling of being letdown, Amy stood on the street. To the astonishment then of passengers on a bus going by, all of whom turned to the windows to stare, she bolted coltlike down Main Street, long blond hair bobbing on her shoulders. The sudden sense of freedom brought delight so that not even the heat mattered. Stores went by in a blur, like a solid front. Having wanted to do something the older people could not do, Amy ran block after block, until she was exhausted. She walked slowly back to her car, feeling overwhelmed at Mrs. Almoner's dependency on her. Never, Amy swore to herself, would she get old.

———

No, Almoner said, he had not known they were coming to Delton. He had been away on a fishing trip and entered the house as the phone was ringing.

Standing in a public telephone booth, Amy became increasingly aware that it had been used for more than telephoning. Yet, across the way, in a park resident above the river, was a small building with doors marked Men and Women. Did people choose to do what was forbidden because life was so dull the act of urinating in a phone booth gave it impetus? Phoning Almoner made her own heart beat excitedly, though she knew his wife was not at home.

"I'm sorry you had to go through this on my account," he said.

"I didn't mind," she said. "It's funny. I liked her."

"She can be very charming," he said.

Amy told of Leigh's visit and of Inga's suggestion they come to the Fish-o-rama. "I'm glad you and my wife have become such good friends," he said, without humor.

"It's a way to see you," Amy said, a note of apology in her voice. "I don't think I can before then."

"No," he said. "You'll be busy with your plans."

Must he sound wistful or petulant or whichever he was sounding? Despite his saying it often, he did not seem to sense her right to a life with friends her own age, and she did not like feeling possessed. When she felt him intruding on her other life, she began to guard it jealously. Talking, she watched a young girl, in the park opposite, swaggering back and forth before a man who lonesomely fed squirrels and paid her no attention. Some look of desperation about them both brought Amy's own to her mind. When the girl had gone, the man sank forward, his hands to his face. But there were leaves, casting lovely dancing patterns of shade on the hot walkways, and between delicate paws, a squirrel was nibbling an acorn. With what astonishing facility it dashed up a tree.

Look! Amy wanted to call, look at the day!

Almoner had been telling her inconsequential things about his trip, and she had stared from the booth, answering with remarks that did not matter either. They wanted connection, to hear one another's voice, and were aware of that. After she had stopped running, Amy, standing, had thought, What am I to do? and had longed immediately for Almoner, who made her loneliness bearable. Now, she pressed the moist receiver closer to her ear. Beyond the park she could barely glimpse the river, which seemed utterly still, though flowing with its strong deep current. The voice in the receiver lowered affectionately. Hearing it, she knew never again would he come first to her mind as Almoner. From now on, always, he would be Jeff.

When the train was late, Amy could not help feeling annoyed. She felt, even, like blaming Jeff, though of course it was not his fault; sensibly, she knew that. Roaming the station, she reminded herself it had been her idea, as much as his, to meet as soon as Leigh left. She ought to be able to control her moods better. Driven off the station's only empty seat by the stench of the man next to her, she felt more disgruntled. The station was dank when it was a glorious blue September day outside. Today was the opening football game of the season. With friends, she ought to have been there, though she did not care an iota about football. Only, it was customary to attend the first game of the season.

The train announced, Amy forced away her irritated look and hoped Jeff would not be overly apologetic. She tried to head off an obvious apology saying, "Don't worry. I haven't been here too long."

"Always, I'm inconveniencing you," he said, coming through the gate.

"It's not your fault if a train's late," she said.

"It cuts down on our time so badly though," he said. "Already, it's short."

She must control her moods. Again, she felt grumpy that she and Jeff had nothing to do. The newspaper vendor seemed to be staring as they went past. Could he realize, remembering her, that since she was meeting this older man again, he was probably not her father? And why let what some stranger thought matter? Forever was she to be hampered by both background and moods?

"I'm sure you had a better way to spend Saturday afternoon than standing around this station," Almoner said, holding open the door.

"It doesn't matter," she said. "But where shall we go?" The bland streets reflected nothing of the excitement and gorgeousness of fall.

He said, "I'll have to take the next train. As I wrote you, she has been truly sick this time."

"I was sorry to hear it. And it was pneumonia? It was too bad it rained that day of the Fish-o-rama. If that's not the most fantastic name!" They had reached the bottom step and stood, laughing. Then, staring in either direction, she said, "Well, where are we going?"

"You choose," he said.

Her mouth set. She started off and barely slowed for him to catch up a moment later. "You were impressive that day, winning all those awards," she said. He had seemed to come doggedly, which was irritating, but she determined to be kind. And that he seemed breathless worried her.

"Thank you, Miss Howard," he said, attempting a light manner, though sensing her changing moods. "You were impressively pretty. But that's not unusual."

"Thank you," she said. "Do you feel like walking? I don't know anything else to do. There's no time to go to the river."

"Exercise is always good. And, I'm afraid I went on a little tear after that day."

"Because of it?" Immediately, she knew she had had some part in it. Once she had written in her diary that leaves, dying and sighing, seemed to ask where she would be in a year? That thought came back, while she stared ahead at the dingy street.

Almoner longed to say it had not been only the weather that had made the day of the Fish-o-rama ghastly. If only someday she would look at him as he had seen her glance once at Leigh.

He said, "Because of repercussions from the day. What I thought had died down started again. I'm an old goat." He smiled. "Inga's opinion, not my own."

"I'm sorry." Here, as they went past little stores, which seemed empty, proprietors glanced eagerly at shadows falling across their dusty windows, and Amy stared back at them. "Still, I think it's best you accepted her invitation." Jeff took Amy's arm as they stepped from the curb and drew her closer. "This is the first chance I've had to tell you how much I like what you call a slip, I guess. The one you wore that day. It made you seem so like a little girl. A white ruffle showed."

"My slip showed! Why didn't you tell me?" she said, almost blushing now.

He thought that even he forgot sometimes the enormity of her sensitivities. "Only a bit when you sat on the bank," he said, no longer teasing. "No reason to mention it. Like so much about you, you don't understand, it was charming, Amy."

"But did it show even when I stood up?" she said. "And all day?"

"It did not. Only once when I looked up at you, there on the bank."

She kept a little worried frown, leading him on. They reached unexpectedly a small patch of rehabilitated land made into a park, containing only a small pond with several sluggish goldfish. A bored young mother trailed a toddler, who threw pebbles into the water. Amy watched enviously the smooth glittering retreat of the fish, to hide beneath rocks. As smoothly had Leigh retreated. She thought perhaps she had treated him as expectantly as Edith and that had been her mistake. The quick, slick glimmer of the goldfishes' backs transferred in her mind's eye, becoming her party, the ceiling transformed into a night sky shiny with tinsel stars. Only, when the lights had come on fully and the last guest had gone, there had appeared instead a somewhat droopy dark blue canvas. By then, too, the hopeful look Edith had worn all during Leigh's visit had disappeared. When he was eventually waving from the departing plane's window, she had said, "Why did he come here? What did he want?"

"To see the South," Amy had said, realizing the truth.

"For God's sake then, why didn't you let him take a Cook's Tour!" Edith had cried. Now, Leigh had gone off to Yale to graduate school.

The young mother kept trailing the toddler, while enviously examining Amy and her clothes. Amy looked back also with an envious expression. She and Jeff kept heading this way and that around the pond. Then Amy stood still and announced abruptly, "I've quit my job." She stuck the tip of her shoe dangerously near the water. "Nothing is ever going to happen to me here. I've got to go away."

Almoner thoughtfully watched smoke drift away, having taken several rapid puffs from a cigar. He said finally, "I think I'm sorry you quit. People need stupidity in their lives, particularly artists."

"I'm not an artist," she said angrily. "And people don't need having nothing in their lives but stupidity. That's all my life is, except for you." She looked at him grateful for that, and her face then set sadly again.

"Maybe we could manage to go away together for a few days."

"I'm not talking about a few days, Jeff."

"I wish I were enough. I don't think another place is the answer. Amy, don't leave your own people. Give yourself more time."

Bending, she had picked up pebbles and now tossed them into the water, her aim not much surer than the child's. He, having been forbidden by his mother to bother the fish, looked at her mystified. She led him away. He turned once to look back at Amy, who watched him similarly, with longing and wonder.

"Maybe we ought not meet in the city," Amy said. "There's just nothing to do here. I guess it would be cold in the woods, though. And our butterfly would be dead, wouldn't it?"

"I am sorry for both of you," he said.

But not wanting to be felt sorry for, she could not keep an angry edge from her voice. "It's time to go." She felt as she had at the edge of the pond, her foot extended toward the water, teetering.

He looked stolidly at the goldfish beneath the water; they seemed mesmerized there, not a tail swished. And when he looked up, Amy had begun to walk away. He ground out with his heel his cigar after a moment, then followed.

She reached the sidewalk and stood with a reluctant air, her bottom lip slightly protruded and her hands stuck boyishly and childishly into her pockets. Her head was cocked slightly and as if attentively toward a voice no one else heard, inner perhaps. The patient way in which he followed her made Amy feel guilty and put an obligation on her she felt unable to meet: her tendency then was to run away. But she forced herself to walk more slowly, convenient for him. Forcing an even tone, she said, "Should we try the woods?" and indentations when she tried to smile made her face seem instead lined, as if she were tired and old.

"If you will," he said. "Next week?"

"The one after that," she said, not meeting his eyes.

"The first of November then," he said. The conductor, as Almoner went through the gate, nodded, recognizing them by now.

Amy held onto the iron bars of the closed gate, watching him disappear. And imagining herself again a prisoner, she thought that she was her own jailer, too.

He decided to risk waiting at the bus stop, the square being deserted. However, he made no move toward Amy when she stepped off the bus. He said only, "I'm glad to see you."

"I'm glad to see you, Jeff," she said.

They glanced around in all directions, heading toward his car. Winter light gave the storefronts a greyish cast, as if they were dusty. Apparent only were the red caps worn by hunters, grouped now around a stove in the hardware store, but the men paid no attention to passers-by. The stone tables around the Court House had a relentless cold look, empty on a winter's day, cleared of course of checker boards. Places rubbed free of grass, beneath the benches, showed where the feet of the old men continually had rested and seemed all evidence of their existence. With trees bare, houses were exposed and appeared to have been set forward closer to the street since summer, making Almoner and Amy feel more in evidence. An old woman, coming onto her porch, shooed away a dog digging at bone meal around her bulbs and stared as they passed. Amy wanted to stare back, curious too. Here were the boundaries of the woman's life, her house and her yard; that showed in the intense squint she gave the strangers.

"Something's on our side, at least," Amy said, settling onto the car's front seat. "It's warm for November. And you were certainly brave, kind Mr. Almoner, to be standing on the square."

"I'm glad you didn't mind, pretty Miss Howard," he said. "I

was afraid you would. But then you're looking thinner. Perhaps you're losing your baby fat. It was a little test. I confess now to giving them to you sometimes."

"And I passed?"

"Today, so far, you have gotten an A in growing up."

They drove from the square, and she resisted making a face at the old woman, still squinting. "Is not caring what other people think growing up?" Amy said. "I was glad you were waiting for me."

"You've tried to please everyone," he said. "And that's impossible. Growing up is being able to decide who and what you care about and sticking to your decision. Sometimes, it may be necessary to hurt other people."

"As little as possible."

"As little as possible, of course," he said. "Growing up is also accepting that it is not your prerogative to try to change other people. They are what they are. You will have to accept hurt from others, too, you know."

She had glanced toward the back seat and said, "I see there's a basket. Jessie fixed enough lunch for two?"

He nodded. Then realizing that Amy still gazed toward the back, said, "I brought that blanket because I think wherever we choose to sit, we may be cold."

She turned saying nothing, tucked a foot beneath her, and gazed out at the familiar landscape, so different with fields brown and cleaned. Tags of cotton left on browned stalks seemed markers to guide them along some unknown way. Distant trees had a fire-gutted blackened look. The sun's winter sheen gave everything a white-gold cast; still here was the same reddish maze of roads. "Let's find some place we've never been before," Amy said.

"Something new then," he said. Yet when he drove past places they had been Amy recounted them lovingly, her feeling painful as longing. There was the spot in the road where the man with the cabbage had stood, and there was the abandoned house that in some ways seemed their own. It was empty still, and someday they must go back there, she said, turning to look back. The house's door stood open into emptiness and silence. In the day's white cast, Amy saw not only on the porch the ghosts of the house's occupants, but hers and Jeff's. She was bound to these places now, for they were part of her past. She reached out and touched his arm, which he acknowledged by a certain silence, that he understood. Life was painful to her, but she could not change hers for one without unordinary experiences.

There, she said, was the pond! It was more easily glimpsed in the unleaved distance. Afterward, they passed a fire tower whose name they liked. Wind Borne, Amy repeated.

Slowing the car, Almoner asked, "Is this place worthy of those others?"

They glanced up from the road at a slope of eroding ground, once a driveway, leading to an abandoned Negro schoolhouse. He turned the car that way when Amy nodded. Though it was only midday, the sun had the pale look of late afternoon. With its edges diffusing, it seemed to be helplessly swallowed by the widening winter sky. Everything was whitening, and Amy felt that at any moment the world about her might give way, to be blotted out entirely. Lengthily, off the tin roof's ragged edges, like rain, the pale winter glow fell. Touching their faces, highlighting their cheeks, it turned their noses redder in the November air. They went about the dry deadened yard gathering twigs and branches to fill what remained of a pot-bellied stove. The vine-trailing outhouse yielded a plank, easily broken into firewood. Inside, the fire was eventually fed paper and scraps from Jessie's lunch. They sat like schoolchildren themselves, the blanket drawn over their knees, whispering in conspiring tones. Supposedly, he had left home to inspect roads into a deer camp and wore rough clothes and had brought whiskey. They passed the bottle between them, as if it might warm their hands; wind stole in through glassless windowpanes and cracks in the walls. Without more fuel, the fire grew steadily weaker. Shivering and returning the bottle again, Amy said, "I'm glad you brought that instead of beer." Momentarily warmed by the whiskey, growing both sleepy and melancholy, she put her head on her knees.

"Blue Monday?" he asked, turning from staring into the deadened fire.

"Just thinking about going away," she said, lifting her head. "I just can't stay here, Jeff." She had drunk more than she had realized. The iron feet of the bloated stove seemed to lift and fall when she moved her head. They seemed the forepaws of some great animal. At Jeff's look, she thought things had been different for him back in his day, or he would understand her situation more clearly. Today, two girls had invited her to the movies, and that was the kind of thing people she knew did with their afternoons. Her nose sank down with a little abrupt bump against her knees, while she snickered to think where she was instead and how surprised those girls would be.

Jeff stretched out on his back, his hands behind his head. Wasn't he cold? Amy drew the blanket he had abandoned back over his knees and stretched out alongside him. The ceiling, as she lay down, receded and then came slowly down into place, which seemed funny. In their winter coats, she thought them like two cumbersome bears settled side by side for their winter's sleep. Against the stove's warm sides, the soles of her feet had begun to burn uncomfortably, though the floor beneath her was hard and cold. The two inconveniences loomed large in her mind, and Jeff's hand touching her was bothersome. He seemed trembly and shaky, like an old man. This time: she repeated that to herself over and over. But the room was all the barish-brown Sunday-school rooms she had ever sat in with her mind skittering away from the lessons in large-printed, colorful Biblical pamphlets. Must she blame herself that when she tried to return his kiss, she felt nothing at all? Reserve, part of her, tightened her like a rein. Coldly, she removed his hand from her leg. She said all the things she always said: she was sorry but she couldn't and she just didn't feel that way. Her longing, however, was for abandonment.

Jeff walked to the window with the whiskey bottle and tilted it to his mouth. Having recapped it, he said, turning, "Poor baby." That struck Amy as being condescending, and she looked at him, a little less sorry for having refused.

"—who can't melt," he had concluded.

Against the edgeless sun visible at the window, he seemed all the same color, hard to distinguish. "You may think too highly of your body, Amy," he said. "It's, after all, flesh and blood. And, I worry that you're never going to be able to love anyone."

How ridiculous, she thought, running over in her mind the people she already loved, her family despite all the things they had done to her, and she loved him, though not in the way he wanted. Could she help that? Old shame filled her as she stood and drew up her pants, uncomfortable that he did not look away. Not speaking, she gathered things to take to the car. She waited for him then at the door. He put the last scrap into the stove and came on, bringing the lunch basket. Still silent, they crossed the schoolyard, passing left-over sad playground equipment, a tire hanging lopsidedly by a frayed rope, a huge tractor tire on which the children had climbed.

"I thought I could help," he said. "I know you're not frigid. You only need to have something frozen inside you melted.

Something your past did to you. But I guess I'm the wrong one."

Miserable, she said, "I'm sorry."

"It's not fatal," he said. "It's a momentary sadness like a star falling. But we've put so much time into this, it seems a shame it's ended."

They spoke little on the trip back to town. But Amy was surprised that he stopped at the bus stop for her to get out, though the bus had not come. They said hardly goodbye, and he drove away. She had felt so disgruntled on the drive that she had argued with him even when he mentioned that it was going to rain. But he had been right. Rain was coming down torrentially by the time the bus reached Delton. She was drenched in the moment it took her to run inside the station. She was so cold that she had difficulty opening a locker where she had stored inconsequential packages, to pretend that, having gone to the movies, she had done a little shopping. With these few things, she felt homeless, that they were all her possessions, and she started from the bus station.

She went home in a taxi, and got out a block away, hoping to dash up the driveway and enter the house through the back way, not to be seen. Her father was standing on the back steps waiting for a lull in the rain before going out to the garage. When she rounded a corner, he stared at her so strangely that Amy wondered, too, whether she were in the wrong place.

This was his daughter? his face asked. His eyes strayed to where a button was missing from her coat, and her hands, without gloves, were wet and red as a scrubwoman's. He would offer no advice, not to be an old fogey like most parents. Standing convivially, jiggling change in his pockets, he observed Amy's small packages. He remarked how glad he was she had been out shopping again. Spend all the money she wanted! Offering, he thought that she had never looked worse. Her hair that could be pretty hung around her face like wet mop strings. And with an observant look on his face, he said, "I ought to get you a car of your own."

Amy, hesitating at the bottom step when he spoke, started toward the porch's shelter.

"I don't need a car," she said. "I'd like the money, instead, to go away."

Amy, I can't bear the silence. I can't. Will you take me back into your experience? I had thought I could stand it, but I can't. I know that now. Naturally, it hurts when you say no. You had said you wanted to be free, and I wanted to help you become so. I may be the wrong one. But until you find someone else, let me keep trying. You need someone so much. Your past has made you so vulnerable to hurt, I can't help but worry about you. Once before I told you, I'll be anything to you you want me to be. I only think now there's confusion on both our parts about what you want from me. There were questions when I got home that day. I had been needed to go for a prescription. The night before, Jessie had made a mess of dinner and that day had burned Amelia's birthday cake. I've been appointed to find out what's wrong with her. Neither liquor nor pills will help me. One of the things we had between us was truth. I think we still have that. So will you tell me truthfully if you really do want to be free of me completely. If so, then I'll quit this. I promise.

Jeff

She wouldn't eat lunch, Edith had thought, but feeling tired must mean that she needed food, and having set down her grocery bag, she opened a package of cookies. The chocolate taste set up inside her a feeling of starvation, for food, excitement, sex, something, and one cookie led to another. Having no name for what she wanted, Edith continued to cram cookies into her

174

mouth until, at least, hunger was sated. Afterward, she could have cried over the cellophane bag, emptied. Instead of asking Mallory if she were too fat, which obviously she was, she now asked him frequently how much too fat she was, considering her age? He muttered something always about looking healthy, neither telling the truth nor avoiding it. This avoidance made her eat more, as if to force him to say what he really thought.

Whistling, the postman went down the other side of the street, his breath smoking O's, as fragile as the sky. That morning, tree limbs had been perfectly preserved in ice, which now melted in unrelenting drips against the house. Edith, holding a letter toward the light, thought, if only Amy had stayed here and married and been like the other girls, I wouldn't be in this dilemma!

The letter against the light, she could make out only that it had been scrawled in red pencil, but it did reveal that Amy had not told Mr. Almoner she was leaving. What did that mean? If Amy had run away from him, perhaps she cared enough to come back if he asked. Edith's heart set up a rhythmic thumping, only partially because she was walking upstairs. Would Amy come back? Edith wondered where the years had gone when she had complained about being exhausted from running after Amy, keeping her from moving knickknacks about the house. How she longed to be exhausted in that way again.

She did not glance at stack after stack of numbered canvases in her closet, having given up painting. Now, in her tufted pink chair and confronting her life, she thought that, Yes, she would give in and eventually buy expensive silk slacks and a silk shirt to be worn out covering her stomach, and she would go with Mallory to some semitropical place and there attempt native dances, further ruining her skin with martinis and sun and catch a fish and pose, or in a flower lei, for a picture to be sent back to the hometown paper. At night, wearing a flowery dress with a match-

175

ing cashmere sweater similar to the other ladies', she would pose again behind an exotic rum drink, or on deck behind a life preserver bearing some cruise ship's name. This is my life, Edith thought, dialing the phone.

"Hello. I understand you have a ceramic class. I'm interested in taking it three mornings a week."

Enrolled, she went downstairs to a house filled with ceramic ashtrays and bunnies and urns presented by friends. Now she could give ceramic presents in return. The letter on the kitchen table, the water boiling, reminded Edith again of her dilemma. *One thing we had between us was truth.* The envelope when it was resealed did not seem steamed. She would make Mallory a big white ashtray for his office, and he would say, "Honey, you're just as artistic and talented as you can be," though it would be a replica of all the ashtrays taken out of the kiln that day. She was tired of pretense and wished Amy had told her what she was looking for. Gaiety was a covering up for fools, pretensive and easy. She was wrong then to have despaired of Amy's mournful face. Only how did you make sense of truth and honesty? Edith wondered. It was by dishonesty she had learned of her failures and more about her daughter. While the cycles of her life revolved still with the moon, Amy saw her only as her mother, which was natural. Though, touched by the right person, Edith knew she might abandon even Amy. Who was to touch her?

Opening a box of crackers and eating, Edith began to clean pantry shelves. The work would take up most of the day. Something else might happen tomorrow. She finished a cracker, dried her hands, and put Almoner's letter into an envelope addressed to Amy before taking from her desk a sheet of plain stationery.

Never would it occur to Amy her mother had had a lover. Amy was too young to appreciate one, having never done without love. Knowing how much she could bring to an affair, Edith yearned with Mr. Almoner, addressing an envelope to him.

About the letter, he thought, a beldame straining toward vicarious intrigue and no longer protecting her only chick. What had changed her? Maybe she thought he might lure Amy home again, though he did not think he had that power. Though she had written the letter, the composition teacher at Miss Somebody's finishing school might well have been looking over her shoulder; however, she had been cagey enough not to use her feminine blue stationery.

Dear Mr. Almoner:

May I take this opportunity to tell you that my daughter, Amy, has gone to New York City for an indefinite stay. I have forwarded her your recent letter. Her address is as follows: No. 2 Beverly Place.

Sincerely yours,
Edith Howard

Mister Jeff had sayed, Come here, Jessie. I want to talk to you. Then Miss Amelia come from choir practice and had the mail. He read his letter and it taken a time for him to understand, seem like. Then he so pale, I ast if he needed a pill. He sayed "No" and something about his last cast, but not fishing talk. Probably about that girl and none of my nevermind, unless he told me. My dough was ready. I let it set and finally had to get him some water. He taken a pill quick. Sho do worry me about Mister Jeff's heart.

Then Vern come. I had done seed his car at the end of the drive and thought, this one time he could wait. But young folks don't expect to for nothing. Think old folks here to hop toad to they biddin', shoot. I thought Mister Jeff and me done been here together long time 'fore Vern got hisself born by mistake. Mister Jeff sayed, "Jessie, guess this the spring I'll finally make that garden I always been going to make." I sayed I sho would be

177

glad. I was telling him about where to set out the 'matoes when Vern come up the back steps. He seen Mister Jeff and me setting there. His eyes pop out asting me, Why? Honey, I could have told him. Evening was coming on and Vern stood in the shadows. He ain't going to come in, mad enough at having to come to the back do'. I had done tole him, "Come on to the front. Mister Jeff, he don't care. It his house even if Miss Amelia act like it hers." Vern had did told me he'd wait till didn't nobody have to go to the back. "Time going to come, Aun-tee," he say; and I sayed, "Let it."

Remember how Momma always sayed, "Live so that if your hen have eggs, your neighbor got eggs?" But Vern don't want to listen, not to nothing. Standing out on the porch thinking I don't see him. I wanted to say, I see you, baby. Thing is, you don't see me. I know what he do see. He see me coming across the flo' with these big old bosoms shaking and Mister Jeff's slippers flopping on my feets. Can't keep nothing on my feets but house shoes. I can't go on no march. I told Vern, though, if it give him hope, then march. Miss Amelia say these corns come from shoes too little. Me and her been treating ours together. Vern don't want to hear, time was when didn't colored or white folks have nothing round in this part of the country. Think nobody have had such a hard time as him. That's young people. Mrs. Uncle Tom; Vern thinking that just as clear. Here I'm at, boy. I just soon tell him so. He in the shadows whispering, "How long 'fore you can go?" I sayed, "I ain't coming." Then he say, "They won't let you off?" He sho quick to bitter. I sayed I been coming and going here like I wants all the time I been here. I ain't coming 'cause I ain't coming. Too old. Lord have mercy so much angry in young peoples today. I sayed I'd stay home and read the Bible. Only place they is any religion left. And pray Vern don't kill somebody yet. Then Mister Jeff seed him and say, "Hidy, Vern," and act like he don't notice Vern don't say "Hidy" back. I told Vern,

"Wait," then go on 'bout his business. Them stairs is gettin' me down. I brought me back this book I had did cut the insides out one time, and Vern knowed what was in it. I told him, "This the place we got to live. We got to get along. But take this on to meeting and when you at the lunch counter, buy something on me." He sayed, "I ain't got served yet." I sayed he would be. He sayed, "Aun-tee, you give me it all? Three hundred dollars. That is all you got in this world." And I sayed, "You wrong about that."

Mister Jeff ast me, "Did he come for you to go to church?" I sayed, "I ain't going to meeting, my corns hurts me too bad." He sayed, "He's gone then?" and I sayed, "Gone, now, but you ain't seed the last of Vern." Then Mister Jeff say Miss Amelia want him to find out what is the matter and don't anybody care I have did burned the dinner and the cake, but they care about what is the matter and have he or her or Miss Inga did something wrong? So I sayed, No, they have not, that something just been on my mind that's settled now. Then he look up quick knowing it have to be something about Vern, what I give him, or me not going to meeting. I sayed, "What the young peoples do is what they is going to do and I am too old to take part. I have give all I can. Tell Miss Amelia everything going to be the way it was befo'."

Then Mister Jeff up like a shot. I thought he had did seed something out in the yard. I didn't seed nothing. The ground could be turned soon and I sayed, "Carry us up to the Western Auto. We could be picking us out some seeds." But Mister Jeff already going out saying, "I won't be here come springtime, after all."

"But why the train?"

Amy thought of her mother and father asking why take two days when she could get there in a few hours. She could not have explained it was because she did not want to go. They would have asked, then, the expected, Why go? And she could not have explained. But on the bus, having left Jeff, she had stared out at kudzu vine being beaten frenziedly by the rain, later dashing itself onto Delton's streets, knowing that she had to leave. Two Negroes on the bus had loudly argued and her seat companion, redolent of false-teeth cleanser, leaning close had said, "They're so shortly out of Africa, you know, we're not safe." Turning away, Amy had thought more resolutely that she was going.

Spring was a fantasy, the conglomerate colors of the countryside, swiftly viewed from the train, were like a carnival, with redbud and forsythia and jonquils fusing, though nothing of the startling sweetness of the outdoors disturbed the stale air in the sleeping coach. In New York, the intense explosion of the season was sidewalks filled. Under striped umbrellas, like fairytale mushrooms, men sold hot dogs, their signs also reading Bagels. Feeling she had plunged into a new life, Amy determined to try everything; though, parsimoniously, she held close her purse pretending she must be careful of money. She had decided to accept only income from stocks in her name. Then, at the last moment, relenting, she took a large check from her father. The spring wind now was chill and blew cinders along the street.

Sitting in a taxi, Amy tried to recall Nancy, her college roommate, and could remember only someone faceless who always wore plaid shorts bicycling. When Nancy had written that she was moving from her parent's uptown apartment, downtown to Greenwich Village, Amy had decided to join her. Nancy had written that she was not even going home for weekends, which Amy had felt showed true independence.

Now, she felt pressed in upon by small worries, riding along, and was disappointed to find she could not yet meet every situation with the aplomb she wanted. The phrase "cool as a cucumber" went through her mind. With suitcases falling over onto her and nibbling a cuticle, she worried about how much to tip the driver and whether Nancy would be at home to let her in; if not, how she was going to manage her luggage alone? She had foolishly expected, in her first moment of freedom, to be without confusions. Instead, she was filled with small ones. Staring out at muddled streets, Amy wondered whether she had made a mistake to leave home. Perhaps her father did love her and maybe her mother had meant something besides what she had said. "Amy, if you go away, I'll never get you into Junior League," Edith had cried despairingly.

"In New York for a visit, young lady?" the taxi driver asked. He waited comfortably behind his wheel while Amy dragged her suitcases to the sidewalk. "To get a job," she said. "Good luck to you," he said. She tipped him too much, not only because she was fearful of not giving enough, but because she wanted to feel one of all the small working people up against the world.

Her new residence she thought marvellously depressing, with haphazard and dented garbage cans lining the sidewalk in front. The building seemed squeezed in as an afterthought to fill up space between two larger ones. Not only were the mailbox slots inside glassless, the foyer could hold only one suitcase at a time. Nancy's white card, in one slot, stood out from the others, clean and engraved. Having buzzed, Amy was admitted through a second door. Propping it open, she dragged her suitcases from the sidewalk into the hall, expecting Nancy to run helpfully down the stairs. When only silence came, she started up, dragging the heaviest bag. Random lights gave the stairwell a dim, dirtyish and appropriate air, but Amy hoped there were not roaches or rats. Rounding the first landing, she was disappointed that a baby cried behind an apartment door and that there were cooking smells and the sounds of tables being set. She had expected all the boring details of the everyday world to have disappeared. Down

the roundy stairwell, making no move but to lean over the bannister, Nancy cried, "Don't give up! There are only three more
flights."

Amy, banging her suitcase a step at a time, calculated how
many more trips she would have to make. Nancy's accent had
sounded much more nasal and Northern than she had remembered. Nancy did cry and dance when Amy arrived breathlessly.
Hugging her, Nancy shouted, at last they were free! They went
into the apartment, where she hoped Amy would not mind that
she had gone ahead and decorated. Nancy announced proudly
that she had made the curtains and bedspreads herself.

"Oh," Amy said, looking around, "I didn't know you *sewed.*"
Catching the slighting tone, Nancy said that indeed she did sew
and making it more obvious she pulled slightly out of its corner
her shiny walnut-cased machine. What else, Amy wondered, in
this first moment of coexistence, could she have said except that
she liked the furnishings? But, regrettably, the apartment looked
cozy. The curtains and bedspreads were all chintz when she had
envisioned filling it more modernly, with colorful burlap curtains
and sling chairs. Nancy had lacquered a coffee table pink. On it
were overlapping copies of *Vogue.* Nancy beamed at having co-
ordinated the apartment, carrying pink from room to room. Amy
was taken around to see a fuzzy pink toilet seat cover and dish-
towels with hand-screened pink carnations. In the bedroom to
which she was assigned were pink velvet accent pillows. "You
don't mind having the alcove?" Nancy asked. Glancing at the
things Amy had brought up, she added, as if it were not an afterthought, that Amy would have more space for her typewriter.

Later, when Amy set her emptied teacup on the pink coffee
table, Nancy immediately whisked it to the sink and rinsed the
cup. Rightly and immediately, Amy guessed the main thought in
Nancy's mind was getting married. After dinner they settled into
an awkward silence, until Nancy decided to phone her family.

Listening to the conversation, Amy grew lonesome thinking of the unavailability of her own parents. Nancy, in bed, fell instantly asleep. Lying in her own bed and hearing hatefully the even breathing, Amy decided only brainless people did not lie awake a long time, thinking. Wide-eyed, she stared at the chintz ruffles shadowed here on the wall, like the ones in her bedroom at home. The difference was that at home, her curtains were reflected by moonlight, and here a street light shone annoyingly into her window. She almost listened for the smooth running of Edith's heavy curtains along their antiqued rod. Young men passed along the street and yelled curses, in loud voices, more vile than any she had ever heard. Amy, smiling, thought that at last she was beginning to live, that each new experience would add up to some large meaning of her life.

The next evening, Nancy sauntered in and announced without the faintest embarrassment that she had taken a job with a friend of her father's, in an advertising agency. Advertising! Amy thought. She trudged the city endlessly that day looking for a job. That, she thought, had been the point, to struggle and to poke about in sections of the city she would not see otherwise. Her suspicions about Nancy were further confirmed when she told about the "darling boy" who worked in the office. Amy realized sadly that Nancy had less sense of adventure than anyone she had ever known.

Every day, roaming the city, Amy thought with disgust of Nancy safely in her Madison Avenue office. Determined to live a life different from what she had known, she sought out shoddy places for lunch. A tiny cafeteria on Fourteenth Street smelled of cabbage and soured sponges used to wipe the tables. But the oily food was cheap. Inside, someone always was asleep or drunk, which was picturesque. Then one day, the counterman leaned over the steam table, with a sweating face, and said, "Honey, one of your stockings is falling down."

Amy stood stock-still, mortified, while an old man, eating soup, looked up at her dumbly and questioning, What was she going to do? She wondered even if there were a ladies room whether she would dare use it. She thought suspicious diseases came from bathrooms. Certainly they might in a place like this. A sense of unbelonging as well as one of embarrassment flooded her. Turning, Amy went out with a stricken face. On the street, she tried to straighten the stocking, but several people watched. She then went on, with it slightly droopy. Standing on a corner, she ate a dry bagel for lunch, wondering if her life were to be forever a multiplicity of confusing details.

To take a job meant she might make a mistake; suppose, accepting one position, she heard later of something better? Her days continued to be filled with job-hunting. To give them more point, she began keeping her diary again, convincing herself that every minor incident would eventually have importance.

Monday. I took the wrong subway and couldn't get off until I got all the way to Queens!

Tuesday. I've been discriminated against! I answered an ad for a stock girl at a famous hat shop, and they said they preferred Negro girls! That should make a great short story but should that be the beginning, the middle or the ending?

When Nancy was told the incident, she stared at Amy blankly. Why did she want to apply for so menial a job? Pitying her, Amy knew there was no sense trying to explain. Nancy went regularly to her office, then out with the "darling boy," leaving Amy alone most evenings. She began to sleep late every morning, telling herself, the first one, that she had a sore throat. But the week stretched out, and the next began. Only desultorily afterward did she search for a job, infrequent afternoons. She often reread the letter from Jeff her mother had sent, keeping it in her pocketbook always with her. Readdressed in her mother's handwriting, the letter, to Amy's surprise, held no cautions or explanations when she really longed for her mother to have advised, See him, or don't!

Nancy's engagement was announced, and Amy thought, haughtily, she could certainly find someone better than Nancy had. When the young man came to dinner, she asked if he had read *Reconstruction*. Without glancing at Nancy, she tried to pretend it was not surprising her fiancé had never heard of Almoner. "He's a writer Amy knows," Nancy said lamely.

The young man never understood exactly why, but, always uncomfortable around Amy, he would not come back to dinner. He then took Nancy out and Amy was more alone. She had a few dates with college friends, but they all ended in mutual lack of interest. But somewhere in the whole Village wasn't there an artistic person she could go out with, or even marry? A painter or an architect. Someone in a creative field. A young Almoner, destined for fame. Though she would not marry the first person who asked her, as Nancy had. If only Nancy had been honest about her intentions from the beginning, she would not have a roommate sewing a trousseau. She had needed someone as interested as she in finding out meanings, Amy thought.

The apartment's silence began to be oppressive. Nancy stayed at her parents' on weekends. Amy, growing tired of wandering about the Village, some mornings washed underwear and straightened her drawers. She feared that when she was not there, Nancy had peeked into them, horrified. Opening them herself, she sometimes had felt overwhelmed and shut them quickly. She understood for the first time people committing suicide, particularly older people whose lives had come to nothing. She bought two goldfish, but it was enervating to change their water so frequently. Was it possible she would go on like this, grow old, and her life would never change?

She wanted to explore further, but wandering about the city as an occupation had lagged. She decided to get up at some un-known hour, like six A.M. Then, pigeons fearlessly strolled the Village streets. But, sadly, there was no sense of a day beginning. Amy missed grass wet underfoot, the smell of earth, though bits of sky she could see had a moist look, and there were fewer people. A man making flapjacks in a restaurant window decided her to have breakfast there. Hopefully, she tried to joke with the counterman when he set down her orange juice. He returned to the kitchen without his surly expression changing. Never would she be capable of light, bantering chatter, Amy conceded, staring into the juice which tasted like orange soda pop. A young man with a reddish, crinkly beard sat opposite, his blue jeans interest-ingly smeared with paint. He certainly must be an artist. Amy decided immediately afterward that he had great depth. She had to have courage, for once; direct her life and meet him. Leaning to see the title of the book he was reading, Amy said, "Excuse me, but I see you like Henry Miller."

Amelia said, "What are you doing in the closet so long?" and came toward it. Having huddled there, Inga came out with her face disarranged, sadly waving the pink straw hat.

"Looking for this," she said, and would have wondered how Amelia knew where she was, except that Amelia knew every-thing. "I'm going to sit in the hammock."

There were limits to things, Amelia thought. The sadness on Inga's face was one. Amelia felt keyed up by the April weather, and though not sure for what, she liked to think for life itself. Birds were throaty in the flowering bushes, her bulbs were com-ing up, nothing could be sweeter than tuberoses in moist dirt, and there were baby rabbits in the pine copse. Why couldn't Inga turn her thoughts to spring?

"What's the matter?" Amelia said.

"He's going to New York."

"He always does when a book's finished." Inga's drawn look was not going to take away her own joy in the day. "Just look at this day," Amelia said. "Go on and sit in the hammock, don't worry about freckling."

As Inga put on the pink hat her wedding ring shone in the light. Amelia looked down at her own ringless hand, thinking not only would Inga require increasing care, but that she required, still, too many explanations. She had been irritated, only yesterday, when she mentioned that the old hotel on the edge of town had been a hospital during the war. Inga had said, "The Vurld Var?" She had cried, "The Civil War!"

Inga, without shading her eyes, looked at the day. "In April, where I came from," she said, "people still ski."

But skiing was something she had never known, so Amelia had no interest in that. Imagining was not her forte. Then suddenly realizing that imagining was Jeff's business, she felt dumbfounded. She had given his work short shrift all along. Now he was leaving, and she was sorry about both things. Saying what she believed would not help Inga, and Amelia said, "Jeff probably doesn't even know that girl's up there."

"He'd have found out the same way we did, through the paper," Inga said.

"He doesn't read the society page," Amelia said. "The only mention of it was buried at the bottom of that column about her father opening a dancing school. Jeff got those things out for the cleaner. To be put away for the winter."

"He's packing them now," Inga said.

"He's always had to go to New York when a book's finished," Amelia said. She was sorry he had disappointed Jessie again about the garden. And all along, she felt Jeff had not thought enough about going. She ought to be able to delay him.

At cold supper on Sunday night, Amelia said, "Dear Brother, are you going to New York just when you're getting your old-maid sister off your hands?" The blush of flowers at the windows seemed no more pink than his face, or the ham he was eating.

"Is this an announcement about you and Latham?" Inga said.

"Unless you can think of somebody else for me to marry," Amelia said.

"This is a surprise. When?" Jeff said, quietly putting down his knife and fork. Handy it was already April. "June," Amelia said. "Isn't that the month for blushing brides?"

From within the deep twilight in the kitchen, she heard Jessie murmur, "Hmmm-mm." No one else seemed to hear. Maybe Jessie only thought of the washing and ironing she had done for Jeff, now to be unpacked. Inga must be thinking of the word *unpack*, too; she looked in the land of the living, at last. But did Inga expect to undo in two months what she had spent all these years doing? She probably had little imagination, too, while the girl would be more like Jeff, Amelia supposed.

The house was invaded by a slow green twilight with a quality that could kill, it was so beautiful and so intense. Amelia suddenly felt the newness of aching over nebulous things, like love and growth and loneliness. Everyone sat still; their faces around the table struck newly by the yellow-green light. Though each might want the moment broken, Amelia knew she was the only one crass enough to do it.

"I hope you'll be here for all the festivities, Jeff," she said, wondering what possibly they would be.

"Of course," he said, putting down his napkin. "I must see my little sister married. I'll give her away, gladly."

Inga's eyes, watching him leave the room, turned the light startled blue of the Dutch iris, just beginning to bloom. Amelia's ample chest heaved as she sighed and wished she might console everyone in the world at once. Who did not need it? But finishing her custard, she felt a sense of satisfaction like a cat having eaten, figuratively licked her paws. She thought of Latham's first wife, Idabel. The way she had their house arranged would be all right with her, and they would keep Marguerite, the Negro woman who lived out back behind the house. Latham seemed fond of her, and she had been with him almost as long as they had had Jessie.

"Let's sit on the porch," Amelia said. "And enjoy the evening."

Inga lay in the hammock. She had a look still somewhat lost, but happier. Among the evening sounds, they heard Jeff thumping upstairs, taking his suitcases back to the attic. Amelia listened and felt confident that tomorrow evening, after Latham had had his little drink before dinner, she could persuade him he had proposed.

And when they were at dinner, she thought never had anybody seemed as picked up by a drink as Latham. The nice thing was he never seemed to need a second drink. "Latham," she said, "I've been thinking. And you're right. We ought to get married." She said consolingly when he looked up that they would have to wait till June. She had legal things to get straight and would need to buy a few clothes. She spoke so rapidly on and on that Latham kept looking confused. Amelia never gave him time enough to ask himself when he had suggested getting married. She thought his strong point was that he would do what she wanted, without fuss.

When she got home, that night, she gave his hand a good squeeze.

"Now, you just behave yourself," she said, "or I'll put the wedding off even longer."

Latham went along the path between his house and Marguerite's cabin behind it. Her light was on, and he gave their signalling knock. "Come," she said. When he told her, Marguerite agreed there was no sense his staying alone in his great big house.

"Miss Almoner might turn out to be a good woman. Sharper than Miss Idabel?" she asked. Latham said he had thought before of cutting a door to the cabin, which could not be seen from the house. He would do it. Marguerite, complacent, agreed. No other change was about to take place in her life.

Deftly, he filched a dime tip from beneath another customer's saucer and set it as payment by his coffee. He looked up at the blonde who had spoken and saw that she had not noticed. "Yes," Tony said. "I like Miller. Why; do you?"

The worried look already on Amy's face deepened. She could give no definite answer. Twirling a piece of hair around her finger, she said, "I've never been able to decide whether I do or not."

They introduced themselves. Amy tried to tell Tony her feelings about Miller; but partly out of nervousness at having spoken to him first, she was not clear. Tony, unnoticeably, was looking at her clothes, the scrubbed quality of her face, and guessing that she had not been in the Village very long, he labelled her Southern and high class. He had seen her wallet was loaded when she paid for her breakfast and moved over to the stool next to her.

They agreed the coffee here tasted like the bottom of a bird cage, but shoved their empty cups toward the surly attendant, who filled them again. When Amy reached for sugar her arm accidentally brushed Tony's. His arm was covered with curly reddish hair, which had little flecks of paint beneath them. She had found out he was a painter. This accidental brushing against him sent a shivery thrilling feeling through her. She had a nice sensation, but also one as if something with light legs, like a spider, had run along her arm. Tony thrust his face so close she could smell coffee on his breath, asking what she did.

Unless you had published something, Amy felt you should not call yourself a writer, though in the Village that seemed not to matter. People announced professions, even if they only dabbled in them at home alone. Tony had said, he had never exhibited any paintings. Amy, however, was hesitant saying, "I'm a writer. I mean, I want to be a writer, but I don't write much. I haven't published anything."

"Who has?" Tony asked nonchalantly.

"But I'm looking for a job," she said.

"Why? You don't have to have one, do you?" His eyes insinuatingly travelled her from head to toe.

She felt as always ashamed of not being poor. Those piercing, fathoming eyes would know if she lied. Amy lowered her head to mumble, "No." Bending over his arm stretched along the counter, Tony swung an indolent leg. He looked at her from this half-reclining position. "Why," he said, "do you want a job if you don't have to have one?"

Not really knowing, Amy shrugged. "Isn't that just what people do?"

"Not here," he said. "Where you came from, probably. But didn't you come here not to be like them?" He motioned a boneless-looking hand toward the street. Activity had begun, and people hurried as if toward shelter down toward a subway entrance and disappeared. Amy, having twirled around on her stool to look out, now twirled slowly back to face the counter. She felt lazy sitting here with nothing to do. But of course she said, "God, no, I don't want to be like them."

"Then forget a job." Tony seemed about to beat his chest. "I'm a writer, too," he said. "I'm writing a poem about Queen Elizabeth. She kills me. I don't know why. It begins, Oh Queen!" He threw an arm wildly into the air, but grinned. "That's as far as I've been able to get."

He laughed at himself, which made him all right, Amy thought, grinning back. She could not criticize him when she never finished anything, either. But, frantic, she thought it was too easy to live as Tony did. Something was wrong, and she looked around as if she might see exactly what.

"The whole publishing bit is a racket," Tony was saying. "Try to get an agent, for instance. You have to know somebody first. Then, you don't need an agent."

"New people are discovered," Amy said shyly. "I know one writer who made it on his own. He says the thing to do is work hard."

By being decisive, Tony reduced her to silence. Success came from knowing the right people, he insisted. At that moment, several people, who looked like bums, paused outside the front window, waving to him. Appearing drunk, they were much older, but Tony greeted them like friends. All this impressed Amy, who felt in herself such an inability to mix. She gave Tony a look bordering on admiration.

"Why don't you write something sexy?" he said, turning from the window. "That's the only way to make any money." When Amy was silent, he drew his eyebrows together, looking at her from beneath them. "What's the matter? Don't you know anything about sex?" He noticed that she leaned forward against her arms, seeing him glance at her breasts. Probably scared to death of getting laid, and wanted to be, he thought.

Amy, twisting a strand of hair around one finger again, made her smile enigmatic, which Tony guessed. He kept on swinging his leg indolently and waiting for an answer. To avoid one, Amy looked out the plate-glass window, as if distracted by something beyond it. She succeeded in drawing Tony's stare past her. He saw nothing of interest in the street.

Amy's heart ached for the blind newsman with a scruffy dog, and for all the worn-looking people going to and from the subway, who must have boring jobs. Yet, here she sat lonesomely, and what then was the answer? The counterman might be surly because he had such terrible acne; why wouldn't his parents have taken him to a dermatologist? She thought about the people she had seen first going down into the subway, now emerging uptown into various lives. Tony seemed content, pulling paper napkins out of a holder. It terrified her that, having so much time left to live, she had no idea what was to happen. Naïvely, she fell back on what represented constant security, that her father and Jeff would always be there for her to go to. She thought again of the subway travellers, looked out at people on the street, at those inside the restaurant. Here we all are, she thought, which posed itself as the possible opening of a novel. She folded her hands neatly into her lap. Tony paused a moment before pulling out another paper napkin.

"Well," Amy said, filling the pause, "here we are."

"We'd better go," Tony said, looking around. "People are beginning to wait for seats." He got up, poking fingertips into the diminished pockets of his shrunken jeans. He had no change. If Amy could pay for his second coffee, he would pay her back later. She gave that no thought and put down the money. On the street, she was thrilled when Tony spoke to several well-known Village characters who had intrigued her from a distance. She thought Tony humane and longed herself to be a great humanitarian, but was too shy to speak to people. He would have made friends with the people in the Fourteenth Street cafeteria. He would have had a ready joke when the counterman spoke about her stockings. Sunlight, blustering thinly down upon them in the crevices that were streets, gave Tony's heavy-lidded eyes the pinkish tinge of a rabbit's. Exhausted, he could hardly keep his eyes open. He had been up all night painting.

"Why, that's wonderful!" Amy cried. She thought him very serious about his work. It was unusual to be up so early. Most people she had met here slept until noon, at least. "Do you paint every day," she asked, "or just when you feel like it?"

"When I feel like it," Tony said, yawning.

He walked in a ragged way, and Amy skipped several times to keep pace, confiding, "I've always felt writing should come out in one enormous passionate rush. That it should be all just feeling!" She threw out her arms, as if to float off her feet. "This friend of mine though, who's a writer, says writing's hard. You need to think of it as a job, something you go after every day."

"He sounds full of crap."

"He publishes."

Stymied a moment, Tony said, "Crap, or good stuff?"

"Very good stuff."

"What's right for him," Tony said, again in his decisive way, "doesn't have to be right for you."

"That's true," Amy said slowly. She could not concede that Jeff's life had ever been as hard as hers; what he said might not apply.

Along the sidewalk, Tony's leather sandals made a sound, insolent and sloppy. He stopped at a corner to slap himself about on various pockets. He not only had no change, he seemed to have forgotten his wallet altogether. Could he borrow money for cigarettes?

Opening her wallet, Amy heard one of her mother's earliest warnings: Never go out without some mad money. If she went anywhere with Tony again, probably she would need some. Amy put down his forgetfulness to his being artistic. She made a comparison to Jeff's wearing shirts with frayed collars, which he seemed never to notice. Her father made a point of carrying enormous amounts of money wherever he went. When Amy left for New York, he mentioned a rating with Dun and Bradstreet. Should she run into trouble of any kind, ask people to look it up, and anyone would cash her check. His look had been like a child at a moment of unexpected accomplishment, or a retriever laying a bird at the hunter's feet. She had tried to praise her father but praise for the accomplishment of money stuck in her throat.

Thanking him, she had said she would remember, without understanding Dun and Bradstreet.

Tony had bought cigarettes at the corner stand and stood, blowing out grey-blue smoke rings. One eyebrow quirked, he wore a tilted half-smile. He cocked a hand to his waist and bent toward her, half as if to take her in his arms, half as if to treat her roughly. That this stance and the look were familiar ran like a melody through Amy's mind. He spoke, and she never quite settled on what movie star, or what movie, he brought to mind. Had she lived through this before? The instant his eyes narrowed behind the smoke rings and his voice became huskier, she had known those two things were coming.

"Come on up to my room," he said. "I'll show you my work."

Amy shook a dubious head, undecided whether she knew him well enough. To stand on ceremony was not the usual etiquette in the Village. She ached all over at being able to do nothing to change some dead cold thing in the center of herself.

"I can't come," she said.

She was terrified at the thought of Tony's going away, realizing how miserable and alone and unhappy she had been. He seemed the epitome of all she had come to the Village to find, spare-framed and slightly odorous as he was. "I do hope you'll ask me another time," she said.

"Well, ah dew hope you'll come if ah dew," he said, holding up mockingly an absent lorgnette. "Would you do me the honor of accompanying me to a free concert in Washington Square tomorrow evening, instead?"

Knowing she had blushed to the roots of her hair, Amy pretended to laugh at herself, as well as at his mocking her, and she made the date. They drifted about together in the next few weeks, attending any free art exhibit or concert. Occasionally, they sat in a bar and had beer, usually sharing the cost. When Tony walked home with her, Amy could not ask him inside.

Nancy was always up past midnight sewing, or her fiancé was there (if Amy was going to be out for most of the evening). The two sat around as if they were already married, Amy thought. She would have been embarrassed for Tony to know she had a roommate who was making a trousseau.

Tony began to wash more before coming to meet her, which touched Amy hopelessly. His hair would be slicked down boyishly and still damp about the edges. His face would have a sheen like a rubbed apple, and his shirts would be usually clean. She was glad he kept on paint-smeared jeans. It made her feel a part of things that Tony was recognizable as an artist. Outwardly at least, she seemed abandoned and free. A couple of times, she bought wine, which they drank beneath a tree, near the archway to the Village, watching lights come on. Then streets appeared awhirl with color, like a carnival. Above the buildings, pale pink tinges of evening disappeared into dark rooftops. For several nights, a block was roped off for an Italian street fair, which they attended.

During the time she was seeing him, Tony would sometimes drop from sight. She would be walking along the street and unexpectedly he would reappear. He would be exhausted and his eyes as red-rimmed as the first time she had ever met him. He would have been up all night painting, which sent a thrill through Amy.

Continuing to read job ads in the paper, she would convince herself it was too late to apply, that the job sounded so good it was taken, or either it did not sound good enough to bother with. She felt often too languid to go out to dinner, or to breakfast, and bought a hot plate. Usually, she ate canned hash, though it tasted like dog food. Amy continually started short stories and wrote fitfully in the diary. Whenever Tony reappeared, she was enormously glad to see him.

Looking more haggard than usual, he came around a corner one day to stand squarely in front of her. "How's your work going?" she said.

"I've gotten some good stuff in the last few days. Come up. I'll show you."

Allowing herself to be taken by the arm, Amy passed through sunshiny streets as if dreaming. Tony seemed now her oldest friend. He was desperate for sleep and clung on to her. He stumbled over a sidewalk crack and she tightened her hold, not wanting anyone to think "the artist" was drunk. His building was entrancing and far worse than hers. At the end of each hall as they climbed stairs were tiny smelly bathrooms, and from one an old man came shambling, his fly open. This was the first cold-water building she had ever been in! Amy exclaimed. On the old man, she turned such a beatific smile, he stopped dead and stared, thinking her strange. Not only did the hallways smell of toilets but also of the wet-bottomed bursting sacks of garbage sitting outside doors. The main room of Tony's apartment faced the street. Amy, going toward the window, heard the door shut with a firm click behind her and stood knotting her hands, longing to say something impressive.

"What a great light for painting," she said. But she was vague about directions and was it northern light that was supposed to be best? Having spoken, she looked at him uncertainly.

Tony seemed uninterested in whether or not the light was good and muttered that it was adequate. Having made his way through the room's clutter, he sat yawning in a broken-bottomed armchair. Amy wonderingly appraised the number of empty gallon jugs of a cheap wine about the room; paper cups, some still wet, were scattered everywhere, squashed and stained red. Otherwise, the room was scarcely furnished and was bland, except for paintings stacked in a corner and for several six-foot canvases near the window. In several places on them, paint appeared still wet. And about the room as if someone had tossed confetti were specks of paint, denying the window its full view and giving pattern to the floor. Watching Amy look at his pictures, Tony slumped onto his fist. "Those pictures look any different from stuff you see in galleries, now?"

"I don't really know much about painting." Without criterion to judge, Amy said, "They seem good," and the abstracts were similar to many in small galleries along the Village's streets.

"Just decide whether you like them or not," he said, jabbing at her indecisiveness, knowing she was vulnerable.

"I do like to know the meaning of a picture. I don't understand modern painting," she said, digging in her heels a little.

"Nobody who painted them knew the meaning, either!" Tony said gleefully. He managed to raise his head from his chin prop. "I get a bunch over, we drink wine all night and throw paint on the canvases. I name the pictures. Great idea?"

Amy turned slowly, indicating her understanding. "You don't paint them yourself," she said flatly.

"Why, when I can do it this way, and get the same effect?" He got up from his chair sleepily. "Know the old saying about leaving monkeys in a room with a typewriter long enough, and they'd write a novel." He had unbuttoned his shirt and came up behind Amy to put his arms about her. His breath was warm as a puppy's against her ear; the lingering smell of wine on him seemed to intoxicate her. Amy's heart beat fearfully. Having closed her eyes, she opened them quickly, as Tony pulled her back against him. There, she felt his intimate parts and was motionless. He straightened one arm past her, to point. "That one is Midwest Snowfield. I only handed out white and blue paint. Then I added that little rose color in the bottom corner. The sun going down."

"Oh. That was a good idea," Amy said hopefully. "Are you ever going to paint them entirely yourself?"

He drew out a shrug, enabling him to rub more intimately against her. Though her impulse was to move in the same slow

198

way, Amy held still. Holding her firmly, Tony set her more securely between his legs. "The one next to it is Mardi Gras," he said. "All the different colors. Get the feeling?"

"Yes, the dots are all people, or just their faces, mingling and making a crowd."

"That. Anything." Tony turned her around, his thumbs pressing her shoulders painfully. "Relax. Or shall I paint you a nice, upper-middle-class picture we'll call Inhibited?"

"But I'm not," she said, her voice holding disbelief.

"Then, hold still." His face thrust close had again the half-tilted smile, the quirked eyebrow.

Inquiring, Amy's mind settled on its being a French movie, and actor, which made the look familiar. Trying to piece together the scene, she wondered what the heroine had said at such a moment. No words came to her until a moment later, she said, "I like your Midwest Snow—"

"Oh, for God sakes," Tony said. "Are we going to bed, or not?"

Amy did not want the decision left up to her; how possibly could she blurt out, Yes! Sensibly, Tony was steering her toward his second room, a small alcove, which turned out to hold only a thin mattress with mussed sheets. Having been pushed gently toward it, Amy sat thinking happily of the scene, the picturesqueness of the mattress on the floor and of a cold-water building. Behind her, faint sounds and movements made her aware that Tony was undressing. She could not take off her clothes in front of him. Having no other idea what to do, she sat clasping her knees. He sighed and settled under the top sheet. Feeling him stare at her, Amy looked at the ceiling, which badly needed painting.

"Are you going to stay dressed?" he said.

Her fingers were stiff as she began to fumble about with her clothes, wanting desperately to take his attention elsewhere. Always, he had tried to convince her of Marx's ideas. Now might be a good time to seem more receptive. Blankly, Amy could not think of any questions. Having resisted his conversations before, he might suspect she was delaying. He would know she was afraid. She knew also he would not be interested in the subject either, at the moment. Glancing back at him once, she tried not to think how hairy his armpits were. His arms were flung above his head, the back of one hand in the palm of the other. Sighing heavily, and as if glad at last for sleep, Amy got in beneath the cover.

Immediately, Tony lowered his hand and gave her slip strap a flip. "Are you going to keep that on?"

"There's a kind of draft. I'm cold."

She accepted reluctantly his assistance in removing her pants. The next instance his mouth opened over her closed one. "Scared, Kansas City?" he said teasingly.

"Delton," she managed, foolishly and with difficulty. Tony's tongue had sought her mouth.

He gave a little groan, which Amy realized had nothing to do with her telling him for the umpteenth time where she had come from. Bearing his weight, she withdrew as flat as possible toward the floor. Past Tony's ear, the grey ceiling, strangely, had streaks of a lovely shade of violet that would be from water leaking from an apartment above, or from rain on the roof. She tried to remember if Tony were on the top floor. Staring at the blankness above her, she thought how her father went out with women who were not very nice, but how disappointed he would be to know where his daughter was. Into Tony's nearest ear, she whispered, "I've never gone this far before."

He reared back to look down at her. "You don't have to say that. I couldn't care less."

"I know. It's true."

"Why now?" He looked mystified.

Amy was sorry he did not conceive of her caring for him.

Though she was not in love with him, Amy wished that Tony thought she was. "I don't know exactly. Does it matter?"

"Not to me," he said straightforwardly. "If it won't to you, afterward. I don't want a lot of tears."

"Oh no, there won't be," she promised, all but crossing her heart.

Almost in the same instant he moved off her again, Tony fell asleep. Her hands folded a little uncalmly on her stomach, Amy stared again at the ceiling, wondering if a novel might come out of this experience. How was she to justify it, otherwise?

A fly, settling on her nose sometime later, woke her. She was surprised to have slept at all. And she woke and found herself, with a quiet sense of terror, alone. Deserted by Tony after the act, she had not expected also this desertion. She did not move and then heard, in relief, the click of a cabinet door in the next room. Her clothes went on quickly, as if there were a raid. She could not face Tony watching her dress. In the next room, he sat in the windowsill, eating peanut butter with a knife. When Amy appeared, he offered her a glob, holding the knife tip toward her. From the doorway as she shook her head, her expectations faded. She had waked with the desire to call him endearing names and had envisioned their daylight meeting as one between honeymooners.

When Amy turned down the peanut butter, Tony stuck the knife tip into his mouth and stared silently. Amy felt herself the last guest at a party which had lasted too long, or she might form a trio, the other two people wanting to be alone. He gave her these feelings, staring silently. Then, she went toward her purse, on the table in the middle of the room, and said, "I guess I'd better be going," and picked up the purse. Something lacking ought to be said. Edith's voice came back coaxingly, Always remember to say you had a nice time. . . .

"See you around," Tony said. "I'm going out to the Island a couple of days. I'll drop by your place when I get back."

Amy yearned not to leave and toward many things for which she had no names. Even today, she could not think what to do, yet Tony was going away with friends. How had he made them? The details of life were myriad when they were too complex to be dealt with. Besieged by doubts, she went to the door and opened it, then closed it after a lingering glance at Tony's expressionless face.

Her heels gave back hollow raps on the hall floor. The bannister she held to was grimy. Opaque with dirt, the glass panels of the front door reflected nothing as she approached them. Though stepping out onto the stoop, Amy felt she must have a more womanly and a more worldly look. Certainly, her round-necked and flower-sprigged dress was too prim, too reminiscent of home, too childish, and another instinct had been sharpened. Before opening her purse and looking inside, she knew her money was going to be missing.

With unsurprised eyes, Amy stared at the pocket of the wallet, missing fifty dollars. Her first inclination was to avoid the incident and once she would have followed it. The money was not the bother so much, for she was always sorry Tony had so little. But fearing confronting him with the theft, she would make herself do it. Going back upstairs, she was willful and shaking. Her voice was a little steely, to be kept free of wavering. She knocked and walked in almost immediately.

Though Tony had not moved, he had not been expecting her. The knife tip, about to be inserted into the jar, remained touching the glass rim, landing there with a slight ring. His elbows only dropped slightly toward his sides. He looked secured to the windowsill and hopeless about his situation. The apartment's interior then leapt, at once, to her mind's eye. Amy accused him of taking her money, and Tony's voice denying it was tired but not at all angry.

Politely and evenly, Amy had said, "I know you took money from me. You think I don't need it, but I do. Please, give it back."

He said, "I don't know what you're talking about. I didn't take any money from you."

"I know you did, Tony."

"You must have dropped it when we were out."

"I didn't. It doesn't matter, keep it. I just wanted you to know I knew you took it."

"I didn't take any money from you," he said.

"Have it your way." She closed the door.

Then when she emerged again onto the street, the day was ecstatically fine. Smells everywhere along the street were delicious. At a candy store the doors stood open, and from an Italian restaurant warm rich food smells floated along the street. Even a shoeshine rag, flipped outward upon the air by a boy as she passed, had a tar, pine scent, mindful of trees. While considering whether she felt cheap, Amy thought that the setting for her experience had been perfect. Again, she saw the mattress, bread-thin on the floor, and all the interior of the cold-water apartment.

Before now, she had been cowered by girls who dressed appropriately for the Village, by those who worked in its shops, selling handmade leather accessories and silver jewelry. The latter, geometrically shaped, displayed on invisibly thin wire, hung from the ceilings of rooms, like stars. Today, with no hesitation, Amy bought a leather purse and thong-tied flat sandals, though her arches ached when she tried them on. She selected tight jersey blouses in brilliant but oddly matched colors. Paying by check, she further forgave Tony, for to be in rebellion was expensive, and how did people manage who had no families to give them money? She was bothered about not having a job, even if that were a middle-class idea as Tony had said. She lingered before windows where Help Wanted signs were pasted. Eventually, she was depressed by the sight of her pale feet in the sloppy sandals, her toes dirty from soot. The leather pocketbook was deep as a horse's feedbag and difficult to fill up, though she put in unused cosmetics from the dime store and a bulky amount of Kleenex. Writers ought to be able, on the spot, to jot down observations, she thought, and added a notebook. Her first entry read:

Today, I saw an old woman tottering down the street with blackened eyes. A child wearing a birthday hat came by me, in a car, and tossed confetti, which fell over my hair.

Reading the entry later, Amy could not discern the importance of these events in their lives, as well as in her own. She had nothing to add, after reporting what she saw and filled up moments of unrewarding thought by doodling on the notebook margins.

Another early admonition of Edith's had been never to run after boys. Perhaps that was a middle-class idea, too, but Amy would wait for Tony to get in touch with her. Alone in her apartment, she memorized poetry, to hear a voice aloud in the room and to use hers. Nancy, soon to be married, had moved back to her parents' apartment. Considering buying a canary, Amy knew she would never want to clean the cage. She hated herself for clucking at her goldfish, as if they were babies, hated that she talked to them in a voice people used for responsive puppies. Her days grew longer and emptier. Thinking of ways she might have experiences, she jotted down in her notebook several headings:

> Liquor
> Drugs
> Men
> An affair with a Negro

But what point was there to getting drunk in her apartment by herself? She would not go to a bar alone, nor would she smoke marijuana. She was looking for reality and not trying to escape it, she felt. On the other hand, if she had wanted marijuana, she would not have known how to get it, which was the disappointing point. At a loss, she wondered how to meet Negroes. The ones she encountered here did not seem interested in girls, though how, she wondered, did you meet even them?

One day, wandering, she saw a Room for Rent sign in a window and decided to move. The room was appropriate in that it was too awful for anyone from Delton to see. However, she did miss going out with well-dressed and well-mannered young men, who had money. Quill and Leigh and Billy Walter. She had envisioned their coming often to New York to take her out and, of course, they never had. When she moved, the gloom in her new hallway was almost tangible. In drifts, it came down the unpolished stairs, yellowed by the stained-glass window half-illuminating the landing, and rose in puffs off the dusty carpet, disappeared into faded brown stripes of the wallpaper, renewed itself to fill a bowl for mail, which the tenants left full of bills and other unwanted pieces.

Her landlord was tousled and lame and wore a bitter expression, even accepting fifteen dollars, in advance, for her first week's rent. Sensing her pity, he saw also that Amy was lonesome and feared her wanting to talk. She went up to her room, feeling his rejection in the firmness with which he closed his door. Finding the bed sheets unchanged from the last tenant, Amy could not face the landlord again, nor did she have the inclination to ask for favors. It showed fortitude to crawl in between those sheets; arms along her sides, she lay stiffly, unwittingly thinking the position would ward off bedbugs or diseases. Small and rectangular, the room's yellow walls had faded to a nondescript color. Many sleepless nights, Amy thought about the procession of previous occupants, who might have lain wide-eyed, too. She was no different from any of them. Here, she would be replaced as she had been in her English tutorial. Her college professor, now, probably barely remembered Amy Howard when she had been one of his favorites.

Moving in, Amy had looked into the closet and beneath the bed and searched the dresser drawers, but nothing had been left behind by the room's previous tenant. The same sense of vacancy and lack of personality would remain when she was gone. At home, around her dressing table, she had tacked up pictures of friends and favors from parties. Her mother, or even the cleaning lady, looking in there would think of her, Amy felt.

She dreamed, often now, of leaves rattling and falling and saying they were dying, which was followed by images of snow. Before she could realize them fully, it would be April and spring again, though as quickly, the leaves would be rattling and falling and saying they were dying. Hurry! Hurry! Amy, they cried. To her disgust, she hung back fearfully even in dream, not knowing in which direction she ought to go. Again, she slept late and woke to see in a loft, opposite, women bent over long tables sewing. Guilty at being in bed, she quickly drew down the shade. How did those women reconcile themselves to life in a loft hardly lit, or to their repetitive work? Lost, she nevertheless believed her life on some better track.

Finally, when she came in, the sheets had been changed. Unmistakably, her pillow case had been used to sop up tears, and had someone noticed? Would the person who changed the sheets have looked into her drawers? She thought they had the appearance of a dryer with clothes tumbled to a stop. Had that person wondered why a young girl would choose this room when obviously she could afford better, if they had noted her clothes in the closet and her luggage beneath the bed? Were her sleekly cased typewriter, or the stack of classical novels on the window ledge any clue to her personality, or to normalcy? Obviously, she was not holed up here to read lewd magazines, for instance.

Would the unknown visitor be astute enough to observe hesitation between two worlds? One coat hook held carefully shrunken blue jeans, with an untracked zipper, while another held a dress with a designer's satin label. On the dusty dresser top was a bottle of expensive perfume, next to a ream of cheap canary yellow typing paper. The whole room seemed in a quandary; even the floor slanted. Able to solve only one problem, Amy took the jeans to a tailoring shop across the street.

She had a more ladylike look than the Greek tailor was used to, and as soon as she entered the shop, Amy won him. She spoke politely, or he would not have agreed to fix merely the zipper on a pair of limp blue jeans. Having time, Amy asked questions about him and his country; in common, they desired a warmer climate and a less crowded place than New York. Though he had an abundance of ash-colored hair, and his stomach paunch required him to sit some distance from his machine, the tailor forgot them because of Amy's interest. He asked if she would go with him to a Greek café. Would she like to see belly dancers?

She could have overlooked his being fat and toad-ugly, but it was annoying somehow that he forgot them. And she imagined, rightly, that in the Bronx where he had mentioned living, there was a sunless apartment full of antimacassars crocheted by a plump grey-haired wife. Amy refused his invitation. Miles lay ahead across the shop before she rang the bell, exiting, which she had rung coming in. The tailor bent with a rejected air to his machine, setting in motion its almost continuously turning small wheel. Not to hurt him more, Amy had said that she was a graduate student with no time to spare from her dissertation. Since he was watching, she had to return to her room. The lame landlord's door was always shut, television an unending murmur behind it. Climbing toward her room in the yellowed gloom, Amy began to wonder what good all this silence, and this aloneness, were doing her.

The stairs groaned bending inward. Other roomers went off daily to work. Possibly, it had been the landlord's mother, trying to help the place, who had tacked net curtains over glass panels in the front door. Now, the worn and separating threads were like a spider's web. Shutting her own door, Amy leaned against it in tears, thinking of a young girl who spoke poetry aloud to hear her own voice and talked to goldfish, whose response was to swim soundlessly through a glass castle. If she telephoned someone was that asking directly for help? The strongest people, athletes even, had limits to their endurance, Amy told herself. The need to break the monotony of herself did not mean weakness, did it? Frankly, she wanted to see someone from her own background. Apprehension grew during a long wait. Faintly up and down protective corridors, young men called to one another. Eventually, footsteps stopped by the phone receiver, which she had imagined as dangling. Her voice was weak at first. Then it grew stronger, though evidently not strong enough. For on the other end, Leigh said in exasperation and repeatedly, Hello. Hello. Hello.

"It's me. Guess who."

"Why, Amy," he said, his voice descending.

"I'm in New York looking for a job. Are you surprised?"

"No. I'm more surprised you stayed at home so long. You didn't seem to fit in there. Are you having trouble finding a job? How about your friend, Almoner. I thought he'd give you a leg-up in publishing. What's going on there?"

"Here? Absolutely nothing. You may have heard static in the phone."

"Not there, stupid. With Almoner."

"Oh, nothing. We don't even write any more."

"Just as well. I never believed that was as innocent as you pretended. I watched him look at you. Surely though, he'd help you get a job."

"I don't want to use him."

"Why not? Everybody uses everybody."

"Do I have to be like everybody else?" she questioned.

"Suit yourself. Look, I have to run."

"Oh. A minute. I was thinking about brandy Alexanders, how many we used to drink. Even before dinner! It's sickening to think about now. But, I just feel like doing something again. Can you ever come down from New Haven, for lunch even?"

The pause while Leigh thought of an excuse was obvious. "I have a paper due soon. Then I'm heading up to Canada for a vacation. Maybe in the fall."

She hung on, saying anything that came to mind. "Remember Quill? That boy who went to Princeton and was so fat but got thin? My mother wrote he and his wife are having a baby."

"That's the most interesting news I've heard recently."

"Of course, it's not interesting to you. But it surprised me so. I don't feel old enough to have a baby. I don't know anything myself."

"Listen, girlie. I've really got to run."

When a bell rang distantly, Amy thought of making some snide remark about an ivory tower. "Run then," she said only.

Tony swung around his newel post like a child about a pole, one arm and leg extended wide. As if on alert, his freckles appeared when he grinned. He seemed not surprised to see Amy, standing in the entranceway.

"I was just passing by."

"I came by your place once," he said. "You had moved."

"Oh." She could not hide looking pleased. "No one told you where I had gone?"

"No one knew you. Some people thought they remembered a blond girl, moving."

"I gave the super five dollars. It looks like he could have remembered after that!" She ended on a wail.

"I thought maybe you'd gone back to Kansas City."

"Delton," Amy said firmly. "I've never laid eyes on Kansas City and never hope to."

Tony's look indicated he thought all such places were the same. However, he saw the difference in her and whistled appreciatively. "So, look at you. You look almost as if you belong here, not fresh off the ooold plantation."

Amy squashed down a thought, that to look like everybody one place was the same as looking like everybody someplace else. She only thanked Tony for his approval. Her arches in the flat sandals ached even during the time of his appraisal. She was slightly breathless, the faddish wide leather belt tight at her waist.

"Were you on your way somewhere?"

"Just out," Tony said.

"Oh."

"Why, you want someplace to go?"

"It doesn't make any difference to me."

"I've got an idea you'd like. Want to go to the lesbian bar around the corner? That'll be a new experience for you. I want to see a girl there, who'll help me get a show."

"Tony, great!"

"You want to go?"

"If it's all right."

"It's all right. Damn, though, my blankety sister didn't get off her duff and send me any money this month."

Amy was silent.

Tony said, glancing sidewise, "Well, it's an experience. Maybe some other time."

She took the bait knowingly. "I have enough for a few beers."

She wondered, ushered by Tony to the street, why he expected his sister to send him money. Married to a fireman, she wheedled five dollars now and then from her grocery budget, Tony had said. There was a difference, but she accepted money, and so Amy was silent.

Hesitating at the top of steep stairs leading from the street, she peered down toward the bar, as dank and damp as the basement the room once had been. Sawdust on the floor, wet from spilled drinks, never dried. The little damp sprinkles clung messily and uncomfortably inside her sandals. How she hated the shoes. Going along the street with Tony, she had noticed the duet they made, her slapping heels having the same insolent lazy sound as his. As a cigarette machine loomed ahead, she paused just before Tony asked if she had any change. She pinched it from her coin purse reluctantly.

She was ashamed and remonstrated with herself about being stingy, crossing to the self-service bar with Tony. If he turned out to be a famous artist, then how small she would feel. Still, she was haunted by conventions and her past would not let go. She was embarrassed paying the bartender. He paid her no attention; she might have been faceless, a voice asking for two beers. Undoubtedly Irish, with thick eyebrows and a ruddy complexion, he had a fatherly air: He seemed a judge, too, looking down from a platform where the bar was built. Saying, "Two beers," he set them down with authority.

Why try, her mute eyes straining, to signal she did not belong in this subterranean world any more than he? Her money lay, as if trying to survive, in foamy puddles left by the two overflowed beers. Each carrying one, she and Tony searched for a table.

They were hailed by Anila, a dark heavy girl with a slight accent, who gave Amy a hard handshake, introduced. She then talked animatedly to Tony about his show. Amy noticed how she stared around the room, and having some qualms, she drank her beer and was silent. Though girls danced together, few appeared any different from her, to Amy's surprise.

She wished, a little, someone would notice her. With nothing else to do, she listened to the conversation at the table and was sorry to hear that Tony's prospective show was to be held in the YMCA and that the director was a friend of Anila's. Was the show being held as a favor for her, and not because Tony's work merited one? Having persistently drunk her beer, and now wanting another, Amy did not want to cross the room to the bar. She feared being watched anywhere, uncertain what should not be observed. She admired girls here, with courage to be as they wanted, though it was not a life she could understand. Her own situation, however, was not understandable to many, even to Jeff. Had she cut herself off too thoroughly from everything she had ever known? Any thought of pain, at night, set her eyes open in panic. Ambulances in New York, she had been told, did not respond to a random caller's voice, and suppose she lay alone, some night, and died?

There was sadness here, too, and even Anila's brusqueness might be a cover-up. Some of these girls Amy had met other places and knew several had been married. Many had a wan quality; akin to hers, she supposed. Here in the dim light in the off-on rosiness of a blinking neon beer sign, faces had an uncertain look. With suddenness, Amy crossed the room and bought three beers. This basement room had seemed a retreat. Amy determined to keep struggling to find out what ordinary and everyday living meant.

"Why," Anila said after thanking Amy for the beer, "don't you cut your hair?"

To Amy's disgust, no answer would come. She had opened her mouth ineffectually and without sound. She was grateful to Tony for rescuing her. "She doesn't have to," he said, which she longed to have said for herself. "Anyway, she's straight."

Anila agreeably turned back to her business with Tony, leaving Amy to her own devices, sipping beer. Eventually, when Anila stood up, jarring the table, she looked from one to another. Then her attention focused on Amy. "Now," she said, "I'm coming very early to see his paintings. Is he ever up by nine?"

Amy had not time to collect her thoughts. A voice seemed to answer for her, which she found to be her own. "Why, I have no idea," she said.

With an impatient look, Anila turned to go, her final words lingering like stabs in Amy's heart. How sweet, how innocent, she had muttered. Amy, watching her walk away, realized she had wanted the girl to like her; and what had she put out to gain friendship but a little money for a beer. She went up the stairs hastily, toward the safer openness of the street, and waited for Tony, who had stopped to talk. Nearby, the doors of a Spanish café stood open, throwing out high-pitched conversations, rapid as castanets. Music inside was lavish and quick-tempered. Amy thought of some badly tinted old travelog, where beautiful, long-waisted Spanish women danced in ruffled dresses, their arms above their heads, bougainvillea tucked behind one ear. Her visions spread outward to any foreign country. And perhaps that was her answer, that she had not travelled far enough.

In the café's doorway stood a man, dark and foreign and treacherous-looking. And was she alone? he seemed to be asking, until Tony emerged, elflike in the dim light. Never before had she noticed how squashed to his head Tony's ears were, or how pointed. But she turned toward him in a sort of desperation. In the doorway, the man seemed to be giving her one more chance. He stared on at her, invitingly. His glance toward Tony had been insignificant, the way grownups acknowledge freedom to gossip before an uncomprehending child. As Amy clutched Tony's arm, a gutteral laugh escaped the man. If only she knew what she was missing! He gave another uncomprehending and flickering glance toward Tony. He then looked at her with pity. She had rushed Tony into the street, where they stood combating traffic, having stupidly gone against the light.

Turning over in midmorning sunlight, Amy avoided the sight of Tony sleeping with his mouth open. Two green flies buzzed in a bothered way against the screen. Getting up, she thrust further open a torn place and freed them to the city. Cautious eyes on Tony, she dressed, not wanting to be seen. She particularly could not imagine being revealed naked in this strong morning sunlight. One of his hands lay limply on his stomach, with a look as useless as a single glove. At the window, clad in her slip, Amy imagined herself as the cover of a cheap true-confessions magazine. Midday in her rumpled underclothes, her hair mussed, she felt slatternly.

Today, even Tony's gigantic colorful canvases added nothing to the plainness of his other room. Dressed and coming into it, she felt disgust at ants, Indian-file along the table going toward dabs of peanut butter and jelly. No longer did it seem to add up to experience to live in squalor. It was not even worth relating to anyone that the plates off which they ate always had to be washed in the bathtub at the end of the hall. Tony's sink was too small to hold them, though it held cups. When Amy moved a stack of dirty ones, circumspect brown bugs darted for the open drain. Tony last night had asked for an appraisal of his pictures. Thrusting out her chin, Amy had said that some looked merely like slashes of paint, or paint thrown, on canvas.

In a fit, Tony had said she was still a hick from wherever she had come from. She liked probably only paintings that looked like photographs and had not a single idea in her head. Had she read Freud or Marx or anything besides Jeffrey Almoner! What a fool, always defending this country. She ought to go back where she belonged. He then expounded lengthily on the meanings of his paintings and so windily that Amy reassured him, hastily, that she knew nothing about painting. But now that he told how he thought them out, she understood much better. But this morning, she came into the room and thought the pictures seemed merely slashes and dashes of paint on canvas.

Evidence of mice was everywhere in the room. In the night, she had sat bolt upright, thinking something had run across her feet. Nothing had confronted her but the darkness, that boldly. Wondering what had made her wake, she had decided it was simply apprehensiveness, constantly with her.

Moonlight had seemed not to penetrate the apartment. She had been glad for daylight when it came, at last. Tony's lax hand, his total surrender to sleep, had given Amy an opposite feeling, that she must do something energetic. After washing cups and straightening the apartment, she gathered a laundry pile by picking up clothes off the floor.

To be outside with something to do made the streets themselves seemed more functional. She was passing quickly a building with a doorman, usually suspicious and rough. Today, he called in a friendly way, "A big load for a little lady!" Courteously, he drew a baby carriage out of her way.

In the laundromat, ladies with flabby thighs, in curlers, turned their heads at the same instant toward her. They mistook her for a bride, as Amy blushed profusely, having dropped some of Tony's underwear. Several women swarmed toward her, like a welcoming committee. She was ceremoniously provided with correct change and informed how to operate the machines. And bring her own soap the next time, she was cautioned. To buy it in miniature boxes from a machine was too expensive. The clothes sloshing in suds gave Amy a comfortable feeling. Lounging in a chair, with a coverless old magazine, she watched the washing cycle hypnotically. To transfer clothes to the dryer was also a satisfactory feeling. They came out with buttons and zippers too hot to touch, warm and smelling good. She then copied heavy-armed housewives, busily smoothing their clothes until they seemed ironed. Carrying her completed stack like an offering, on extended arms, she went back happily into the street.

Tony, having just waked, blinked owlishly. He accepted his cleaner apartment and his clean clothes as his due. That was what girls did, wasn't it?

"Not usually, unless they're your wife or your mother—or something," Amy said, at a loss as to what she meant to Tony.

Seizing the opportunity, he said bitingly, "You'll make a good little suburban housewife. That's how you'll end up, with a husband on Wall Street." He kept on feeling irked, as usual, that she always had money.

You want to bet? Amy's angry look said. Lavish with green cleanser, she bit her lip, scrubbing his filthy sink. On hands and knees, she had spread poisonous pellets for mice, while he watched with folded arms, his pale face soft and runny-looking, like the margarine left out and gone rancid.

With arms wet to her elbows, Amy rung out the sponge capably. She wanted to rush to her room and accomplish cleaning it. Sitting back on her haunches after spreading pellets, she had come up with an enviable idea about giving life impetus: get one thing done in order to get on to something else. She went huffily and hurriedly from Tony's apartment.

Mornings afterward, when she woke in her own, she would circumspectly watch the women in the loft opposite; always, the wheel on the tailor's machine would already be spinning. She had for these people more compassion. With something akin to joy, she would hurry through dressing to go out for breakfast. She would come from that still with her sense of eagerness, but suddenly all her energy would lag. Back in her room, she lay on her bed to summon up strength, for something.

She heard no more from Tony, and lonesomeness took her

finally to him. He yanked open the door angrily and said he was painting. Anila had said he did not have enough finished work for her to take to the YMCA director.

"Are you painting alone?" Amy asked.

Apparently with a memory lapse, which Amy envied, he yelled, "Of course!" and slammed the door.

She went back to her room to straighten drawers. She threw away letters from friends, then from family, but took those back shortly from the wastebasket. She kept all the letters she had ever received from Jeff in a blue satin stocking box. Rereading them, she would think they were all posterity was ever to know of Amy Howard.

Her father wrote only exclamatory postscripts at the end of Edith's letters, which made Amy feel he was too busy to write. Though was it possible he could not find common ground with her, or that he was shy. Could her father be shy? If she went to the Waldorf, Edith wrote, look up an assistant manager with whom her father had gone to school back in Arkansas. Have you seen any Broadway shows with good-looking gals? her father added. Or been to any fancy night clubs? He wrote that he thought New York women smelled "prettier" than anywhere. Did she need any extra money, for some little thing like perfume? When Amy next went shopping on Fifth Avenue, Edith asked for a pair of short white pigskin gloves; she could find none in Delton. And Amy's friends at home, according to her mother, were always having a whirl. Wasn't Amy sorry to be missing all the parties? Billy Walter continuously, it seemed, asked about her. Every letter of Edith's ended with two questions: Have you met anybody? Do you have a job? With them, her mother's handwriting grew tinier, and the words appeared on paper timorous.

One day, in the jumbled window of a popular bookstore, Amy saw a sign asking for Sales Help. Inside, she made her way between shelves from which books were about to tumble, between rickety tables which were laden. Staring from beneath a heavy fringe of bangs, the owner wondered if the girl asking so hesitantly about the job had courage enough to sell books. However, she had a nicer appearance than many young people and was hired.

Amy, thrilled, thought each moment would be one of intellectual frenzy. She was disappointed to be handed a feather duster and told to use it each morning. She was warned never to approach the men who read books at the first rack by the window, the sex books. The owner was sad, too, that it was necessary to sell trashy stuff to stay in business. Seeing people near the window reading and browsing, passers-by had the idea of coming in. Those who came regularly to the sex rack never bought anything. That bothered Amy unreasonably. She liked fairness. A morning when the owner went to the bank, Amy sidled up with her duster and spoke quietly to one of the men. Always, he wore pearl grey suède gloves.

"May I help you?"

When this young man swallowed, his Adam's apple protruded as unfortunately as a growth on his throat. Gently closing his book, he set it on the rack. His mouth opened slightly, but saying nothing he vanished ghostlike from the store. Amy wondered if since being grown, even she had been as fearful and shy. She remembered the cache of beer cans at the abandoned house and how sympathetically Jeff had said, "Probably the only little pleasure the man had." Another day an old man read with his hand on his zipper and gave her a hellish look out of sea blue eyes, brightening. Amy gave him a benevolent smile, though keeping at a distance.

Monotonous time stretched without customers and all the books would be dusted. Arms folded, she stared up at the street, the store several steps down from it. Several times, she recognized Tony's legs, thin and covered with auburn hair, and his sandals, always accompanied by a slim pair of feet in ballet slippers.

Once, a handsome, blond merchant marine ran in for Jane's and several navigational books, the names jotted down on paper. He was frantic and almost late for his ship. Amy darted helpfully around finding books for him. He tossed down by the cash register a large bill and told her to keep the change. Before she could ring up the sale he had disappeared. She held the bill, experiencing the newness of being tipped, probably for the only time in her life. She wanted to laugh, to tell someone. Only in the store at the time was Mack, the stock boy. She had never been able to determine whether he was Negro or Puerto Rican, and it had not occurred to her he might be both. With a diffident and defiant attitude, he wore, indoors, his hat, with feathers stuck in the band.

Amy went toward the back of the store, laughing, the money in her hand. Mack slouched among the stock and watched her come. She stopped short, but his dark eyes remained on her and his mouth was unsmiling. She folded the money neatly into a square. "I can certainly use this," Amy said, and sensed not to offer it to him, as she wanted.

Desperately, all this time, she had longed to be friends with Mack. Did he know she was not prejudiced, that her accent did not mean she held the opinions, by now clichés, attributed to all Southerners. After all, she had gone to that crazy liberal school, but that was not explainable to Mack. Her attempts at conversation were always stymied by his refusal to participate. Habitually, she used the weather as an opener but that was where the conversation ended. Arriving in the morning, she would say either that it was a nice day or a bad one; either it was clear or looked as if it might rain. To whatever she said, Mack replied flatly, Yeah. Sometimes, his voice gave the word a little inflection. Yeah? he might then say. He did not show up for work and his telephone number turned out to be bogus. Wearily brushing back her bangs, the owner said, you tried to help these people, but they were all alike, and none could be depended on.

This phrase sounded so much like her mother's in dealing with maids that Amy was surprised, realizing she had been under the false assumption prejudice existed solely in her part of the country. She would listen more carefully now wherever she was. It was apparent Mack was not coming back. He had left them at inventory time, and Amy fought down the owner's words, as well as her mother's, echoing from her past.

When Tony finally came clomping down the steps, she could not help being glad. Though after his absence, she was struck by his frailness and a look of insubstantialness. She could not imagine appearing at the Country Club in Delton with him. "How've you been?"

"You ought to know," Tony said.

"How could I know?"

"Every time I've passed, I've seen that tiny face peering out."

"I wasn't watching you! I was staring out. Thinking."

On the edge of anger, her voice faltered; she was too lonely for Tony to leave. He leaned against a table, taking in that fact. As if in generosity, he said, "A guy I know, who's a drummer, gave me some peyote. Want to come up to my place this evening and try it out?"

Was it habit-forming? she wanted to know.

She might get nothing at all from it, once, Tony said.

She would give it a try, but acknowledged wanting no outside thing on which to be dependent. Tony patted his hollow-shaped stomach, having eaten peanut butter until it was coming out of his ears. And someplace else, he said, grinning. Would she pick up a couple of orders of spaghetti and meat balls on her way? He had some wine.

She would be glad to, Amy said, and meant it.

Gladly, after dinner, she washed plates in the bathtub at the end of his hall, having first washed a ring from the tub. Tony, at the stove, boiled the root. Amy came back and he had a pot full of what looked like pea soup. Was the whole idea hallucinatory, that drinking the mixture would fill her mind with visions such as she had never imagined? One saw, Tony had been told, anything one wanted to—the entire range of architecture since the world began, for instance. Toasting one another, they drank.

She lay flat with her hands folded expectantly on her stomach, thinking Tony would claim success whether he had visions or not. She could not find anything to think about. Enough times alone, she thought about herself. Once, she peeked at him, thinking how funny if he had fallen asleep. Though that moment, not surprisingly, Tony sighed; pearly gates might have opened ahead of him, she thought.

She resettled herself on the mattress, wondering what to see if she saw anything. Her imagination stretched toward some broad subject. She might know, at once, all of the great literature. Then to her mind's eye came the trellis full of June roses which had arched the driveway of the first house she remembered. Her mother was laughing and holding her father's hand.

A rabbit given to her some Easter, early in her life, came to mind. That gave way to colors of the rainbow always discernible when she closed her eyes. Tony sighed more blissfully. One of Amy's feet itched, but she was afraid to scratch it. She saw the Court House, the old men playing checkers, herself alighting from the bus, into blankness. She could not, she thought, face things, even in fancy.

"Fantastic. Wasn't it?" Tony stood and stretched.

With nerve then, she glanced at her wristwatch. Having been lying down several hours, she felt absurd. Nor was she going to believe Tony had experienced anything.

"I just saw the sort of things I see any time I close my eyes," she said.

"You've got to be kidding." Tucking in his shirtail, he threw back over his shoulder, "Maybe you're not so sensitive as you think."

"I'm as sensitive as you," she said, feeling mean.

"You don't really feel much in bed," he accused her for the first time.

"Maybe that's your fault."

His eyes took on a tiger's yellow gleam. It was not necessary to say what the look meant. Amy clearly saw those little feet in ballet slippers always close to his, passing the bookstore. She had to impress him.

"Did I ever tell you," she said, "that I see Almoner?"

Tony turned, rebuckling his belt. Plainly, he assumed she was remembering an hallucination, after all.

"I know him," she said. "I've been to his house, and we used to meet. We've written a lot. If you don't believe it, I can show you some letters."

"What right," Tony said, advancing in a menacing way, "do you have to know Almoner?"

Too hung in the air unsaid; with all else she had, Tony meant.

Stepping back, Amy wished she had not intentionally tried to hurt anyone. Now all her family's warnings about her possibly being murdered in a place like New York rang in her ears. She saw herself, strangled or blood-splattered, found by disinterested policemen. Who, here, would mourn? Only when she was home would her resting place not be thoroughly ignominious. She had tears, unnoticed.

Tony stopped halfway toward her, then combed his hair. His sharp nose seemed lengthened and similar to a fox's. Recently, the fact had begun to sink in that he was never going to have a show. He longed for Amy to leave so he might have all of what was left of the wine.

"I don't know what you mean by the right to know him," Amy said. She then thought well enough of herself to think, why shouldn't she?

"I didn't know Almoner liked young girls," Tony said. "I'd heard lots about him, but never that."

"That's not it, at all. We're friends because I want to be a writer. We are—" but Amy bit off the words "soul mates," knowing what fun Tony would make of them, "friends," she said.

"So I didn't go to college, I'm not dumb, babe." Above that lengthened nose, his eyes narrowed. "I guess to an old man, you'd be a good lay."

Reversed in Amy's mind instantly was who might lie dead and bloody in this filthy apartment. She stalked toward the other room and picked up her purse. She looked openly into the wallet before going to the hall door. Supporting himself against the bedroom door, Tony yawned.

"If this is the way you want it!" Amy said, before slamming the door behind her. She had wanted to yell further that he was not a good painter! Starting down the stairs into dimness, she laughed at their childishness. She might be playing a part in an old melodrama, she thought, as the stairs creaked.

Her block, when she reached it, stretched ahead, an unremitting row of similar grey stone buildings. The tailor took a few steps out of his shop and stood with flabby arms folded. His face seemed to reflect the greyness of the buildings, not the sunlight. The sun's shaft, entering the street, avoided him altogether. Light, for him, was confined to that tiny single bulb illuminating his machine. As he watched Amy coming down the block, she could not deliberately cross the street.

"It's a nice day," she said.

"A nice time of the day to walk."

Loneliness led her to the verge of changing her mind about going out with him. Then he smiled, and red veins sprayed across his cheeks like map routes. God, he seemed a bloated grey fish, out of water. And nodding slightly, Amy crossed the street. Her building inside was silent and odorless, and neither her footsteps nor her entrance created a ripple. It was better not to be inflexible, she decided, setting her back against the door, facing her room. She again had to seek help but in this emergency she could think of no one to telephone.

I'm lonely. Would the police emergency squad answer that summons? A meager list of people came to mind, all of whom she had contacted last. They seemed all to have given her the joking message, Don't call us, we'll call you. She could think only of Nancy. She spoke to her, saying she was dying to see Nancy's new apartment; in a humiliating pause afterward, Nancy obviously tried to decide about an invitation and gave a vague one. "You'll have to come to dinner, sometime."

Through innuendoes, Amy managed finally an invitation for that evening. If she would take potluck, Nancy said. What she ate was the least of her worries, Amy confessed.

Nancy's building, newly renovated, gave Amy a comfortable feeling, with dirtless corners and shiny floors. There was a smell of fresh paint and an outdoorsy scent, as if carpenters had just departed carrying wood shavings. The same freshness rushed out when Nancy opened her door. Amy did not belittle her, standing there in a sweeping taffeta hostess gown.

Though the husband had grown fatter and was chewing the first of an evening's supply of antacid mints, he seemed a nice man. Kindly, he dismissed standoffishness had ever existed between them and shook her hand warmly. Amy came gratefully inside, telling Nancy how beautifully she had co-ordinated the apartment. She went all about admiring what Nancy had

224

achieved, all that she must ever have envisioned for herself, Amy thought, oyster-white wall-to-wall carpeting and satin-covered headboards. For a moment, while Nancy smoothed the unwrinkled bedspread, Amy considered one person ought not to judge the aims of another. The point was to determine on and achieve what one wanted, as Nancy had. Liking the new building, Amy liked also the table set with pretty things, as she had known at home. Candles reflected in a window, which revealed the black void that was night. Inconsequential chatter done, Nancy asked reluctantly the question, "What have you been doing, Amy?"

Turning her gaze from the window, Amy answered with a small but matter-of-fact smile, "I'm working in a bookstore."

While waiting for her answer, the husband had poised a dubious fork over a mushroom cap. Now he sank in the prongs deliciously. He looked up, chewing. Nancy generously thrust toward Amy the salad bowl. Sighs had escaped them. If only they had known, they seemed to say, that Amy led some plausible life, they would have invited her much sooner. Nancy knew a bachelor, she said, whom Amy must meet. The husband, gazing past candlelight, had a look of appreciation, as if then discovering she was female. In the glow, bending toward her plate, Amy had the satisfactory feeling that her hair falling softly over her shoulders looked pretty.

After a second crème de menthe—and the trouble of making a frappé had not been at all too much, the husband had said—Amy felt she ought to go. She protested she was not at all afraid of the dark streets, but they would not hear of her going out alone. Though it meant Nancy had to change into street clothes, they went with Amy and waited until she was on the bus.

"Too bad you couldn't stay longer," the husband said. The bus came into sight. He gave her shoulder a companionable pat, adding, they knew what it was to have to get up and face the old grind in the morning.

She entered her own room with a refreshed sense of its bleak-ness. A great deal of that was her fault. She could have put pic-tures on the walls, at least. Was it ferns Nancy had said were marvellous for filling up bare corners? Tomorrow should she buy four pots of ferns, Amy thought, looking around. Tears went their frequented and familiar course down her cheeks. She sat on the bed in resignation, that all that ever was to happen in her life already had. A sense of destiny had been ridiculous. Fate had never had anything in store for her. To live was only to put off dying. She created a sad picture of her life, coming to an end willfully at so young an age.

She agonized over the discovery of her body, taking a razor out of her dresser drawer. The room was so small, to draw out the drawer meant pressing herself against the bed. At its head, a small washbasin was attached to the wall.

There, she bent over with the razor poised above a wrist. She realized the blade had not been cleaned since she shaved her legs last. Warning about infection, dinned into her ears in a lifetime of maids and a mother, came into her mind. Only when she was wiping the dull edge did she wonder what difference infection made if she were dead. Sticking the clean razor to her wrist, she was unable to cut deeply. No blood appeared, and she looked closer at the minutely parted edges of skin. Her interest was aroused. How intricately people were made, and she considered the whole fantastic process of birth. A fetus she thought of as being like one of the tiny sea horses advertised in the back of the New York *Times* magazine section; if she ordered one would it live? She stuck the razor unsuccessfully again to her wrist and thought how sad it would be never to have a baby.

If you had to gather courage to die, you might as well use it to live, she supposed. Or, either she had to kill herself in some irre-trievably quick way, like shooting off her head. Amy put the razor back in the drawer again. She would try life a little longer.

But if she was still an old maid when she was thirty, then she would kill herself! And she promised, staring into the mirror.

She looked from the window, thinking of having more than one baby. She would teach her children so they might avoid all the wandering and searching and all her mistakes. Taking her experience as their own, they would have a head start in life. She had rejected this attempt on Jeff's part, she saw, having wanted to find her own way. Her children, however, would listen and be forever grateful for her advice. She would be consoled by them for her own loneliness and suffering. How grateful they would be to her, Amy imagined, ready to cry again, erroneously consoled.

She would tell her children how once she had thought of killing herself, without being able to tell everything, for always much she had felt would be nameless. Having described the terrible rented room in which she had lived, she would tell of standing a long time at its window, looking out toward an avenue, the glow of lights like colored mist. A florist's window, filled with spring flowers, had glimmered most brightly. Rushing there, she had bought the most enormous pot of pink tulips she had ever seen. It had been a test of living or dying, whether or not she reached the shop before it closed. The streets had seemed less aloof when she returned with the flowers. When she had put the pot on her windowsill, the blooms had seemed to overflow the room.

But was she too solicitous and did she water them too much? It seemed more than ordinarily soon that they died. She began to sleep repeatedly through her alarm's ringing. Often she found, waking later, that she had at some point turned it off. The bookstore owner's indignation seemed to make her bangs stiffen. She would not reconsider, and Amy was fired. Customers, in the store, observed a girl evidently not to be gone near with a ten-foot-pole, for the owner looked at Amy that distantly, backing away.

Feeling she crept, Amy left the store. Beneath those bangs, the owner's eyes revealed Amy was no more reliable than Mack; she would, like him, simply disappear somewhere into the city.

Going empty-handed toward her room, having received no severance pay, Amy passed a public telephone booth on a corner. Quite simply, no one was left to call. Nancy and her husband had been busy whenever she had attempted to repay their invitation.

Reaching her street, Amy knew it must not matter the tailor seemed a bulky fish, left out to thaw. Any offer of friendship was too valuable to turn away. On her block, long and lonesome slants of afternoon sunlight fell across the buildings.

Her own window, between two slants, remained dark. Glancing up at it, she realized the pot of dead tulips was forgotten on the windowsill. Something figuring in the corner of her eye drew her attention. A man on the front steps of her building was making out the house number, almost eradicated. Curlicues, in stone, on the old house formed a frame behind him. Only a moment was her attention distracted by that thought. This silhouette was recognizable, even from a distance, and she started immediately toward it.

"Hush," Jeff said, his arms going around her. "Hush. Didn't you know I was coming?"

"No." Amy dabbed her eyes. "How could I? You didn't write."

"Because you know I know things about you before you do. Didn't you realize I'd know you needed me. That I would come."

"I don't know what I know. Whether I ever think anything. How did you find me?"

"Your mother sent me your address. Of course, you've moved. But the janitor told me this one."

"Thank God. I gave him five dollars. But he told someone else he didn't know where I was."

"I think he thought I was your father, come to drag you home by your ears. Probably thought you belonged there, too," Jeff said.

"It's funny, but my mother seems different," Amy said. "I was surprised she sent me your letter. No screaming about you, either. I sort of expected her to say not to see you."

"I felt she wasn't fighting us," Jeff said.

"I didn't know what to do, so I didn't do anything. I've read your letter so often, Jeff." She looked at him hopefully but his face did not change. She said then, somewhat petulantly, "Why didn't you come sooner?"

"One thing after another delayed me," and not until then did he see there had been a chain of events, as if planned. He supposed he had been taken in, though if he had come sooner, Amy might not have been so glad to see him. "I'll tell you why later," he said. "We seem to have an audience." The tailor had come out as far as the curb, ostensibly to sweep, though staring.

"Where shall we go?" Amy said, in a low voice.

A quality of innocence had disappeared from her face. And although he had wanted to mature her, he felt sad. When he looked at her his emotions clashed, he imagined the way hers did. "Listen. *Ton nom c'est une petite sonnette d'or pendant dans mon coeur, et quand je pense à toi je tremble, et elle sonne.* Do you know French?"

"I studied it, but not as well as I should."

"Your name is a little golden bell hung in my heart and when I think of you, I tremble and it rings."

"Jeff, that's beautiful!"

"That's why one of the great lovers said it to his love, long before I. Cyrano to Roxanne."

"Then I must read that, too," she said. "I don't think you've told me to before."

"Alex is in Europe," he said. "And I'm staying in his apartment while he's gone. Will you do me the honor of having dinner with me this evening, Miss Howard?"

Glancing about protectively, not knowing whether he was teasing, she feared someone overhearing and laughing at him.

"It would give me a great deal of pleasure." She made a mock bow as a couple was passing.

"What is your wish, then? Hamburgers and soda pop?"

"I've become more sophisticated, Mr. Almoner. Nothing will do me but pheasant under glass. Oh no! I was kidding. Don't take me any place expensive."

"Always," he said, smiling, "you are considerate of my pocketbook, which makes me feel nicely protected. But, tonight, we'll throw caution to the wind."

"If you say so. I'm sorry, but there's no place inside for you to wait while I change. Can you sit on the steps a minute. You look tired."

"Yes, I will sit down. Amelia was married and with all the hoopla of a young woman. The kind of thing I imagine you will want, though," he said and was silent. Then, "You look fine as you are, but run along if you must change."

"I won't have all that hoopla," she said. "I'm an old maid already by Delton's standards. Didn't you know that?" She took one step up toward the door.

"Maybe I haven't kept you from it, Amy. But I'm glad you haven't rushed into marriage. All this celebrating for what may be the worst mistake of your life. People can get married too easily. It ought to be hard, and divorces easier. Not the other way around."

"Your trip probably tired you, too. We aren't going to stay out late."

"You are very considerate."

"It's about time," she said apologetically.

"Part of growing up is learning to think of other people. But you have been considerate before."

"I'm tired of thinking of myself, I can tell you. I've been alone, mostly."

"You haven't been, at least, overindulging in small talk. That's been the exhausting thing about the parties. In a small town, as you know, it's always the same people over and over. Finally, there's nothing to say and nothing to do but drink."

"Shame on you! I thought so. Tonight, you're not going to have anything but wine. I've still got to take care of you for the world, I see."

Either the sunshine lingering over buildings filled his eyes with tears, or feeling did, and Amy wondered which.

"Is there any wonder I love you?" he said, love so obviously on his face, Amy felt guilty. She could not return as much.

"I don't know why you do," she said, then.

"If this love for you hadn't come along, Amy, I'd never have finished my last book. Though until a few moments ago, when I looked at your face, by God, I couldn't believe I had. But it's done! Thank you for that."

"I don't see that I do anything for you, Jeff," she said. "But don't talk to me, ever again, about not writing another book!"

"Run along and change," he said, softly and smiling.

As glass covers were whipped away, Amy thought again how surprising that Jeff had wanted to undergo the flurry ordering pheasant had caused. The Maître d' hovered, other diners watched. Jeff, his nose almost touching his plate, bent over to draw in the aroma of a browned bird on toast, which was soaking up deliciously basting juices. He might be saying, Ahhh, to himself. About more, she thought, than the food. Possibly about his book being finished, or possibly about their being together. Always, she was sad thinking it not fair that Almoner had known loneliness; unless, as he said, loneliness was the nature of living. For a hideous moment, she thought she might scream that it should not be so. She saw about the room opposing vignettes, a young couple holding hands on the table, a middle-aged couple who had yet to speak to one another. She ducked her head toward her plate, busily cutting meat, though she was not hungry any longer. Jeff had said that he wrote to fill up the void. She wondered why in the name of God, He had made life so difficult?

Having finally to lift her head, meeting happiness in Jeff's eyes because of her, she thought, God bless him. God should. If only she could give, as he gave to her. Always, she was stopped by the cold dread inside herself. Jeff had bent again to his food, enjoying it. Why when he cared so little for possessions, she wondered, watching him, had he become so entangled by them? Wrangles about bills, new wallpaper? Sitting back, wanting to escape all responsibilities and duties, Amy realized, apprehensively, that she had neither.

Wine in the glass Jeff lifted accepted light from the small one lighting their table. The color reminded him of purple-red blackberries, overripe in the sun. Closing his eyes while the wine went down, he thought back to walking carefully barefoot through tangled vine, while scratches on his legs tingled with sweat. Carefree however temporarily now, he was grateful, knowing some people never were, at all. At home, kudzu vine ran wild over the countryside and Johnson grass overtook the yard; mostly, he was overwhelmed, told in the midst of working that the neighbor's German shepherd was a threat he had to do something about, that there was a leak in a sink. How long he had wanted to say, "Take the house and take everything; I've been done with it a long time." The wine, having gone down, left a taste like the mellowness of the warm overripe berries.

232

Opening his eyes, he said, "You ever eat blackberries straight from the vine?"

"Of course, at my grandmother's in the country," Amy said. "Aren't they great. The wine's the same color. I was thinking that, too."

Her eyes roved pensively toward the dessert cart. He watched her pick and choose some frothy tart, thinking that she was still young enough that what was in her heart was usually on her face. Thank God for that. The thin-stemmed glass was twirled slowly between his fingers as he watched her eat industriously. Then laying down her licked fork, she said, "We're so quiet, we're like that sad married couple who haven't said anything since they've been here."

"I noticed them, too. It is sad, Amy, that people can live in an isolation which blood ties, and even marriage, can't break, sometimes."

"I don't understand why people are always marrying the wrong people," she said, thinking of her parents and of him. "I hope Amelia hasn't. It's funny she wanted now to get married. Why is everybody acting different? My mother and Amelia, for instance?"

"I've begun to wonder if, as we've changed our own lives, we've changed theirs," he said.

"Wouldn't that be funny?" Amy amused him then by leaning forward in what so clearly she felt to be a womanly way, her chin delicately balanced on the backs of her cupped hands. "Tell me about the wedding and why you stayed so long afterward," she said.

He leaned comfortably toward her, relating details. Amelia had skipped a honeymoon, and things scheduled for before the wedding had been rescheduled for afterward. With relatives already assembled, it had seemed a good time for a cousin's baby to be christened. "Little things like that kept turning up," he said. "Now, I realize it was perhaps all done to keep me there. But, of course, I had to stay on for the bride's first dinner party." He began to chuckle. "Latham has a cook, Marguerite, who has been with them almost as long as Jessie has with us. Amelia's dinner was quite elegant. Only when we looked down, Marguerite was serving barefoot!"

"Oh no." Amy fell back against her chair, laughing. "Poor Amelia, when she has such pretensions. What did she do?"

"Sent Latham out to threaten her with being fired, I guess."

Long after the incident had been told, he was still smiling. "Why?" Amy asked.

"No reason," he said, "except that I'm happy."

"I'm glad," she said.

"I too, Amy," he said. "I'm glad to be happy."

"Are writers often, though?" she said anxiously. "Or is it a cliché that they're not?"

Writers, he thought, had more extreme emotions than other people; seldom did they feel nothing. "When I'm happy, no one has ever been happier." He looked pleased. Even boyish, Amy thought. "They don't fall in love lightly, either," he said. "And now, as I thought, you want to run. You don't like either pressure or responsibility. But I've begun to believe you confuse them, Amy. You can't avoid responsibility. That is, if you want to grow up, which always you've said was what you wanted. All right, if you won't even look at me while I talk about it, I'll quit. For tonight, anyway. Happiness comes over me sometimes quite unexpectedly, without apparent reason."

"Over me, too!" She looked excited. "Just sometimes if the sun is shining and I'm driving along the street, everything seems wonderful. We are the same."

"The last time it happened to me I was walking across a frozen cotton field," he said. "My God, how I longed for you to be there to kiss you. But, even without you, I was suddenly and simply struck by an unbearable happiness."

"One time when I was in a phone booth talking to you, I remember thinking, Look at the day! Everything seemed so marvellous and fascinating, Jeff. The feeling never lasts."

"No, it never lasts," he said. "But knowing what you are going to say before you do, sometimes, makes me happy. Always, something serene and nice and never foolish."

"Most of the time I feel stupid."

"You have never been stupid."

"I don't know why not. I *feel* stupid. I don't think I'm growing up at all." Knowing it would exasperate him, she did not confide she thought of trying another city, or country, to see what turn her life might take.

"Things are going on in you all this time, which you don't realize," he said. "I believe that. You've had a lot in your past to clear away. It's not done yet."

"It won't ever be."

"Probably, not completely."

"What then?"

"I hope you will learn to live with some things. I've stuck my neck out for you. I wouldn't have if I didn't believe in you completely."

"If only I could believe in me. It wouldn't be so hard just to go on."

"But what else is there? I can't imagine anyone's taking their own life. That's one thing I've never thought of."

Amy was altogether astonished. Jeff did not, after all, understand the extent of her despair; therefore, he might not understand much about her, as she had questioned before. He had never understood how she feared her life passing; she knew that.

"Don't let me have this grey head for nothing," he said, seeing how she stared at him. "If I believe in you, then know there's something in you worth being believed in. Damn it!" He struck the table forcefully. And having thought that she would never laugh again, Amy began to. His attempt to seem angry seemed so much only that—an attempt.

"All right," she said. "Almoner can't be wrong. I'll believe in myself, or I'll try to. That's all I can promise."

"Jeff's not wrong, either. You haven't stumbled into my orbit for nothing. We aren't spinning about together for nothing. I'll never believe this time is wasted."

"No, it's not wasted," she said quickly. "I've never thought that. And someday, I will know what it means, won't I?"

"Yes, Amy. I think you will."

She let out a long breath. "I feel better." She reached out and lightly lay her hand on top of his.

The touch had the same gentleness of the butterfly; he was as afraid to move. "I had begun to think maybe I was an untouchable," he said, grinning. "When I see your aunt, she runs as if I were a leper. Or a rapist. Or head of the NAACP. You don't mind if I indulge in foolishness, do you? You seem never to mind. For now, I would like to present you with a little bouquet of violets with a star inside."

"But that," she said, her eyes filling with tears, "is not foolishness. That's beautiful, like the bell in Cyrano. And so sweet."

"Never now, Amy, can you be some beldame concerned with position or money. I know that." He dared turn his hand over and took hers. "If only I could help you avoid pitfalls in your life."

But she did not want to avoid whatever pitfalls were to come, Amy thought. She felt jealous of her own life. With all its own misfortunes, she wanted to live it. Sometimes, she felt that in trying to help her, Jeff was about to take over what belonged to her. Those times, she longed to be with friends her own age, who had the same problems. Her attention had been distracted, and he saw that he had again said something confusing for her. Silent, he drank his wine. But she was wondering how in the world the women in this restaurant, who all looked so chic, had kept their hair looking so nice despite the windy streets. Peeking at Jeff, she saw him looking moody and deep in thought, and she worried that her own thoughts were so shallow. But she felt so disheveled and so wrongly dressed. Though the beige shirtwaist she wore was raw silk, she simply had disappeared into the candlelit atmosphere. These other women, the sort who knew everything, wore dark dresses which stood out, and their throats had some silvery glistening sheen, and even their faces seemed pearlized; what make-up had they found? Beneath great swoops of starched tablecloth, Amy rubbed her thumb nervously against a hangnail, anxious to bite and get done with it; but she could not here. She felt fearful of the women, never realizing they might covet the unbeatable thing she had, youth. While presenting his check, the waiter seemed to smirk. Amy looked up at him, then bent her head and shrank a little, so that the tablecloth rose up like a bed sheet around her arms. The waiter's smirk had seemed to say so clearly that he knew all about May-December couples.

Jeff made small talk with him during the exchange of money. Having received his tip, the waiter grandly swept Amy's dessert plate from the table, causing the fork to clatter. From him escaped some watery sound like "Tch," as other diners looked their way. That sound, his rolling eyes, made clear the disturbance had not been his fault. Someone had placed the fork on their plate incorrectly. He stood aside, and people watched the nervous-looking young woman lead from the restaurant the much older man; but certainly a father and daughter would not be dining in this tête-à-tête sort of place.

Immediately upon reaching the street, Amy bit the hangnail. She was more than glad to be out of sight of those languidly turning heads. She was comfortable, being alone with Jeff. There were not many people with whom she felt so comfortable. That thought reached him, and he returned it by pressing her hand. Whenever she drew close to him, she had observed that a slight smile settled onto his lips. Despite whatever conflict was inside her, knowing that she made him happy made her happy. She felt she had a purpose, then. Her hair flew about her face, wind rushing down the narrow streets as if through tunnels. She determined, however, not to bother about her looks.

A movie? The theatre? he suggested.

They bought *Cue* in a small tobacco shop. Their heads touched bending over it, while they consulted one another solicitously. Nor were they surprised by the affableness with which they agreed that there was nothing to see. Jeff dropped the magazine into a wire trash basket. They kept strolling. Amy said, "Maybe you ought to go to bed early. Get a good night's sleep."

"I'd never be able to sleep this early," he said.

Arm in arm, they went on and paused to look into windows, if something attracted one or the other of them. She thought how he cancelled out her feelings of being alone in the world. Sometimes, the smile he had when she looked at him took the form of a slight trembling of his bottom lip. All that mattered to him these times was their being together. Amy read that quite clearly on his face. She would smile back, but sometimes had to look away. She worried that it was not fair to be with him when she had thoughts of a life apart.

Never did she want to use him. Whenever he was with her, he seemed to walk more erectly. She knew then that her presence did give him something. And often, when she had another desire, as now to go home and go to bed, she stayed on.

"Would you come to Alex's for a brandy?"

They had paused indecisively in the middle of the block. Cars drew alongside, halted by a red light commandingly changed. Jeff had begun to walk more slowly. She had tried to hide a yawn. The cars rolled away rather darkly, their occupants' faces turned studiously ahead, intent and preoccupied. The green light, coming on at the corner, gave an eerie cavelike feeling to the spot where they stood. Without quite nodding her head, Amy said she could come for a little while.

Turning on the doorman a wan smile when he opened his spotless glass doors, she thought how the man well knew that Alex was out of town. But he was trained to be blind and subservient toward anyone who could afford to pass through his doors. She supposed him not watching them as they crossed the lobby. As immediately as Jeff opened the door to the apartment, however, it seemed hostile and withdrawn. Like a sleeping porter, it did not want to be bothered and had assumed itself with Alex on vacation. It had lent itself magnificently to a large party and, otherwise, had long been accustomed to a settled bachelor's existence. It gave itself up to the impersonal thoroughness of a cleaning service, and did not care in its owner's absence to have a cigar crushed into an ashtray, even to have pictures and books inspected. About to take a book from a pile stacked on a table, Amy suddenly drew back her hand. Jeff brought out the brandy, set out glasses like a boy stealing from the family liquor supply, as if not to be heard. He came across the stretches of quietude and soft carpet, holding out her glass.

The hushed quality of everything irritated Amy. He seemed humble approaching, too eager to please her; so often, she wanted to tell him to be more assertive. Patience with her might simply be the wrong approach, she thought. She wanted really a man to drag her around by a hank of hair and tell her what to do. Jeff, by waiting to see what she was going to decide, made her often feel put on a spot. Making a design in the carpet with her shoe, she watched the resultant dark pattern change gradually lighter again. She stuck her nose into the brandy glass repeatedly to avoid speaking, sorry about the perverseness of her nature. If only she could make herself affable when necessary. That would seem to be the ultimate in growing up.

Yet, the thought of Jeff's not being kind to her seemed unbearable. She raised eyes a little moist. "Brandy fumes really get me," she said. She held her breath and drank. He made a motion with his own glass and thought she sometimes seemed a child he wanted to tuck into bed; directly afterward, he could have the desire to yank away the covers.

Amy was thinking she was lucky to be with him, though. Curling her legs beneath her, she reached out to faintly touch his hair above each ear; his hair shone dimly in light from beneath the fluted shade of a lamp. Having nothing to say, it was understood, they would say nothing. With that situation, they were comfortable. After drinking, they set their glasses down into silence, and the brandy, shifting from side to side in the bulbous glasses, turned more golden in the light.

Suppose she said, Think of rain falling in places we'll never see. He would understand and know she was thinking how lonely they both had been. Turning, he seemed to ponder, too, the enormity of this moment in which no longer were they lonely. Amy moved toward him, and his arm went around her.

"I do love you." She spoke softly, but the words seemed to have the force of a trap sprung. "Oh, I do love you," she repeated, feeling released.

"Yes." His bottom lip trembled a little. "I believe you do." He spoke against her hair. "And, someday, you'll learn to love more." The trembling of his lip was all the indication that his happiness had sunk deeper. She held as still as a baby exhausted from crying.

"It seems so funny though," she said, sitting up, continuing aloud a conversation she had been having with herself, "that no one ever recognizes you when we're out together." She moved over one pillow on the sofa. "I'll bet no one would ever imagine your spending time in New York like this. They'd think you were constantly surrounded by people."

"In Europe," he said, "it's very different. There, young people worship writers the way they do baseball players here. One time, a group waited outside my hotel, for hours, until I came out and followed me along the street. Afterward, one of the young women I met even sent me a present. A travel clock and embarrassingly expensive."

"Well, that was very flattering, and you deserve adulation," she said. "I ought to give you a present."

"You are here."

"That's not much."

"She lives in New York now," he said, rather shortly.

"Who? The girl who gave you the clock? Oh," Amy said. She stuck her nose into her glass and breathed. She sipped brandy with deliberate slowness, considering whether she had been jealous, and whether that had been his intent. Between them, the invisible clock ticked in the silence. He reached for her and said, as if in apology and in a rush, "Yes, the girl who gave me the clock. And she is beautiful, too, Amy. But she is not you. And even crumbs, I'll take those."

It seemed an accusation that she gave only crumbs. Amy said nothing. His hand had rested on her knee, trembling a little. She freed herself by going across the room to set her empty glass on the bar.

"Another?" he said.

"No, thank you."

"Shall I take you downtown then? You look sleepy."

"Wine and brandy," she said, trying to smile.

"Well then, I'd better take you back downtown." As he got up, the elevator clicked past going to another floor. Voices were heard saying goodnight and the elevator came back past, causing a reminiscent flickering of yellow, like the flickering of yellow summer moths, along the foyer floor. Silence returned, heavy as sleep.

"Can't I just stay here?" Amy said.

"Of course, if you will." He had given a little start, before setting down his glass with a slow movement.

Looking indecisive, she said, "I think this one switch turns off all the lights in here." Moving to it and reaching out as hesitantly as if expecting a shock from the electricity, she drew down the switch. Darkness seemed inordinately quick. Peering through it Amy experienced the childhood sensation of hiding, but feeling terror at not being found at once. Light came on placidly in the adjoining hall where Jeff stood and waited. Beyond him, the bedroom was revealed only by light from apartments the other side of the fire escape, across a courtyard from Alex's window. Objects in the room were difficult to see, the lights opposite somewhat obscured by a half-drawn Venetian blind. When she entered the room, Amy stumbled against the bed. With her knee aching and clutching it, she went about as if crippled.

Jeff's toilet kit had a homeless air atop Alex's dresser, which being cleared was ownerless-looking. Of some dark wood, the dresser did not take kindly to clutter. Searching for bobby pins somewhere in the bottom of her handbag, Amy had scattered the top with lipstick-dabbed Kleenex and other possessions: a pale blue wallet, a companionless earring, a rattail comb, a tiny brush. Reprimanded by the furniture's heavy look, she stuck things back into her pocketbook hastily.

After making little pin curls above each ear, she stood dead still, no longer really seeing herself in the mirror. Assuming she had changed her mind, Jeff made an offer. "If you'd prefer, I could make myself comfortable on the couch in the living room."

She bent then toward the mirror, dissatisfied, and redid the curls; her throat muscles seemed strained with the effort. Her hipbones pressed the dresser so ardently, she might have been holding it back against the wall. In a resigned way, her hands left the curls alone. "Why should you have to sleep on the couch? I should, if anyone does," she said.

Jeff, having undressed to his undershorts, had gotten into bed. Amy travelled back and forth to the bathroom, apparently able to remember only one thing at a time. She took the tiny brush and went away stroking her hair, then came back for the comb. A bedside clock had stopped, which Jeff wound and set. Leaning on an elbow, and pretending interest, he flipped through a publisher's catalogue, on a table next to the bed. Amy came back in, to search again through her purse, which she then shoved against the mirror, a dead end.

The catalogue was bound stiffly and falling shut seemed never to have been opened. Jeff set his reading glasses atop the bedside table. "Would you like for me to lie on top of the covers for a while?" he said.

Amy dawdling beside the bed shook her head. Suddenly, her arms went up full-length on either side of her head, and she drew in her breath. Her back arched. A diver, she would have been about to plunge headfirst from a high board. Here, her hands clutched beneath either armpit, and she drew off her dress. She got in gingerly beneath the sheet; their heads turned instantly toward each other. For the first time, Amy did not look away from his close observation. But she was not stirred.

"You've been yawning all evening," he said.

"I know it. I can't help it. Aren't you ready to sleep?"

He said, "I'll doze off and on. I don't need many hours of sleep."

"I feel like you'll be watching me."

"I will be," he said, laughing.

"It makes me feel funny."

"All right. I'll close my eyes."

When his hand touched her, she stiffened. Behind closed eyes, she longed for some great emotion to take hold of her. She thought of movie scenes with limp heroines being lifted in strong arms, their hair streaming floorward. Sex, with Tony, was an experiment. She had wished he loved her, knowing she could not love him. It was always evident in the way he rolled off her and went to sleep immediately, that he never thought of her until the next time. She lay then wishful for love and staring into the darkness. Jeff's hand moved cautiously. Her brain became alert. If only she could stop thinking. She remembered going to a birthday party where she had known none of the children, the hostess's mother being a friend of Edith's. When Edith left, the others drifted toward games. Then ice cream was served, and she had been revealed, still standing in the doorway, and had begun to cry. Edith had been summoned and arriving had said, "I'd be ashamed," although she had thought her mother so beautiful, coming through the door, all she had longed for was never again to be left by her. Questioned at home, she remembered blurting out that she had not been to the bathroom for two days; then irritatedly Edith had said, "But why didn't you tell me!"

But how much, Amy thought, clenching her teeth against the feel of Jeff's hand, she had never told anyone. Was she now responsible for feeling nothing? He was older and married and everything in her past told her what was happening was wrong. She cried silently, Don't! with her teeth gritted. Her soul and her spirit were unmanageable and ungiving.

He said, unexpectedly, "I'm sorry. I'm sorry."

Having been about to move over her, he lay back. Opening her eyes, Amy was not sure exactly what had happened. Then she understood nothing had happened and, therefore, she need not feel guilt.

Jeff said, "I had waited for you too long."

Never thinking to brush aside apology for what she had not

wanted, and ignorant of anything she could have said or done, Amy slid down a little on her pillow and, shortly, fell asleep.

Jeff coddled her, and she knew it. She did not blame herself for falling asleep, but him for leaving her behind. Where could he have gone? Waking, she felt deserted by his independence. The sun likely shone elsewhere. It could not penetrate the crevasse protuberant with fire escapes between Alex's building and the surrounding ones. Her eyes came open. She saw first the furniture, shadowed and hostile-looking. Then, only her head moving slightly, she looked up toward the window, which emitted a solid greyness.

I'm awake, Amy had thought, a little terrified. Fear was a continuous state of being, suspended briefly while she slept. She accepted its return. Slats of the venetian blind were unthoroughly closed; the shifty light gave her a sense of having been drugged. Beyond, the apartment seemed full of animosity, silent and soundless. Barely could she see in the dimness of the tiny hallway, which seemed confining as a boat. Reaching out, she touched the wall once, to stop some shaking in herself.

Everywhere in the kitchen copper utensils had been hung, a decorator's fine touch. They served as decoys, diverting attention from the fact that most of the drawers and cabinets were empty. Alex seldom ate at home. Perfected, the kitchen seemed an unused stage prop, particularly because of the stillness. Amy's own sense, as she walked in, was of playing a part. Her face registered disbelief while she stared at the unshaven man, dispiritedly at the kitchen table, on which a whiskey bottle sat. Hollowly she spoke as if a memorized line: "You shouldn't be drinking in the morning." But because she was Amy, she added a little uncertainty even to that of which she was sure. "Should you?" she said.

Jeff said he was sorry. Crumbs were not enough, after all. But she had gotten into bed with him! Amy said.

"The whole time wishing you were not, Amy. Don't you think I could see that? I don't want pity."

"I don't pity you," she said. "And, please, don't drink."

His head nodded but his hand seemed to have its own mind. He reached for his glass. Amy's heels sank firmly, impressionably, upon the cork floor. Reaching him, she pressed a cheek to the top of his head, one hand shyly touched his back. "You've got to go outside," she said. "You'll be all right if you take a walk and eat." The queasy feeling so often with her subsided unexpectedly. She was struck by the disappearance, like that of a close friend. How unlike her to have reached out, she thought. That she could offer only what she wanted might have enabled her to. Jeff set down the glass, understanding that she was trying.

Speaking, she had mimicked her mother who made the same suggestions helping her father over a drinking spree. The words were familiar, the pattern was known; but to follow only what was set out for you limited life. Amy felt that strongly, now, after drawing back from Jeff more quickly than she had wanted. She sensed again she avoided full-blown relationships; the queasiness that had left her began to return.

Coming out onto the broad avenue, though the sun settled on it stingily, Jeff looked better. He wavered, however, and took her arm. Noticeably, he had not shaved. The doorman was amused and unsuccessfully tried to hide a grin. But an older couple about to enter their Mercedes openly stared. Amy found then she had limits to her timidity and knew she was capable of loyalty. Wildly and publicly, if necessary, she would have defended Almoner's right to be drunk on Sunday morning if he wanted to be. When he apologized for being a nuisance, she assured him he was not.

In a restaurant, she placed a paper napkin in his saucer. Raising his cup shakily, he kept spilling coffee. The shop's stuffiness gave his face a false healthy look, his cheeks pink. Unable to stand the stale air any longer, and putting down her protests, he insisted he could walk. Then within a few blocks, he had to admit she was right. Blindingly beyond them, a marquee drew Amy's attention. Docilely, he allowed himself to be led toward it. The movie was the sort that not even Amy had heard of the stars. Predictably, Jeff fell asleep. His head dropped politely forward, as in a formal bow. She fit a cautious shoulder against him, pushing him enough upright that he did not appear to be sleeping. At the sound of snoring, people had turned. But it came from an open-mouthed bum a few seats down the row. Shifting her eyes, Amy directed their attention to the snoring's source. The people looked past Jeff, without realizing that though he faced forward, he saw nothing. She endured the movie halfway through again, for his sake, then woke him.

"Shall I take you downtown, now?" he said when they stood on the street.

"I'd go alone. There wouldn't be any sense in your having to make that trip," she said. "But I'll stay at Alex's. I don't trust you enough to leave you alone."

She came to bed less reluctantly and put her head on his shoulder. "Amy," he said, "you're the most dear and precious thing I've ever held in my arms. Does that embarrass you?"

"No."

"Good," he said. "I don't want you ever to be embarrassed by sentiment. That's one thing wrong with the world today." He then whispered, "I'm afraid of failing you again, tonight. But someday I hope we'll be as close as people can be. Poor baby. I keep trying to help free you of all your Sunday-school morality. On the other hand, I'm stuffing some back into your head, preaching. But, Amy, to give is to get back so much more."

She turned her face into his shoulder and said, "There's something that's been bothering me. I have to tell you, even though there's no point to it now."

"There is. This is the time to tell everything, anything."

"My story about the lonely little girl burning sparklers on New Year's Eve by herself was about me. It was true."

"Why, Miss Howard! You don't mean to tell me," he said softly.

Leaning up on her elbow to look at him, she then laughed. "Oh, of course you knew. Why did I think you didn't." They looked at each other affectionately before Amy moved to her pillow.

He said, "You are so quiet that I look at you to see if you're still breathing when you're asleep."

"Don't you ever sleep?" Her voice was a little defensive. She had put up a guard, at once.

"Yes, I sleep, too," he said reassuringly. "Don't worry. That capacity you have for privacy and silence is intact. I can't take it away, even knowing you as I do." The sheet settled over them both, as she relaxed beneath it. He said, "I've learned something about my life recently, too." Immediately she was listening. "Everything I've done was for you, Amy, even when you were still in darkness. I know that now."

"Before I was born, you mean?"

"Yes," he said. "Yes, even before you were born. It was all for you. I know that, now."

A call came urgently the next morning from the publisher's. When could Jeff come in to see the copy editor? Amy thought he was too shaky to go; everyone would gossip about what was the matter. They went to a newsreel and roamed about that day, ending with a large dinner in an expensive restaurant. Amy did not quibble about the price since he needed to eat. She slept in the apartment again. After washing stockings, she hung them to dry over the shower rod. He came later from the bathroom and said, "I like seeing your things there, washed out. It makes living here together almost as if we were married." She was surprised not only at how happy he looked, the incident seemed so small, but at the implied lack of intimacy in his life; and she must struggle not to freeze it out of hers.

Reluctantly on the following morning, she said he ought to go, that a publisher could get mad even at Almoner. Jeff agreed a certain amount might be put up with from him but it was time for him to face up to working. She hid feeling peeved and left out and that her day was pointless. She combed and recombed her hair ruthlessly. Sticking in bobby pins, she pulled them out, moaning that she looked too terrible to go anywhere. Already with his hat on, Jeff sat down again. Patiently, he said that, as always, she looked beautiful to him. Why was he so patient! It annoyed her when he was the one who had to hurry. Knowing she had been trying to delay them, jamming the comb into her purse, Amy kept her annoyed look and urged him out. He was keeping people waiting.

The publishing house was a gleaming new one with sepia windows in monotonous rows. On the site formerly had been an old and cherished building. Amy remembered the outcry when it had been torn down. She remarked snidely that such a building was helping to take away New York's character. In the entranceway, when they faced a solid wall of aluminum elevator doors, she shuddered.

Jeff said, somewhat shyly, "I like my going off to work this way, and you to do whatever it is women spend their days doing. And we are to meet again for the evening."

Amy was spared an answer, for people rushing toward the elevators separated them. A swarm of bees might have passed by. The buzzing subsided. "I may start a story today," Amy said.

"That's good news," he said. "And, listen, if you get hot on the typewriter you may not want to come back up here. Call me, and I'll come down there."

"I doubt that'll happen to me." She managed to look worried. "I do have a lot of other things to do, too."

"Of course you do," he said.

"I have to—" but what was lost. A young man passing seemed to jam on brakes and whirled around. He introduced himself as Alex's assistant, but scarcely acknowledged being introduced to Amy in return. He rushed immediately into telling Jeff how marvellous that he was in town. She had stared at him with interest, he was so handsome. He gave a brief apologetic nod before hurrying Jeff into an elevator. And there, Jeff turned his head attentively to the assistant's conversation, his mind gone ahead to business in which Amy had no part. One instant, he looked back before the doors closed, making intact the solid sheenless aluminum wall. Even looking at her, Jeff's eyes had reflected interest in what that snobby man was saying, and Amy had felt also a look of being sorry in them, as if she had been rushing toward the elevator, and he regretted not being able to keep the door open. And so she stood, as if she had missed it, watching the indicator rise. She was not going to just stand there watching it come down! The lobby seemed a tomb, deserted. Whoever ran the magazine stand was busy someplace else, missing anyway. She stood to buy gum, but no one came to wait on her. She went fruitlessly out to the street and with a twinge of envy and jealousy wondered what a copy editor did.

Along Fifth Avenue, the stores seemed monumentally old and grotesque and grey and bulging. She could pretend no reason for going to her room. There the day would pass as if she had a fogged memory, with nothing to recall later. Apart from the crowd, she stood beneath a canopied window and apparently looked strange, for several people looked back at her. She had seen too much of New York to go sightseeing. Then she remembered, happily, that she had never sent the pigskin gloves her mother had wanted. Much as Edith would, Amy wandered between counters, looking, touching merchandise for no reason. The right gloves were found after a thorough search. She had waited until the rush hour for lunch and had to stand an inordinate amount of time in line at a luncheonette; the afternoon had almost passed. Then, after eating, she thought of not having started the story, as she had told Jeff she might. Beside the restaurant's uninteresting front window—some lackadaisical hand had jammed a bunch of paper flowers into a pot as an adornment, once a spring collection, now bleached colorless by the sun— Amy thought life worked this way, that if fate had meant her to start a story, she would have had an inspiration. It was some indeterminate late-afternoon hour when lethargy settled over the city. A typist looked down, sleepily, from an office across the way. About to sweep, a man bolted the luncheonette's door behind Amy. The lucrative hours of the day were over. Buses went by, actually empty. A pigeon ventured to a curb. At Alex's, she would have nothing to do but wait for Jeff. It seemed pointless to go downtown and come back up for dinner. The man stood behind the door, his hand on the bolt and the other clutching his broom, and stared at her, puzzled. She darted toward the pallid pigeon in a vengeful manner, but so that no one else noticed, and sent it purposefully skyward.

Squatly above the subway entrance, a sign gave directions uptown or down. Ducking her head not to notice how arrows pointed, Amy intended to let fate determine her way. Only when the train glided noisily through the tunnel did she look out a window to see the dreamlike sequence of platforms passing. People stared back as she headed toward the Village. After even a brief absence, she felt it more than ever like a carnival. From the top of the subway steps, streets spoked in many directions. Each would take her home. Again, she let an outside factor decide.

Halfway down a block, she saw Tony playing handball against a building, jogging this way and that after an old tennis ball. Missing a bounce and waving as she came toward him, he gave her a hard look.

"I had to go uptown to see some friends from home," she said, only half-apologetically. "I had to get dressed up."

"Not your buddy Almoner?" Tony said quickly. "I saw in somebody's column he was in town."

She refused to look surprised and shook her head. "Are you going to see him?" Tony said.

"I don't know."

"If you called him, he'd take the call? You know him that well?"

"I guess."

He grinned and called, "Catch!"

Taken by surprise, Amy received the ball against her stomach, but then threw it skillfully through the extended hoop of Tony's arms. "Hey, good!" he cried.

"I was the star on my high-school basketball team," she said happily.

They went dancelike along the sidewalk, tossing and retossing the ball. People watched. At her windowsill, an old lady watering a single geranium called shaky encouragement. Amy saw people she wanted to know, to whom Tony talked easily. A shabby wino, wearing pants split open wide along his rear, called her "Beautiful" out of a toothless mouth. Despite his stench, Amy touched him as they exchanged the ball. He went off after returning it. And except that he wore green undershorts, which were showing through his split, what else did she know about him? Their lives had not in any real way touched. That life could be repetitious and dull was evident in the faces she saw along these streets. Long ago, Jeff had said places made no difference.

Anywhere, she was faced with fighting or accepting those two things. Here, colored lights and unusual clothes were only outward differences.

Tony smelled of peppermint candy as he came closer. "Come on and go with me to a party, beautiful," he said, close to her ear. "I haven't seen you in a long time."

"I have to go back uptown for dinner," she said.

"Oh no. You're backsliding, Kansas City. I know, it's Delton."

"It was important to go," she said, instead.

"Why'd you come down, if you're going right back?"

"I don't know," she said.

"Come on. Go with me," he said. "It'll be a blast." He circled her waist and pressed it winningly, drawing her close. Little girls across the street stopped their game to line the curb, balanced like little birds on a telephone wire. One screamed, "Tony's got a girl!"

"See. Out of the mouth of babes. You're my girl," he said, and unexpectedly moistened her ear with the tip of his tongue. Amy shivered. She gazed down toward the end of the street to pretend indifference; there, blood red as a peach stone, the sun was going down. Tony had felt that shiver, and tried again. Amy gazed fixedly at the reflective streaks of sun along the pavement, her ear being touched, before abruptly closing her eyes. Tony quickly began to urge her along the street, past the treachery of objects in the way, a shopping cart, a scooter, a baby carriage.

Another couple flaunting courtship called encouragingly as Tony, still circling Amy's waist, leaned around to kiss her. She let herself be pressed against a building. He leaned against her full length and kissed her harder. She resisted opening her mouth. But he knew enough to ask for sympathy and wiggled closer. He was not going to have his show at the YMCA. He was so unhappy! And she, being a writer, could understand. She was not easily enough swayed. Suddenly then, he simply told Amy she was going to the party and yanked her by the wrist. Caveman-like, he might have been yanking her by the hair on her head.

Hooting and calling, the little girls suddenly came after them. The sun spilled along the way in pink tatters. Glimpsing herself in a store window, unable to see her feet, Amy felt fleet and buoyant, that she was flying. Heedlessly past outraged people, hand in hand, she and Tony ran away from the persistent children, who continued to follow, screaming gleefully. As a bus stopped at a corner, Tony suggested they get on. Amy agreed, for she was breathless. And not much longer could she elude anything, she had thought, by running.

Telephoning, she gazed about the apartment of Tony's friends, thinking it was a room like this she had wanted living with Nancy. A hand to one ear and trying to hear above the noise, she saw, tiny as a pinpoint, the girl she had been, struggling upstairs with her suitcases and fraught with worry over paying a cab driver. Ebony African statues stood starkly against white walls. A shiny zebra-skin rug was splayed on the hall floor. Sling chairs were dabs of color, obvious like spots of rouge on a pale face. Since it had nothing to do with her, she wondered why she had longed for this room. She imagined only because it had been different from what she had known, a reason that seemed silly now. Tony stood riffling through slick art magazines. With an aloof look, he kept his back to clusters of people. He was feeling inadequate, Amy thought, therefore looking defiant. She suddenly decided he deliberately put splotches of paint on his jeans. And why had he worn them when everyone else was dressed in usual street clothes? She had not been the odd-looking one, walking in.

Enormous flurry had accompanied Almoner's receiving a personal call. Shifting the receiver to her other ear, Amy continued to wait, while the call was transferred from place to place in the publishing house.

Lucky she had caught him, Jeff said when he was found. He had been about to leave for Alex's. His voice was tender when he talked to her, but took on a harder note when she had spoken. It dropped a tone. Of course, he could understand she had forgotten having another engagement this evening. He had taken up too much of her time. "It's natural," he concluded, "for you to want to see someone your own age."

"That's not it, at all," she said. "I'd just forgotten about promising to go to this party." She held the receiver from her ear. He would hear the noise. She had considered it better to lie than to hurt him by telling the truth. But the truth was, she thought, staring at Tony, who looked as if he had wandered in off the street, the truth was, she thought again, that she might have made a mistake. She shrank against the wall, out of the way of someone passing a tray. It was held a moment as if for shelter over her head. "Jeff, we'll get together tomorrow. Won't we?" she said.

"If you want," he said. "But I'll wait for you to call me."

She hung up reluctantly, as he had spoken. And she remained there, hesitantly, at the edge of the room. This time she had meant to fit directly into the crowd. But the conversationalists had formed circles, their faces turned toward one another. They seemed to shut her out, like doors. Tony seemed skittering as a leaf, coming toward her.

She accepted a drink. "This is a lousy bunch," Tony said. "I don't know why I thought it'd be a good party. I'm sorry we came."

"Maybe it's us," Amy said.

He shook his head. "Let's get out as soon as possible."

"But, maybe it is us," she said.

"This guy's had a little success," Tony said angrily, nodding toward the host's paintings on one wall. "It's gone to his head. He used to be a nice guy."

"He's getting to have a name. That's good. He's our age, too."

"He's got lousy liquor." Tony thrust his glass up and stared at the bottom, as if hopeful of finding something like sediment. "Let's get out of here," he said.

"But shouldn't we talk to *somebody?*" Amy said. "I feel dumb, leaving. I feel it's my fault now if I can't talk to people. We can't say they're all stupid."

"Hell, they are," he said, starting her toward the door.

"I think we ought to stay," she said worriedly.

"Then stay," he said, heading for the door. Reaching out as if for his coattail, Amy followed. Picking up her purse, from among many left on a side table, she saw her face in a mirror and looked away. No one noticed their leaving. It had seemed a nice party, she thought. She went out automatically when Tony opened the door. She might have joined a group by going up and saying something first. Anything would have done, as an opener. Too often, she waited for people to make overtures to her. As the door closed and set them into abrupt silence, she thought that waiting was why her life might seem to consist so much of nothing happening. She settled, with simplification, on the thought that she must learn to start conversations.

Though he used all his coaxing methods, tried pressing her again ardently against a building, himself onto her, Amy remained firm about not going home with Tony. He was angry, but surprisingly, for him, that mood disappeared. The next moment, he was all smiles and nuzzling. She thought, dumbfounded at not having had an argument, that perhaps Tony also wanted to change. They might be growing up, she thought, a little sadly over wasted time. And it must be true, for he was spending money. At an open stand, Tony insisted on buying two slices of pizza and presented her with one. The mixture began to slither off the crust, melting cheese and tomatoes and anchovies deliciously running into her hand. They were laughing and ate rapidly, despite the hotness. To walk along the street, laughing and eating, gave Amy one of her unexpected and fragmentary moments of happiness and well-being, which she and Jeff had discussed. Thinking that, the call to him bore down on her conscience again.

Above them at her steps, the landlord's window let out light in a thin stream, as she and Tony stood, kissing. She liked even the taste of pizza lingering on Tony's breath, its warmth. He apologized, in a whisper, for his behaviour the time they tried peyote. That didn't matter any more, Amy said, forgiving happily.

He said, "Your knowing Almoner, in fact, gave me an idea. I'm going to make a play out of *Reconstruction*. Would you show him the script?"

He leaned so close that Amy had to lean backward to see him. Then in the inadequate light his face had its pointed look, like a fox's. Despite his closeness, Amy spoke stronger than her normal voice.

"Have you finished it?"

"God, no." He lifted meager shoulders. "I haven't even started it. I wanted to know first if you'd show it to Almoner. I don't want to do all that work for nothing."

"I don't know him that well."

"I thought you knew him pretty well," he said grumpily.

Amy's foot sought a step behind her. Rising, she teetered but kept herself carefully from Tony's reach. "No," she said firmly, "I don't."

Even in the dim fake moonlight streaming from the landlord's window, she saw dismay on Tony's face. Having taken a step backward he stood below her like a waif; his arms thrown out were beseeching and scrawny. "I see. Well, see you, Amy." His

257

hands went into saggy empty pockets as he turned away. Impulsively, she thought of asking if he wanted back the quarter for the pizza. But he looked meek disappearing. She was sorry again for the times she had begrudged lending him money. Standing at the avenue, looking both ways, he seemed about to look back. Amy automatically lifted a hand to wave. He rounded the corner. Her hand dropped against her thigh, as if, all along, she had intended to strike herself.

Never will I know what she's doing walking uptown, but my feets ain't going to make it. Jessie said, "Miss Inga, ain't you tired?"

She would find strength in her body to make it if it were the last thing she ever did, and Inga said, "No. I'm not tired." She pulled nervously tighter the drawstrings of a crocheted handbag, already as tight as they need be. Having bought it from Mrs. Decker, Amelia had said, "It's the new shade for fall," meaning it as incentive for Inga to get up. Then she had rolled her eyes toward Amelia asking, For what? Jeff was gone.

These sidewalks once had been wooden planks set above the road. They had walked them fearful of wasps' nests beneath. No longer now around the station ahead were there any vacant lots. Still it was a lounging place for men, some now leaning against dusty car fenders. A car slowed. Its driver stuck out a ruddy face and said, "Give you a ride?" Turning on him a bright smile, Inga shook her head, despite Jessie's eagerness. When he drove on, she apologized. "I'm sorry, Jessie. I just had to make this walk again. I made it so easily when I was young."

Well, she sho was foolish if she was going to try to act young again, Jessie thought. She had to undo the drawstring Inga had tangled. Stopping beneath a sycamore, Inga fumbled with the purse. The mirror she took out flashed in half-realized gleams along the shady sidewalk. Inga saw it had been a mistake to order over the phone. When the girl at Chester's had read off "Light Suntan," she had asked if that wouldn't give her a healthy look. Then the girl had answered, "Yes, mam, it says on the label a healthy glow." But the make-up was caked in creases along her face. Would nothing work out right as hard as she tried? Inga wondered. The Vaseline touched to her eyelids, instead of giving her eyes a shiny look, made her look as if she had been crying.

"Who was that man?" Inga said.

"Mister Vida, runs the bait shop out on the highway. I thought sho you knowed him, you looked so friendly."

"I get confused about who I know and who I don't," Inga said. "But wasn't it nice he stopped?"

"Anybody round here see anybody out walking in this heat going to stop," Jessie said. "Miss Amelia would have carried us uptown."

"I hate to ask her with Latham at home. Queer to me why he wants to change around that old cabin out back."

Menfolks was queer. Never any telling what they would do. Looked like she'd know it by now. Jessie lagged passing the movie. Inga said, almost excitedly, "Cary Grant. I'd like to come to that tonight."

"No'm, don't come tonight. You be's tired to-night. Stay home." Jessie then nodded her head, barely saying "How do" to a Negro man sweeping the sidewalk, who in return barely spoke. They looked away from one another quickly.

Counting the man in the car as one, the man coming along now, lifting his hat, was two. He was looking, wasn't he? "How do," Inga said. She could sound like them, every one, if she wanted and wondered whether white people here had ever realized how much they talked like the Negroes. In other days, men had looked at her first. "Jessie, whatever happened to that great big market basket I used to have?"

Going down one side of the station and now heading for the

259

other. My feets giving out. Jessie wondered, What was she shopping for? She said, "Honey, that basket done been gone, wore out with age."

In his little garden, still full of cinders after all these years, the stationmaster stood up and said, "Afternoon, Mrs. Almoner." Seeing her come toward him, he had thought she had something to say. She only stared, a wet look to her eyelids, while the Negro woman with her sat down and eased off her shoes. "I was pinching my mums," he said. When she only repeated, "Mums," he realized Mrs. Almoner had nothing on her mind, after all. He suggested a tour of the garden.

Inga found herself walking between flowery rows. The old man, whose hand was shakier than hers, guided her along the cinder-block path. It would be better, Inga thought, if she were helping him. She wanted to laugh despite everything. Afterward, waving to Jessie, and signifying her eventual return, she went on past an empty-looking feed store and to the post office. Outside there, a little boy lifted his puppy to drink from the bronze fountain. Thinking how listlessly the flag hung in the hazy autumn, only at the last instant did Inga think to count, "Three," when the man coming down the post office steps lifted his hat. When he had gone on, looking a little miffed, for she had barely spoken in return, she recognized that girl's uncle. He always wore the same perforated shoes. Inga made up for that lack by speaking over cordially to a Negro on his knees, polishing the post office's brass spittoon.

When she came in, the mail clerk slapped down the Delton paper. " 'Fraid you didn't catch another thing today," he said.

She said, feeling foolish, "No news is good news." She tried to smile. As she turned away, he called, "Heard Mr. Almoner had left town. He didn't leave instructions about his box. You want the mail, if any comes, for March Walsh?"

It rang a bell, like a tinkle, as removed in memory as the long-ago bell that had sent her trudging up a hill to school.

Inga shook her head, wanting no letters for any (whoever he was) March Walsh. It probably wasn't really amazing that people lived together almost a lifetime without ever knowing one another. Inga went down the steps again as delicately as a dancer, her toes in yellow shoes carefully pointed. Crossing back to the shade beneath oaks, she said, "Jessie, it's taken more out of me than I realized. I think we'll have to take the taxi home."

Praise the Lord; Jessie said, "I just seed Vern. He can carry us." Catching sight of the old green car meandering past the Negro stores, she yelled, "Boy, come on over here!" He came only after turning his head and staring a long moment, then his green fenders shimmied, the car stopping, a drum's rhythm in time to the motor's overly apparent running. Stretching an arm along the seat, Vern watched Jessie open the back door, watched Inga get in. Her smile was so quick it seemed gone before it got there and her eyes were like blind people's eyes. Don't see me, he said to himself, his hand roving airward toward the steering wheel, without causing her to glance his way. "Be careful, you going to knock somebody in the head," Jessie said. "How come you ain't working?"

"Ground's too wet," Vern said. In the rearview mirror, he saw Mrs. Almoner reading the paper, not caring who driving her long as somebody was. "Whoa, boy! Slow down," Jessie warned. The car bumped a curb going around a corner. "What time the show start tonight?" Jessie said.

"Seven," Vern said.

Only when they passed the movie did Inga look up to say, "Cary Grant. I'd like to come."

Who going to keep her from it? Vern wondered. Come on and come, he thought, I'll sit next to you. Driving on as fast as possible, he saw her slide to a corner and hang on to a strap as if for her life. "Going to let you out before the gap," he said. "I got meetin' to go to."

"Us done walked uptown, guess us can walk from the gap to the house," Jessie said, beginning to climb out. Inga, already out and waiting, said, "Jessie, I'm going to clean up Jeff's study."

Jessie sat a moment, catching her breath. "Ain't supposed to go in there when he ain't home," she said. "Us don't need to do nothing this evening, but rest."

"That's a good time to get it done when he's not here."

'Zactly why she's doing it, too, cause he ain't. Looking for something. "Umm-umm," Jessie said, and heaving herself to the ground stood with Inga beside the panting car. Closing both doors, Inga said, "Thank you for the ride."

Looking like she's dead, Vern thought; has to look at me now. "Got through with your paper?" he said.

Reaching back through the window to take it, Inga said, "Oh, I didn't know I had one."

It might have been her own baby, if she'd had one, who had written these sad lonely letters, Inga thought. They struck more than one void in her heart. So young as Amy, she did not believe she had been as full of urgent grief and asking. (I'm unhappy. I don't think the feeling is ever going away. It's not the feeling sorry for one's self kind of unhappiness. You told me to do away with that. I've tried. It's dissatisfaction and unrest, wanting something and not knowing what. An ever-present lump of deep-down sadness never goes away, except briefly. I must have been born with it inside me. I wish someone—not you who've had enough—but someone could have it for me. I'd sail along without thinking. Yet I do want the capacity for sadness, even if I don't see the reason or purpose for it. I hope I will, as you think. I only don't want sadness that's of no purpose, except unhappiness. It's raining. I don't want eternal sunshine.) The letters, read often, opened easily onto Inga's lap. Careful of their creases, she read at random. Tender as first green shoots, Amy must be protected. (Probably, I'll always have to be pushed.) Jeff would be the right one to help her, Inga thought.

Having despaired over getting her to unlock the door and come to supper, Jessie had gone to bed. Her feet in echo again ascended the stairs. The iron headboard of her bed thumped the wall, bedsprings protested, and she got in. Inga, soothing letters, thought wearily of sleep, herself. Everyone must have the same sense of relief about stretching out at night, glad that a day had been gotten through. (I want to live every day as if it were a whole new lifetime, a whole new world! I want every day to run the gamut of emotions, to feel everything anew—suffering, unhappiness, trouble, sorrow and laughter. In the streets I want to see those things reflected in the faces of people, imagine and think about each person's story; keep conscious all the time of the things going on inside people.) Inga lifted her face, as again the headboard thumped the wall, and again the bedsprings tried resisting Jessie's restlessness. She saw the letters without seeing them, tears in her eyes. She saw underneath all their various surfaces people suffered the same. Before, she had not had much curiosity about people, their lives, and what they anguished over or dreamed of. To suddenly think people anguished the same anguishments, only separately, made her want to put back her head and bawl like a calf. She might have, except that only night, hushing an instant, would hear.

On pink paper with its edges all fringed, one letter broke her heart on sight, being delicate and girlish. She had to make clear surface differences were only that, surface differences. Could she say to people, here, the color of skin makes no difference. Probably to some people, she could. She might start with Amelia, and make her understand by showing her the letters. She would say,

Look! The girl and I are years apart in age, but the same in our hearts. And Amelia would surely see; anyone could. (I feel these are among the last months in my life I'll be young. Twenty will not come again.) The tears on Inga's face met the corners of her mouth, turned up into a smile. (I'm older and wiser after reading anything you've written. Never again will I be the same person. When I read your work now I wonder, How did he know that? Why did he think that? Your last story gave me a funny feeling when you wrote about dying. Don't think old. Once I stood on a corner, my throat dry, trying to eat a bagel for lunch. So much beyond one incident sent me there. It makes life lonely and difficult not being able to tell everything. I do love you and not only, as you once asked, because you know how to construct a proper sentence, but because you understand. This moment, I love you so much. I think I understand your pressures, too. Thank God, for letting us meet. Sometimes, I've thought I didn't, but now I think, How good to live. You've done that for me. Goodnight.)

Inga had long known where Jeff kept hidden the key to his lockbox and had wondered what he kept there, besides manuscript. To have the key in her possession was to have the one to him, she thought. She began to replace the letters gently, in sensible piles. Askew, they had overwhelmed everything. She gave to one pile a settling rap, like a deck of cards, against the title page of *Reconstruction*. Staring down, she focused slowly on the list of characters, the name March Walsh immediately standing out. Then she felt clearly how much Jeff's work meant that he entangled it, as he did, with the rest of his life. In this room where he had created time of his own, how appropriate that the desk calendar remained dated backward to the day he had left. How much and too late, Inga wished to commend him. She settled another letter onto the pile, her face grown haunted. (Please keep writing me. Your letters are so beautiful. I hope knowing that just your writing me gives me a certain faith in things, makes you happy.

Aside from unhappiness about me, are you happy? Try not to worry and to work. That's the important thing. Despite it's all being so hard, this is a wonderful wonderful time in my life because of knowing you. I hope all this adoration isn't irritating. I read once, and I don't know where, adoration is a universal sentiment; it differs in degrees in different natures. I can't help being emotional about knowing you. Others feel as strongly as I, but happen not to write you. I'm afraid you don't understand that nothing in your life has been worthless. You must be proud knowing your writing can inspire me so much that I write you the way, at eleven, I wrote to movie stars. And now I feel silly!)

A confusion of insects crying and, at once, falling silent gave night a pulsing feel. In one of the silences, Inga was aware of the determined beating of her own heart and felt not afraid of the rapidity, as she had often. It had never been a doctor she needed. In the hall, she flipped on a light to reveal the wallpaper, now meaningless. The light spread outward, upward to catch, as remotely as starshine, the dining room's chandelier, which sprang alive in varicolored gleamings. A firecracker might have exploded, the floorboards leapt alive with sparks, and reflected everywhere in multitints, like Christmas bulbs, or the silver seedlike ornaments of birthday cakes, reflecting candlelight. When Amelia right away had given her silk stockings, she could have said, No, thank you. Jeff liked the ones she had. She could have done the milking, which he had not minded. In the hall, listening to the nothing that was there, Inga clutched a letter. (I might be nothing but a dreamer; that's what I fear most. Being like that Henry James character who thought all his life he was destined for something different and died realizing the only thing different about him was that he had never done anything, that he was the only person to whom nothing had ever happened. Suppose that turns out to be me! If I haven't quite been able to break out of my shell, you do reach me. Something, somewhere inside me is touched deeply. Obviously, I can never forget you. But more important, you have partially formed what I am to be. I remember your saying, someday you would be so damned proud of me. I sleep at night, now, telling myself, someday he is going to be so damned proud of me. I'm going to make this a chain. The hope you've given me, I will someday hand on.)

Going back to the study, Inga put away the letters, once and for all. Hungry now, she went to the kitchen, certain Jessie would have left a plate of food for her in the oven. Silence companionably went along with her. In this place undeniably Jessie's, Inga was aware the thumping of the headboard against the wall had been continuous. She shut the oven door without removing the plate. The door's minute squeak was forerunner of the squeaks her feet made on the back stairs. At the top, she stood timidly an instant before knocking.

"Who?" Jessie said immediately.

"Only me," Inga said. "I kept hearing you turn over and wondered why you were so restless. Can I get you something to eat or drink?"

"Come on," Jessie said. "If you want."

Inga, opening the door, thought that here was fear she could not even imagine, for reasons learned over many years and handed on from generation to generation, like less realistic tales. If she had stopped to think, she might have guessed that in this stuffy and remote room, Jessie slept winter and summer with the windows down and bolted when, from outside, the room was not even accessible.

"Ovaltine?" Inga said inadequately.

"No'm." Jessie lifted a perspiring face from her pillow. "But, I thank you."

"Jessie, you know all of us would do anything for you. You would be taken care of even if something happened to all of us."

"Yes 'um. Anything I got is yours, too."

266

"I know."

"Haven't nobody come up in a long while. I'm glad you come."

"I'm glad, too." Then after turning, Inga looked back. "Thank you," she said. She went back down the stairs and watched herself descend, a shadow on the wall.

"I swear to my soul," Dea said. "You give 'em half of Hades, and they want the other half. Why did they have to go and carry on the night we wanted to go to the show? If they want to sit with white people, why don't they go to Delton. They've taken over that town. Every one of them on welfare's got a car, too." She turned down, dispiritedly, Joe's offer of a "sody" at Chester's, instead.

"They won't picket more'n one night," he said. "If they shut down the show every night it's like cutting off their noses to spite their faces. Negroes like shows, you know." He had taught himself to stop saying "nigger," though he never had meant anything wrong by it. It had been habit, learned from his daddy, he guessed. If you did think about it, the name had a ring that didn't set right. He wished them no harm, but was darned if he was going around calling them black people, the way he had heard on television they wanted to be called.

"Well," Amelia said when she and Dea met in the parking lot, "you disappointed as I am over missing Cary Grant? I'm crazy about that man."

"Who?" Joe said, coming up. "Your bridegroom?"

"Naw, we're old married folks now," Latham said. "She's talking about Grant."

At the wet base of the fountain before the post office, frogs croaked. In the headlights of the police-directed cars, circling around the movie, they watched several hopping. Near the fountain, illuminated by its base lights and on display, was the first bale of cotton ginned in the county. Latham began to mention it and leaned in pain, instead, against his car fender. The others solicitously helped him to the front seat. Amelia explained he had, that afternoon, fallen off a ladder while fixing up Marguerite's cabin.

"You've probably done something to the kidney you've got left," she said, half-angrily, thinking this pain in his back was the second ruination of their evening out. "I'm glad we didn't ask Inga to come," she said. "As crazy as she is about Cary Grant, it would have been too much."

Inga's being mentioned made Dea feel she had to ask, "How are the Almoners?"

It was a good thing she had, she thought, afterward.

Amelia said, "She's been sick, but is better. We haven't heard too much since he's been in New York."

"Swear to my soul!" Joe muttered, not particularly meaning to be heard.

"She hasn't mentioned seeing him?" Amelia said quickly.

"Not to me," Dea said. "I'm sure not to her momma either, or she'd have been on the phone to me." And Joe was right. She'd like to swear herself.

"They'd do something if they knew he was up there," Joe said.

"What?" Latham asked. The others pretended not to hear, having no answer.

Amelia said, "To tell the truth, we've expected some kind of news." Or else, she thought, she wouldn't be here married to a man apt to have no kidneys, who spent his time hammering on a Negro's house when he ought to be hammering on his own. "We've just been waiting."

She meant existing, Dea thought, thinking of people who went other places, and she gazed at frogs and cotton and the limits of her life. Perhaps she had settled for too little and now she lacked something. She hoped Amy fared better.

"Well, I don't know what to say," Dea said. Joe slipped an arm about her, saying, "That's a first," making the others smile. "Take care of yourself," she told Latham, thinking how intent people were on their lives. She wondered whether the children were only waiting to divide the little acreage and the house which was all she and Joe had to leave them, or whether they would care when they were dead.

"We got to get on," Amelia was saying. "We're practically baby sitters for our Negro out back. She's scared when we're not home." Only when she said it out loud and laughed, it did not seem so funny. She tucked unconsciously into her mind the way Joe almost glanced at Latham, then did not.

"I'm so glad Edith's coming down Sunday," Dea said, after she and Joe drove off. "I can save a toll call." But to wait even a few days was going to be hard.

"You still ain't going to say nothing to Mallory?" Joe said.

Since she had discovered long ago that he knew perfectly well how to talk and willfully talked like a fieldhand, Dea had given up correcting Joe. His reason for it was one more thing she would go to her grave wondering about. Though in a way, Joe's talk often gave him a flavor, which made people notice him. Maybe that was why he did it, to set himself apart. Oh, Joe. Dea suddenly placed her hand tenderly on his thigh. She had not before thought Amy cared what her daddy thought and had not herself thought Mallory thought about much of anything. Now she asked herself, Who knew? She might give up trying to account for other people. "If anybody tells him, it's Edith's business to," Dea said.

Every year she had Mallory's birthday dinner, though since the children had been grown and gone, Dea had known he had rather stay in Delton. Still, she had insisted, telling herself it would be good for him to be out in the country and somewhere a lot of whiskey was not served. Now, seeing Joe in a different way, she would not mind their being home alone. She had taken a book out of the library yesterday, and today she did not want to cook any dinner. Wishing Mallory was celebrating where he wanted, Dea felt no triumph this year about holding the party.

Brushing past ferns, Edith came in wearing a pink mohair stole, which made her look pretty but stouter, her eyes revealing what Dea already knew: have dinner as soon as possible. They could not, however, avoid having out the one bottle they always kept.

"Got snake bit on the way!" Mallory cried, seeing the bottle. "Jesus," and he added another jigger, "you don't get to be sixty-five years old every day in the year!" He poured with the others grouped about the table familiarly, as if over open ground to mourn.

"Ain't that roast ready to come out?" Joe prided himself on one sophistication, rare meat. Dea jerked her head suggestively toward the living room. After a slow moment, Joe got the hint. "Come on, Mal, let's leave things to the womenfolks," he said.

But he had left things too long, Mallory thought, draining his glass. "Better freshen this up first," he said, tugging at an ice tray.

Knowing she could not wait all day, Dea said innocently, "How's Amy?"

Edith popped a radish into her mouth and answered evasively, chewing. "Fine, worked in a bookstore."

When Joe said, "I imagine she runs into folks from this part of the country up there, don't she?" Edith thought, They know.

"Joe!" Dea said. "You and Mallory run on."

"Boy, they're trying to get rid of us," Mallory said, his glass full. "Edith doesn't want me to say Amy's quit her job. She's not doing anything up there."

Stirring mashed potatoes, Dea dropped open her mouth, as if about to taste them. "I said 'worked,' " Edith said, blushing.

"She's going to come home," Mallory said. "I've decided that."

Edith said, "She's doing something." They turned faces of inquiry toward her which asked, What? When Edith said she could not explain, they looked away feeling justified, having felt she could not. Tired, which he must be now, Mallory had a look in his eyes similar to one in Amy's, and only then could Edith ever realize this was the father of her child. The night she had conceived, sensing it, looking out, seeing the moon full, she had tried to weld them together inseparably afterward and had clutched him; saying he could not breathe, Mallory had drawn her hands away, as if knowing people always lived apart. Though, surprisingly, he had seen through her trying to hide Amy's joblessness. What else did he understand about her? Edith wondered, less lonely. Funny that one little radish had killed her appetite, or perhaps feeling happier, she was not hungry.

Lilylike, or as if all their necks had been simultaneously broken, they bowed their heads. Mallory intoned, Give us grateful hearts Our Father—

—and for what? he wondered. A daughter who had left home and was probably living with an old man, and for his so long not knowing what to do about much of anything. Had he failed Amy that she needed this love?

For these and all thy blessings, Mallory said.

—he probably meant to be nice telling her how beautiful all her ceramic things were. She should be grateful he liked to try making everyday living livelier, dancing and carrying on. Why not? Edith thought. She could have had a little drink with him on his birthday, though his blood pressure must be up, he looked so hot and tired. Oh, Amy.

Mindful of the needs of others . . .

Lord, she ought to have put a top on those potatoes, Dea thought. They were getting cold. She had always thought Amy's unpredictability had come from Edith's side, but uptown the other morning, she was not sure that what Bubba had on his breath was mouthwash. He wouldn't take after Mallory and Poppa, would he?

For we ask it in Jesus' name. . . .

Shootfire, that roast is cooking away, Joe thought. That cuss Almoner was almost as old as he was. Amy's had everything in the world money could buy. What in the world did she want from him? Though if you studied Mallory long enough, you might finally figure it out.

Amen. All spoke with finality. Like children saving dessert, they saved until last their most favored topic of conversation. Not until Dea brought in the cake was Amy mentioned. "I'm sure Amy's looking for another job, though," Edith said, as Mallory blew out the candles. "I want just a sliver of cake. I mean it."

"Of course, if she didn't have any money," Dea mused, "she would have to come home."

When Edith said, "You could take back her stocks, couldn't you?" Dea nodded her head in satisfaction toward Joe, meaning, she had told him.

"What good would that do?" Mallory said.

"Of course!" Dea said, thinking she understood. "She might take it from— Get it someplace else, or something."

They definitely know, Edith said to herself morosely.

Dea would tell him everything later, and Joe settled to football on television, while Mallory went to the bedroom to nap and the women cleared the table. Joe loved fall. Every year now though, when the leaves fell, he thought of friends who were gone, and every six months or so there was another.

"He's up there!" Dea cried, in a whisper, the minute the door shut her and Edith into the kitchen. "Amelia told me."

"Let me set these plates down," Edith said, needing a moment. Instead of asking, Who? she said flatly, "Mr. Almoner."

"You don't sound surprised," Dea said.

"I'm not." Edith, weary of pretense, thought the moment she had sent him the letter had been like the one at the end of the day when she got her girdle off.

"We should have known she'd write him," Dea said, rinsing dishes.

"Maybe she didn't." Edith lacked courage. "Maybe someone else told him, a well-wisher. I don't blame Amy for wanting a different life from ours, Dea."

"My life's not yours," Dea said quickly. "You've had a maid as long as I can remember."

"Money's not everything," Edith said.

"That's what people who have it always say. Let me try having it, then I'll tell you whether it is or not," Dea said, drying her hands.

"We need to try to understand what she's doing," Edith said, reaching for a dishcloth.

"You just said she wasn't doing anything!"

"Doing *being* there," Edith said, gazing at a dish. "She's trying to find herself."

"Is this some kind of psychology mess?" Dea said suspiciously. "If it is, I just don't believe in it. All it does is excuse people. Only yesterday, Rod Randolph blamed all his alcoholism on his mother's not loving him when he was a child. Would I be to blame?"

"Who?" Edith said.

"Don't you see The Doctor's Hour on television every day? At two, this town comes to a standstill. It's as real as life."

That's too real for me, Edith thought. It was enough to have cried herself silly over Almoner's books, which she had just read. She could not imagine anyone going through what he must have to write them. She guessed she'd just have to stick to ceramics. A band on television beat happily, saluting the glorious afternoon. Through covert fields opposite, a boy trailed, carrying a gun, and a spotted dog leapt after him. The opened cotton was blindingly white. Dea swirled around dishwater blue as the fall sky and said, "We got by without all that psychology mess. When we did something wrong, we got blistered. And look at us."

"Yes," Edith said, holding up a dry dish. "Look at us."

"Boys," Dea said, gazing out of the window and thinking of Bubba (Edith wondered if she had said "boys" pointedly), "boys might need to run wild a little before settling down. It sometimes shows up later if they don't," though she had thought it so nice to have Bubba graduate from the university and immediately settle down with a sweet little girl. Stirring up dust, crowded cars were passing along the road, and Dea drained the sink, thinking, If the Negroes were coming from church, it was late. "Seems like we been in the kitchen all day," she said. She and Edith stood on the back porch and hung out damp aprons as ceremoniously as flags.

"You don't think then, it's all right for them to meet?" Edith said.

"No sir-ree bobbed-tailed cat, I don't." Dea knew she could change in some respects, but not all.

"It's—" Edith began.

"An old man and a young girl!" Dea cried, as if presenting on cue what she saw.

Joe swung open the door and said, "Half-time. Got anything to eat?"

Dismay already reflected on the women's faces only deepened. Joe had waked Mallory calling, "Want a snack and to see the rest of the game!" Mallory called back that he wouldn't mind a roastbeef sandwich.

"I just been wondering," Joe said. "Is Amy safe up yonder?" Night and the roads seemed to him no longer safe even at home.

Her baby. How could she have kept her safe? "You talking about physically safe?" Edith said.

Dea banged a glass to the table, while Joe stared. "Edith's gone stark raving mad off on some psychology mess," Dea said. "What kind of safe do you think?"

"I thought you meant safe," Edith said, backing down. "I'm sure she takes taxis if she goes out at night alone."

"Well, I can't imagine her not having that much sense." But Dea could not help adding, "Whatever other kind she's got."

Joe would have expected a little fireworks, but the women, in resignation, only put back on their wet aprons. Dea picked up a stack of dried plates. Edith, feeling suddenly ravenous, began to cut the cake and nibble. Mallory had his shoes finally tied and came in and began to take up ice. The afternoon lengthened and soon it was dark.

In softened ground and among peat-moss bags, a man knelt setting out white and yellow clumps of chrysanthemums. They seemed to blossom mindlessly, their shaggy heads bending. His shoulders sagged and sadly he mounded dirt about their roots, as if burying something which had breathed. Killing frost seemed imminently in the air. Only temporarily would his arrangement ease the monotony of the jaundice-colored building rising above him. The sun was a flamboyant gold seal directly overhead. Trees were wildly aflame in a park opposite, and there old people sat warming their knees. A young woman, leaping up the front steps, was about to pause and admire his flowers, then went on. His handiwork, the gardener thought, would last about as long as her smile had.

Amy had wanted to make him happy about his flowers, he looked so downcast, but had been afraid to stop. Her buoyancy was too unusual, she was afraid of losing momentum, and so had plunged ahead toward the door. She felt, for once, absolutely come together, complete as a pie whose cut wedges, put back, make it perfectly round again. Her feeling might have been be-cause of the day, which was gorgeous. Crossing the park and hearing music from a merry-go-round, she had first seen the possibility of believing in herself. Even stared at on the subway intrusively she had not minded, but had merely stared back levelly. Outside, a young nurse had given her a look confirming the chicness of the new suit. Amy had found it with a sense of miracle, along with the right accessories. She touched a silk scarf adroitly knotted at her neck and came with confidence out of a revolving quadrant of the door. Then she was brought up short by the uninterruptedly bland and curry-colored interior and by the stilted smell of food cooked and kept too long over steam. Oval aluminum carts were depressingly the size of babies' caskets, being pushed on squeakless tires down a corridor straight ahead.

The eyebrows of the receptionist were querying and rose as she glanced at Amy's clothes. "Almoner," she repeated, then scooted her chair backward to look through index cards. Rolling back to the desk with a suspicious look, she was aware that well-dressed but aberrant people were quite common in private hospitals. "We have no such person," she announced coldly.

Amy turned wordlessly to recross the bland expanse of carpet. Feeling alive with good will and the right intentions, she had hoped to make up for other lapses by visiting, and perhaps it was right she was not to be allowed to. Set adrift, wondering if she had misunderstood the address, she was called from the door by Alex, who got off the elevator. When he had led her toward a colorless plastic couch, he handed her a package. "This arrived at the publishing house for you, in care of Jeff." Seeing her puzzlement, he added, "Maybe he left it to be sent, and someone forgot until now."

"It seems strange he wouldn't have brought it himself." She held it tightly to open when she was alone. "But the receptionist said he wasn't here."

"I put him in under an assumed name," Alex said, "though I'm afraid even the doctor didn't recognize his real one."

Amy wondered what everything was for, and turned her head to watch a man merely mopping the empty hall at its far end. Keeping slightly turned from Alex and plucking string on the package, she wondered if he thought it her fault Jeff was here. She said, "I'm so unhappy about Jeff. And is he unhappy? Permanently, I mean?"

In conservative grey, Alex's long legs were stretched ahead of him. He stared down at them. "I don't think fixedly unhappy," he said presently. "That's not his habit, as you know. And I hope you do know that happiness comes from determining on it." He glanced at her slyly. "Though, perhaps, you are still young enough to believe it's something to be found?"

"I've been looking." Amy had spoken off guard and in embarrassment added, "I mean, I've tried to be happy."

However, Alex had not been fooled and gazed at her kindly. "Maybe I shouldn't discourage you. Keep on looking, then. Maybe you'll find it."

"Why should I?" she said. "I don't deserve anything special. Someone like Jeff does." And she sat still, realizing it had been childish to go off looking, that you could not find happiness as you found Easter eggs. Today, coming through the park, she had seen children with pirates' flags and briefly searched beneath rocks with them, for gold. Now she gazed down the hall and sighed, looking at the man wringing out his mop.

"If you want to see Jeff, you'll have to hurry. Visiting hours are almost over."

At the elevator, Alex said, "He's sedated and very groggy. I didn't know what to do when I found him, except bring him here," and had he fallen short, he seemed to be asking. "I've never dealt much with people in his condition."

For the moment, Amy felt older and wiser in the ways of the world. She felt capable, as Alex stood looking uncertain. Not trying to excuse himself, he said, "It may be good that I did bring him. He's not at all well. Liquor has this effect on him partially because of medicine he's taking. The doctor didn't feel he drinks all that abysmally much."

"If only I hadn't left him." Amy tucked her hand into Alex's and they shook firmly.

"Call me if you need anything," he said.

"Do you think he'll be out of here soon?"

"I hope so, and it's important this doesn't happen again. Do you mind my asking, has he asked you to marry him?"

"In a way, he has. I haven't thought about it, but I have to. I know he wants me able to make up my mind. Do you think I should marry him?"

"I would," Alex said, "be very tempted if I were you."

Having rung for the elevator, he walked away. On the other side of the glass front door, Alex stopped and tipped his hat and gave a little send-off wave of his hand as if saying bon voyage or good luck. Touched, Amy nodded. She watched him go, recognizing he was on her side.

In the elevator Amy unwrapped the package, and she held it open against her going down the corridor in search of Jeff's room. There, white blinds had been drawn against the day, and with his silverish hair and pale face, a sheet drawn to his chin, he seemed a waxen figure on display. Only on the windowsill were there moving gold glimmers, for there the sun edged in. The room, heavily accented by some dulling drug, made her think of bees droning, of clover, of the sluggishness of midday on a Southern summer afternoon. The remoteness and secretiveness of their meetings in the woods came back to her also in this darkened room. Uncertainly by the bed, she repeated his name until he opened his eyes.

"I was dreaming. I thought in the dream, you called."

"I'm here," she said.

"Amy."

"Yes."

"You had begun to grow up, but not in the way I meant. More and more, you were becoming secretive. I'd urged you to be frank." He spoke haltingly, from the drug. "I suspect a young man. You should have told me."

"Is it my fault you're here?" Bending close, as he spoke softly, she wiped perspiration from his forehead.

"If only you had told the truth about not meeting me." After a struggle, he focused on her face.

"I'm sorry."

"You always are," he said. In the resultant silence, he closed his eyes, while Amy looked gladly toward a nurse who had come to the doorway and pointed to her wristwatch. Amy whispered, "I'm still here," and the nurse had gone.

"Is it the same day?" Jeff stared up a little blankly, before whispering, "Today, you are more like Amy. Softer. People are like animals. You're secretive. A cat. Played possum too, hiding from things. I'm a mule. Stubborn. Wasn't I persistent?" And he relaxed into half-sleep, smiling.

A little sadly, she said, "Maybe you'll be sorry now you sent it, but the manuscript came and means so much. Do you hear?"

"I knew it was your voice." His eyes gave up the effort to open.

"Do you still want me to have the manuscript of *Reconstruction*? It's come and means so much."

Stronger, managing to look at her, he said, "You're the very person to have it. Not even I had thought of it." His hand waved and lost direction. "That top drawer. There's something for you. Said once you wanted it. Bought it that day the book was done. You never came. What we had deserves a better goodbye than it was getting."

"Goodbye?" Moving toward the top drawer, she turned, surprised.

"Wasn't that what you were trying to tell me?"

"I hadn't thought so."

"Then I'm confused," he said, attempting to push himself up.

"Yes, I know. We'd better talk another time. Jeff, the bell!" She had taken a small box from the drawer. The bell, gold, was not large enough to cap the end of her little finger. She held it out on a thin chain. "I thought you had forgotten."

"I'm able to forget so little," he said, lying back.

Following whim, chance, the less rational and the easiest way had not been goodbye to her, Amy thought, teetering on the curb outside. Though that assumption on Jeff's part might have been kinder than others he could have made. She thought again that he was too kind to her, knowing herself to be capable of dishonesty. Stepping off the curb, she headed toward the park, though at evening it was too foreboding to enter. Evening had blackened buildings and gave their windows a void look. The city seemed to grow upward toward disappearing rooftops, the streets became funnels, the reverse of wells. Staring up, Amy saw the bland grey sky, a link between avenues, and thought how responseless the city seemed. To whom might she speak? Wells, at least, revealed one's own wavery image. And she remembered suddenly the old barn near her school with the clock with the stopped hands, and the clock had not lied; time stood still. From the park, indrawn with dark, a man who had been selling balloons emerged. He stuck a pint of whiskey to his mouth a moment, the balloons on invisible strings motionless above him merged into an enormous greyish mass. Feeling herself colorless, Amy passed him and went along the block to the subway entrance, having too a feeling of being emptied, like the park. Was she responsible for her alienation? Trees dipped toward her and bore oncoming night as they might bend with rain. Glancing over her shoulder at no one, nowhere in particular, she thought of freedom and of its various degrees.

The other evening, after Tony had traitorously turned the corner, she had found a note inside tacked on her door. To return a call to Connecticut. From there, Billy Walter shouted as if he were calling from overseas, his voice hale and hearty, enlivening the hallway's gloom. Panes in the stained-glass window seemed to reverberate, and blithe yellow light shook like foil when she switched on a light near the phone.

"Billy Walter! I thought you never were going to get up here."

"Honey, my back yard's the closest I've ever wanted to get to New York," he said. "This pretty weekend I'd be hunting, and I'm indoors freezing, instead."

"Freezing," she said, laughing. "Billy Walter, it's nice and only October."

"Shoot, the wind almost blew me off the streets of Hartford last night."

She spoke in a remembered teasing voice, "I wonder how you could get warm?" But suddenly her voice rose, as if near hysterics. "You are coming down here, aren't you?"

"Whoa, of course," he said. "Sugar, would I come this far and not see you? Last night, I waited up half the night for you to call me back. Evidently, you didn't come in. Shame. Want me to tell your daddy on you?"

"He might not care, if nobody else knew."

"Don't sell the man short. I'm sort of his emissary."

"What?"

"I said, don't sell your daddy short. The man wants you home."

Though not given to inner reflection, Billy Walter thought back to Amy's father, as he had stood at the club's bar one Saturday night, or had it been a Sunday? Nights there ran in memory similarly together. He only knew it had been that late hour when the neon tubing around the bar's mirror had melded indistinguishably and blurrily into it, the whole glowing like a halo. Gaily and effusively, he and Mr. Howard had fallen onto one another, the older man giving him a hefty slap on the back. Here, Mr. Howard had announced loudly to anyone within earshot, was a good old boy! That pleased Billy Walter, being an epithet he bestowed on himself at his best moments, on his friends at theirs. He went hunting only with cronies who were good old boys.

"Son," Mr. Howard had said, "aren't you going up yonder to the big insurance convention in Hartford?" Stabbing for it, he had at first missed the bar with the edge of his elbow. Billy Walter had helped to right him. Modest, his rounded cheeks reddened as apples, Billy Walter admitted to having been chosen as his company's representative. When Mr. Howard asked, Billy Walter had promised to see Amy, promising further that if he found out anything not suitable for Delton's ears, he would not tell it.

"I mean," Mr. Howard had said, "if she's become a Communist, or something," his eyes watery. Promising, Billy Walter knew the man was not worried about Amy's politics at all.

"Honey," he was saying, "get on your face. I'm coming down to show those Yankees some dancing."

"Oh," Amy said. "But I have other plans."

"All I don't have is time," he said. "I only have tonight."

In Delton, he had turned toward the picture window overlooking the golf course, while his drink was being refilled, in order not to see Mr. Howard's tears. "She'll come home, won't she?" Mr. Howard had said. "Amy," Billy Walter had said, "is kind of cerebral, not like us drinking and tearing up!" For a moment, they had forgotten everything to roar in appreciation of their own kind, heads lolling. "My wife, I guess she's more the other kind, too," Mr. Howard had said when he could. "Well," Billy Walter had said, "that's worked out all right." "Oh, has it?" Mr. Howard had asked. Slipping from the bar stool, he had gripped Billy Walter's arm. "Son, I appreciate it. I was happy as a bluebird when you and Amy were running around together. By the time you get back now, I'm going to be needing some insurance on my dancing school." "I'd sure be glad," Billy Walter had said, "to come around and talk to you about that." He had gotten up respectfully when Mr. Howard stood, and they had parted, veeringly.

Billy Walter thought Amy might not need much coaxing to come home, hearing her voice trembling. "Billy Walter," she said, "I'm so glad to hear from you I don't know what to do. Come on down here quick as you can." She heard her accent return.

"Honey, you bawling? Tell old Billy Walter what's the matter?"

She said, "I'll stop. Just you come on down here, quick as you can."

Dancing exuberantly from the phone and almost lightheartedly, Amy thought of her first kiss, from Billy Walter with closed dry lips when they were fourteen. Jeff was full of understanding and would realize her need to see someone from home, but she should not tell him exactly who it was.

"An old friend from Delton," she said, phoning.

"Amy," he said, "you won't be young and attractive always. That does enter in, now. You aren't going to be able always to do with people what you want. If people can't trust you, you won't have anything left. How many times have you changed our plans?"

She was irritated knowing that he knew and had answered, "Twice." Confidently afterward she apologized and said she

283

would call him later. Later, when she telephoned, the ringing had gone on and on in the apartment, the following day and the following. Where would he have gone without telling her? The only possiblity which occurred was that an emergency had called him home, until Alex came back from Europe and found Jeff in his apartment, unconscious.

Knowing none, Billy Walter had not picked a sedate small hotel, but the city's brassiest and largest. It fitted him, too, Amy thought, watching him cross the lobby, which was full of nearly riotous conventioneers. In a forelock like a pony's, blond hair fell over his forehead, and though he wore an expensive suit, it was buttoned straight up like a uniform. He elbowed his way, happily, toward her. The morning after his call, with some quicker perception of what was right for her, Amy had found a black crepe dress with a (moderately) plunging neckline, as well as the suit. She felt more than well-dressed in the bar which Billy Walter picked. With her bosom shaking, a fat lady, who played a thumping piano, began immediate rapport with him. "Bourbon and branch water," he had ordered, which bored the waiter. But, overhearing, the lady had laughed loudly and played the piano accordingly. "That's Tennessee wine!" Billy Walter had called. She shook, bending over her pudgy thumping hands, the waiter looking sour. Disapproving, in parody, Amy drew down her own face. Billy Walter was glad to see she had not become pretentious living in the city. "Big girl," he had said, "when are you coming home?"

Teasingly, she had said, "Oh, Billy Walter, you don't care."

"I didn't call you for a while," he had said, so seriously Amy was surprised, "because I thought you had something going with Quill." Having pretty much looked over the field and finding nothing left but much younger girls, and tired of his mother questioning his comings and goings, Billy Walter had decided he needed to get married.

"How is Quill?" Amy asked, hoping for some clue as to what had gone wrong between them.

"Crazy as ever, maybe crazier. Cutting up every time I see him. Though don't mistake me, Quill's a pretty good old boy. Last time I saw him out to dinner, he had everybody in the place looking at him and knowing who he was, too, by the time he left."

"Isn't he happy?" Amy had asked quickly.

"I don't know why he wouldn't be. But I've never found any cure for unhappiness but keeping busy, have you?" Billy Walter had given her an affectionate poke with his swizzle stick, shy about his pronouncement, and had gone back to talking about Quill. "You and Quill are up on the same cloud."

"I think I'm coming down off mine. But you're a philosopher, Billy Walter. I never knew you had such thoughts." And feeling naïve, she said, "I'm impressed," and looked at him a bit differently. "Is Quill still thin?"

"As a rail. Too thin."

"I hope his father is happy."

"You going to show me around tomorrow? What's on the agenda, art galleries and museums?"

Dismissing those plans, Amy said, "Whatever you want to do."

He looked doubtful, but said, "You wouldn't be interested in Yankee Stadium?"

"I'd love it, if you would!"

"Careful, you almost looked as if you enjoyed smiling."

"Oh. Don't I usually?" she said, continuing to.

"No, you're always solemn as an owl."

"I'm afraid to have a good time," she said.

"Why?"

"I don't know. It makes me feel guilty."

"You always were a screwball," he said, but kindly. He took her hand. "But you're not going to bawl!"

"Oh, dear. It seems like it. I don't want to here." She looked around.

He began to urge her up from the table saying, "Come on up to my room. You can cry your heart out."

Going through the lobby, he put an arm about her waist and kept her close. While observing the deriding glances of several obvious New Yorkers, Amy did not move away from him. Suppose they looked like hicks, she thought, entering the elevator. And who decided how many buttons to button on a coat? She was concerned, however, with how many people she ought to go to bed with, numbering Tony and Jeff and, momentarily, Billy Walter.

This hotel room, like most, was innocuous, the carpet without pattern was merely a covering for the floor, and a couple of unnoteworthy pictures hung over the bed. The curtains were there only to frame the gayer view outside. Amy, in the middle of this room, was aware of nothing except Billy Walter, who seemed enormous coming from the door, which he had locked. He crossed from it in two strides and put his arms about her. She was suddenly frail as a flower stem in strong wind, and bent against him. Totally new feeling filled her at his touch. With a sense of awe and astonishment, she was lifted, and Billy Walter carried her to the bed.

There, Amy felt no desperate need to cover herself, even when she had removed her dress at the moment Billy Walter began to tug open his tie. As quickly as he got into bed, she turned toward him, liking this closeness: that she could see minuscule flecks of green in his eyes, never before noticed. She felt compulsive about being even closer to him. When he turned off the light, she was sorry, for she had liked the sight of their bodies together and wondered at her previous embarrassment. Time, which seemed so often to her endless, seemed now not long enough. Closing her eyes, and wishing to prolong it, she felt a potential in herself never before felt.

They were two birds fantastically soaring, she imagined. They came back to earth, seemingly many-limbed, perspiring and exhausted human beings. Billy Walter got up eventually and stubbed his toe, headed toward the bathroom. He swung open the door as if clubbing it. When it had banged the wall, he shoved it again toward the bedroom, though it did not close completely. Unmindful and whistling a gay tune, he stood urinating loudly. Amy lay back on the bed to hug her pillow with a sense of deliciousness, laughing.

Preceded by a towel on which he was drying his hands, which he then flung across the room to a chair, Billy Walter came back. Amy got up swiftly, to stand as if experimentally, beside the bed. He looked at her appreciatively. She was still laughing when she went into the bathroom, never bothering to turn on the obliterating faucet.

The clothes of spectators, in stands opposite, had seemed scattered dots of color, like confetti. Distant trees waving in the fall wind had a similar look of frenzy and excitement. Nothing seemed to press inward on her, and Amy felt that she had grown, that inwardly she had expanded. Rising with the crowd to cheer, she watched in exhilaration as pennants flew in the breeze, and programs slung outward by excited fans sailed far. On this sunny afternoon, almost blinded by the brilliant green ball field, she wanted to think of nothing beyond this moment, of nothing more than being at a game with Billy Walter. In her seat, she leaned against him. She had had this morning nothing to put on but the black crepe dress and could not go to Yankee Stadium! Billy Walter quickly solved her dilemma, rushing them downtown in a taxi, which waited while she changed, and took them as swiftly to the field. Figuring it out herself, Amy knew she would have contrived a difficult situation on subways and buses, causing them to arrive for the game both distraught and late.

All around her now faces showed an unreasoned happiness, without guilt. She applauded the players and their striving enthusiastically, having a sense of well-being in the autumn day. Perhaps this was everything. Perhaps, after all, it was enough, she thought, glancing around. Anyway, since she was here, she meant to participate. Players jogged from the dugout and seemed, pointedly, to glance up at Billy Walter, in camaraderie; calling off their names, glimpsing their numbers, he seemed to know them, making Amy envious. Even the peanut vendor, who circled routinely and wearily, stopped to joke, calling Amy "the big boy's better half." She blushed, remembering that in bed, she had dwelled on having a baby with Billy Walter.

From the stadium gate, where he held up a brand-new suitcase, waving, Billy Walter took a taxi to the airport. Streets over which Amy returned to the city were clogged with dingy houses, the bus driver was melancholy and had no interest in his pretty passenger who tried to make jokes. Gabby as his two-year-old learning to talk, he thought, his frown driving Amy back into silence. Slumped into her seat, she stared out, depressed, knowing that she might turn obsessively inward again. Her loneliness was intensified when, leaving the bus, she had phoned Jeff and received no answer.

Coming from the hospital to stand in pale sunshine on the steps, Jeff then took the arm Amy offered. She hoped to make him smile and descending the steps said, "See, the chrysanthemums are still pretty." Across the way, however, the trees partly had lost life and, half-bare, cast emaciated shade. Having caught cold, he had been confined past his designated week, and the flowers held little interest, though he smiled dutifully and said they were pretty. He held in one hand toilet articles in a small brown kit. Pressing that arm, Amy shepherded him carefully past traffic, halted with an impatient look, as if tethered by the red light.

Motorists, noting that he came from the hospital slowly, and noting the attentive young woman, thought that even though he relied on her, he had a self-possessed air. It made them conscious of being enclosed in cumbersome and expensive machinery, for his air said he wore and carried all really necessary to own. His tan raincoat was slightly soiled, its wide belt drawn so tightly to his middle, he seemed to have received some blow there, or to expect one. His set face had a pale sheen, like paraffin. Though November had only begun, there was to the air, to the day, some hint of white. Icicles might glisten so, hanging in the sun. Amy reached out a hand to turn up Jeff's coat collar, before they disappeared from the motorists' sight into the park.

An olive-skinned delivery boy, peddling fast on his bike, had lifted malicious eyebrows as if inquiring whether Amy might be a Girl Scout? Having looked quickly away, fearing comment, she glanced back, once, with a feeling that someone came behind her along the path. Visible, only, was the hospital's forbidding roof.

Almost immediately while following the path, Amy and Jeff had begun to alternate passing from sunny spots into chill shadier ones. That set for the afternoon a fitful aura. Although they admitted wanting to scuffle through leaves, lying about in sparse drifts, they did not. The leaves were bright as Indian war paint, red and orange and yellow, and rose up with wind in whirlish dances. Following the walkway, Amy and Jeff happened past the merry-go-round and arrived at the top of an incline to face a lake. Trees stood away from its edges, permitting them to see the variable and uncertain sky, which was thinly blue. Giant clouds of grey overrode the blue, full of rain and possibly of snow. There were no longer swans on the water or people out in boats and a sign on the padlocked dock read, Closed. A bent candy box drifting on the water presently dissolved to spread in many unrelated directions. In this silence, the merry-go-round's deadened music came to mind as well as reminiscent thoughts of childhood: lost things and times. Before those presently here had come, said the desolate place, there had been children and activity and good times, but the desuetude did not promise their return. The effect made Amy linger over the thought of how long she had known Jeff, without significant change in her life. Was she to go on and on as she was? Her moods shifted and changed, like the heavy clouds drifting here and there on the delicately blue sky. She was glad they did not feel the necessity of small talk, and oppositely, she felt as a burden the obligation to break their silences.

"I'm glad you're out of that place, at last," she said.

"Yes, I'm tired of illness. This may all be over soon."

"It was a depressing place. And for you to be in it depressed me, too. In fact, I don't like it here any more. I wish we were in our woods, Jeff."

"That, Amy," he said, "was beautiful. But it's past. You can't recapture. Though people keep, if they're wise." And he glanced at her sideways, as if ascertaining whether she were. He put out his hand then. "A leaf's fallen in your hair." He removed it and gave it to her.

Amy took it like a more valuable gift and stuck it into her purse. "Thank you," she said. "I'll keep it because it's from you. Somebody said to me once that leaves falling were like people dying. Was that you?"

"No," he said. "But someone near my age, I'm sure. Your father?"

"I don't think he's ever said anything even that profound," she said. "It might have been my Uncle Joe, though I never think of him as saying anything poetic. But it must have been one of them."

Having observed her opposing moods, he said, "I'm going to risk further boring a beautiful young woman by recalling an old saying. The one about the child who grows up and is amazed to discover how much his parents have learned."

A sudden glimmer in her eyes matched his own, and Amy laughed. "I have to confess. I don't think I've ever understood that saying fully, until just now." The face she turned toward him expected approval, perhaps appreciation of her being agreeable. Jeff remained absorbed in watching a squirrel running blithely along an iron railing. Feeling rebuffed and looking away, Amy snuggled her cold nose into her coat collar. Aware of her movement, without exactly looking at her, no matter the weather, he thought of sunlight when Amy appeared in that coat. He had to smile when she snuffled her nose, made runny by the day, against the collar. He felt indulgent and spoke more kindly. A feeling from their better times came back. "Shall I take you inside somewhere? Are you too cold?"

"No," she said. "Not unless you need to rest?" She glanced around at benches, themselves cold-looking with the trees leafless. "Let's walk on to Fifth Avenue and then decide what to do. Unless you want to do something different?"

"No. I need to clear my head and need exercise, too, only slowly. Though I thank you, beautiful Miss Howard, who is growing up. I'm afraid, however, I'm not to be much fun."

"I didn't know you thought I was looking for fun."

"Once, I thought I knew a great deal about you. This past week or so, I've not been sure."

"Does the time you were in the hospital count?" she said defensively. "I tried to come often, but it was tiring just to sit when you were so sleepy and confused. You never could remember things, even that you had sent *Reconstruction*."

Stopping in the middle of the path, he gripped her elbows and turned her toward him. "Amy, I've had a hard time convincing you of anything. You've been too stubborn and proud and stiff-necked, and gotten away with it because you so often broke my heart. Also because you're beautiful. But damn it, I'm telling you, once and for all, I haven't forgotten. I didn't send the manuscript. I only wish I had thought of it."

She said, shocked and believing at last, "But then, who did? It's impossible that anyone else did."

He seemed as stunned as she. "That's something I've got to think out myself," he said.

"But what's happening to everyone?" she said. "My mother told you how to find me, and now this." She stared at him as if he had materialized on the path. "It's as if they wanted us to be together."

"I said once they were enough to make us tear our hair." He looked as if he had been laughing and were trying to stop, the back of his hand against his lips. "It was when your momma first looked at us cross-eyed, I remember. Now she seems to be looking at us in an entirely different manner."

"They couldn't change," Amy said conclusively.

"People do," he said. "At your age, you grow so fast our people might feel you've bridged the gap between us."

"Seriously. What are they up to?"

"I am serious." But when he saw that she looked more angry than mystified, he said, "I'm sorry. I had to laugh. Here we are with our heads together, puzzling over them the way they've probably puzzled over us." A little against her will, Amy laughed. "Apparently," he said, "some of them have come up with a solution, which seems to be, Yes."

She went ahead up the path, faster, as if in pursuit of something. Leaving him behind, she stopped as a traveller halts to figure out direction at a crossroads. She waited for Jeff, who came up the incline seeing the stubborn set of her chin. He had always had the calm belief everything would turn out all right, now worried the time invested might have been wasted. Confusion had made him drink, for if Amy had changed their plans because she was serious about some young man, why hadn't she told him? Always ahead there had been the possiblity of his being replaced, which he had told her. The way she went about with her head down, she did not look happy enough to be in love. When she had come to the hospital, she had worn an impatient and puzzled frown often and sometimes even a devious look.

At their age, what possibly could either her family or his have learned that would change them? Amy felt Jeff knew, or guessed, and would not tell her. That was annoying. But did he know? Having stuck out her chin, she stared straight ahead at where she was going, feeling wrong about questioning Jeff. Yet doubts crept in. Sitting beside him in the hospital, she had even asked herself disloyally whether she really liked all of his work, whether it was good that several of his books had recently begun to have popular acclaim? He had a small wise smile, as he hurried to keep beside her, which she felt was presumptuous. She knew that, at least, her life was going to be happier than his. What had he meant by saying the others meant Yes. To what? she asked herself, suspiciously. Turning at his touch, she followed him to a bench, answering that it would not be too cold to sit down. She did, however, tuck her hands up her coat sleeves for warmth, having forgotten gloves. Jeff studied the upturned toes of his shoes, his heels digging a little into the ground. Opposite them was a bench heavily layered with newspapers, which had obviously been a bed. At its base a pigeon pecked dolefully.

"Imagine having there to sleep," Amy said.

"Yes," Jeff said, glancing that way. "Poor lost soul."

She at once removed her hand from her sleeve and placed it on his arm. "Are you sure," she said, "that you aren't cold?"

He twined his fingers into hers and said, "I think shortly we should go inside someplace warm."

"Not where you can have a drink, though."

"No," he said, pressing her hand. "I can't risk your anger again. At the hospital, you seemed so often angry. I know you didn't want me there, but I'm real, Amy. And you can't know true feeling unless you love someone despite their faults."

She looked up the path, hoping for a distraction, for always what he said seemed to his advantage. And not having known how to answer, she watched several young men who were hunkered down beside a bench, playing some game involving a penknife. On the ground, their transistor radio played loudly. Through their shouts, Amy could hear fragments of one of her favorite songs. Billy Walter, liking it, had requested it from the lady with the thumping pudgy fingers. Amy now tapped her fingers lightly to the music, asking, "Do you like this song?"

Jeff's look was distant, either not knowing the song, or that a radio was even playing nearby. He looked in the direction she turned, but said nothing. Amy said defendingly, with a little condescension, that it was really a good tune and the favorite of everyone she knew. He might not have heard, or was paying no attention, and Jeff held up her hand, as if she must see it before her face. "Amy," he said, the words abrupt and withheld a long time. "You want the world to be a simple place, and it's not. Didn't you see I understood your difficulties growing up because I had been through them, too? I wasn't a pretty young woman whose family pushed her lovingly down every proper path. But I had other things expected of me it wasn't my nature to fulfill. I told you it was difficult to be a writer if you had to start by fighting all the disbelief, and conventionality, of the Southern middle class. It's unfortunate you continue taking the childish attitude that no one understands. That no one has been through what you have."

She said quietly, "You're mad. You never have been before."

"Before, I may have made a mistake," he said. "If so, I can only blame myself. I treated you with tenderness because I thought that was what you needed most. I thought if someone were kind to you, you might be to others. You know I felt I learned compassion from someone far worse off than I. That woman who sent me home when I ran away, long ago. She thought of me, not herself. I keep telling you, something will come out of all you've felt. How can I know when?" He gave her a sharp look, to cut off her question. "Surely, you know, by now, I don't have the answer to everything, even to very much. But, earlier than you, I knew as much as I could of regret and grief and loneliness. I was a better man for it, but I couldn't help wanting to spare you."

"I didn't want to be spared, though," she said. "I wanted to know things. That's why I left home."

"Yet still you expect life to be the way you want it," he said. "You want friends and no enemies. To take only what you want and to give only what you want, and when. That's not the way the world works. An artist must—"

"I'm not an artist," she said, taking away her hand. "I don't fool myself about that any longer. I just kept promising you to write."

"I never wanted you bound to me by promises," he said, "about writing, or anything else. That promise should have been made to yourself, anyway. I liked you as you were. I never cared whether you became a writer. But this life here, I believe, is not the right one. It's sophomoric, and there aren't even any exams. Do the people you know talk about making something, or make it? I suppose, sometimes, they mar up paper or canvas to justify themselves, but anything beyond that?" Then he said softly and pleadingly, as her eyes filled with tears, "It won't all have been wasted, though. You do have time. You have so much time. If I can wait for things at my age, you can at yours."

"You're being kind to me again," she said, "and probably you shouldn't be." There was not so much time, she was thinking, with a little inward wail, having never wanted to be an old maid. Couldn't he realize how she worried about that? Bare branches overhead refused to reflect the sun and to see leaves, through tears, they appeared not anchored to anything. The little over-turned boats, behind the padlocked gate, returned to her mind. "I'm never going to have anything to write about."

"You'll have a book, someday, that won't let you alone," he said. "You'll write that book. Pride's not going to let me think you won't. I've invested too much time in you. I'm not going to be-lieve my heart would choose you if you didn't have in you what I thought."

"What *about* your heart?" She turned so abruptly, they bumped knees.

"It often aches," but he smiled. Amy smiled then, innocently. In a calm voice he said, "I like to think I made you, as you made me over." His forefinger sought the chain around her neck. When he gave it a slight tug, they heard the bell ring. "I wanted to see if you were wearing it."

"I haven't taken if off since you gave it to me."

"I haven't seen it exactly the way I wanted," he said. Amy looked away, without answering. "Always, you're worried. Amy, it wasn't physical attraction that brought us together or kept us together, either. We had a stronger need, because it outlasted all that long time when I held your hand and there was no more response than a child's. Poor innocent little star. You never thought you were putting yourself in the way of a comet. I often still think of the way you came to me, just coming, without knowing exactly why. Haven't you ever questioned writing me after I sent you off the way I did?"

"I think I've mainly questioned the wrong things," Amy said unevenly.

"What wrong things! The point is that by questioning, you can see what are the wrong things. You can judge what's worth keeping, bothering about. If you hadn't questioned, you might never have known the difference. Someday, when you're older, you'll see that you're ahead. You won't decide against the life you've chosen too late, the way I think your mother has and also—"

"Your wife!" Amy said, sliding forward on the bench. "Jeff, did she send the manuscript?"

"She is the only person I can think of who could have but, more importantly, would have," he said. "She wants for you, and is even generous enough to want for me, what we want. But I'm no longer sure what you want."

Did he suspect something had happened, in her life, like Billy Walter? Amy said, "Why does she think she understands me? Unless, she read my letters! Oh my God, think of the things I said about them. And about myself!" Her head bent toward her knees while she moaned, "I don't want to be felt sorry for."

"Then perhaps I don't have to worry about you, after all," Jeff said, tugging her sleeve until she sat up. As she searched a Kleenex from her purse, he said, "Don't cry," and when she brought out the leaf, and held it up, they shared again the moment he had taken it from her hair. "Amy, you know it's possible to cherish privacy and silence too much. Fear might cause your doing it. Have you thought of that? Never to let anyone know you, means never to know anyone else. That's no way to be marooned in this life. I've talked about bravery and it takes it to be exposed. But what do you have to hide? The confusion of growing up? Never. Not to want to be felt sorry for is a very grown-up feeling and puts you in the driver's seat. I only wish I could see what you are going to do with all the rest of your life. You've come so far, though I still have a question."

She held the tissue piecemeal in one hand. "A question to ask me, or one that exists?" she said, lifting her face.

"You'll know, in time."

"It feels so stupid to have had my letters read. Suppose she shows them to your sister, and she tells my aunt and so on. Oh, it's all so embarrassing, having me known." Her mouth formed roundly a silent wail.

"But why? There's nothing the matter with you. I like you very much," he said simply. "Your letters made me not only love you, but fall in love with you."

"I just feel afraid," and her face reflected that she did not quite know of what.

Understanding that, he said, "Well. We do have a little work ahead."

Having rolled around and around the remainder of the tissue until it was a small ball, Amy stuck it into her pocket. The park, misting over, looked shrouded. The blue in the sky had gone and a whiteness, moving in steadily, inserted itself between trees. The young men on the bench had halted their game to stare her way and seemed to nod slightly, meaning that in alliance with her age, they were on call. By looking right away, Amy meant to imply things were all right, that she was in cahoots with this generation by choice. Jiggling and swaggering young men, their lives consisted entirely of the external; they would accomplish nothing more exciting than being bullish and young and so had reached, Amy thought sadly, the apex of their lives.

She squirmed away slightly from Jeff's arm, which lay along the back of the bench and rested tentatively across her shoulders. She lowered her eyes to avoid the stoic gaze of a nursemaid pushing an English pram. Only when those serviceably clad white feet had gone could Amy look up, and after the shapeless white-clad figure, wondering how the woman reconciled herself to caring for someone else's baby. Suppose life were inevitable instead of full of choices? Probably, the nursemaid had loyally nursed some aged parent and been left to age alone; justice had no compassion or plan; willy-nilly, people were fortunate or not; some people sacrificed without rewards, while others got them through leading selfish lives. Why? If you made a happy decision, you could be hounded by the ghostly alternative, that you might have been happier. Amy wanted to bound from the bench, realizing that to accept life meant to accept disillusionments.

This acceptance gave her the heady feeling of gaining entrance to a secret society, after a long wait. That she had been intolerant and may have seen things wrongly made her want to rush away and see them all again. Sitting forward on the bench, her pocketbook swung from the ground to her knees, she appeared prematurely ready for some departure.

Bolting up then, she said, "It's freezing," and went off so hurriedly, Jeff remained like a possession left behind. He felt nervous watching her go and, standing, lighting a cigar, not wanting immediately to follow, he saw the young men watching more carefully. Seeing them, Amy felt hesitant to pass, fearing either a caustic remark or preposterously some overt act—that they might drag her off into bushes. Though their glances urged conversation, she turned to head off Jeff and watched him come slowly up the path, his cigar smoke a white drift ahead—as white as the day—a small cloud within the larger one in which they were all enclosed, separate here from distant sounds and other lives. Leaning close and taking his arm, she whispered that she did not want to pass those boys and here was another way. Then, taking the smaller path, Amy said, "But where are we going?"

"Alex has made arrangements for me at a small hotel near him, has even moved my things. It's a residential hotel and will be quiet, though they take a few transients who are recommended."

"I'd be glad to give you a high recommendation," she said teasingly, "but I'm afraid one from me wouldn't count."

Hoping to match her gayer mood, he said, "Anyone would recognize a young woman struggling to make her soul and spirit as beautiful as her face and take her word."

Obliterating buses rose before them suddenly as the off-beat short path ended. They faced an exit blocked to ordinary traffic and seldom used. On either side, stone walls were precisely matched to those through which they had come into the park. Had they really crossed it, or only circled through the mist and come out where they had started? The walk seemed to have taken them so long. Stopping to look back, Amy stared searchingly over where they had been.

Not only this melancholy evening but every afternoon at the Edwardian, the aged desk clerk hid its inhabitants discreetly from the street. Even when afternoon ended by casting over the deadened side street a mauve glow, the color of pigeon's wings, the thick wheat-colored curtains came in lumbering folds across the windows. This activity, like the mailman's arrival, was some fluctuation in a day's emptiness, its silence within, and the dependability of the two things gave the Edwardian's residents, upon arising, a faint, barely renewable, sense of anticipation. Now, at the afternoon hour, most gathered for tea in the muted lobby, while the old clerk, in his tan uniform grown shiny through pressings, let the drawstring of the curtains once more fall and turned and faced them with a smile of satisfaction and completion. They gave him barely perceptible nods of appreciation in return. The street, its activity, no longer existed when squat lamps were turned on, scarcely revealing the brown plush settees. All present bent forward to eat iced cakes in the small amber circles cast by the lamps. In their light, on lengthened bosoms, year after year, the same glintless old diamond brooches hung lopsidedly. Then gracious gentlemen, in the autumnal light, at tea, admired them.

This evening, the drawstring fell ceremoniously from his hand but the clerk's smile wandered from its usual direction and toward the lobby, causing those gathered to glance that way; titters were heard, perhaps a gasp. A man and his daughter (was it?) had wandered in, making a mistake one would have assumed could not be made when the Edwardian's brass nameplate was regarded from the street. Distinctly, a gasp was heard when the clerk, having gone to the desk, handed the man the register, and the tray of iced cakes clattered in the hush.

"So happy," the clerk said to Almoner. "We've been fortunate enough to have Mr. Alex Boatwright's mother for a short time. I'm sure you'll find things as satisfactory as she has."

"Certainly, it's the sort of quiet place I need," Almoner said, "for a while, until I can make other plans."

The young woman was peeking around. "Did you want for your daughter—?" the clerk said.

"This young lady must do some typing for me. I brought her around because she may be coming and going even when I'm not here. Could I get a typewriter?"

"It's late. Tomorrow."

"Fine. Not this evening. I've just come from the hospital and walked across the park. It may have been a mistake. I'm not going to be able to go out again, at all. Is it possible for dinner to be sent up, for two?"

"Two?" Unable to think of a rule against it, the clerk trembled. The young woman, since being introduced, had not removed her eyes from the clock above the mailboxes. Myopically, the clerk stared past Almoner's left ear and toward the attentive faces, whose owners watched transfixed while the three by the desk went single file toward the elevator. Inside, clutching the folded afternoon newspaper against her, Amy sighed. "Oh dear, there's so much to do." Her eyes rolled up, wearily.

Helping her out, amused, Almoner said quickly, "Yes. I'm going to be keeping you busy."

The clerk, carefully not looking around, slid open the grill-work and sank gratefully toward the lobby, having opened Almoner's door. "But I hate this," Amy whispered, after several moments during which she and Jeff laughed.

"I'm afraid it's my fault, for not making things clear enough to Alex. But you're so determined our relationship appear to be only your worshiping at my feet, I was afraid to be explicit about a place where you could stay." He picked up the phone. "Shall I order you a drink with dinner? I can promise, it will be all right for you to have one. I have a pill to sleep. I won't be wandering about tonight." Amy shook her head.

The dinner was heralded by a slow creaking cart in the distance, and when the waiter had gone and Jeff drew out her chair, he stared at her plate. "I'm sorry you wouldn't have even a little white wine with your chicken and rice."

"It's probably as well," Amy said, sitting down. "Even the salad is white. And cauliflower, ugh!" Feeling listeners behind the walls and to dull their second attack of laughing, she and Jeff stuck napkins against their mouths. Then whispering, "It's so quiet," Amy lowered hers.

"We've finally managed to play house but in the most genteel surroundings!"

"There's color in your cheeks, at least."

"I've tried to tell you, I don't need drink. I need you. I was afraid that would make you look away and feel pressured. I'm telling you again, you confuse pressure with responsibility. Amy, that's what you don't like."

"Does anyone?" she said hopefully.

"Probably not. But some people don't run from it. That's the difference. All right, that's all the lessons for now. Don't look so worried."

"I have to keep learning."

"I'll tell you a last . . ." He broke off, then said, "Not a last piece of advice, I hope, but another piece. Learn something each day you didn't know before. It'll be worth living through today to get to tomorrow. Life will never be for you the way it is for those people below." He leaned over the table. "I see so much in those violet eyes that wasn't there before. Tell me something you think you've learned, Amy."

"Life's full of disillusionments. I accept that. Dullness, too." She looked down at her plate; he watched her. "Once," she said, looking up, "I did want to kill myself. I can't imagine that now. Despite everything, I simply would hate—and I know this might sound a silly way to put it—but I would hate not to see tomorrow. I don't think life ever will be empty for me, the way it is for those people downstairs. You're responsible for that." She said, looking at him directly, "But I don't think I'll ever like responsibility. Anyway, I'm tired of being serious. Look at these little cakes." She peeped under a napkin, then held a dessert plate toward him. "I wish you weren't watching your weight."

"Do you know," he said, and looked at her bashfully, "that I can still get into a pair of white flannel pants and a blazer I had when I was a college freshman?"

She had put a cake toward her mouth and let it remain half-way there. "You still try them on?" she said, thinking how curious. She did not like this glimpse of vanity and was sorry when Almoner nodded. But while he spoke briefly about his short college experience, and she ate several sticky little cakes, she considered that she must stop putting people on pedestals. What could you be then but disappointed? Jeff had said, she wanted the world to be as she wanted it: that was bound to cause clashes when other people wanted it their way. How did you ascertain

303

what was real? Licking icing from her fingers, touching them to water in her glass, she dried them on her napkin, and Jeff watched from behind cigar smoke rings. Amy looked after the pattern he made, complimenting him on being able to send one ring through another. He was another human being and, therefore, had his little vanities. I must must must, she thought, mentally pounding her fist on the table, accept people as they are. She kept herself to herself, afraid of being wrong. That came clear suddenly. Suppose, she thought, she was wrong?

The last smoke ring jumped through the air and dispersed. He was saying, "It seems so long, Amy, I've watched you struggle. I could see it on your face just now. Perhaps you've tried to find something which doesn't exist. That may have been my curse, too. Nothing can match our dreams." He saw some wiser look on her face but thought of their broken appointments, the reasons never exactly given. "Remember this. Nothing you do can hurt someone who loves you as much as lying to them."

Amy avoided both the seriousness of the moment and his look by picking carefully among the differently iced cakes. She studied with pretended interest the inside of one, having bitten into it. "I realize the pressure you've been under from your family," he had continued. "You know that, and also from your friends. You didn't even need money, which might have made things between us explainable. I know your young friends must have asked why you'd waste what you have on an old—"

Comforting him immediately, as she could, Amy said alertly, "You're not old."

"You wanted a young man, naturally," he said. "But when you went to one, I think you found something missing. Belief in you. The tenderness I've tried to give. You've always come first with me. That's why you kept coming back. Someday you'll know, Amy, no one will ever love you as I have." As if to state it with more finality, he crushed out his cigar with a grave air.

Something seemed taken from her, and Amy's shoulders drooped. She wanted even less to look at him and said, "Coffee?" picking up the pot.

"All right." He held out his demitasse.

Pouring studiously, as if because of the smallness, she fought resentment against his implication. She was to live out the rest of her life without love. Did he mean that?

He said, "Something's come between us. If it is a young man, I hope like hell you really want him."

"It's not," she said.

"I feel often now as if we're still running the same race, but on different tracks."

Her face distressed, Amy pushed away the empty plate. "I shouldn't have eaten all those cakes! I feel sick."

"Well, I'm going to tell you this simple piece of advice. Chin up. I've found more than once that stood me in good stead." He leaned back, and she lifted her face then, to look past him and around the room. There were not even pictures, and the furniture was dry as bones. "Life grows more difficult," he said, watching. "When you're older, it comes down to a few friends, and many small things. Not much, after all. Writing, I've said, filled up the void for me. Maybe you won't write, but you've got to find something. End of lecture," and he drank coffee.

She said, "How awful."

Thinking he followed her gaze, Jeff said, "Yes, I'd hate to end up in a place like this."

"This cart's taking up the whole room. I'll push it into the hall," she said, and stood up. The wheels lamented her pushing; their creaks seemed to fill the building. With hollow and echoing clangs, the elevator had stopped several times at their floor, and whispery, the old people had passed their door, to shut themselves into their own rooms. Amy struggled and got the cart with difficulty through the door and stood with it in the hall then, feeling senseless accomplishment. From behind one door came an uneven snoring. Once, it ceased. She stood as if her heart had stopped, until the snoring resumed. The elevator shaft had a dark threatening look, like a grave. Smoked glass shades wore away light in the hall to a melancholy dimness, like the worn-away goldness of an old pocket watch. She felt ghosts here, and these might be their footsteps, the thin rubbed places down the corridor's red runner. Her inclination was simply to follow them out of here, but Amy turned and re-entered the room.

From where he had not moved, Jeff said, "Are you wearing the bell?"

Circumventing his chair, she stood beside one which held her coat. "That man downstairs knows I'm here," she said.

"I thought when you moved, I heard the faintest tinkle."

"I've worn it ever since you gave it to me," she said.

"Just once," he said, as if that were all the time he had, "I've wanted to kiss you, with the bell there."

Amy looked indecisive and at the window, leaving her coat on the chair.

"It was raining, but I think now it's freezing." Backed against the windowsill, she said, "Could we just sort of be together and listen to the rain?"

"I've never wanted to force you to do anything," he said.

She went to one of the twin beds, where he sat beside her. She undressed to her slip, and he bent to where the bell rested. Lifting his head, his face remained close. He said, "Amy, have I done you any harm?"

"No."

He moved onto his own bed and stared at her seriously. "No matter what course your life takes, there are some things between us that can't change. There's a bond that nothing can break. There's been love between us, but sin. No, I'm not talking about morality. I know I was the father you wanted. We've committed incest, then. That alone will always hold us together. Now, are you going to run?"

"No," she said, complacently lifting the cover.

He lay back, and watched her settle for sleep. "I'm better for all that's happened between us. I hope, someday, you'll feel you are. If what I've believed since the beginning is right, you will."

"I know so now," she said, looking directly at him.

He settled to a pillow and turned off the light. Rain in a sudden gust burst open on the window. A blinking red sign on a near rooftop revealed them to one another. Jeff rested cupped hands beneath the back of his head. Amy turned, having felt he was laughing, and made out a mischievous look, as well as an amused one.

"You know what I'd like very much to do," he said. "Cut a hole through the title page of the book and make love through that. I've always dreamed of being that close to someone."

She said, "Oh," in a small voice. "That would be impossible."

"Don't ever tell youself anything's impossible. If we let ourselves believe that," he said, "we wouldn't be here."

Next morning, Amy sat up to see that it had not snowed, as expected. A weak sun sent dejected piles of slush sliding along the window. As immediately as she had opened her eyes, she knew that Jeff had, that he now watched her. He was waiting to know her mood, and she felt selfish. As happily as possible, smiling, she said, "I hope you slept. I dreamed terribly all last night."

"I'm sorry. You slept quietly."

"Didn't you sleep, at all!" she said.

"Yes, don't worry. I dozed. I dreamed a lot, too."

"Mine," she said, making a face, "was so obvious. I was shopping and my clothes kept falling off. A lot of old ladies were staring and talking about calling the police."

He laughed. "No, we don't need even a good working Freudian to analyze that one." He got up. "Shall I order breakfast?"

"But how? They'll know I'm here."

"Don't look so alarmed. Suppose they do. But I'll order a large orange juice and a large pot of coffee and toast. That ought to work."

"They send so much," she said, relieved, and leaned tentatively against the headboard. "Tell me your dream."

Jeff, at the window, the cold nickel-colored day as backdrop, seemed part of the cityscape. His voice seemed unattached, bodiless in the room. He looked thoughtful and about to begin a tale. Amy cocked her head, attentive.

"My father had a horse named Molly," he said. "Last night, I dreamed I was lying in the hammock on the porch at home. My father, on Molly, came up out of our side lot. The horse's tail, in sunlight, looked on fire. It trotted up close to the porch's rail. I could see Molly's nostrils dilating. My father took his foot out of a stirrup and said, 'Come on, climb up.' And I said, 'No. I have to see Amy grow up some more.' His foot kept on dangling outside the stirrup. He said again, 'Get on.' And I'm lying there still shaking my head and saying, 'No, no, just a little longer. I have to see Amy grow up some more. Just a little while longer,' I said. 'Then, I'll go.' So, he rode on around the side of the house, but waited there."

"My goodness. That is a dramatic dream. No wonder you're the world's greatest writer," she said, touching him affectionately.

"Yes," he allowed, grinning, "ain't I got some imagination though?"

She leapt up at the sound of dishes rattling a distance down the hall, closeted herself hurriedly in the bathroom, and emerged only when Jeff knocked on the door and said, "All clear." Indicating the tray, he could not keep a straight face. "I'm afraid, though, we haven't fooled anyone. They've sent two cups," he said.

Amy was still somewhat vexed when she had on her coat, the collar turned up carefully, though her face had, too, the eagerness of a child about to be taken for an outing. In the hall, she tiptoed in a storkish, erratic pattern down the red runner, though no one was to be seen. Jeff, behind her, thought of the old rhyme about stepping on a crack and breaking your momma's back, as she continued in her half-hopping way, hurrying. He was not, however, going to wait much longer to give her the final test, he thought. He could not help being annoyed that she refused to take the elevator and led them down seldom-used back stairs.

"You're going to have to face crossing the lobby," he said. But while he said, "Good morning," to vague, watery-eyed residents, Amy darted on with her head down, out to the street. There, she turned to greet him triumphantly when he emerged. "I made it!" she said when they were away from the door. "I don't think anyone saw me."

He took her impatiently by the elbow, leading her to the curb. "There's never a taxi in midtown when it's rainy," she said, after a time.

"The buses are jammed, though," he said, watching one pass. "I can't take that much cooped-up humanity. Do you mind walking until we find a taxi?"

"No. Though if we do see one, I'd like to take it. I don't want to wander about this city. I've begun to hate it. I think maybe I'll go to San Francisco. Have you been there? Or, I might try Europe."

Jeff drew her suddenly and roughly into a doorway, protected by an awning. "You still don't know where you're going," he said, in a rush. "Let me take all of your life into the rest of mine, Amy. Let me tell Inga we want to marry."

She gave an involuntary twist of her body, as if squirming out of a tight place, her arms drawn against her. "Oh," she said. "I don't think so," and when he stepped back immediately toward the sidewalk, Amy realized she had spoken without thought. She had not given an answer but a response. Her mother or Aunt Dea might have spoken for her. It seemed irrevocable now, like time wasted. Having followed him to the curb, she stood, uncertain and shivering there.

"Because," he said, "someone your age couldn't want physically someone mine? If that's the reason, you should have told me before. I've never wanted to disgust you. And I hate this stinking humility, too."

"You've never disgusted me. I couldn't have stayed if you had."

"Then it's a young man. You should have told me. I think you're not sure you love him, but you want to marry him. And don't want to hurt me by saying so. You have always been tender."

He veered away, too intent on finding a taxi. They stared in frustration at those passing, which appeared empty, and then had passengers on closer view. "You must have known," he said, from a short distance along the curb, "that knowing you the way I do, I'd suspect. It only seems to me, Amy, you wanted me to know, without having to tell me."

He had found an excuse for her. Billy Walter was a way out of things she did not want to do. She silently thanked Jeff for never thinking no young man had asked her to marry him.

He said, "You're still running, damn it. But it makes a lot that was confusing understandable. Some of your silences, for instance."

Fear, mostly, had made her silent, and he ought to know that. Wind came in a strong gust around a corner bringing random things, a blown-off man's hat, a sheet of newspaper, a candy wrapper. Stonily, Amy watched them fritter themselves to a stop against a building.

"Maybe you're never going to grow up," he had said brusquely.

She was angrier about that. "There's a taxi, at last," she said, and opened the door before Jeff could. She stared out the opposite window, while he got in behind her. Her legs were stretched toward the heater's comfort, a warm gust of air blowing from beneath the front seat. Other pedestrians stared at her from the sidewalk. "We were lucky," she said.

"We were lucky," he said, "to have had all we had." He put his hands toward her lap. "Now, I've mislaid my gloves. Maybe you'll warm my hands."

She covered both with her own. "You'll have to get some more gloves," she said. "You are cold."

He said then, wryly, "I wouldn't have any reason, then, to expect a young woman to hold my hands, would I?"

"Of course," she said shortly. As if it were a magnet, the back of the driver's neck held her attention. Jeff sat glumly, too. The day was the color of ashes, mist like their fine sift falling. When they arrived, the tailor's shop was inexplicably closed, and in darkness seemed firegutted, ruined. Already despondent, she felt responsible for whatever had happened; this too was her fault somehow, she felt, guilty over treating Jeff badly. Solitude seemed safety. She watched unhappily the taxi go off. "I wish you had kept it," she said. "Though maybe you'll find one easier here. But as I said, I really have to wash my hair."

Jeff reached out and pulled her coat collar tighter against the drizzle. She said, barely audible, "Thank you."

"Thank you," he said. "You were generous, Amy. I didn't give you enough credit. You did give and when you didn't want to. In time, something will come back. Never be sorry, or ashamed, you accepted an old man into your experience. Someday, it'll all be a memory. As fine a one for you as for me, I hope."

"I never wanted to look back and be sorry I'd been afraid to know you," she said. "But I want to see you, still."

He said, "I'm never going to believe there was too much distaste. Afterward, you'd hold my hand. The countryside will have memories of you as long as I live. A beer can tossed away under a tree will make me think of our woods."

"And butterflies will," she said, dreamy and enumerative and singsong as a recitative child. At a sudden intenser shower of rain, she thrust her hands into a hoop over her head and might have been a child about to begin some inept ballet.

He made signs of leaving. "I've known all along I'd have to suffer. It doesn't make it any easier." His voice was jerky. "I won't keep on like this, though. If you want to see me again, it'll be on my terms."

At a point when Amy avoided looking at him, he had signalled a cab, meandering on the avenue. It came with funereal slowness down the block. Amy tried to think of some restraining remark but, as if suddenly, he had disappeared. She stared in an amazed way before darting upstairs, like a scared animal. When she entered the soundless, and even odorless, house, the landlord, having seen her come in, opened his door. He thrust toward her a letter so abruptly, it seemed to hang midair before Amy touched it. "Special came," he said, and went back in his room.

The envelope when she opened it in her room produced a heavy white card with a detachable purple ribbon. It bore the name of her father's dancing school in gilt letters. How sad, she thought, that people would come there to pay more for companionship than for instruction. She pictured the place as ostentatious and full of gilt mirrors, with hostesses wearing dresses tight across the rear. Both her father and Billy Walter would enjoy dancing with them. At the bottom of the card, her father had scrawled that he hoped she would come for the opening.

She went downstairs and telephoned about a plane. Coming back, she knelt and drew from beneath the bed her suitcase, stifling a scream as a pale spider ran toward her. But, steady after a moment, she began to pack. She glanced several times at the scrawl along the bottom of the card. Two to tango and all that, pet! Come if you can. Nicknames were touching; that small one might be sending her home. However, her father was unsure of himself and had added, *Billy Walter* says please come.

The landlord remained silent, after opening his door, and heard without interest that she was leaving. She stood with a scarf over her head, more like some impecunious immigrant who was arriving, bundles and a suitcase and a paper sack at her feet. The flicker of his eyes toward them made Amy look down, to see she had a run in her stocking. Her mother would smile and say it didn't matter, make some excuse about stockings running more easily all the time. Then, she would want to know how, possibly, her baby had managed to get home with all this stuff? Amy, in giving the landlord her forwarding address, wondered if the tailor would ever inquire about her. A taxi drew up with its lights wavery in mist, turning into fog. She piled in her things and, driven away, glanced back once toward the place she had lived. Soon, in the window, where the landlord passed now as a shadow, the Room for Rent sign would reappear.

Later, he thought Amy had been anticipating a call. That would be the reason she had stood so hesitantly, and so long, outside his door, to explain her leaving, why she had looked so expectantly around and back up the stairs. The landlord had supposed her wondering whether she had left anything behind. Customarily curt to late callers, he gave out her address and answered that the caller was welcome. A gentleness in the older man's voice had coaxed his own.

———

313

"Have you met anybody?" Edith said. "And what's happened to your coat? And, baby, how did you manage alone with all that stuff?"

"I had to manage," Amy said flatly. "There was no one else to."

Staring appraisingly, Edith said, "Your hair's longer." They exchanged a glance, in silence. "You're thinner," Amy said. "You must have been sticking to your diet." What, Edith wondered, if she's grown, is to happen next? Her father had parked the car and came down the airport's ramp with a bright smile, wearing a blue ascot, an addictive color to match his eyes, but they had ashy and noticeable shadows beneath them; Edith had written he had not been well. "Have you grown?" he cried. "You seem taller."

"You haven't seen me in so long," she said, "and my skirt's shorter, that makes my legs longer. How about putting me to work in your dancing school?"

"We like 'em a little fatter other places," he said and stopped his hand from giving her a swat across the rear, which Amy wished he had done. Grown softer, his face seemed to give way when she pressed it with hers and his cheekbone, sharper, left a smarting place, where she raised her hand. Her father. Home. She looked at everything, speculatively. A peach, a swell girl, the icing on the cake, the whole cheese—these were the things her father called her for coming home, and mentioned them all in the short time it took them to reach the car. He said them almost all in one breath. On the front seat they sat, three abreast, a unit formed again. Her father grandly held the steering wheel, with hands whose nails were highly buffed and shone. He mentioned that, incidentally, the dancing school was on the way home. Of course then, they must go by to see it. Hearing her mother's grateful sigh, Amy realized they wanted little from her and expected nothing. How selfish she must have been. Approaching the school, she stared ahead as the road generously widened.

314

Though possibly the building could have been worse, it was hard to imagine it so. The façade was modern, and the school appeared a tuberous outcropping of light, on a tree-lined street of old houses, which had now a huddled-down and almost embarrassed look. Amy and Edith climbed apprehensively purple-carpeted steps between walls painted geranium pink, and found the ballroom emitted a sensational glitter, a turbulence to shame storms. Spangles shaking as quicksilver on the hostesses' gowns, hanging along a corridor, added to the feeling. Last-minute workmen stored hammers in the kangaroolike pouches of their work clothes and seemed to tiptoe away, as though feeling they did not belong.

On the following morning, the leaves lay flat in rain puddles, with a look of having drowned. After waking and glancing at the clock, Amy thought how the tailor would be opening his shop and heard reminiscent horns coming up like cries from the Village's streets. Should she have stayed in New York, and had she been short on persistence, and had she given up or given in? Had she waited longer would something have happened, she wondered.

Edith had put bronze chrysanthemums in a copper bowl. Amy, left alone, went about the house, her parents having spared her lunch with city officials. Billy Walter would pick her up for the dancing school's champagne opening, at five. Tugged open, the French doors in the living room revealed violently green winter grass and that raindrops had given to tree bark the texture of frogs' backs. A sluggish wind was inept against matted piles of wet leaves; among them were only a few colorful ones. Along the driveway, oaks stubbornly held all their foliage, which was just beginning to crackle and to brown. Here was conflict and confusion, winter intruding but fall not yielding. All the chrysanthemums in Edith's garden had not dropped their blooms. Violets peeked from beneath leaves yet to be raked. Should she, Amy wondered, standing by Edith's pretty arrangement, have tried another coast, or some more distant place?

Lopsided beneath his pouch's weight, the postman caught sight of her behind the door's glass panes and ceased whistling. "Haven't seen you in a long time," he said, extending mail, leaving unspoken between them the question, Where had she been?

Wherever Amy went, friends came forward to hug her, asking immediately, Had she met anyone? To marry, they meant. Her smile was always hesitant, which made her look mysterious, and made them less worried. On her first afternoon home, Billy Walter had come in and lifted her off her feet in a hug. This afternoon at the reception, he held her hand. As if painted on with one of Edith's little brushes, Amy's smile was set and represented pleasure—a doll's face, or a puppet's. The corners of her mouth thinned with smiling, her cheeks burned bright red with effort. No one could help thinking she was having a good time. Billy Walter, feeling the trembling in her hand, thinking he caused it, was not surprised later when she threw herself on him rather desperately when they parked.

Soon their dates began to take place in motels. He said once that he put into his love-making all the love he could, and Amy felt grateful. But she had feelings of sadness afterward, while Billy Walter strode about busily, filling the dingy room in which he was dressing, having a drink. She lay inertly asking him questions (to his secret annoyance) about himself: had he had a happy childhood; what were his feelings about his mother and father and all his sisters (she liked the idea of being drawn into a large family), what childhood pets did he most miss; did he believe in God; how had he decided to go into the insurance business? When his answers were short and brusque, she would gaze sorrowfully at him, as he seemed not to worry in the least that one person could never know another fully.

Handling insurance for the dancing school, Billy Walter came by frequently in the late afternoon to see her father. Edith would do crewel work and the men would drink and talk about money, and while blue and orange flames leaped in the gas heater, they were all comfortable together and grew drowsy. Shaking herself from reveries, Amy made herself look wide-eyed, attentive to the stock market's future, knowing she need never worry about it. Her days were a repetitive confrontation of clothes, and not only did she spend time arranging them, she shopped for more. She and Billy Walter were taken as a couple and invited everywhere together. Relieved and hopeful, eventually fairly certain, her friends and Edith's waited for an engagement. They thought Amy wore less an air which always had been to them unsettling, though never had they been able to give it its name: puzzlement. About what could Amy have been puzzled? they would have asked.

After Christmas shopping, Dea stopped by, wearing her perennial nubby navy blue coat. Her hair was greyer, but her face bloomed with information not offered and questions not asked when she met Amy. "You seem to have grown," she said.

"My skirt's shorter, that's why."

Dea and Edith closed themselves too obviously into the kitchen to drink coffee, but Amy heard Dea's first whisper, "He's back!" They became busy about the room when Amy swung through the door. Edith had been baking cookies. They all bent to the oven while she drew them out, turning full attention to whether sugar should be sprinkled on when they were cooled, or still hot. Having offered an opinion, Amy pulled on blond pigskin gloves. "The sherry party's from three to five. Then, I'm taking dresses to be shortened," she said.

"Have a good time," Edith said.

Dea, with her coat on, ballooned out. She had to go, and closed her eyes against the uncertain afternoon sunlight and leaned dependently upon Amy's arm. "I'm getting old," she said, "but feel I can't do anything about it." Amy felt surprised. To her, Dea had always been old. "You don't look any different to me," she said.

"Well, you're sweet to say so," Dea said. "But I can see myself."

Behind them, in the door, Edith stood watching. As they bent together, she observed in the shape of their heads a family resemblance unobserved before. Had they been talking about Mr. Almoner when Dea had said she would not mention a word? Edith had said she dared not and knew nothing. Past the house, chimney smoke drifted in ripples, like ribbon shaken out. To everything, there was a quality of overcolor, picture stillness, the grass was even too green. The scene appeared unreal, yet this was life. This was it, Amy repeated to herself. She watched Dea climb reluctantly into her old, almond-pale Chevrolet. Her breath still warm from coffee, she kissed Amy.

Holding open the car door, Amy wished there were not lying on the front seat a little whisk broom. It lay there so hopefully over a frayed place, as men attempt to spread thinning hair over bald spots. Bravado often seems sad.

"Land, the faucet's going on," Dea said, beginning to cry. She whispered, "I couldn't tell even your momma, but I have to tell someone. Bubba has just left out. We're pretending on a business trip, hoping he'll come back. Had to sow his wild oats, I guess. He never had. Once, my patience would have been tried. Your momma and daddy and I didn't grow up in an age of this psychology mess. When we did something wrong, our britches got set afire. But I guess he's trying to find himself."

With Dea in her car, Amy stuck her head in the window saying, with no idea, that she was sure things would be all right. Dea said, "I don't know whether it would be good or not if we ever knew what was ahead." Often when she put her head on the pillow at night, she wondered. Her advice now might not be the kind somebody like Mr. Almoner could give Amy, but was practical. "Honey, you may think your children are trouble when they're little," Dea said. "But you won't know anything till they're grown." Her face attentive, Amy said she would remember. In the rearview mirror, Dea watched Amy's much sleeker car follow her own a short distance and turn a different direction. She stuck her arm out the window to wave. At the same moment, Amy waved. Driving on, Dea thought it was necessary to existence to have these little reassurances, waving, having somebody at home waiting for supper.

"I'm glad," Amelia announced, "to have a change from turkey for Christmas." What she had always wanted, though, was roast beef, or goose, though everybody said it was greasy. But did Inga have to stare as if she absolutely adored this venison because Jeff had shot the deer. Jessie, stepping back after putting the platter down, waited, disapprovingly, her arms folded. Amelia had made her soak the meat in red wine for days. Jeff was carving. Latham had sat with his fork upright ever since the blessing. Sometimes, he had no more table manners than Marguerite. Amelia glanced at him affectionately, realizing she had gotten more tolerant with age. A year ago, for instance, she never would have expected to buy bar-b-ques where Negroes were sitting eating them. And though, still, she would not sit down herself when the place opened and the Negroes were the first ones in, she had made no comment. They would be served in Chester's, yet. And what she hoped, now, was only to live to see the day. Jeff looked peaked. Change seemed to have done him no good. If she had known he was coming back would she have married Latham? It was, she decided, better that she had.

"Now that, Jeff," Latham said, handing along his plate, "is one mighty fine buck."

"Sweet potatoes?" Inga asked from the other end of the table.

"Don't give him too many," Amelia said. "Getting heavy may be why his ankle keeps giving way."

"Yes, sir, one fine buck," Latham said again. "Ain't that right, Jessie?"

"Sho *was,*" she said, eyeing the juices running red.

"It's just a rangy taste otherwise, Jessie," Amelia said. "Now cheer up. If you eat some it isn't going to be like you taking spirits. Inga, I declare, what a nice Christmas present to have had the head mounted." They gazed outward to the hall where it hung. "Let me tell you," Amelia said, "that we've—that you've —needed something out there all along. That paper I picked out was too plain."

"I'm happy with the mounting, if Jeff likes it?" Inga said questioningly.

"I thought I made that very clear when I first saw it," he said, putting down the carving knife. Gazing at her, he said, "Have more confidence in your gifts. They're appropriate."

She said, almost loudly, turning to Amelia, "I thought when you picked it out the paper was too plain. But you had to have your way."

"I see I did," Amelia said humbly.

"Can you take more?" Jeff asked, holding up Inga's plate.

"I can. I think I can stand more," Inga said, folding her hands calmly into her lap, watching him add meat to her plate.

"Very fine," Jeff said, after eating. The others had waited for the tasting verdict from him. Only then did Jessie carry out the platter, muttering again that the meat ought to have been fried.

The day was warm and the front door stood open. Intermittently, through the afternoon, they heard firecrackers set off along the road, then the enthralled cries of youngsters. Cows let out outraged bellows. Trees in front of the house looked unbalanced, dark and leafless, in opposition to the solid bright sun.

From her seat, Inga could see down to the pine copse, where birds nestled. The house gave off a gummy smell of pine, the tree lit, wreaths at all the windows. The others had wanted candles in them. She had said, "Too dangerous," and had won. "You hardly ate, Jeff," she said, solicitously. There had been these moments since he came home.

"Watching the waistline boy?" Latham said.

"You ate enough for both, and I'm bursting," Amelia said. "But, Brother, you didn't touch your nice cranberry salad."

"It was my day to eat venison," Jeff said. "I find I no longer need to eat much. Many things all taste the same."

Warm air from the floor furnace swayed icicles on the Christmas tree, and sunshine, rebounding from the white walls, fell in shaking patterns everywhere. Jeff hardly touched his dessert, though it was homemade boiled custard, which Amelia had decorated with a cherry and tiny real leaves. She said, "Did I take over dinner in your house, Inga?"

"No. Look at the custard. So pretty. Only you could have gotten the meat done right." Inga nodded toward the kitchen, about Jessie and the deer; after all, people with strong wills, who knew what they wanted, ought to be admired. Amelia had stuck by her when Jeff left home and now that Latham's back hurt, and his ankle would not heal, she had to help Amelia. After dinner, they went out, not even needing coats, and drew in the day. Brittle-seeming, but tenacious and strong, the stripped muscadine clung to supports of the porch, which seemed endless and vacated, the hammock down for the winter. With a scattergun sound, firecrackers broke the far-away quality of the country stillness, the children's voices grew remoter. "Christmas is for kids." Amelia paused from walking off her dinner, up and down, to watch beyond the unvigilant and leafless hedges young people parking. A party was being held some distance down the road. "Still," she said, "I love Christmas."

"Excitement goes when you're too old for toys," Inga said. Yet, she had anticipated this day; something filled her deeper, warmer than excitement. Jeff had worn a sense of waiting, too, which she had thought for the holiday, though evidently it had not been, for he wore still a look of waiting as the day was ending.

When Vern's green coupe appeared, its rattling outdid the clanking of the cattle gap. Possibly because it was Christmas, he had the decency to nod, passing them. That boy might be the death of us all, Amelia thought, the car going toward the back.

"Christmas gift!" Jessie called before leaving with Vern. "Christmas gift!" they called, in return. Soon Latham and Amelia went home to take naps. Inside, Jeff made a fire that was reluctant, as the logs were damp. Cleaning up Christmas debris, Inga offered balled gift wrappings, which he stuffed among the kindling. "It's not going too well," Inga said.

"Well, I tried." He stood staring down at the flameless fire, convinced that Amy had gone off on her own too soon. She had grown tougher, as he had wanted her to, but, damn it, this tough? "If you could be reincarnated, how would you like to come back?"

"My goodness," Inga said. "I don't think I'd want to be."

But if you were to have no peace. Leaning against the mantel, Jeff knew he would have none until he had seen the end of what he and Amy had started. He felt so incomplete. "I," he said, though Inga had not asked, "might like to be a butterfly."

Inga considered that without answering. It was not in her background, her nature, to be fanciful. Instead, she said, "No luck?" when the logs only hissed.

"None," he said moodily.

She sifted through Christmas cards on a table. "Surprising some of the people we didn't hear from this year."

What good does it do to be remembered, someone had asked. Who? he wondered. "People get busy," he said. Inga, wanting to please him, tried to think of something. "Perhaps I'd like to be a mountain goat," she said, with an eager look.

He said appreciatively, "Not a bad choice." Looking at her, he wondered about this blonde, in the room, looking through Christmas cards. Perhaps prolonged truth was not possible between two human beings, even though married. How long it seemed they had lied to one another, by saying nothing. His heart beat warily, and he chided it: If only you had stayed out of the way! He was equally unhappy about losing Amy so soon, and that she was still a partly frozen child. Moving from the mantel, he said, "Many of these books must go to a library. I'll start cataloguing them tomorrow."

"Tomorrow?" she said anxiously. As he had knelt to poke again at the fire, the door knocker fell and Inga answered it.

"Christmas gift!" Icicles shook on the tree from the night entering, though the neighbor's shout itself might have set them aflutter. "Got you first," he cried.

Jeff heard Inga mutter something in return, the customary answer, he imagined. "Grandbabies been running over the house all day," the neighbor said. "But we wanted to bring you some eggnog. And oh, the carrier made a mistake and left all these cards at our house. Sorry I didn't get them over sooner. But grandbabies got me run ragged."

The night's cold crept away as the door closed, and the icicles set. Jeff had seen stars in all their magnitude before Inga shut the door. In the doorway, she held a napkin-covered bowl, her face happier. "Look! cards got left next door by mistake." Her other hand was full. "Let me get cups, though." The silver bowl caught roundly all the glorious color of the Christmas tree lights. And entering the dark kitchen, Inga for some reason was surprised when the reflection disappeared, though that bright warmth could not go on and on, for nothing did. Carrying the bowl and two glass cups, she took also the cards back to the living room.

After setting down the tray, she said with a fluttery wave of her hand, "I forgot cookies." She waved again, fluttery in the doorway. "There are the cards. But one is a letter." She disappeared, leaving him before the fire. She had rather he read the letter than have it lying there between them. So, it was still going on. In the dark kitchen, remembering Jeff's face, she again had the strong sense that something had ended. She turned away, having gone close to inspect the clock. Almost, Christmas was over and Jeff still had that sense of waiting. It was not then the day's being over on his mind. Why had he had such a sense of urgency about the books? He looked toward something reluctantly. Maybe that another year was ending, she thought.

When Billy Walter gave her a puppy for Christmas, Amy could only feel that she was crazy about Billy Walter. She had opened a large box, to find inside a blond cocker, damp but ecstatic.

"Taffy," Billy Walter had said, and touched Amy's hair.

"Billy Walter, he's adorable, and how sweet!"

Now, Christmas lights on trees along Quill Boulevard looked dim compared to car lights, but stars seemed unusually large, to shine brighter in the cold. "I know it seems silly," Amy said, peering intently through the windshield. Lights blinking seemed swimming in the night. "I know it's silly, not to want to go to a motel just because it's New Year's. But it seems wrong."

The fishtail wavering of the motel's too many signs muddled with light from the boxed decorated trees on the street. However, the headlights of traffic, going two ways, guilelessly outdid them. A pucker on his lips was all that showed Billy Walter found her reasoning female and incomprehensible.

"If that's the way you feel," he said, with a shrug. "I certainly don't want to push in where I'm not wanted."

"It's not that. I want to be with you. I just feel if we go to this crummy place the first night of the year, the whole year will be like that. I *know* it seems silly."

Billy Walter looked at his watch, bending toward it in the light of a motel sign, his chin set. "O.K., sugar, I'll take you on home."

Opening her mouth to protest that it was early, that she did not want to be dumped home at this hour, Amy realized she had only one alternative. As he reached for the key, she thought of being alone and said, "Oh, all right. It *is* silly. It was just a momentary feeling. I don't really know why I said it."

"The message of Christmas get you?"

"You know I'm not religious. Though a long time, I believed heaven was a place with God and Jesus walking around. A Sunday-school teacher told me Jesus was a man who went around telling stories and had tuberculosis. Billy Walter, what a comedown! I do like idealizing things."

Guffawing, repeating "tuberculosis," Billy Walter got out of the car and ambled to the motel office. There, he leaned charmingly toward the woman behind the register. Within a moment, her hennaed head thrown back, she was howling with laughter. Watching, Amy could not help her own lips twitching. Billy Walter was, as her mother said, an overgrown puppy. Seldom did Amy think Billy Walter's jokes really funny, but enjoyed watching him tell them for he enjoyed his own hugely and life with him would be a continuing series of practical jokes. Recently, agreeable as always, he had gone with her to a show of modern art, held in a medieval-looking building which lent an air of solemnity. Rightly, he had not pretended to be impressed by a square within a square as a picture, and neither was she. Like Billy Walter, she had soon found the whole collection a bore, but kept sheepishly trailing from picture to picture. After following her for some time, like a dutiful consort, only his hands behind his back were restive, Billy Walter left the room. Looking

325

around, Amy found that, not surprisingly, he was gone. He reported later having seen a good buddy—a really good old boy—whom he had not seen in a long time. That boy, foresightedly, had a fifth of vodka in his car. With it, they had spiked not only their own punch but cups they thoughtfully carried to the elderly hatcheck lady. At the afternoon's slow end, she was handing out coats in vague directions and usually to the wrong owner. Taking Amy by the hand, howling and at a gallop, Billy Walter raced with her down the museum's steps.

The woman behind the desk now gave him a paper cup, and raised one to touch it. Cheers! they would be saying, Amy thought impatiently. Right then, being cold, she would have gotten out of the car, except that a car full of Negroes came swervingly from behind the motel; tailpipe dragging, it went off down Quill Boulevard. The screeching sound drew Billy Walter to the front window, where he seemed to remember Amy. He made an obvious farewell to the woman and headed for the door. But she went on talking, her mouth widening and closing like a snapping turtle's, persistently, as if never would she get through telling Billy Walter all she had to tell him. He always, from the merest encounters, came away knowing more about people, Amy felt, than if she had spent the day with them. He chided her when she said that. Wasn't she, after all, the one who wanted to have experiences and know about people? She shouldn't waste time, then, being shy. However, she knew she went on being dependent on Billy Walter for information. He very shortly forgot details, often could not recall them a second time, while Amy vicariously lived these lives. People seemed to endure such sad small ones, without malice. She was fretful, often, wanting something in return for living.

Standing in the motel's doorway, Billy Walter was calling, "The little woman's going to give me hell!" He came along, followed by the woman's shooing motions and laughter and gave

Amy a paper cup. After drinking from it, making a face, she said, "What's that?"

"Rye, I think. Isn't it terrible? But the woman inside gave it to me for you. 'Happy life,' she said." Amy took the cup back and drank its contents obligingly.

With the Christmas season past, its decorations gave everything a leftover quality. On the door to which Billy Walter fitted the key, with difficulty, were strung lopsided letters reading Merry Christmas. In the motel's office window, the pointed and blush-colored bulbs of an artificial candle had gone out. "Go on in, sugar." Billy Walter stood aside, the door thrust open. Closing it, he said, "I told that woman about getting that old lady at the art show drunk, and I thought she'd split a gusset!" The room was filled up with his size and his own laughter.

"What's her story?" Amy said, a little jealously.

He was roaming the room inspectingly, and said, "Oh hell, there's some rumpus in the kitchen. The help's all drunk and fighting. Her husband's gone home to get his pistol."

If asked to close his eyes and relate what he had seen roaming the room, Billy Walter would have remembered little. While apparently watching him, Amy could have said that there were cigarette burns the size of dimes in the green chenille spread, faded by bleach. Glasses had left white rings on the top of the tilty bureau, and its lamp had little for a shade but a wire frame. The shower curtain, having lost holders, hung limp as a scarecrow. Amy pranced from the bathroom wearing a diaphanous and frilly slip, naturally enticing to Billy Walter. Taking her by the wrist, he drew her toward the bed, down on top of him. There, Amy faltered. She, in her mind's eye, kept thinking of the square within a square, the picture at the art show that had been incomprehensible. Why had she pretended to like it? And why had she not come now glumly, as she felt, from the bathroom to be enticing?

327

No longer than he lingered over her many questions did Billy Walter linger after making love. He heaved himself from the bed, restless and ready for some other activity. He considered himself practical, that he faced life head-on. But Amy, watching him from the bed, wondered if he were not actually trying to escape things, rushing about and always busy. He told her she was morbid and obsessed by death, and she had answered that she was not afraid of being sad. Now he was hurrying toward the shower. She impulsively reached out for his hand, but with an occupied air, he barely brushed hers and went on, by-passing her attempt to make them closer. He seemed to know there was no such thing as being inseparable.

She sat up to disappear from the bureau mirror, with steam coming from the shower obscuring it. Lavishly soaping, Billy Walter sent a sweet warm scent into the room. Lighthearted and complicated as a bird's chirping, he whistled above the shower's noise. As against the stall's tin sides the spray lessened, Amy quickly read a letter, taken from her purse.

Jeff:

I've wondered so much what's happened to you?? I've hesitated to call or write you at home. I'm dying to know when your book is coming out??? Will you let me know? I had to come home on short notice for the opening of my father's dancing school—eek!!! You can imagine! Otherwise, I would have phoned you. He's not well. All the same things here; how 'bout there?? I am doing some social work with crippled children and like that. I have written little things in bits and pieces, not much. But remember how warm it was once in the woods in December, or was it November??? Anyway, want to meet again?????

Love, Amy

The top sheet held a mercuric and disinfectant smell, not at all pleasing, as Amy read the letter hidden beneath it. Though the water still ran, she felt fearful of Billy Walter suddenly coming in and asking what she was doing. More clearly, she saw how shabby the letter was, with all its inane flip question marks. And it reeked with the confidence that, summoned, Jeff would come. He had not thought it worthy even of a fresh reply and had merely scrawled an answer on the bottom.

This letter is the only stupid thing you've ever done, Amy. That's because you wrote it out of your head and not from your heart. And this one is the one I never meant to write. I never intended to fall in love with you when all this began. I took you in only to shape you into what you wanted to be. But yours is the girl-woman face and figure I see when I close my eyes. No, I won't meet you again, for a ghost would be between us, as now I think when you are with him a ghost is between you, whether he knows it or not.

Billy Walter, roughly toweling his head, came out flinging water drops like a dog shaking rain. "You look like a mouse burrowing in your purse. What's always in them so important to women?"

"Things to hide behind mainly," she said, smiling. "The face you see isn't really me. It's made up. I don't think you realize that."

"It's good-looking. That's what counts," he said.

"And I carry mad money. I'm always afraid someone will go off and leave me."

"I'm going to now, to get ice," he said. "I need a little hair of last night's dog."

With his usual alacrity, Billy Walter was dressed. He seemed never hampered by buttons or zippers as other people were. Things went smoothly for him, and Amy looked at him in faint surprise. With a cardboard container, he started for the door. "If you go out without a coat and your hair wet, you'll get a cold," she said unexpectedly.

He came back with a thoughtful air, his eyes on her. He gave his head one more swipe with a towel before putting on his coat. "Nice to be taken care of in more ways than one," he said.

She felt shyer under his look and said, "Well, you would."

The door banged behind him. His matter-of-fact footsteps disappeared with crunching sound on the cold pavement outside. The bathroom looked as if a child had been there bathing. Only toys left behind were missing. All the towels but a small one had been used and left in damp huddles on the floor. He might have attempted to mop up water with them. Spray was left running down one wall, the shower curtain hung out, dripping. Amy went about instinctively, and happy to do it, cleaning up. Cold water splashed repeatedly onto her face left her, momentarily, while bent over the basin, with blank thoughts. If she was thinking anything, she thought fondly of Billy Walter. In his way, he needed someone after all, she had considered.

She lifted her face and searched for the one dry towel, at the moment of a terrific impact against the side of the building. Immediately, Amy's thoughts raced around between earthquakes and explosions and fallen airplanes. The Sheetrock wall had bent inward, the blow enough to give the shower stall's tin sides a slight ringing. Struck still, she might have been holding the towel to her mouth to silence her own terror. Once the impact was over, the area's normal silence seemed ominous. Standing on the closed toilet cover, Amy could see out the tiny window, set close toward the ceiling.

"Man," a voice had said beneath the window, then repeated the word. "Man."

Behind the motel was a courtyard of cinders, and its dim outlines, its contents, were revealed by light flooding out from the kitchen. There, the door was open, with a stocky white man filling it. In the courtyard, three other men tussling had disarranged the even rows of garbage cans. Now, a lid clattered and rolled off like a tire. She could see they were Negroes. Evidently, they had fallen, as one body, against the side of the building by her room. Bending and swaying and groaning now, they seemed engaged in some tortuous form of calisthenics.

Two of the men had pinned back the arms of the third. He was straining back toward the kitchen, where the white man still silently observed. Behind him, visible as a shoulder, part of a face, the rest of the kitchen help watched, awed and quiet. The Negro, with his arms held back, was shepherded past Amy's window, toward the end of the building.

"He going to kill you," a voice whispered by Amy's window.

At the end of the building, having shoved the smaller man around it, they seemed figuratively to dust their hands before lightly running back to the kitchen. In the light from her window, Amy had seen that the pinioned man had blood streaming down his face. When the two men entered the kitchen, the white man closed the door and the courtyard was left to bleak darkness. Indecisively, but then with more determination, Amy grabbed the one half-dry towel off the rack. While she had stood there, almost clinging to the window ledge by her fingertips, the sound of their feet on the cinders had been haunting. A whiff of something remembered and not immediately placed was insistent. As she came into the next room and dressed, the sound, like a reprise in music, returned at intervals—while she fastened her stockings, stepped inside her skirt, considered there was not time for her sweater and only put on her coat. Behind the house where they had lived when she was small had been a great trellis of roses and a narrow cindered alley. In it, wild sunflowers had grown, enormously beyond her head. And there, in rooms attached to or atop garages, Negroes had lived. On hot Sunday afternoons and evenings, they sat outside for air. Amy had be-

331

come gradually aware that their conversations or laughter ceased whenever white children, who cut through or played in the alley, passed by. She had realized finally that the alley was the entranceway to their houses and was their only yard, and that she had been a trespasser on these, even though the city owned the land. All her sympathy had gone toward the Negroes and yet alone and meeting a colored man, she had fled in terror. The exact reason had been nameless, but feeling received from white grownups had made her instinct sure. Her feet running, the slow steps of the alleyway's occupants going to and from home, had come to her again, looking out the motel window.

Determined to curb her fear, she went out the front door to find the hurt man. On closer inspection, he was about her age. Groping along the strung-out row of rooms, he might have been blind, and sensing something blocking him, lifted his head. He moved to avoid the encounter by stepping off the walkway. He stopped when Amy called, though making no move toward the towel she held out. Slightly suspicious, he stared at her, his head cocked in order to see her more closely. Blood overhung one eye, like a great clot, half closing it. The eye's swelling dropped the lid, making his face have even a sadder quality. She kept the towel thrust at him without saying anything; her face longed to offer more than something for his cut. Her urgent feeling made her hand tremble, and noticing that, he took the towel. He said, "Thanks," in almost a whisper. Then he clapped the towel, a great white lump, to one temple.

"You need to go to a doctor."

About to shake his head, he stopped it, aware any motion would cause it to hurt. Unaware Amy had further interest, he started away, his profile dazzled a moment by lights from the boulevard, revealing a puzzled and lost look. She went quickly after him then.

"You've got to go to an emergency room. You might need stitches."

He had looked around, stiffly, reassuring himself that what he had thought was true was, and she was following him. He looked away first, their eyes having met. How, Amy wondered, could she make him feel all right about talking to her?

"I might see about it," he said, veering away from the motel, toward the street. Hesitantly, Amy remained, wondering if there were a point to following him, until he slowed. In the slowed walk, in some hunched lift of his shoulders, she knew he would not ignore sympathy. "What happened?" she said, beginning to follow again.

When he stopped to light a cigarette, in the match's flare, her face reflected concern. "Can you tell me what happened?" she said.

The match almost burned his fingers, before he flipped it to the ground. "Don't nobody call me a nigger," he said shortly. Since there was nothing to add to that, Amy said nothing and only tried wearing an appropriate expression of dislike, too. This bordered on sorrow, which seemed to deepen as she frowned. He blew out smoke and watched her and said, "Not nobody."

"I don't blame you. And why did he?"

"Niggers don't eat his steak!" As if it were not already out, he ground out the match again with his heel. His face set angrily, without touching the sadness in his eyes. He looked back at the motel. "He come in the kitchen where we eating and say we can have hamburgers or cheeseburgers or a pork chop. But not to eat his steak."

"What did you say?" she said, trying to imagine herself into such a situation.

"Said I don't like steak noway." He gave her a quick, sidelong glance; they could not help laughing. "He come after me with

333

the butt end of a pistol, say I'm sassing him. I ought to have killed that white man."

"That wouldn't do you any good." Amy peered closer at the cut as he took down the towel and said, with sudden authority, "You have got to get help. You do need stitches."

"Could you call me a Checkers cab?"

Capably, she urged him down until he sat on the curb. "Don't move," she said, and darted back to her room. The thin yellow pages of the phone book were difficult to manage in haste; she turned past the taxi section several times. Then, seeing the number at last, she dialed it. Only when the number was ringing did she read the Checkers cab advertisement. She glanced about the room, in a guilty way, having read the words Colored Taxi. She had flushed and felt hot. Suppose, though, they would not send the cab, hearing her voice. She embarrassed herself, wondering how to explain it was for a Negro. Flooding back were all the times she had played jokes telephoning Negro places of business, as a child; and never once had she been scolded. Let this call be taken seriously, she thought. "This is an emergency," she said, and her voice trembled on the final word. On the other end, a polite voice answered that a cab would be there shortly. Amy added, feeling the necessity, "Someone's been hurt."

Her feeling was that she had to give but how and not be patronizing? She knew he would need money and that conviction outweighed her usual hesitancy. She took all the money she had from her wallet, and was sorry Billy Walter had taken his with him. The boy, rising waveringly when she came back to the curb, did not want to take the money. Amy kept thrusting it toward him. "It's silly not to if you need it," she said.

"Well, thanks," he said, finally allowing her to tuck the folded bills into his breast pocket.

She said, "I'm here with someone, I've got to go back. Just wait. The cab will come," and then as if they had shaken hands, and were reluctant to let go the moment of touching, as if slowly their hands were sliding apart, they remained looking at one another; after that moment, Amy went with a sudden sense of freedom back to the motel, while he turned toward the seasickening motion of lights on the boulevard.

Shivering, she wrapped herself in a curtain and stood at the window, where wet patterns formed. She watched him. Beams of headlights struck him, glanced off, and traffic continued to be heavy in two directions. The boy went in a little aimless pattern up and down the curb, unsteadily. That he might be taken for drunk, and arrested, suddenly terrified Amy—for it was likely to happen. Neither of them had considered calling the police, and that, she thought, if anything had happened to her would be the first thing to be done.

She was relieved when the taxi came, a green light swirling atop it pinwheel fashion. The breath she had released spread over the window, in a frosty snowflake design. She rubbed the glass clear, the boy had gone, and peered down the walkway, anxious for Billy Walter to come back. She felt abandoned to the room, as if she were in the little one in New York. Taking so long, Billy Walter would have fallen into conversation with the woman again, or someone else; Amy felt she waited for some dawdling small boy. His voice preceded him then, as the office door opened. Light slapped brokenly along the sidewalk was erased again as the door was closed. The rattling of ice, whistling, rapid footsteps all ceased as Billy Walter halted, to open the door.

She said, sitting in a prim way on the end of the bed, "I thought you'd left me, after all."

"No, baby, don't look so woebegone. I just got involved in there again. My tongue's hanging out, I need a drink so bad. God, that fat bastard that runs this place," he said, opening a bottle of bourbon. He slipped paper jackets off glasses on the bureau.

335

"What happened?" Amy said.

"There was some big ruckus going on in the kitchen. I couldn't even understand it all. The whole time he was trying to tell me, he kept spitting tobacco juice into an empty pear can. I'll never eat canned pears again. But he'd hit some Negro with his pistol. Says this boy sassed him. That's one thing po' white trash can't take. What else has he got, but to kick a Negro."

Amy accepted a drink from him and, sipping, felt calmer. The liquor warmed her, straight downward. She looked more admiringly at Billy Walter. He was going about with little angry strides, gulping at his drink. She said, "You're not nearly so prejudiced as I thought," and he looked at her strangely as if she did not think, at all.

"I would take me," he said, "a Negro over that kind of white man any day. There's nothing, as they say in the country where I grew up, trashier than a trashy white man. They don't belong anywhere. And one time a Negro said to me, 'They must be the loneliest people in the world.'"

"Billy Walter, that's incredible. You seem so much more in touch than I am. I seem just to know what other people have learned."

"I doubt that. You probably know a lot more than you think."

"Somehow, I manage," she said. "But I really don't know how. I do know I've got to go out to people more. To give of yourself is to learn. But I feel so limited about what I can get into." She laughed. "Sometimes, I wish I weren't a girl."

"I'd sure hate to be caught in here with you if you weren't," he said, with sort of a bellow. He moved to a chair and sprawled in it in a manner lordly and baronial. He commanded her, patting his knee. Amy got up and went to sit on it—being obedient appealed to her. He gave her several unsettling bounces, intending them affectionately. She wondered whether affection were the deepest Billy Walter could know of love. He looked as if he wanted to say something serious, that he knew no words. Instead of saying he loved her, he kept bouncing her on his knee. Amy was unable to keep from her mind the chant about riding a horse to Banbury Cross. She suspected this void of words would always be between them, and that only she would feel their lack.

Billy Walter sat up stiffly. Clearly, he had a speech to make. In pulling back, Amy gave him room, if he wanted, to pull it, prepared, from his pocket. She turned a polite face toward him to listen, her hands folded. He then began to dig into a pocket for something, avoiding looking at her. She began slowly to feel certain about what he was going to say. Her impulse was to avoid the moment, to run out of the room, which clearly was impossible. He had one arm still around her. With a sheepish look equal to his, she stared down at the small blue leather jeweler's box he presented, in lieu of saying anything. Since there was no mistaking the meaning, she said merely, "Oh," took it and opened the box.

He said, "It was my grandmother's ring. I hope it fits. That is, sugar, if you want it."

Her first thought was that she wanted it because it was beautiful. She said, "It's beautiful. I love it." But she let the ring remain inserted in its little slot, until she wondered if Billy Walter noticed this hesitancy. He stared at it as if not quite certain what to do, either.

He said, "Well. Will you marry me?"

She said, "I don't know what to say," while tears came to her eyes.

Not understanding them, Billy Walter pretended not to notice. "Say yes or no," he said, smiling but not quite looking at her.

She said again, "I don't know what to say," and burst into

337

tears, hiding her head against his shoulder. He put a hand somewhat cautiously against her head, like a bear trying to be gentle with its paw. Her tears began to dry. She sat up, smiling. Absolutely everyone they knew expected them to, wanted them to get married. She tried to ascertain whether the stubborn little thing inside her which kept her from saying yes was pure perversity. Her mother had always said she had a stubborn streak. Every consideration came to a dead end in her mind. She was tired of being lonely, and was that reason enough to marry?

"Suppose it doesn't work out?" she questioned.

"Everybody takes a chance getting married," he said. "By the way, I love you."

"I love you," Amy said, loving him a certain way. Criticized as being rather wacky, she supposed there was no such thing as the sort of love she had always imagined. "Could I keep it and wear it around my neck for a while, and decide?" A muscle was set jumping in his neck, which meant the suggestion was not to his liking. But his leg was beginning to go to sleep, and he set her off his knee and said, "All right."

As they were going out, Amy said, her voice timid but hopeful, "Can we still keep going together if we don't get married?"

That arrested the muscle's twitching. With a decisive motion, Billy Walter opened the motel door. He stood over her at an advantage, being so much taller. "Not on your life," he said. "I don't have any more time to lose. I'm not getting any younger." After a moment, with level eyes, he said in his practical way, "Neither are you."

"I'd give anything I own to get to play bridge more often," said Cindy, wearing a crushed-velvet hat, which quivered whenever she spoke.

Lydia said, "I take the baby and a folding crib whenever I want to play."

Meanly, Amy thought Lydia, with her spreading thighs, ought to be taking some other form of exercise. Cindy said, her hat quivering, "Well, you can do that with a baby. But I have a toddler as well!" After sighing enormously, she placed a hand apologetically on Amy's arm. "We just keep on and on, don't we, talking about things that bore you to death."

"I don't mind," Amy said, feeling exhausted.

The room was too warm and musky with perfume scents, and those of sherry and cigarettes. Cindy's hand left Amy to take a tiny cream-cheese sandwich, tinted pink and green, from a silver platter. Offered one, Amy shook her head and watched the tray go around the circle of girls, in which she sat. This afternoon, she had heard how to ice a store-bought cake messily enough that a husband would think it was homemade. A recipe for frozen fish sticks and mushroom soup, which made dinner not quite so obviously quick, was exchanged. Once the crushed-velvet hat had belonged to Cindy's mother, and Amy thought she remembered that hat. It was the mothers of these girls to whom she had been told to speak when they played bridge with Edith. What had changed? Cindy wore the hat and her breasts now were swelled with milk. Darkness lightly glossed over the girls; purposely no one turned on lights. Only candles on a lacily clothed table lit the room. Amy felt further cast onto the sidelines. Faces of the others seemed more aglow, eagerly animated as they talked about bridge. Once, when she leaned forward to pick up her glass, Amy pressed against the bell on the chain around her neck.

Placing an inclusive hand on Amy, too, another girl said, "I'm going to quit that bridge class though," explaining, "We started taking lessons with a lot of mother's friends. But those older women could play all afternoon. We had to go home and fool with kids. We just got so far behind!"

"Oh," Amy said.

"I'm going to quit it, too," Lydia said, nibbling a canapé.

339

"I would give," Cindy repeated, her hat pitching forward, "almost anything I own to get to play bridge more often." Asked, Amy confessed that she no longer played bridge at all, and their faces reflected surprise, shock, interest: What did she do instead? Having no satisfactory answer, smiling and looking mysterious, Amy managed to have the question by-passed. Cindy said, her look envious, "Those older women get to play at night, even." Her girdled thighs rubbing one another made a whispering sound as she stood. "What am I going to have for dinner?"

"We've been out every night this week, almost," Lydia said. "Quill says we're staying in tonight, he's tired." But she pouted.

Have mushroom soup and fish sticks, someone suggested.

The hostess expected to be taken out to dinner, being exhausted from a day making cream-cheese sandwiches and other tidbits for the party. Dully nibbling, she passed a tray. The pink candles on the table, subsided to tiny flames, tenaciously clung to their final moments, as the guests clung to the tag end of the party. No one wanted to return to housewifely duties. Cindy mentioned the hostess's new curtains, which were then drawn out like cloth to be measured. A careful explanation was given of how they had been lined. The other girls exclaimed over the sewing trick that had made that much simpler, while Amy's face reflected mystery. Once, while Billy Walter was kissing her, she had tried to tell him she would not make a good wife, that she could not sew on even a button. He did not care whether she could sew! But in her mind had been the solemn warning of her friends: men changed after marriage. The hostess drew the curtains against the deathly greyness of late afternoon. Everyone agreed to one more sherry, and picked over what was left to eat.

"I had," the hostess continued, passing the decanter, "the worst time deciding on a color for in here." Thought-filled faces said she had made the right decision. Her eyes, having looked from

340

face to face, paused at Amy. "You've hardly said anything all afternoon," she said.

"I was just wondering how you ever knew what to choose when you have so many choices." Amy nodded toward the curtains. "They are perfect." The smile she put on she hoped was winning; she had a need to be liked. Freedom, she had considered, had presented her with an enormous number of indecisions; under that circumstance, freedom either had done her no good, or was not truly freedom. Having put on her coat, she was followed to the door by the hostess.

"A date with Billy Walter tonight?"

"I guess so."

"Well," said the hostess, looking older, "have a good time."

Dear Jeff:

I have finished the book. Thank you so much for wanting to send me a copy, for sending it. I never doubted that it would be what it is; but how lame to use words like great or marvellous. I only hope you can truly know how I feel about it, and I'm sure you do. And it is marvellous that the reviewers all think as I do; then, too, I knew they would. It has always been so touching to me to receive a book from you, one of yours or not, with the wrapping done by you. The first you sent, "Don Quixote," was all badly wrapped in green tissue paper. Do you remember? And I worried then so over not having a present to give you in return, not realizing, though you told me, that I gave you something. That I did it unconsciously was best. Calculatedly, I'm afraid I never did give much; I wish I could change all that. Why must everything always seem too late; too late, I always think I've learned. I can only hope not to keep repeating mistakes, though how can I know I won't. Life does seem to go on and on and on, harder as you once told me, which I didn't believe at the time. Maybe my children will never believe anything I say.

Writing the letter, with Jeff's newly read book beside her, Amy saw suddenly whether or not love could have been made through the title page was not the point, at all: joy was: exultation at the book's being done: after so much work, the book was simply an extension of himself. They could have tried love that way, if only to laugh. The result, probably failure, would have brought them up short against the condition people needed to be reminded of occasionally, fallibility; Amy suddenly wondered what she was to make of herself; that was what mattered.

My heart aches for those days, in the woods; it hurts: those lost days. Where has the time gone? I'm older. I don't fool myself any longer. There won't be anybody to fill your place in my heart, thoughts, to ever even understand me as you do, to console, love, feel for me as you do. If I'd let myself stop and wonder and worry about it, I would be afraïd (I said I wouldn't be, and I'm not in the way once I would have been, of what the future is to hold in this way). Probably, I'll go through life looking for another you. Oh Jeff, the sun, the red roads, the house, the school, the woods, the trees, beer and talk. Have I written you all this before? It seems I might have, but I had to say it all again, to tell you that I love you. To think of you, I think of sun and laughter and a sort of lovely sadness. It's in every face, building, and in everything I see and do. I go to sleep thinking, Someday he will be so damned proud of me. Oh, thank you for that.

She put down the pen, thinking she had to let her mother redecorate her room. How childish to have said she wanted everything to stay the same. The curtains were frayed, their linings stained brown from sun and in-blown rain. Edith had a swatch of material pinned to the old ones, of some satiny material, sleeker, and with a barely discernible silvery pinstripe. The flowery look of the room would be gone, and about time, Amy thought.

Of course, I shouldn't have run off the way I did, without saying anything to you. You were right that I was thinking about a young man, and that I was not sure what I was thinking but

When she found the letter some time later, Amy wondered what that qualifying *but* had been about. What had she been going to say? Fluctuating, she had been going to pose some alternative. The letter being broken off seemed appropriate to the reason it had been; life could stop as short; it could seem unfinished. She had left the letter on her dresser and wondered who had moved it. The cleaning lady might have, while dusting. If it had been moved by Aunt Dea would she have read it? Her mother would not have moved it, as she had been too distraught to have been cleaning up. Time had passed; the letter still had relevance, but Amy felt herself not the person who had begun it. The bottom of her wastebasket was scattered by the pieces. Once, she had written Jeff that she was sick, and he had replied, that if he could, he would be the sickness. She thought of her father, his look, and knew she could not have been so generous. When we are so vulnerable, must we die looking horrible? To look at her father's skeletal face, she could only think how glad she was to be living. All the time she had been going forward, seeking life, he had been retreating, his done. Could they not have at some point, passing, touched? When he lay in his hospital bed, and she looked at his face, she tried to remember in their life together what words they had said. Children think their parents' lives center entirely on them. What thoughts, what feelings had her father had about which she had known nothing? He had once passionately loved her mother; Amy tried to imagine the night she had been conceived. She could see only the man she had always known, elderly-seeming always to her. Her thumb touched to her middle finger, she formed a circle with which she enclosed her father's wrist. She remembered his carrying her at a gallop on his

343

shoulders. Now, he could not lift his head. He had difficulty speaking. Open, his eyes stared. But did he understand? Did he know her? Amy asked, bending over him. Did he know her, at all?

She felt that she was drowning in his breathing, which was hampered by phlegm. Below his wandering mouth was a dark hole, from which he sent out sighing and melancholy and caught sounds, some like the sound a straw makes sucking, emptily, at the bottom of a glass.

She had been writing the letter when Edith rushed in, wildly, to say he had been taken to the hospital, having collapsed at a meeting. Edith eventually stood at his bedside, her face knotted like writhing hands, insisting he would get well, he would! But Amy grasped the situation and said that no, he was dying. Having found the letter again, and wondering who had moved it, Amy thought of a myriad of helpful things Dea had done: none of them large. More importantly, they were the little things that bridged one day to another; the coffeepot was always clean, her stockings washed, her room straightened. Everyone is glad for a little break in routine. In his own way, Joe performed similar small thoughtfulnesses. As if to accumulate miles, he travelled the hospital's corridors, finding out of the way machines which produced sodas, mints, crackers, small toys; once, he brought to the room miniature Scotties, one black and one white, which were magnets; finally, Edith smiled. The food accumulated like an animal's hoard. He kept bringing things. Amy felt about Aunt Dea and Uncle Joe the emotions she had felt at their house with Quill; these emotions endured. People needed places to go back to, people to resee; it gave life a design, she thought; that was necessary for her. Staring at her father's familiar face, from which unbelievably life was going, she knew she had to rely on something, and chose love.

Frequently irritable, he struck out at anything that came too

344

near, even a shadow's flicker. He often knocked the tube from his throat. Demanding, he rejected afterward what he wanted. Private nurses were continually quitting. That he flailed against muteness Amy found admirable. The final nurse was motherly and scolding and more strong-willed than he. She threatened to tie down his hands if he did not behave. In recognition of tenderness, he looked at her, suddenly, without vacancy in his eyes, and was quiet. Days began and ended. Amy wrote Jeff a short note saying where she was, thanking him for the book. He wrote back sympathetically, and that he looked forward to the long letter she promised.

Guided into the hall, she wondered what the sense was in whispering. What possibly could the doctor tell them, she wondered, that her father did not know. Having motioned her and Edith into the corridor, the doctor said it was only a matter of hours. Her throat worked against her and Edith thought, if only she had known something to offer besides ceramic ashtrays. She went back into his room. Facing the window, she saw a cold early spring rain beginning. In the corridor, Amy had sensed the three of them there had been, unwittingly, a little impatient at the idea of someone else's death. Why die? they had wanted to ask, parting from each other a little shamefacedly, as if someone might ask it. The doctor, turning away, plunged a thick thumb to the elevator button. Amy went back into the room where Edith had opened the window and drank a soda left by Joe, which was flat. "Couldn't I get you a fresh Coke?" Edith said hopefully.

"This is all right," Amy said, while opening a package of mints from among Joe's accumulated pile. He was not good with money. Billy Walter came forward to help with practical things. He had come by the hospital every day after work. Though feeling timid, Edith asked Amy if she were going to marry him.

"Can I," Amy had asked, "think about it while Daddy is like this?" the latter an afterthought in her own ears.

She never would have tied down his hands! said the nurse, coming out of his room and crying. She could not think when a case had moved her more. Did they know the last thing he had said, clearly? "All he had ever wanted in life was to be a good man."

Edith, full of pain, felt her thoughts confirmed by the look on Amy's face. "You never know," Edith whispered. By not changing her expression, Amy agreed. She determined, as she came down the hospital steps, late that afternoon, with her mother and Billy Walter, that her life must come to something. An old blind Negro stood there and, at the moment of their passing, put his hand up to the rain, then stuck wet fingers into his mouth. Billy Walter had bought newspapers in the lobby. Edith gratefully accepted one and stuck it as shelter over her head. Amy declined.

Passing the dancing school on their way home, Billy Walter sped up. He and Edith, almost desperately, continued their conversation, staring in other directions. But, "Look!" Amy cried. Neither looked, and Billy Walter hurriedly repeated something he had been saying, something practical about their lives, capturing Edith's attention. Look, Amy repeated, to herself. At the window, couples were silhouetted. From the street, the three in the car caught a whiff of music. Amy saw, as they passed, wind instruments lifted triumphantly to blare, and gaiety and glitter emanated from the building. Outside, in an impatient line, people stood waiting to get in; in the grey day, expressions on their faces were happier. Having concluded his advice, Billy Walter was silent. Edith said, "Billy Walter, whatever would we do without you?"

At the same instant, Amy announced, "The dancing school's a success."

Putting down her pen and resting, Dea said that she did not know just how soon after the funeral they could announce the engagement. "Why announce it?" Amy said. "Everyone knows."

Edith called from upstairs frantically, "It's customary!" knowing Amy could be serious.

"If you're tired, I can finish writing these thank-you notes," Dea said. "You look pale."

"I've been indoors too much," Amy said.

Dea remembered telling Edith, once, it was Amy's salvation that she was pretty since she always had her nose in a book and seemed to know nothing but what came out of them. That Amy had made so many of their present decisions had been a surprise. Dea said hesitantly, "Indoors because of writing your book?" and offered a compliment: "I never thought you had any stickablity, Amy. But your momma says you spend too much time writing, that you aren't even looking after buying a trousseau."

"I can buy a trousseau any time," Amy said.

Dea, hoping Amy was going to make that boy a nice wife, said, "What's the book about?" at the same time picking up her pen. She could continue writing thank-you notes for flowers, as her notes were similar and mechanical.

"It's kind of a history of a city," Amy said evasively. "About a man struggling to succeed in the world and how differently people see him. In a way, he's sort of like Daddy—"

"My brother!" Dea said, slapping down her pen. "Listen here, Amy, I want to know what you're going to say about my family! Now, don't you say something you shouldn't. I'm sure you know your granddaddy had the same little weakness as your daddy." Amy, she knew, would not, and she hoped could not, write the raw things Mr. Almoner wrote. Dea preferred to believe his influence forgotten. Having been told he was not well enough to leave home often, wondering if Amy knew that, and deciding it best to let sleeping dogs lie, Dea kept quiet. This book business, anyway, she considered something to help Amy pass time. After she was married, she would have other things. Amy could never publish anything. Long ago, she and Edith had decided that. Imagine! she thought. She watched indulgently and full of love the way Amy sat thoughtfully composing each note, as if to every individual one needed to say something different.

"Write something happy in your book," Dea said, watching Amy frown. "You're too serious. You ought to be writing about your life, anyway. It's old folks supposed to be concerned with the past."

But already what Dea had said was past, Amy thought, looking up, to stare at her aunt's well-meaning face, and past it at spirea bushes in bloom and beginning to shed; below them, the ground seemed covered with sleet. As quickly as Dea had spoken, as quickly as the blooms fell, life could be taken, all was past. She bent her elbows sharply to the table, licked shut another envelope and added it to her pile.

"Are you," Billy Walter said, not really a question, "dreaming about the living or the dead." How long was she going to mourn? he wondered. He took her hand and toyed with it, his other beating time on the table to the band's music. After an intermission, being refreshed, the men played blaringly. He pulled his glass toward him, shoved Amy's toward her. "Let's get some drinking done around here," he called to everyone at the table.

"When you think," Amy said, after emptying her glass, "that I'm thinking about my father, I'm a lot of the time thinking about my book."

"Have another drink and cheer up," he said. "Hell, we need Quill here to liven up this party." People kept asking, Where were he and Lydia? No one could remember, lately, Quill's being late for a party. Their appetizers, grapefruit halves, were wrinkling, the maraschino cherry in the center beginning to spread color. Waiters were removing dessert plates from the others. The

348

two empty chairs made everyone feel silent, and Cindy leaned forward to say she hoped Quill's and Lydia's baby was not sick.

Billy Walter restlessly tapped his heels to the floor. "They're evidently not coming for dinner. Let's get a nigger over here to clear their places and bring more setups."

"Billy Walter!" Amy said, shushingly.

"A Ne-gro." He looked at her in a set way. "Honey, today I ate spareribs with some Negro clients. How many Yankee friends you have who even know any Negroes? I'm doing business with them every day. Now, I can't take this dullness." Waving toward a waiter, he poured himself and Amy another drink.

"Quill's probably had some trouble with his daddy today," Cindy said. "You know how it is when you work for your daddy. You can't tell your daddy a thing. Lydia's probably trying to get him calmed down. She says Quill comes home every night so maddd at his daddy, she thinks he's going to explode."

Amy knew she had lost count of her drinks. What else was there to do? Setting the rim of her glass against her nose, she began on another glassful. Billy Walter, jumpy, both knees bouncing, decided he was going off to dance, since Amy sat like a stone and said she did not want to. She watched him head toward a blond divorcée, who rubbed pelvises when she danced. He lumbered off, his shoulders so broad, she remembered watching him, with her heart pounding, run across a football field when they were in high school. He had been the captain of the team. She had been willing to die, if he would look at her! The most ecstatic moment of her life had been when, finally, he had invited her to a movie. That evening, walking back to his car, he had dropped a matchbook into a gutter. When they reached a corner, he suddenly had whirled and run back to get the cover, which had his name printed on it. He had explained that, remembering it, he wanted nothing with his name on it in the gutter. How strange, she had thought. Now, she considered that at an age when she had never thought of it, Billy Walter had felt aware of who he was.

To be attentive, Cindy's husband refilled Amy's glass. She had looked down in surprise to find it empty. With the ghost of Billy Walter and herself in the room, younger, Amy began the drink, wondering how when you were old, it was possible to contain all your memories. People at the table chatted about inconsequential things, assuming that since she was silent, she was brooding. Had she and Billy Walter had a fight, they wondered. She looked at them a little blankly and tried to keep up a conversation, sorry her reverie had been broken. She sought silence again, by drinking.

"Potato chips?" Cindy offered a bowl. Amy shook her head, aware someone was pouring into all the glasses lining the table. She felt sick, smelling liquor. She hoped to avoid what amounted to a steady stream of questions about the wedding, her plans. Vaguely, she wondered why she was not jealous about Billy Walter and the divorcée. Others, she knew were watching her, solicitous. Her glass kept being refilled; a way of comforting her, the others felt. Dizzy, she began to eat potato chips, one after another, hoping they might make her soberer. She was either uninteresting, or had nothing in common. The husbands had drawn together at one end of the table, to talk about their afternoon's golf game. Billy Walter had gone out to the golf course with the divorcée.

Cindy, grouped together with the wives at Amy's end of the table, was saying intently, "What are we going to do about a car pool for day camp this summer?"

"Mondays," said another girl, "would be my best day to drive. Except every third Monday, I have sewing club."

"I could take Tuesday," Cindy said, "except that has been my grocery shopping day."

"Count me in. I'll take Wednesdays," said another girl.

Cindy looked worried. "I don't know but one other soul sending a child to the camp. If we only have four, there's an extra day each week for someone to drive."

Amy looked up, seeing blurrily that new setups had arrived. She found the potato-chip bowl empty. She felt pale, and tried to look interested. There was nothing to say, and nothing to do but finish her drink.

"Well, who is going to take the extra day which week?" said one of the girls.

Cindy said insistently, "I can never drive on Fridays. That's my bridge club. Though I can change my grocery shopping day for the summer."

Another girl said, in mock worry, "We're boring Amy."

"Oh no," Amy said, beginning to stand up. "I just have to go to the ladies' room."

"Who's going to take Monday?" said the girl, and they leaned toward one another as Amy left.

Objects were ahead in the room, which had to be carefully circumvented. Like a sailor, she set a fixed point, the ladies' room door, and attempted a steady course toward it. The last potato chips would not go down, and made a burning sensation where they seemed stuck, ready to rise, at the back of her throat. The club's band was engaged in a particularly agonized number, and people had stopped dancing to watch them play, and crowded close to the bandstand. Billy Walter and the girl had come back inside, hand in hand, to watch with the crowd. Amy prayed only to go unnoticed. The music seemed to make the room sway. Florists had decorated with forced spring blooms, which in the warmth and in the lateness of the hour, had begun to shed. Petals lay along her way, some from roses or redbud, pale pink. Looking down, Amy thought how meaningless to have once cov-

351

eted a wreath of buds for her hair, and she gave up that old dream willingly.

A somewhat blousy girl on the bandstand sang "true lovvve" as Amy's hand touched the door to the ladies' room, in relief. Inside was solitude, silence. She only avoided mirrors, which reflected green shaded lights. At last, in a booth, she was sick. When she had washed her face, she stood in the dressing room, looking into those mirrors, and put on lipstick. She took off a shade from one of the lamps, to stare at herself, thinking how her mother said her friends loved to make up their faces in this powder room, because it was so dark, you couldn't see anything. Close to the bulb, Amy held her purse, searching for a dime.

Outside the room, a telephone booth had been artfully covered with flowers, and she headed toward it. She glanced once toward the main room, discovering that though the music was equally loud, though the singer with her full figure was still gyrating, the watching crowd had thinned. Curiously, she peered a little further into the room, wondering what other diversion there was. At her own table, she saw a group of people standing. Something hilarious, she thought, would be going on, of which Billy Walter would be the center, or likely the cause. That thought gave her a dragged-out feeling. She would have continued toward the phone, but saw that as Cindy and her husband came away from the table, Cindy was crying. Others, at the table, were picking up purses and leaving. Billy Walter, looking around for her, was holding her coat. He came toward her, indicating she must stand there, wait. Her coat hung limply over his arm, until, silently commanded, she put it on. People formed a line, moving like a sad pilgrimage. Filing out, Billy Walter pressed arms about her and said close to her ear, "There's been an accident. Quill's been shot."

Shot! Amy covered her mouth with both hands. Images from that word had no association with Quill, who was meticulous and no outdoorsman. "Where?" She thought of burglars in his house, or muggers in the street.

"In the stomach," Billy Walter said. Almost missing a step, going out of the club to the street, she repeated, "Stomach?" causing a friend, passing, to say, "That boy's liable to have done himself in."

Billy Walter held her close saying, "He shot himself with that shotgun of his daddy's, that was hanging in their den."

Quill was not dead; the word went quickly around. Though he would live, would he recover? A stomach wound could harm so much that was vital. The only thing to do was to go home, the hour was late, and people were yawning. Amy stared away from them, her throat deliberately tightened. Yawning can be a chain reaction, and be as contagious as a disease.

Why had Quill done it? everyone asked. Billy Walter looked at Amy quizzically, sensing she would know. She and Quill had had a lot in common. "Why," he said, "would Quill risk mutilating himself for life?"

In Billy Walter's car, Amy leaned her chin to one hand and mumbled that she had no idea. . . .

"It's me," she said, softly, knowing she need not give her name. She knew every inflection in Jeff's voice, as he knew hers.

"It is," he said. "Amy."

"Are you all right? You sound faint."

"Now, I'm stronger." He moved closer to the receiver.

She said, "I'm in a phone booth, and I don't have any more change."

"I was resting," he said. "I'm sorry to have taken so long to get to the phone."

"Oh, that's all right. I was going to call last night, but something happened. I needed very much to talk to you."

"I'm glad of that. Having been the cat who walked by himself, and finding eventually it was a mistake, I had wanted you to try a different way. I only hope to know if it works."

"You will," she said. "I should have called person-to-person. The operator won't just cut us off, will she?"

"No, there'll be signals."

"Not more than one?"

"Many," he said.

"You're not talking about the operator," she said sensitively.

"No. Life."

"But how will I know them?"

"You will, now."

"Why? Because I'm grown?"

"Well, apparently," he said, "or why are you calling?"

"I think I have grown up," she said. "Operator!"

"I'll take care of everything," Jeff said. He had the charges reversed to his phone. "I've waited a long time for this, Amy. I thought, once, I could get over you. I know now, if I lived till I were ninety, I couldn't."

"That's good," she said. "Because will you still marry me?"

He said, "When you get here, you can make plans about the rest of your life. You'll know better what to do. Come with just what you need."

"My toothbrush?" she said, laughing.

"Good," he said, also laughing. "You've learned your lessons well."

"I get an A?"

"Yes, and a star."

"I can't help worrying."

"Choices cost."

"That's a hard thing to accept. But, I will."

"I'm going to rest easy."

"Do. When should I come?"

"As soon as possible. Tomorrow. On that first train past noon. You can be easiest met then. Will you?"

"Risk it, of course. I'll dance a jig smack-dab in the middle of town. In broad daylight, too. I can hardly wait, can you?"

"I was beginning to wonder how long I could wait, Amy," he said.

Seeing her mother growing older, Amy was glad to have learned not to count on anything. Anything might end, as nothing happened of itself. This morning, Edith's sleep-swollen eyes grew doleful. Undefiantly, in a calm voice, Amy had said, "Last night I broke my engagement."

"But why?" Edith said. "For what reason? Billy Walter's such a sweet boy."

"I don't love him." Amy then headed Edith off. "I'm not talking about being 'in love' with him."

But, "Love," Edith had said automatically, impatiently looking out at redbud opening rapidly into pink bloom. The hot burst of spring was on them, though in the earliest part of the morning she found herself shivering and thought it was because the ground was still dank. However, she was hopeful, for jonquils were up. Directly down between where two peaks of the roof formed a right angle, breaking here and there the silvery dimness of her room, the sun came in. Clusters of yellow flowers were everywhere along the ground. On a bush, wind spun small white blossoms like pinwheels. "Marriage," Edith began, watching the flowers, her bottom lip bitten. But she remained silent, and her lips settled into place, for she had nothing after all to say about marriage, having never understood her own.

"I believe in love," Amy said firmly, seeing her mother was going to say no more. Edith got up and went into her bathroom. Bending over the basin to splash water, she looked up, with a slightly different face, then Amy noticed that her mother was growing older. The water seemed to have added weight, like worry, to Edith's face, and lines drew it down. She hung up her towel, but leaned upon the rack a moment, dependently. Having peered at Amy, seeing how strong her face looked, Edith relaxed. She let her chin sag, remembering being told from the time she first held Amy that she would be amazed how soon the shoe would be on the other foot, and Amy would be taking care of her. Spring, Edith thought, staring out again at the flowers, was as unbelievable as time's passing. And looking back, she agreed, to Amy's surprise. "Yes," Edith said. "Love is necessary."

Amy knew her decision would not have changed without her mother's unknowing blessing. But she was glad to have it.

As the train arrived, she saw an old man in a black suit, standing in a garden which was not fully planted. The garden mainly was mulched with pecan hulls, their brownness slick and shiny as mink. When she got off the train, the conductor reached up and helped her down the steps. "I see the old man's letting his garden go to seed," he said conversationally.

"But why?" Amy said, pausing.

"Passenger trains being discontinued. The mail's all going by truck. Might be a freight'll stop occasionally."

"That's too bad," Amy said. Picking up his conductor's steps and getting on board, he said, "Progress, you know. It don't take human beings into consideration." He faded with the train, tucking his brass watch into its vest slit.

Amy went along a path through the remaining flowers and spoke to the old man. His head shook back and forth involuntarily; his look said that was the way things happened to him. He looked at the garden as he had looked at the train, sorrowfully. Around them in a netlike haze, the afternoon had begun to dissolve. The trees seemed bent, but the leaves had a stilled quality,

356

awaiting a presence, twilight. Without the accumulative dust of summer, the town had a more sparkling quality than Amy remembered. In the lighter air, people went by at a brisker pace, noticing the stranger. Like some unwanted appendage, Amy felt her pocketbook dangling by her side. She felt superfluous, wandering about the station. For Jeff to be late was unlike him.

Over the post office, the flag occasionally flew and subsided, in bright-dark ripples. There, a little boy held up a frantically wiggling puppy to drink from the bronze rim of the water fountain. Amy supposed this a foreign country and that she were here alone, with little money and in possession of little besides her toothbrush. She perched on the edge of a bench to watch pigeons, imagining herself in that lone situation, knowing she would then have to have help from others. She began to glance more directly at the Negroes and whites who had watched her promenade. They spoke or nodded in return; several people offered comments on the weather, to which she replied. Idle conversation was, after all, perhaps not so idle. "Warming for sho," said an old man, who had dropped his cane. Amy retrieved it and, after speaking further of the day, she felt less a stranger. In a foreign country and without knowing the language, she would have to make contact with smiles, gestures, small attempts. She might be sending out some secret code. Sitting on the bench, she beat a little rhythm on the pocketbook in her lap. She gazed around, not realizing she was smiling. An older couple stopped and offered help. Both sundrawn faces stared at her with interest, kindly. After shaking her head, Amy watched them with equal interest, as they went on.

In the late spring evening, the sky gave to stalwart and gigantic old trees the appearance of being one-dimensional. Everything had a metallic look, the grey fuzzy appearance of an empty movie screen, and figures seemed superimposed on the day. After wandering to a rusty penny-gum machine, Amy looked toward the station, gum in her mouth, and felt the scene had been transfixed while her back was turned. The boy held up the puppy for a second drink at the fountain, the old man dug with his retrieved cane into dirt, and the old couple were climbing into their pickup truck. She walked eagerly back to the activity around the station and that look on her face again drew attention.

Suppertime was nearing. Storekeepers made preparations for closing. At the hardware store a man brought inside galvanized tubs which had been on display. Letters on the sagging marquee at the movie were being changed for the evening performance. Amy had been warmish in her spring jacket. Now there was prelude to a shower, and a breeze began. A crowd of Negro and white teen-agers clustered about a brand-new Mustang, just drawn up to the curb. Amy went near a short while and noted that other cars, pulling away, had on parking lights. She had to make some plan of her own, and went inside the station to inquire about returning trains.

There was no printed schedule, and only one train tonight, which would pass through in several hours. As once she would have, she did not feel terror or panic. Coming from the station, trailing momentarily through the disappearing garden, she did not fear desertion. Why Jeff had not come was disturbing, frightening—the chance being that something had happened to him. Otherwise, she felt quite settled in her mind.

She had stopped paying attention to traffic, in congestion around town at this hour. Farmers headed home. In stores which stayed open late, lights had come on. Activity had begun in the town's one restaurant. Sitting down again, she became engrossed in watching sparrows in a tizzy over popcorn dropped by the bench's previous occupant. He had, at the moment Amy went by him toward the gum machine, held out the bag toward her, and she had declined fearing popcorn would make her thirsty. A shuddering green coupe stopped nearby, and she noticed the car's occupants when they were getting out. The Negro boy, who had been driving, headed toward the red Mustang, but she was unsuccessful in reading the yellow lettering on the back of his jacket. Her attention went to the woman with him, having difficulty struggling from the running board to the ground. As the woman started toward her, careful of stiff joints, Amy knew certainly who it was. She got up, meeting her halfway. "Jessie."

"Yes 'um." The whole of Jessie's hazel eyes appeared covered with a milky haze; that registered something besides recognition and greeting. Deeper than she yet knew it, Amy recognized sorrow. "Bad news," Jessie said.

"He can't come?"

"He's gone." Jessie's voice broke. "Went this morning. But— have told me, no matter what—be here this time."

Amy's lips formed the word, Where? She knew better than to ask, Gone where? She merely watched Jessie cry. She cried without sound, her shoulders heaving. Amy's lips had set so tightly, they caused her face to turn whiter. She and Jessie went together to a bench and sat down.

The station and the stores surrounding it now looked entirely different, the silvery stillness dissolving, clouds gathering. Beyond the post office, where the flag alternately dropped and flew, where surrounding fields began, Amy supposed rain had already begun.

"That's impossible." She had spoken finally, with difficulty.

"No'm. It ain't."

Nothing was impossible. Those words bore home. Impossibility was as far-reaching as the horizon, as enormous as the world. She must now know as much of compassion and sorrow as there was to know; but another self stood aside, watchful and wise, to tell her there was more of everything to learn. Learning must not cease. She and Jessie had gripped hands. Amy would be able to recall instantly, forever, the feel of Jessie's skin, recall the proximity of her body; someone, she had to find, would be an extension of her own being; that alone would be life: would be living. She and Jessie were not alone in their grief. Lights blazing in the newspaper office across the way gave its plate-glass window a look of bulging with importance. A man, in shirtsleeves, came out to stick a bulletin to the window. Darkness gathered in from the surrounding small hillsides, lavender with vetch. On the rising wind came the smell of spring land, rowed-up and waiting. Flower petals lifted in the old man's garden, the sparrows' feathers ruffled, the edges of Amy's and Jessie's skirts lifted. After that moment, Jessie said, "Seems like it would be impossible. But it ain't. His heart been so bad, honey. Gotten worse. It ain't all that surprise."

"It doesn't seem to me," Amy said lonesomely, "it was his time to die."

"In the kitchen the other day, he sayed, Gettin' time for me and him to move over for the young peoples."

The astonishing silver glow of the afternoon, relentless, would not give in. The sun even stubbornly reappeared, and strongly, as if it had not been satisfied with its finale. Amy held back tears for later. "He was out driving," Jessie said, "and shouldn't have been. The car left the road, went over a ditch into a field. The doctor think his heart had quit."

"He wasn't on the way to meet me?"

"No'm."

"I'm glad of that." Then Amy said, puzzled, "But he told you to meet me. Why did he say that this morning?"

Jessie might not have heard. Deep in her eyes, a shadowed look only told she understood. She gave Amy, barely, a glance sideways. "Just sayed, meet Miss Amy 'bout fo-thirty. She'll be on her own."

"He knew he wasn't coming, Jessie, then— But, God!"

"Sho is the truth."

"Does anybody else know he told you that?"

"What, Miss Amy?" She gave Amy a practiced dumb look, for white people.

"Nothing." Amy took the cue. Her own face set in a closed firm look. The rain had not yet come, though a breeze smelling more strongly of it began to disrupt town. The bulletin on the newspaper window flapped insistently. Around the Mustang, the boys began to make signs of leaving. Town had begun to look empty.

"Do I have time to go out to where Jeff will be buried before the train comes?"

"Ain't far, but it's fixing to rain," Jessie said. "I can get my sister's boy to carry us." Vern had separated himself from the car and, looking around, now came toward them. "My sister's boy, Vern, Miss Amy."

"Amy Howard. Vern?"

At the introduction, Vern slightly nodded. He stared a full instant before understanding that Amy was asking him a question. "Vern Dell."

"I'm glad to meet you."

"Glad to meet you."

"How far is it to the cemetery from here?"

"Almost two miles. Aunt-tie and I can take you."

"I'd rather walk. I have time."

Beside the Mustang, a boy in a satin shirt, holding up his guitar, called to Vern about meeting later. Vern lagged behind, shouting confirmation. As Amy and Jessie went toward the car, an old man hailed Jessie, took off his hat and held it against his chest. Amy moved away while he spoke comfortingly, sadly shaking his head. All his life, she heard him say, he had known Mr. Jeff, and he looked about seeing other changes. A large blinking neon sign helped color the evening blue, and suggested EATS at the restaurant. That once had been a mansion. Vern at the Mustang joined the boy, playing the guitar, in an impromptu dance, their gyrations in pulsating beat to the on-off blinking of the blue sign. Their voices blended. Amy opened the car door and Jessie climbed inside, having hugged her.

"I'm glad to have seed you."

"I'm glad to have seen you."

Part of the plan, Amy thought, turning away, had been for her not to hear the news from a stranger.

First, she saw willows, topping the hillsides the cemetery covered. On its far side, it slanted toward a muddy yellowish pond. There in the cautious twilight, people were fishing. Having trailed between gates and now following a walkway, Amy pretended not to see the plot, while going directly toward it, knowing the spot from Jessie's directions; past the World War I monument, a carefully tended rose garden, a grove of cedars. As a cry went up collectively from those at the pond, she saw a large Negro woman hold up a fish on the end of a bamboo pole. Afterward, in the quietness, she heard the soughing of the cedars. Their bark peeled, leaving them, whitely, with a look of being frail. They might yet totter and bend with the wind, like bamboo. Yet, if trees could, she felt they had a look of wisdom, being so old. How much they had seen; how many people had come here and gone. People were sorrowful here, or secretly in their hearts glad, lovers hid in the grove. Inside there, Amy sat with her chin to her knees, her hands plying dry auburn needles. On some of the graves were wax or paper flowers, impermanent and fading and shredding. Other places, ivy fled along the ground, its tendrils as stong as cord. Lichen clung to old headstones. At the pond, everyone now was industriously and silently fishing. Bobwhites, in weeds along the road, called to each other by similar name. Amy wondered if ordinariness and everydayness would have destroyed what she and Jeff had; those things, she suspected, were death on marriages and might ruin less binding relationships. Nothing she and Billy Walter shared would have held up under them.

A caretaker, wandering about, made it obvious he wanted to lock the gates for the night. Women and children at the pond suddenly squealed, for rain had begun there. Amy could see it pockmarking the muddy water and that it came toward her, with colors of the rainbow misting. With saw-toothed edges, lightning broke across the sky.

She had come out of the grove of cedars but did not shy at either the thunder or the lightning. "Better hurry somewhere," said the caretaker, locking the gates behind her.

"Yes, I will," she said, darting across the road and toward the sidewalk back to town. Another thunderhead burst, its roll afterward like a drum's. Either that noise or being intent on her thoughts kept her from hearing the noise of Vern's old coupe, idling alongside her. He leaned across the front seat to the open window opposite him and said, "Want a ride?"

She had reached a sheltered spot along the walk, where enormous oaks provided a dry area. She looked at him in surprise. "Sure," she said, and came down a slick-wet incline and got in the car.

He drove on. "You afraid to ride all the way into town with me? I can drop you off a piece of the way?"

"I'm not afraid," she said. "How did you happen to come get me?"

"I knew it was time you'd have to leave, and then when the rain come up, I just thought you'd get soaked. I was just, you know, driving around. So, I come to get you. If you want to know, because you were friendly to me. Not like most white girls."

"I see. But you live here. You're the one who might get in trouble if we go riding through town together."

"Well," he said. "Who going to see us in the dark?"

363

"We are brave," she said, smiling back.

"I don't want trouble. There is hardly anybody would believe that. I just want, I don't know, you know, something." Amy longed at the sadness in his voice to touch him, and dared not. He gripped the steering wheel as if to quiet desperation.

She settled more closely to the door. "I would like to do this, though," she said. "I don't care if someone sees us, if you don't. But I'd like to drive by and look at the house a minute."

He turned away from the station. They saw lights burning in town, fuzzily through the rain. Chester's awning was only a dark oblong, the station seemed tinier. Vern said, starting away from a stop sign that lost them sight of town, "One thing I would like to be able to do is go in back yonder, in the drugstore, and get me a soda."

She shook her head. "It seems amazing you can't. What would happen if you went in to order one?"

"They close the counter down." He gave a laugh, short and a little bitter.

"Well, I certainly think you ought to be able to, my lord."

He said, in a slow way, "Well . . . thanks."

With a sound of hushing, the road's wet gravel accepted their tires as they neared the house, which seemed asleep, its curtains drawn. Vern stopped short of the cattle gap, and once in the silence, they heard cows bellow. Both stared toward the house, without speaking, not moving. When finally Amy unfolded her hands, shifted herself in the seat, and made known that she was ready to go, Vern said, "We shan't pass this way but once. That's why, well, I, my friends, we want the best of everything." He backed the car swiftly and headed it on the road again toward town. His words "the best of everything" went on and on through Amy's mind. He spoke of the moment of realization in his life that he was different, that he could not shop in stores, do the things that white people could. When they got to the station

364

Amy put out her hand, which he shook. Distantly, they heard the train; its headlight swept the darkness, an all-seeing eye. "Things are changing, aren't they?" she said, opening the car door.

"Yes," he said. "I would have to say that they are better."

"Goodbye."

"So long."

When the train went on, it broke the town into various lit pieces. Amy braced her head against the coach window, and cried then. She had, too long, run away from everything, and alienation of the spirit was bad. She had to have the courage to be, which meant not to fear emotions. She wanted to take hold of life and shake it as a terrier shakes a rat; everything, everything, she thought, must be gotten out of it.

Sometime later, she put these thoughts down in her notebook. She felt surprised at how dog-eared the book had become, at how much of it was filled. Diligence meant accomplishment, as Jeff had always said. Later, when she read them, the pages she had filled immediately after he died were scrawled over with an urgent and frantic writing.

Did he know that I would grieve so? First, I hid knowing him and now I have to hide grieving over him. The grief is like a heavy object that I carry around with me, and I can't find a place to put it down. I can't find anything to do with it.

It's been three weeks and things are no better. Whenever I am somewhere, I have to excuse myself and find someplace, usually the bathroom, to cry. When everything comes over me, I cannot control myself. I know that what I'm to know of greatness in my lifetime, I've known. It makes me feel old; I have a past. Every afternoon I've been taking very long baths, to be alone and to cry. Now, Mother thinks I need glasses. Why are my eyes always red? Why do I stay alone so much? To satisfy her, I went to the doctor. He put that enormous silver eye of his close to mine and said, "I can't find any reason for the headaches, or the red eyes your mother is so worried about, young lady. Maybe, you need to eat more." Then Mother decided I had to go to a diagnostician. She says, I look like I have a fever, even though one never registers. It doesn't matter to me. I had just as soon go to doctors. There have been several and I lie on their tables and think, This will pass—what does it matter. I have memories to hold fast to.

Persistent and mystified, the diagnostician kept probing. His head wore a halo from a strong white hot peering light behind him. Every doctor has given me a prescription. Don't they know pills can't cure deepdown astonishing depression? They ask me, "What do you think is the matter with you?" I smile and say, "I don't know. Nothing maybe." But I want so much to ask if they've never seen grief before. "It's grief," I want to say, "and nothing else." Haven't they ever diagnosed grief before?

Soon after the train no longer stopped in his town, the stationmaster died. Untended, the annuals even disappeared from the garden. The station building grew shabbier, until the Women's Club adopted it for a beautifying project. No one wanted a visible blight on the town. However, the station never regained its air of self-respect, since it had no purpose.

In Delton, a superstructure was built around town, which diverted traffic from Quill Boulevard, and that looked outdated and purely commercial. The enormous complex new highway stretched connectingly out and drew in toward the city nearby small towns. Dea often said, there was soon going to be no countryside left. Having had to give up her own flowers, she had elected to keep watered petunias in the window boxes attached by the ladies to the station. This summer, a dry one, she had come often and, this afternoon, stood almost mesmerized performing her duty. She did not hear anyone behind her, until Amelia spoke.

"Wonder how long it'll be before they tear this old thing down?" Amelia had spotted Dea while shopping, and crossed the street to her.

366

"You scared me. I declare to my soul," Dea said, whirling around, the watering can spout ahead of her.

When Dea whirled around, her immediate thought was that Amelia had either gone grey or stopped dying her hair. Thinking, She's aged, she saw that exact thought reflected in Amelia's eyes, and Dea said quickly, "I'm surprised you even knew me, I've gotten so mud-fat and white-headed."

"I've seen you passing through town with your daughter, but never close enough to speak," Amelia said. "How long's it been? Nobody stays home, do they? Everybody's always in the road."

"Not me," Dea said. "I'm living out back of my daughter's in a guest cabin, and I don't go anywhere but in the back door to baby-sit."

"I was sorry about your husband dying and read in the paper you'd sold your house."

"I didn't want to stay out there by myself, near that Negro church and all. Things get worse all the time, don't they?"

"Latham says they'll get worse before they get better." Amelia saved Dea's asking. "He suffers terribly. Rheumatoid arthritis. So crippled up he can't bathe himself. I manage only because of Marguerite, but I never get out of the house except to go to Inga's or pick up medicine at Chester's."

Dea went with her there now, past Negro teen-agers crowding the soda fountain.

"They take over everything, don't they?" Amelia whispered.

But the presence of the Negroes receded in their minds, and they decided to take the two empty seats at one end of the counter and have a quick Coke. They wanted to be gone before school let out, though already one class was coming down the front steps, in shifting groups of twos or threes, the Negro students, Amelia noted, sticking to themselves.

"Jessie," she said, "suddenly announced she was tired of living in other people's houses. White people's, I guess she meant. I just couldn't imagine. Instead, she's living out in you-know-what-town in one side of a little old house, with her sister and her boy in the other side. He brings her to work and takes her home. He's working in one of the new factories out on the super. I forget which one. She's hardly able to work. I think mostly she and Inga sit all day and talk. I know *Inga* fixes Jessie's lunch."

"If it weren't for factories coming into this part of the country, my husband once said, there wouldn't be enough folks left in this part of the country to stir up a stink. It is certainly emptying," Dea said, noting at the same time the absence of shaved ice in her Coke. "All we've ever known seems to be changing."

Amelia did not want to tell that Inga was planning to work at a school which had nothing but little Negro kids, and that she would not change her mind. When had Inga gotten so stubborn? she wondered. "How are your folks?"

"She—you mean my niece, I imagine—" Dea said, knowing Amelia had no interest in anyone else in her family, "for a long time has been writing a book. It was all against my better judgment, but then so were a lot of things. Her mother tells me she sent it to a man in New York, a friend of your brother's, I think. He thinks well of it and wants to see it when it's finished. So, I don't know. I could certainly be wrong." And Dea felt better to admit it. Climbing from their stools, they glanced understand-ingly at one another.

Before turning to the medicine counter, Amelia said, "We could have saved ourselves a lot of worrying."

"It probably didn't hurt us," Dea said.

Heading out, she felt the need to hurry, for doors at the schoolhouse had opened and soon the whole town, the whole world it would seem, would be overrun by teen-agers. Her car and Amelia's had been, without their knowledge, parked side by side. And that, Dea thought, was how lives came into touch, by accident. Living here all of her life, she had never expected to know anything going on inside the Almoner family. Her smile and Amelia's, when they parted, had been kinder, she thought.

Sometimes, and particularly on bright hot days, I am certain Jeff is coming back. The feeling, of course, goes.

Amy sat close to the window to write, therefore to the warming spring sun. Often, she felt cold but would gradually lose that sensation. As a good-luck piece, she wore the bell, writing. The chain made a warm moist ring about her neck. In spring's leaf-age, its vividness, was a hint of the summer to come, with enervating heat and dryness. She daydreamed of the cedar grove, where always there was a breeze. In the winter, once, she had put violets on Jeff's grave but never again took flowers, as they did not last. Whenever she went back, she thought of the final time she had seen the house. That night, when the rain had quit, and she had rolled down the car window, she had been aware of a fantastically sweet scent. Only now, when she was here writing, did Amy realize it had been the forsythia bushes, past budding, in bloom.